The first romance stories **Stephanie Laurens** read were set against the backdrop of Regency England, and these continue to exert a special attraction for her. As an escape from the dry world of professional science, Stephanie started writing Regency romances, and is now a *New York Times*, *USA Today* and *Publishers Weekly* bestselling author.

Stephanie lives in a leafy suburb of Melbourne, Australia, with her husband and two daughters, along with two cats, Shakespeare and Marlowe.

Learn more about Stephanie's books from her website at www.stephanielaurens.com

# Scandal's Bride

*Stephanie Laurens*

piatkus

PIATKUS

First published in the US in 1999 by Avon Books,
An imprint of HarperCollins Publishers, USA
First published in Great Britain in 2007 by Piatkus Books
This paperback edition published in 2007 by Piatkus Books
Reprinted 2008 (twice), 2009, 2010, 2011

A CIP catalogue record for this book
is available from the British Library

ISBN 978-0-7499-3718-8

Typeset in Times by Action Publishing Technology Ltd, Gloucester
Printed and bound in Great Britain by
Clays Ltd, St Ives plc

Papers used by Piatkus are from well-managed forests and
other responsible sources.

MIX
Paper from
responsible sources
FSC® C104740

Piatkus
An imprint of
Little, Brown Book Group
100 Victoria Embankment
London EC4Y 0DY

An Hachette UK Company
www.hachette.co.uk

www.piatkus.co.uk

# The Bar Cynster Family Tree
## (at the beginning of this story)

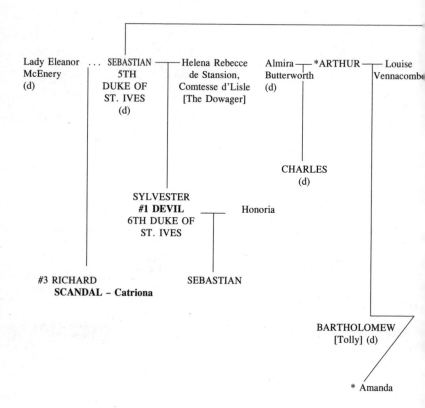

Lady Eleanor McEnery (d) ... SEBASTIAN 5TH DUKE OF ST. IVES (d) — Helena Rebecce de Stansion, Comtesse d'Lisle [The Dowager]

Almira Butterworth (d) — *ARTHUR — Louise Vennacombe

CHARLES (d)

SYLVESTER #1 DEVIL 6TH DUKE OF ST. IVES — Honoria

#3 RICHARD SCANDAL – Catriona

SEBASTIAN

BARTHOLOMEW [Tolly] (d)

* Amanda

THE BAR CYNSTER SERIES
#1 Devil's Bride
#2 A Rake's Vow

MALE CYNSTERS named in capitals * denotes twins

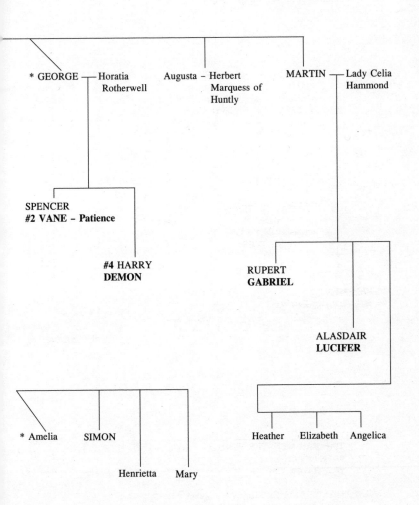

* GEORGE — Horatia
Rotherwell

Augusta – Herbert
Marquess of
Huntly

MARTIN — Lady Celia
Hammond

SPENCER
**#2 VANE – Patience**

**#4 HARRY
DEMON**

RUPERT
**GABRIEL**

ALASDAIR
**LUCIFER**

* Amelia    SIMON

Henrietta    Mary

Heather    Elizabeth    Angelica

# Prologue

*December 1, 1819*
*Casphairn Manor, the Vale of Casphairn*
*Galloway Hills, Scotland*

She'd never had a vision like it before.

Eyes – blue, blue – blue as the skies over Merrick's high head, blue as the cornflowers dotting the vale's fields. They were the eyes of a thinker, far-sighted yet focused.

Or the eyes of a warrior.

Catriona awoke, almost surprised to find herself alone. From the depths of her big bed, she scanned her familiar surrounds, the thick velvet curtains half shrouding the bed, their mates drawn tight across the windows beyond which the wind murmured, telling tales of the coming winter to any still awake. In the grate, embers gleamed, shedding a glow over polished wood, the soft sheen of the floor, the lighter hues of chair and dresser. It was deep night, the hour between one day and the next. All was reassuringly normal; nothing had changed.

Yet it had.

Her heart slowing, Catriona tugged the covers about her and considered the vision that had visited her – the vision of a man's face. The details remained strongly etched in her mind. Along with the conviction that this man would mean

1

something, impinge on her life in some vital way.

He might even be the one The Lady had chosen for her.

The thought was not unwelcome. She was, after all, twenty-two, long past the age when girls invited lovers to their beds, when she might have expected to play her part in that never-ending rite. Not that she regretted that her life had been otherwise, which was just as well, for her path had been set from the instant of her birth. *She* was 'the lady of the vale.'

The title, one of local custom, was hers and hers alone; none other could claim it. As the only child of her parents, on their deaths, she'd inherited Casphairn Manor, along with the vale and its attendant responsiblities. Her mother had been the same, inheriting manor, lands, and position from her mother before her. Each of her direct female ancestors had been 'the lady of the vale.'

Cocooned in warm down, Catriona smiled. Just what her title meant few outsiders understood. Some thought her a witch – she'd even used the fiction to scare away would-be suitors. Both church and state had little love of witches, but the vale's isolation kept her safe; there were few who knew of her existence, and none to question her authority or the doctrine from which it sprang.

All the inhabitants of the vale knew what she was, what her position entailed. With roots buried generations deep in the fertile soil, her tenants, all those who lived and worked in the vale, viewed 'their lady' as the local representative of The Lady herself, older than time, spirit of the earth that supported them, guardian of their past and their future. They all, each in his own way, paid homage to The Lady and, with absolute and unquestioning confidence, relied on her earthly representative to watch over them and the vale.

To guard, to protect, to nurture, nourish, and heal – those were The Lady's tenets, the only directives Catriona followed

2

and to which she'd unstintingly devoted her life. As had her mother, grandmother and great-grandmother before her. She lived life simply, in accordance with The Lady's dictates, which was usually an easy task.

Except in one arena.

Her gaze shifted to the parchment left unfolded on her dresser. A Perth solicitor had written to inform her of the death of her guardian, Seamus McEnery, and to bid her attend McEnery House for the reading of the will. McEnery House stood on a bleak hillside in The Trossachs, north and west of Perth; in her mind's eye, Catriona could see it clearly – it was the one place outside the vale in which she'd spent more than a day.

When, six years ago, her parents had died, Seamus, her father's cousin, had, by custom, become her legal guardian. A cold, hard man, he had insisted she take up residence at McEnery House, so he could better find a suitor for her hand – a man to take over her lands. With his rigid fist clamped on her purse strings, she'd been forced to obey; she'd left the vale and gone north to meet Seamus.

To do battle with Seamus – for her inheritance, her independence, her inalienable right to remain the lady of the vale, to reside at Casphairn Manor and care for her people. Three weeks of turmoil and drama later, she'd returned to the vale; Seamus had spoken no more of suitors, nor of her calling. And, Catriona was quite certain, he had never again taken The Lady's name in vain.

Now Seamus, the devil she'd conquered, was gone. His eldest son, Jamie, would succeed him. Catriona knew Jamie; like all Seamus's children, he was mild-mannered and weak-willed. Jamie was no Seamus. In considering how best to respond to the solicitor's request, she'd been much inclined to start as she meant to go on, and reply suggesting that, after the will was read and Jamie formally appointed as her guardian, Jamie should call on her here, at the manor. Although she foresaw no difficulty in handling Jamie, she preferred to deal from a position of strength. The vale was her home; within its arms, she reigned supreme. Yet . . .

She focused again on the parchment; after an instant, the outline blurred – once more the vision swam before her mind's eye. For a full minute, she studied it; she saw the face clearly – strong patriarchal nose, determinedly square chin, features chiselled from rock in their angularity and hardness. His brow was concealed by a lock of black hair; those piercing blue eyes were deep-set beneath arched black brows and framed by black lashes. His lips, held in a straight, uncompromising line, told her little – indeed, that was her summation of his face – one meant to conceal his thoughts, his emotions. From chance observers.

She wasn't a chance observer. Presentiment – nay, *certainty* – of future contact compelled her; she focused her mind and slid beneath his guard, behind his reserved facade, and tentatively opened her senses.

Hunger – hot, ravenous – a prowling, animalistic urge, swept over her. It caressed her with fingers of heat; its tug was even more physical. Beyond it, in the deeper shadows, lay . . . restlessness. A soul-deep sense of drifting, rudderless, upon life's sea.

Catriona blinked, and drew back, into her familiar chamber. And saw the letter still lying on her desk. She grimaced. She was adept at intepreting The Lady's messages – this one was crystal clear. She should go to McEnery House and, at some point, she would meet the restless, hungry, reserved stranger with the granite face and warrior's eyes.

A lost warrior – a warrior without a cause.

Catriona frowned and wriggled deeper under the covers. When she'd first seen that face, she'd felt, instinctively, deep inside, that, at long last, The Lady was sending her a consort

4

– the one who would stand by her side, who would share the burden of the vale's protection – the man she would take to her bed. At last. Now, however . . .

'His face is too strong. *Far* too strong.'

As the lady of the vale, it was imperative that she be the dominant partner in her marriage, as her mother had been in hers. It was written in stone that no man could rule her. Not for her an arrogant, domineering husband – *that* would never do. Which was, in this case, a pity. A real disappointment.

She'd immediately recognized the source of his restlessness, the restlessness of those without purpose, but she'd never met anything like the hunger that prowled within him. Alive, a tangible force, it had reached out and touched her, and she'd felt a compulsion to sate it. A reactive urge to soothe him, to bring him surcease. To . . .

Her frown deepened; she couldn't find the words, but there'd been a sense of excitment, of daring, of challenge. Not elements she generally met in her daily round of duties. Then again, perhaps it was simply her healer's instincts prodding her? Catriona humphed. 'Whatever, he *can't* be the one The Lady means for me – not with a face like *that.*'

Was The Lady sending her a wounded male, a lame duck for her to cure? His eyes, those hard-edged features, hadn't looked lame.

Not that it mattered; she had her instructions. She would go to the highlands, to McEnery House, and see what – or rather, who – came her way.

With another humph, Catriona slid deeper beneath the covers. Turning on her side, she closed her eyes – and willed her mind away from, once again, seeking the stranger's face.

# Chapter One

*December 5, 1819*
*Keltyburn, The Trossachs*
*Scottish Highlands*

'Will there be anything else, sir?'

An artful arrangement of sleek, nubile, naked female limbs sprang to Richard Cynster's mind. The innkeeper had finished clearing the remnants of his dinner – the feminine limbs would satisfy that appetite still unappeased. But . . .

Richard shook his head. Not that he feared shocking his studiously correct gentleman's gentleman, Worboys, standing poker-straight at his elbow. Having been in his employ for eight years, Worboys was past being shocked. He was, however, no magician, and Richard was of the firm opinion that it would take magical powers to find a satisfying armful in Keltyburn.

They'd arrived in the hamlet as the last light left the leaden sky; night had fallen swiftly, a black shroud. The thick mist that had lowered over the mountains, hanging heavy across their path, obscuring the narrow, winding road leading up Keltyhead to their destination, had made passing the night in the dubious comfort of the Keltyburn Arms an attractive proposition.

Besides, he had a wish to have his first sight of his

mother's last home in daylight, and before he left Keltyburn, there was one thing he wished to do.

Richard stirred. 'I'll be retiring shortly. Go to bed – I won't need you further tonight.' Worboys hesitated; Richard knew he was thinking of who would brush and hang his coat, who would take care of his boots. He sighed. 'Go to bed, Worboys.'

Worboys stiffened. 'Very well, sir – but I do wish we'd pressed on to McEnery House. There, at least, I could have trusted the bootboys.'

'Just be thankful we're here,' Richard advised, 'and not run off the road or stuck in a drift halfway up that damned mountain.'

Worboys sniffed eloquently. His clear intimation was that being stuck in a snowdrift in weather cold enough to freeze the proverbial appendages off brass monkeys was preferable to bad blacking. But he obediently took his rotund self off, rolling away into the shadowy depths of the inn.

His lips twitching into a slight smile, Richard stretched his long legs to the fire roaring in the grate. Whatever the state of the inn's blacking, the landlord hadn't stinted in making them comfortable. Richard had seen no other guests, but in such a quiet backwater, that was unsurprising.

The flames flared; Richard fixed his gaze on them – and wondered, not for the first time, whether this expedition to the Highlands, precipitated by boredom and a very specific fear, hadn't been a trifle rash. But London's entertainments had grown stale; the perfumed bodies so readily – too readily – offered him no longer held any allure. While desire and lust were still there, he'd become finicky, choosy, even more so than he'd already been. He wanted more from a woman than her body and a few moments of earthly bliss.

He frowned and resettled his shoulders – and redirected his thoughts. It was a letter that had brought him here, one from

7

the executor of his long-dead mother's husband, Seamus McEnery, who had recently departed this earth. The uninformative legal missive had summoned him to the reading of the will, to be held the day after tomorrow at McEnery House. If he wished to claim a bequest his mother had made to him, and which Seamus had apparently withheld for nearly thirty years, he had to attend in person.

From what little he'd learned of his late mother's husband, that sounded like Seamus McEnery. The man had been a hothead, brash and vigorous, a hard, determined, wily despot. Which was almost certainly why he'd been born. His mother had not enjoyed being married to such a man; his father, Sebastian Cynster, 5th Duke of St. Ives, sent to McEnery House to douse Seamus's political fire, had taken pity on her and given her what joy he could.

Which had resulted in Richard. The story was so old – thirty years old, to be precise – he no longer felt anything over it, bar a distant regret. For the mother he'd never known. She'd died of fever bare months after his birth; Seamus had sent him post-haste to the Cynsters, the most merciful thing he could have done. They'd claimed him and reared him as one of their own, which, in all ways that mattered, he was. Cynsters bred true, especially the males. He was a Cynster through and through.

And that was the other reason he'd left London. The only important social event he was missing was his cousin Vane's belated wedding breakfast, an occasion he'd viewed with misgiving. He wasn't blind – he'd seen the gleam steadily glowing in the eyes of the older Cynster ladies. Like Helena, the Dowager, his much-loved step-mother, not to mention his fleet of aunts. If he'd attended Vane and Patience's celebration, they'd have set their sights on him. He wasn't yet bored enough, restless enough, to offer himself up, fodder for their matrimonial machinations. Not yet.

He knew himself well, perhaps too well. He wasn't an impulsive man. He liked his life well ordered, predictable – he liked to be in control. He'd seen war in his time but he was a man of peace. Of passion. Of home and hearth.

The phrase raised images in his mind – of Vane and his new bride, of his own half-brother, Devil, and his duchess, Honoria, and their son. Richard shifted and settled, conscious, too conscious, of what his brother and cousin now had. What he himself wanted. Yearned for. He was, after all, a Cynster; he was starting to suspect such plaguey thoughts were ingrained, an inherited susceptiblity. They got under a man's skin and made him . . . edgy. Dissatisfied.

Restless.

Vulnerable.

A board creaked; Richard lifted his gaze, looking through the archway into the hall beyond. A woman emerged from the shadows. Wrapped in a drab cloak, she met his gaze directly, an older woman, her face heavily lined. She measured him swiftly; her gaze turned frosty. Richard suppressed a grin. Spine stiff, her pace unfaltering, the woman turned and climbed the stairs.

Sinking back in his chair, Richard let his lips curve. He was safe from temptation at the Keltyburn Arms.

He looked back at the flames; gradually, his smile died. He shifted once more, easing his shoulders; a minute later, he fluidly rose and crossed to the fogged window.

Rubbing a clear space, he looked out. A starry, moonlit scene met his eyes, a light covering of snow crisping on the ground. Squinting sideways, he could see the church. The kirk. Richard hesitated, then straightened. Collecting his coat from the stand by the door, he went outside.

Abovestairs, Catriona sat at a small wooden table, its surface bare except for a silver bowl, filled with pure spring water, into which she steadily gazed. Distantly, she heard her

9

companion, Algaria, pace along the corridor and enter the room next door, but she was deep in the water, her senses merging with its surface, locked upon it.

And the image formed – the same strong features, the same arrogant eyes. The same aura of restlessness. She didn't probe further – she didn't dare. The image was sharp – he was near.

Dragging in a swift breath, Catriona blinked and pulled back. A knock fell on the door; it opened – Algaria stepped inside. And instantly saw what she'd been up to. She swiftly shut the door. 'What did you see?'

Catriona shook her head. 'It's confusing.' The face was even harder than she'd thought it; the essence of the man's strength was there, clearly delineated for anyone to read. He was a man with no reason to hide his character – he bore the signs openly, arrogantly, like a chieftain.

Like a warrior.

Catriona frowned. She kept stumbling across that word, but she didn't need a warrior – she needed a tame, complaisant, preferably readily besotted gentleman she could marry and so beget an heiress. This man fitted her prescription in only one respect – he was indisputably male. The Lady, She Who Knew All, couldn't possibly mean this man for her.

'But if not that, then what?' Pushing aside the silver bowl, she leaned on the table and cupped her chin in one hand. 'I must be getting my messages crossed.' But she hadn't done that since she was fourteen. 'Perhaps there are two of them?'

'Two of whom?' Algaria hovered near. 'What was the vision?'

Catriona shook her head. The matter was too personal – too sensitive – to divulge to anyone else, even Algaria, her mentor since her mother's death. Not until she'd got to the truth of the matter herself and understood it fully.

Whatever it was she was supposed to understand.

'It's no use.' Determinedly, she stood. 'I must consult The Lady directly.'

10

'What? *Now*?' Algaria stared. 'It's freezing outside.'

'I'm only going to the circle at the end of the graveyard. I won't be out long.' She hated uncertainty, not being sure of her road. And this time, uncertainty had brought an unusual tenseness, a sense of expectation, an unsettling presentiment of excitement. Not the sort of excitement she was accustomed to, either, but something more scintillating, more enticing. Swinging her cloak about her, she looped the ribbons at her throat.

'There's a gentleman downstairs.' Algaria's black eyes flashed. 'He's one you should avoid.'

'Oh?' Catriona hesitated. Could her man be here, under the same roof? The tension that gripped her hardened her resolve; she tied off her ribbons. 'I'll make sure he doesn't see me. And everyone in the village knows me by sight – at least, this sight.' She released her knotted hair, letting it swish about her shoulders. 'There's no danger here.'

Algaria sighed. 'Very well – but don't dally. I suppose you'll tell me what this is all about when you can.'

From the door, Catriona flashed her a smile. 'I promise. Just as soon as I'm sure.'

Halfway down the stairs, she saw the gentleman, short, rotund, and fastidiously dressed, checking the discarded news sheets in the inn's main parlor. His face was as circular as his form; he was definitely not her warrior. Catriona slipped silently down the hall. It was the work of a minute to ease open the heavy door, not yet latched for the night.

And then she was outside.

Pausing on the inn's stone step, she breathed in the crisp, chilly air, and felt the cold reach her head. Invigorated, she pulled her cloak close and stepped out, watching her feet, careful not to slip on the icing snow.

In the graveyard, in the lee of one wall, Richard looked down

11

at his mother's grave. The inscription on the headstone was brief: *Lady Eleanor McEnery, wife of Seamus McEnery, Laird of Keltyhead.* That, and nothing more. No affectionate remembrance; no mention of the bastard son she'd left behind.

Richard's expression didn't change; he'd come to terms with his status long ago. When he'd been abandoned on his father's doorstep, Helena, Devil's mother, had stunned everyone by claiming him as her own. In doing so, she'd given him his place in the ton – no one, even now, would risk her displeasure, or that of the entire Cynster clan, by so much as hinting he was not who she claimed he was. His father's legitimate son. Instinctively shrewd, ebulliently generous, Helena had secured for him his position in society's elite, for which, in his heart, he had never ceased to thank her.

The woman whose bones lay beneath this cold stone had, however, given him life – and he could do nothing to thank her.

Except, perhaps, to live life fully.

His only knowledge of his mother had come from his father; when, in all innocence, he'd asked if his father had loved his mother, Sebastian had ruffled his hair and said: 'She was very lovely and very lonely – she deserved more than she got from her marriage.' He'd paused, then added: 'I felt sorry for her.' He'd looked at him, and his slow smile had creased his face. 'But I love you. I regret her death, but I can't regret your birth.'

He could understand how his father had felt – he was, after all, a Cynster to the bone. Family, children, home, and hearth – those were what mattered to Cynsters. Those were their quintessential warrior goals, for them the ultimate victories of life.

For long, silent minutes, he stood before the grave, until the cold finally penetrated his boots. With a sigh, he shifted, then straightened and, after one last, long look, turned and retraced his steps.

What was it his mother had left him? And why, having concealed her bequest all these years, had Seamus summoned him back now, after his own death? Richard rounded the kirk, his stride slow, the sound of his footfalls subsumed by the breeze softly whistling through snowladen branches. He reached the main path and stepped onto it – and heard crisp, determined footsteps approaching from beyond the kirk. Halting, he turned and beheld . . .

A creature of magic and moonlight.

A woman, her dark cloak billowing about her, her head bare. Over her shoulders and down her back spread the most glorious mane of thick, rippling, silken hair, sheening copper-bright in the moonlight, a beacon against the wintering trees behind her. Her stride was definite, every footfall decisive; her eyes were cast down, but he would have sworn she wasn't watching her steps.

She came on without pause, heading directly for him. He couldn't see her face, or her figure beneath the full cloak, but well-honed instincts rarely lied. His senses stirred, stretched, then focused powerfully – a clear case of lust at first sight. Lips lifting in wolfish anticipation, Richard silently turned and prepared to make the lady's acquaintance.

Catriona strode briskly up the path, lips compressed, a frown knitting her brows. She'd been a disciple of The Lady too long not to know how to couch her requests for clarification; the question she'd asked had been succinct and to the point. She'd asked for the true significance of the man whose face haunted her. The Lady's reply, the words that had formed in her mind, had been brutally concise: *He will father your children.*

There were not, no matter how she twisted them, very many ways in which to interpret those words.

Which left her with a very large problem. Unprecedented though it might be, The Lady *must* have made a mistake. This man, whoever he was, was arrogant, ruthless – dominant. *She* needed a sweet, simple soul, one content to remain quietly supportive while she ruled their roost. She didn't need strength – she needed weakness. There was absolutely no point sending her a warrior without a cause.

Catriona humphed; her breath steamed before her face. Through the clearing wisps, she spied – the very last thing she expected to see – a pair of large, black, highly polished Hessians, directly in her path. She tried to stop; her soles found no grip on the icy path – her momentum sent her skidding on. She tried to flail her arms; they were trapped beneath her cloak. On a gasp, she looked up, just as she collided with the owner of the boots.

The impact knocked the air from her lungs; for one instant, she was sure she'd hit a tree. But her nose buried itself in a soft cravat, mid-chest, just above the V of a silk waistcoat. His chin passed above her head; her scalp prickled as long hairs were gently brushed. And arms like steel slowly closed about her.

Instinct awoke in a flustered rush; raising her hands, she pushed against his chest.

Her feet slipped, then slid.

She gasped again – and clutched wildly instead of pushing. The steely arms tightened, and suddenly only her toes touched the snow. Catriona dragged in a breath – one too shallow to steady her whirling head. Her lungs had seized; her senses skittered wildly, informing her, in breathless detail, that she was pressed, breast to thigh, against a man.

Not just any man – one with a body like warm, flexing steel. She had to lean back to look into his face.

Blue, blue eyes met hers.

Catriona stilled; she stared. Then she blinked. It took half a second to check – arrogant mien, decisive chin – it was he.

Narrowing her eyes, she fixed them on his; if The Lady had made no mistake, then it behooved her to begin as she meant to go on. 'Put me down.'

She'd learned the knack of commanding obedience at her mother's knee; her simple words held echoes of authority, undertones of compulsion.

He heard them; he angled his head, one black brow rising, then the ends of his long lips lifted. 'In a minute.'

It was her turn to listen and hear the intent in his deep purr. Her eyes flew wide.

'But first . . .'

If she'd been able to think, she'd have screamed, but the shock of his touch, the intimate warmth of his palm as he framed her face, distracted her. His lips completed the conquest – they swooped, arrogantly confident, and settled over hers.

The first contact stunned her; she ceased to breathe. The very concept of breathing drifted from her mind as his lips moved lazily on hers. They were neither warm nor cool, yet heat lingered in their touch. They pressed close, then eased, sipped, supped, then returned. Firm and demanding, they impinged on her senses, reaching deep, stirring her.

She stirred in his encircling arm; it locked tight about her. Heat surrounded her – even through her thick cloak, it reached for her, enveloped her, then sank into her flesh. And grew, built, a crescendo of warmth seeking release. His hot hunger had infected her. Utterly distracted, she tried to hold it back, tried to deny its existence, tried vainly to dampen it down.

And couldn't. She was facing ignominious defeat – with not a clue of what followed – when the hard hand tilting her face shifted. He altered his grip; one thumb pressed insistently in the center of her chin.

Her jaw eased; her lips parted.

He entered.

The shock of the first touch of tongue against tongue literally curled her toes. She would have gasped, but that was impossible; all she could do was feel. Feel and follow, and sense the reality of that hot hunger, the surprisingly subtle, deeply evocative, seductively physical need. And hold hard against the temptation that streaked through her.

Even while he took arrogance to new heights.

She hadn't thought it possible, but he gathered her more closely, imprinting her soft flesh with the male hardness of his. Ruthlessly confident, he angled his head and tasted her – languorously, unhurriedly – as if he had all the time in the world.

*Then* he settled to play.

To advance and retreat, to artfully entice her into joining the game. The very idea shocked her to her toes – and sent shards of excitement flying down her nerves. They stretched, tightened. His lips and tongue continued their tantalizing dance.

She responded – tentatively; instead of the aggressive response she expected, his lips softened fractionally, encouragingly. She dared more, returning the pressure of his lips, the sensuous caress of his tongue.

Without even knowing it, she sank into the kiss.

Triumph streaked through Richard; he mentally crowed. He'd laid waste her starchy resistance; she was soft and pliant, pure magic in his arms. She tasted like the sweetest summer wine. The heady sensation went straight to his head.

And straight to his loins.

Staving off the burgeoning ache, he feasted, careful not to startle her, to let her wits surface enough to recognize his liberties. He wasn't fool enough to think she wouldn't break away if he gave her sufficient cause. She was no simple country miss, no naive maid – her three words, her attitude, had reeked of authority. And she wasn't young; no young lady would have had the confidence to command him, of all men, to '*Put me down.*' She was not girl, but woman – and she fitted very well, supple and curvaceous in his arms.

How well she was fitting, how tempting her curves were, locked hard against him, registered, and raised his lust to new heights. The soft, silken sway of her heavy hair, a warm, living veil drifting over the backs of his hands, and the perfume – wildflowers, the promise of spring and the fecundity of growing things – that rose from the silky locks, converted lust to pain.

It was he who pulled back and ended the kiss – it was that, or suffer worse agony. For he would have to let her go, untouched, unsampled, his lust unsated; a snowbound churchyard in the depths of a winter's night was a challenge even he balked at.

And, despite the intimate caresses they'd exchanged, he knew she wasn't that sort of lady. He'd breached her walls by sheer brazen recklessness, evoked by her haughty command to put her down. Right now, he'd like to lay her down, but that, he knew, was not to be.

He raised his head.

Her eyes flew wide; she looked at him as if he was a ghost. '*Lady preserve me.*'

Her words were a fervent whisper; condensed by the cold, they misted the air between them. She searched his face – for what, Richard could not guess; with his customary arrogance, he raised one brow.

Lips, soft and rosy – much rosier now than before – firmed. 'By the Lady's veil! This is *madness!*'

She shook her head and pushed against his chest; bemused, Richard set her down carefully, then released her. Frowning

17

absentmindedly, she stepped around and past him, then whirled to face him. 'Who *are* you?'

'Richard Cynster.' He sketched her an elegant bow. Straightening, he trapped her gaze. 'Entirely at your service.'

Her eyes snapped. 'Do you make a habit of accosting innocent women in graveyards?'

'Only when they walk into my arms.'

'I *requested* you to put me down.'

'You *ordered* me to put you down – and I did. Eventually.'

'Yes. But . . .' Her tirade – he was sure it would have been a tirade – died on her lips. She blinked at him. 'You're *English!*'

An accusation rather than an observation. Richard arched a brow. 'Cynsters are.'

Eyes narrowing, she studied his face. 'Of Norman descent?'

He smiled, proudly arrogant. 'We came over with the Conqueror.' His smile deepening, he let his gaze sweep her. 'We still like to dabble, of course.' Looking up, he trapped her gaze. 'To keep our hand in with the occasional conquest.'

Even in the weak light, he saw her glare, saw the sparks that flared in her eyes.

'I'll have you know this is all a *very big mistake!*'

With that, she whirled away. Snow crunched, louder than before, as, in a flurry of skirts and cloak, she stalked off. Brows rising, Richard watched her storm through the lych-gate, saw the quick, frowning glance she threw him from the shadows beneath. Then, with a toss of her head, chin high, she marched up the road.

Toward the inn.

The ends of Richard's lips lifted. His brows rose another, more considering, notch. Mistake?

He watched until she disappeared from sight, then stirred, straightened his shoulders, and, lips curving in a wolfish smile, strolled unhurriedly in her wake.

18

# Chapter Two

Richard rose early the next morning. He shaved and dressed, conscious of a familiar excitement – the excitement of the hunt. Creasing the last fold of his cravat, he reached for his diamond pin – a rough shout reached his ears. He stilled – and heard, muffled by the windows tight shut against the winter chill, the unmistakable clack of hooves on cobbles.

Three swift strides had him at the window, looking down through the frosted pane. A heavy travelling carriage stood before the inn door, ostlers holding a pair of strong horses, breaths fogging as they stamped. Boys from the inn wrestled a trunk onto the carriage roof, the innkeeper directing them.

Then a lady emerged from the porch, directly below Richard. The innkeeper sprang to open the carriage door. His bow was respectful, which did not surprise Richard – the lady was his acquaintance of the churchyard.

'Damn!' Eyes on her long tresses, flame bright in the morning, clipped together so they rippled like a river down her back, he swore beneath his breath.

With a regal nod, the lady entered the carriage without a backward glance; she was followed by the older woman Richard had seen in the inn. Just before ascending the carriage steps, the old woman looked back – and up – straight at Richard. He resisted the urge to step back; an instant later, the woman turned and followed her companion into the carriage.

The innkeeper closed the door, the coachman clicked the reins and the carriage lumbered out of the yard. Richard swore some more – his prey was escaping. The carriage reached the end of the village street and turned, not left, toward Crieff, but right – up the road to Keltyhead.

Richard frowned. According to Jessup, his groom and coachman, the narrow, winding Keltyhead road led to McEnery House, and nowhere else.

A discreet tap fell on the door; Worboys entered. Shutting the door, he announced: 'The lady after whom you were inquiring has just departed the inn, sir.'

'I know that.' Richard turned from the window; the carriage was out of sight. 'Who is she?'

'A Miss Catriona Hennessy, sir. A connection of the late Mr. McEnery.' Worboys's expression turned supercilious. 'The innkeep, an ignorant heathen, maintains the lady is a witch, sir.'

Richard snorted and turned back to his mirror. Witchy, yes. A witch? It hadn't been any exotic spell that had bewitched him in the night, in the crisp cold of the kirk yard. Memories of sleek, warm, feminine curves, of soft, luscious lips, of an intoxicating kiss, returned ...

Setting his pin into his cravat, he reached for his coat. 'We'll leave as soon as I've breakfasted.'


His first sight of McEnery House colored Richard's vision of Seamus McEnery and his mother's last years. Clinging to the wind-whipped side of the mountain, the two-story structure seemed hewn from the rock behind it and weathered in similar fashion, totally uninviting as a suitable habitat for humans. Live ones, anyway – the place could have qualified as a mausoleum. The prevailing impression of hard and cold was emphasized by the lack of any vestige of a garden – even the trees, which might have softened the severe lines, stopped well back from the house as if fearing to draw nearer.

Descending from his carriage, Richard could detect no sign of warmth or life, no light burning in defiance of the dull day, no rich curtains draped elegantly about the sashes. Indeed, the windows were narrow and few, presumably from necessity. It had been cold in Keltyburn, at the foot of the mountain – up here, it was freezing.

The front door opened to Worboys's peremptory knock; Richard ascended the steps, leaving Worboys and two footmen to deal with his luggage. An old butler stood waiting just inside the door.

'Richard Cynster,' Richard drawled, and handed him his cane. 'Here at the behest of the late Mr. McEnery.'

The butler bowed. 'The family are in the parlor, sir.'

He relieved Richard of his heavy coat, then led the way. Richard followed; the impression of a tomb intensified as they travelled down uncarpeted flagged corridors, through stone archways flanked by columns of solid granite, past door after door shut tight against the world. The chill was pervasive; Richard was contemplating asking for his coat back when the butler halted and opened a door.

Announced, Richard entered.

'Oh! I say.' A ruddy-complexioned gentleman with a shock of reddish hair struggled to his feet – he'd been engaged in a game of spillikins with a boy and a girl on the rug before the fire.

It was a scene so much like the ones Richard was accustomed to, his cool expression relaxed. 'Don't let me interrupt.'

'No, no! That is ...' Abruptly drawing breath, the man thrust out his hand. 'Jamie McEnery.' Then, as if recalling the matter with some surprise, he added: 'Laird of Keltyhead.'

Richard gripped the hand offered him. About three years

21

his junior, Jamie was a good head shorter than he, stocky, with a round face and the sort of expression that could only be called open.

'Did you have a good trip up?'

'Tolerably.' Richard glanced at the others seated about the room, a surprising number all garbed in dull mourning.

'Here! Let me introduce you.'

Jamie proceeded to do so; Richard smoothly acknowledged Mary, Jamie's wife, a sweet-faced young woman too passive for his tastes, but, he suspected, quite right for Jamie, and their children, Martha and Alister, both of whom watched him through big, round eyes as if they'd never seen anyone like him before. And then there were Jamie's siblings, two whey-faced sisters with their mild husbands and very young, rather sickly looking broods, and last, Jamie's younger brother Malcolm, who appeared not only weak but peevish.

Accepting a chair, Richard had never before felt so much like a large, marauding predator unexpectedly welcomed into a roomful of scrawny chickens. But he hid his teeth and duly took tea to warm him after his journey. The weather provided instant conversation.

'Looks like more snow on the way,' Jamie remarked. 'Good thing you got here before it.'

Richard murmured his assent and sipped his tea.

'It's been particularly cold up here this year,' Mary nervously informed him. 'But the cities – Edinburgh and Glasgow – are somewhat warmer.'

Her sisters-in-law murmured inaudible agreement.

Malcolm stirred, a dissatisfied frown on his face. 'I don't know why we can't remove there for winter like our neighbors do. There's nothing to do here.'

A tense silence ensued, then Jamie rushed into speech. 'Do you shoot? There's good game to be had – Da' always insisted the coverts were kept up to scratch.'

22

With an easy smile, Richard picked up the conversational gauntlet and helped Jamie steer the talk away from the families' obviously straitened circumstances. A quick glance confirmed that the gentlemen's coats and boots were well worn, even patched, the ladies' gowns a far cry from the latest fashions. The younger children's clothes were clearly hand-me-downs, while the coat Malcolm hunched in was a size too big – one of Jamie's doing double duty.

The answer to Malcolm's question was transparent – Seamus's children lived under his chilly roof because they had nowhere else to go. At least, Richard mused, they had this place as a refuge, and Seamus must have left them well provided for; there was no hint of poverty about the house itself, or its servants. Or the quality of the tea.

Finishing his, he set his cup down and wondered, not for the first time, where his witch was hiding. He'd detected no trace of her, or her older shadow, even in the others' faces. He'd seen her witchy face clearly enough in the bright moonlight; the only resemblance she shared with Jamie and his siblings lay in their red hair. And, perhaps, he conceded, the freckles.

Jamie's and Malcolm's faces were a collage of freckles, their sisters' only marginally less affected. His memory of the witch's complexion was of ivory cream, unblemished except for a dusting of freckles over her pert nose. He'd have to check when next he saw her; despite his wish to hasten that event, he made no mention of her. With no idea who she was – where she stood in relation to the family – he was too wise to mention their meeting, or express any interest in others who might be present.

Languidly, he rose, causing a nervous flutter among the ladies.

Jamie immediately rose, too. 'Is there anything we can get you? I mean – anything you might need?'

23

While struggling to strike the right note as head of the family, Jamie had an openness of which Richard approved; he smiled lazily down at him. 'No, thank you. I have all I need.' Bar an elusive witch.

With an easy smile and his usual faultless grace, he excused himself and withdrew to his room to refresh himself before luncheon.

Richard did not set eyes on his witch until that evening, when she glided into the drawing room, immediately preceding the butler. As that venerable individual intoned the words 'Dinner is served,' she swept the gathering with a calm and distant smile – until she came to him, standing beside Mary's chair.

Her smile died – stunned astonishment took its place.

Slowly, with deliberate intent, Richard smiled back.

For one quivering instant, her stunned silence held sway, then Jamie stepped forward. 'Ah ... Catriona, this is Mr. Cynster. He's been summoned for the reading of the will.'

Deserting his face, she fixed her gaze on Jamie's. 'He has?' Her tone conveyed much more than a simple question.

Jamie shuffled and shot an apologetic glance at Richard. 'Da's first wife made him a bequest. Da' held it until now.'

Frowning, she opened her lips to quiz Jamie. Having silently prowled closer, Richard took her hand – she jumped and tried to snatch it back, but he didn't let go.

'Good evening, Miss ...' Richard slanted a questioning glance at Jamie.

Instead, his witch answered, in tones colder than ice. 'Miss Hennessy.'

Again, she surreptitiously tugged, trying to free her hand; Richard unhurriedly brought his gaze to her face, waited until she looked up, trapped her eyes with his, then smoothly raised her hand. 'A pleasure,' he purred. Slowly, deliberately, he brushed her knuckles with his lips – and felt the shiver of awareness that raced through her – the shiver she couldn't hide. His smile deepened. 'Miss Hennessy.'

The look she sent him should have laid him out dead on the Aubusson rug; Richard merely lifted a brow, deliberately arrogant, deliberately provocative. And held onto her hand, and her gaze. 'What Jamie is understandably hesitant over explaining, Miss Hennessy, is that Mr. McEnery's first wife was my mother.'

Still frowning, she glanced at Jamie, who colored. 'Your ...?' Understanding dawned; she looked back at him. 'Oh.' The veriest hint of pink tinged her ivory cheeks. 'I see.'

There was, to Richard's surprise, no hint of condemnation, or consternation, in her voice – she didn't even yank her hand away, as he'd fully expected; her slim fingers lay quiescent in his grasp. Her eyes searched his, then she inclined her head, coldly gracious, the action clearly signifying her understanding, and a regal agreement to his right to be present. There was no suggestion in any element of her bearing that she was perturbed at learning he was a bastard.

In all his years, Richard had never met with such calm acceptance.

'Catriona is my father's—' Jamie broke off and cleared his throat. 'Actually, *my* ward.'

'Ah.' Richard smiled urbanely at Catriona. 'That explains her presence, then.'

He fielded another of her lethal glances, but before he could respond, Mary bustled up and claimed Jamie's arm.

'If you could lead Catriona in, Mr. Cynster?'

With Jamie in tow, Mary led the way; entirely content, Richard placed the intriguing Miss Hennessey's hand on his sleeve and elegantly steered her in their wake.

She glided beside him, a galleon fully armed, queenly detachment hanging about her like a cloak. As they left the drawing room, Richard noted that the older woman had also appeared; she had been standing near the door.

'The lady who accompanies you?'

There was a palpable hesitation, then she elected to answer. 'Miss O'Rourke is my companion.'

The dining room lay across the cavernous hall; Richard led his fair charge to the chair beside Jamie, at the table's head, then, at Jamie's intimation, took the seat opposite, on Jamie's right. The rest of the family and Miss O'Rourke took their places. The room was large, the table long; the distance between the diners was enough to discourage those conversations not already dampened by the atmosphere. Despite the blaze roaring in the hearth, it was chilly; a sense of long-standing austerity hung over the room.

'Could you pass the condiments?'

With that the limit of conversation, as the courses came and went, Richard used the time to indulge his curiosity about Seamus McEnery. With no other avenue available, he studied Seamus's house, his household, his family, for what insights they could offer of the man.

A cursory inspection of those he'd met earlier told him little more; they were, one and all, meek, mild, selfeffacing, their very timidity a comment on Seamus and how he'd reared his children. Miss O'Rourke had an interesting face, deeply lined and unusually weathered for a gentlewoman's; Richard didn't need to study it for long to know she distrusted him deeply. The fact did not perturb him; companions of beautiful ladies generally distrusted him on sight. Which left – Catriona Hennessy.

She was, without doubt, the most interesting body in the room. In a gown of deep lavender silk, with her lustrous locks – neither gold nor plain red, but true copper – piled high on her head, tendrils escaping to frame her face in flames, the round neckline of her gown scooped low enough to give a fair indication of the bounty beneath, her shoulders and arms sweetly turned and encased in skin like ivory satin, she was a sight designed for lecherous eyes.

Richard looked his fill. Her face was a delicate oval, with a straight, little nose and a smooth, wide brow. Her brows and lashes were light brown, framing eyes of vibrant green – something he hadn't been able to see in the moonlight, although he did recall how the gold flecks within the green had flared with indignation. He felt sure they would blaze in anger – and smolder with passion. Her only lessthan-perfect feature was her chin; that, Richard considered, was a touch too firm, too determined. Too self-willed. She was of below average height, petite and slender, yet her figure, though sleek and supple, was not boyish. Indeed not. Her figure made his palms itch.

Unrestrained by the usual demands of polite dinner conversation, he surreptitiously let his gaze feast. Only when the desserts were set before them did he sit back and let his social senses take stock. Only then did he notice that while the others occasionally exchanged idle glances and the odd desultory comment, none looked at him, or at Catriona. Indeed, with the sole exception of the silent but watchful, and disapproving, Miss O'Rourke, they all kept their gazes carefully averted, as if fearful of drawing his attention. Only Jamie interacted with either Catriona or himself, and then only stiltedly, when need arose.

Curious, Richard tried to catch Malcolm's eye, and failed; the youth seemed, if anything, to sink further into his chair. Glancing at Catriona, Richard saw her look up and scan the table; everyone took care not to meet her gaze. Unperturbed, she patted her lips with her napkin. Richard focused on the soft pink curves, and remembered, with startling clarity, precisely how they tasted.

Shaking aside the memory, he inwardly shook his head. Apparently Seamus's family were so trenchantly timid, they

27

were moved to treat both Catriona and himself like potentially dangerous animals who might bite if provoked.

Which definitely said something about his witch.

Maybe she really was a witch?

That thought provoked others – like what a witch would be like in bed; he was deep in salacious imaginings when Jamie nervously cleared his throat and turned to Catriona.

'Actually, Catriona, I've been thinking that, now Da's gone and you'll be my ward, that it really would be better – more fitting, I mean – if you were to come and live here.'

Caught in the act of swallowing a spoonful of trifle, Catriona stilled, then swallowed, laid down her spoon, and looked directly at Jamie.

'With us, the family,' he hurried on. 'It must be very lonely at the vale all by yourself.'

Catriona's expression grew stern; her green eyes held Jamie's. 'Your father thought the same, if you recall?'

It was immediately clear everyone at the table, bar Richard, did; a communal shudder passed around the room, even including the footmen, silent by the walls.

'Luckily,' Catriona went on, her gaze still locked with Jamie's, 'Seamus thought better of it, and allowed me to live as The Lady wishes, at the manor.' She paused, eyes steady, giving everyone time to feel the weight behind her words. Then she raised her brows. 'Do you truly wish to set your will against that of The Lady?'

Jamie blanched. 'No, no! We just thought you might like to . . .' He gestured vaguely.

Catriona looked down and picked up her spoon. 'I'm perfectly content at the manor.'

The matter was closed. Jamie exchanged a glance with Mary at the other end of the table; she shrugged lightly and grimaced. Other members of the family shot quick glances at Catriona, then rapidly looked away.

Richard didn't; he continued to study her. Her authority was remarkable; she used it like a shield. She'd put it up and Jamie, poor sod, had run headlong into it. Richard recognized the ploy; she'd tried the same with him with her '*Put me down*,' but he'd been too experienced to fall for it – she'd been all woman once he'd got his hands on her, soft, warm, and pliant. The thought of having his hands on her again, of having her warm, pliant, feminine flesh beneath him, made him shift in his seat.

And focused his mind even more. On why, exactly, he found her so . . . appealing. She wasn't, in fact, classically beautiful; she was more powerfully attractive than that. It was, he decided, noting the independent set of her too-determined chin, the underlying sense of wildness that caught him – caught and focused his hunter's instincts so forcefully. Her aura of mystery, of magic, of feminine forces too powerful for simple words, was an open challenge to a man like him.

A bored rake like him.

She would never have been acceptable within the ton; that hint of the wild was far too strong for society's palate. She was no meek miss; she was different, and used no guile to conceal it. Her confidence, her presence, her authority had led him to think her in her late twenties; now he could see her more clearly, he realized that wasn't so. Early twenties. Which made her assurance and self-confidence even more intriguing. More challenging.

Richard set down his goblet; he'd had enough of cold silence. 'Have you lived at this manor long, Miss Hennessy?'

She looked up, faint surprise in her eyes. 'All my life, Mr. Cynster.'

Richard raised his brows. 'Where, exactly, is it?'

'In the Lowlands.' When he waited, patently wanting more, she added: 'The manor stands in the Vale of Casphairn, which is a valley in the foothills of Merrick.' Licking trifle from her spoon, she considered him. 'That's—'

'In the Galloway Hills,' he returned.

Her brows rose. 'Indeed.'

'And who is your landlord?'

'No one.' When he again raised his brows, she explained: 'I own the manor – I inherited it from my parents.'

Richard inclined his head. 'And this lady you speak of?'

The smile she gave him was ageless. 'The Lady.' The cadence of her voice changed, investing her words with reverence. 'She Who Knows All.'

'Ah.' Richard blinked. 'I see.' And he did. Christianity might rule in London and the towns, and in the Parliament, but the auld ways, the doctrines of days past, still held sway in the countryside. He had grown up in rural Cambridgeshire, in the fields and copses, seeing the old women gathering herbs, hearing of their balms and potions that could cure a large spectrum of mortal ills. He'd seen too much to be skeptical, and knew enough to treat any such practitioner with due respect.

She'd held his gaze steadily; Richard saw the gleam of triumph, of victorious smugness in her eyes. She thought she'd successfully warned him off – scared him away. Inwardly, his grin was the very essence of predatory; outwardly, his expression said nothing at all.

'Catriona?'

They both turned to see Mary rising and beckoning; Catriona rose, too, and joined the female exodus to the drawing room, leaving the gentlemen to their port.

Which was, to Richard's immense relief, excellent. Twirling his glass, he considered the ruby liquid within. 'So,' – he flicked a glance at Jamie – 'Catriona is now in your care?'

Jamie's sigh was heartfelt. 'Yes – for another three years. Until she's twenty-five.'

'Are her parents long dead?'

'Six years. They were killed in an accident in Glasgow while arranging to buy a cargo – a terrible shock it was.'

Richard raised his brows. 'An especially big shock for Catriona. She would have been – what? Seventeen?'

'Sixteen. Naturally, Da' wanted her here – the vale's an isolated spot, no place for a lone girl, you'd think.'

'She wouldn't come?'

Jamie's face contorted. 'Da' made her. She came.' He shuddered, and took a long sip of his port. 'It was horrific. The arguments – the shouting. I thought Da' would have a seizure, she goaded him that much. I don't think he'd ever had anyone argue back like she did – *I* wouldna dared.'

As he drank more port, Jamie's accent emerged; like many Scots of his age, he'd learned to suppress it.

'She didna want to stay – Da' wanted her here. He had plans afoot to marry her well – she needed someone to take care of her lands, he thought.'

'Her lands?'

'The vale.' Jamie drained his glass. 'She owns the whole damned valley from head to mouth. But she wasn't having any of Da's plans. Said she knew what she was doing, she had The Lady to guide her, and she would, on her mother's grave, obey The Lady, not Da'. She was dead set against marriage. Mind you, when those lairds who'd offered for her on the strength of her lands actually met her, they sang a different tune. All the offers dissolved like mist in a strong breeze.'

Richard frowned, wondering if Scottish notions of feminine attractions were so different.

'Of course, everyone o' them was imagining bedding her, until they spoke to her.' Jamie's lips quirked; he exchanged a conspiratorial glance with Richard. 'She scared 'em silly – the beggars came from Edinburgh and Glasgow, or one of the cities, lairds in need of estates. They didna know about The

Lady, and to hear Catriona tell it, if they displeased her at all, she wouldha' turned 'em into toads. Or eels. Or some such slimy creature.'

Richard grinned. 'They believed her?'

'Aye, well – when she wants to be believed, she can be that persuasive.'

Recalling the power he'd heard her wield twice, Richard had no difficulty believing that.

'And that other one, Algaria – Miss O'Rourke – was there to help. So,' – Jamie reached for the decanter – 'after that, there were no more offers. Da' was livid – Catriona was unmovable. The fighting raged for weeks.'

'And?'

'She won.' Jamie set down his glass. 'She went back to the vale, an' that was that. Da' never spoke of her again. I didna think she'd agree to live here now, but Mary said we should at least ask. Especially after finding the letters.'

'Letters?'

'Offers for her lands, rather than her hand. Heaps of 'em. Some from the lairds who'd given up notions of bedding her, others from all over, some from her neighbors in the Lowlands. All, however, for a pittance.' Again Jamie drained his glass. 'I found the pile in Da's desk – he'd scrawled comments on many.' Jamie's lips twisted. 'Like "Bah! Am I a fool?"'

'The land's good?'

'Good?' Jamie set down his glass. 'You won't find better in Scotland.' He met Richard's eye. 'According to Catriona and her people, The Lady sees to that.'

Richard raised his brows.

'Aye, well.' With a rueful grimace, Jamie pushed back his chair. 'We'd best get back to the drawing room.'

Entering the long room beside Jamie, Richard paused just

beyond the threshold. To one side, Catriona stood chatting to one of Jamie's colorless sisters. Perhaps chatting was the wrong word – from her gestures, lecturing might be nearer the mark. The ever watchful Miss O'Rourke stood silently, hands clasped, by Catriona's shoulder; her gaze, black and expressionless, was already fixed on him. Richard resisted the urge to grin wickedly at her; instead, with his usual grace, he crossed to pay his compliments to his hostess.

Mary was easily flattered, easily flustered; Richard spent some time calming her, until she could smile at him and answer his questions.

'She doesn't seem to see any need for a husband.' Her eyes darted to Catriona, then returned to his face. 'It seems odd, I know, but she has been running the manor for six years now, and I gather everything goes smoothly.' Another darting glance lingered on Catriona's elegant dark lavender gown. 'She certainly seems to want for nothing, and she's never made any claim on the McEnerys.'

'I'm surprised,' – Richard affected his most indolent drawl— 'that there are no local aspirants to her hand. Or does the valley boast only a few souls?'

'Oh, no. The population's quite considerable, I believe. But none of the young men would look to Catriona, you know.' Mary regarded him earnestly. 'She's their "lady," you see. The lady of the vale.'

'Ah.' Richard nodded, although he didn't see at all, but there was a limit to how far he could question even sweet Mary without raising suspicions. But he wanted to understand who and what Catriona Hennessy was, and how she'd come to be so. She was an intriguing 'lady' on a number of fronts; he'd been so bored, she was a breath of fresh air – a fresh taste to his jaded palate.

He glanced her way and saw her look sharply at Algaria O'Rourke as the older woman struggled to suppress a yawn.

The conversation that ensued was easy to follow; Catriona, moved by concern, pulled rank and ordered her watchdog to bed. Richard quickly looked away – and felt, a second later, the older woman's suspicious glance. But she went, passing the tea trolley on her way. The butler stationed the trolley before Mary.

'Let me help.' Richard collected the first two cups Mary poured. 'I'll take them to Miss Hennessy and ...'

'Meg,' Mary supplied with a smile. 'If you would be so kind.'

Richard smiled and moved away.

'Meg? Miss Hennessy?'

Both turned in response to his drawl. Meg's eyes fixed on the cups in his hands. 'Oh! Ah ...' She swallowed, and turned a delicate shade of green. 'I ... don't think so.' She cast a desperate glance at Catriona. 'If you'll excuse me?'

With a helpless look at Richard, she hurried across the room and slipped out of the door.

'Well!' Brows high, Richard looked down at the tea. 'Is it that bad?'

'Of course not.' Catriona relieved him of one cup. 'It's just that Meg's increasing and a bit fragile at present. The most unexpected things turn her stomach.'

'Is that what you've been so earnestly discussing?'

'Yes.'

Richard met Catriona's gaze over the rim of her cup as she sipped; her head barely topped his shoulder, yet her manner proclaimed her belief that she was as powerful, if not more powerful, than he. There was no hint of feminine weakness, or any acknowledgment of susceptibility.

Lowering her cup, she eyed him evenly. 'I'm a healer.'

The declaration was cool; Richard affected polite surprise. 'Oh?' He'd assumed as much, but better she think him an ignorant southerner, a gullible Sassenach, if she were so disposed. 'Eye of newt and toe of frog?'

The look she cast him was measuring. 'I use herbs and roots, and other lore.'

'Do you spend much time hovering over a bubbling cauldron, or is it more like a well-stocked stillroom?'

She drew a tight breath, her gaze on his steadfastly innocent expression, then exhaled. 'A stillroom. An *encyclopedic* one.'

'Not a cave, then.' Bit by bit, Richard drew her out – and with each factual answer, her fridigity melted a fraction more. He held to his harmless, bantering pose, letting his gaze touch her face only briefly, politely. Her hair drew his eyes more frequently, a magnetic beacon. Even among all the redheads in the room, her crowning glory made her stand out. The soft curls shimmered in the candlelight; those about her face and neck jiggled as she moved, exerting the same mesmeric attraction as dancing flames. They held the promise of heat – Richard felt an overwhelming urge to warm his hands in them.

He blinked and forced himself to look away.

'Naturally, there are some things not available locally, but we send out for them.'

'Naturally,' he murmured. Shifting so he stood beside her, supposedly scanning the room, he glanced swiftly at her profile. The ice had melted significantly; with her flaming tresses and those gold sparks in her eyes, he felt sure there'd be a volcano beneath. For the first time since joining her, he focused intently on her face. 'Your lips taste of roses, did you know?'

She stiffened, but didn't disappoint him; the look she shot him over the rim of her cup held fire, not ice. 'I thought you would be gentleman enough to forget that incident entirely. Wipe it from your mind.'

There was compulsion in her last words; Richard let it flow

past him. He smiled lazily down at her. 'You have that twisted. I'm far *too* much a gentleman to forget that incident, not even its most minor detail.'

'No gentleman would mention it.'

'How many gentlemen do you know?'

She sniffed. 'You shouldn't have grabbed me like that.'

'My dear Miss Hennessy! You walked into my arms.'

'You shouldn't have held me like that.'

'If I hadn't held you, you would have slipped and fallen on your luscious—'

'And you certainly shouldn't have kissed me.'

'That was unavoidable.'

She blinked. 'Unavoidable?'

Richard looked down, into her green eyes. 'Utterly.' He held her gaze, then raised his brows. 'Of course, you didn't have to kiss me back.'

Color rose in her cheeks; she looked back at her cup. 'A moment of temporary insanity, immediately regretted.'

'Oh?'

She glanced up, hearing danger in his tone, but wasn't quick enough to stop him from stroking, not the nape of her neck, so temptingly exposed, but the coppery curls that caressed her sensitive skin. Unobserved by the company, Richard caressed them.

And she shivered, quivered.

Then hauled in a breath and thrust her empty cup at him. 'I find the company entirely too fatiguing – and the journey here was boring in the extreme.' Her words were couched in sheet ice, her tone a chill wind blowing straight from the Arctic. 'If you'll excuse me, I believe I shall retire.'

'Now, *that,*' Richard said, taking the cup, 'I didn't expect.'

She paused in the act of stepping away and shot him a suspicious glance. 'What didn't you expect?'

'I didn't expect you to run away.' He looked down at her

as she studied him, and wondered how she did it. No hint of volcanic heat remained, not even a tiny glow of feminine warmth; she was encased in polar ice, colder than any iceberg. And the air had literally turned chill – the lady of the vale could give the ice-maidens of London lessons. He let the ends of his lips curve. 'I'm only teasing you.'

It came to him then – no other man had – no other man had ever dared.

She frowned, measuring him and his words. Eventually, she exhaled. 'I won't go if you keep your hands to yourself and don't mention our previous encounter. As I told you, that was a complete and utter mistake.'

Catriona imbued the last words with conviction, but, as before, it had little effect. He seemed immune, as if he could deflect her suggestive powers easily – an observation that did little to settle her skittish nerves.

When she'd walked into the drawing room and seen him there, his blue gaze direct, as if he'd been waiting for her, she had, for the first time in her life, literally felt faint. Dumbfounded. And . . . something else. Something more akin to searing excitement, something that had made her nervous, aware, set alive in a way she'd never been before.

For the first time in a long while, she wasn't sure she could control her world, her situation. She was not at all sure she could control him.

Which, first and last, was the crux of her problem.

She watched as he set their empty cups on a side table, and wished he'd been forced to keep them in his hands. Hands she'd already spent some time studying; longfingered, elegantly made, they were the hands of an artist, not a warrior. At least, not a simple warrior. Standing beside him, she was all too aware that her bedevilled senses had reported accurately on the man who had stolen a kiss – several kisses – from her. He was large and strong – not the strength of

37

sheer brawn, but a more supple, skillful strength, infinitely more dangerous. There was intelligence in his eyes, and something else besides – the embers of that hot, prowling hunger glowed behind the blue.

He straightened. And nodded to the rest of the company. 'Is this all Seamus's family?'

'Yes.' She scanned the room's occupants. 'They all live here.'

'All the time, I understand.'

'They have little choice. Seamus was a miser in many ways.' She glanced about the room. 'You must have noticed the ambience – hopefully, once Jamie and Mary and the others finally realize it's theirs now, and they no longer need Seamus's approval for every penny spent, they'll make it more livable.'

'More like a home? Amen to that.'

Surprised by his acuity, Catriona glanced up; his polite mask told her nothing.

He trapped her gaze. 'You clearly didn't like Seamus. If you won't consider moving here to live, why have you come?'

'I'm here to pay my final respects.' She considered, then added, more truthfully: 'He was a hard man, but he did as he deemed right. He might have been an adversary, but I did respect him.'

'Magnanimous in victory?'

'There was no battle.'

'That's not how the locals tell it.'

She humphed. 'He was misguided – I set him right.'

'Misguided because he wanted you to wed?'

'Precisely.'

'What have you got against the male of the species?'

How had they got onto this topic? She slanted her tormentor a sharp glance. 'Just that – they're male.'

'A sorry fact, but most women find there are compensations.'

She humphed again, the sound eloquently disbelieving. 'Such as?'

'Such as . . .'

His tone registered; she turned and met his eyes – and the glow that danced therein. Her breathing seized; her heartbeat suddenly sounded loud. With an effort, she found breath enough to warn: *'No teasing.'*

His lips, untrustworthy things – she tried hard not to focus on them – lifted; his eyes glowed all the more. 'A little teasing would do you good.' His voice had dropped to a deep purr, sliding over her senses; Catriona detected the power in the words, although she hadn't met its like before. It was . . . beguiling; instinctively, she resisted. She felt like she was swaying, but knew she hadn't moved.

'You might even find you . . .' – his brows quirked – 'enjoy it.'

Behind her back, screened from the company, his hand rose; Catriona sensed it with every pore of her skin, every nerve in her body. An inch from her silk-encased form, it rose, slowly skimming without touching, until it reached her neckline and rose . . .

*'Don't!'* The word was a breathless command; his hand halted, hovering, close, very close, to her quivering curls. If he touched them again . . .

'Very well.'

A seductive purr, with no hint of contrition; *he* was being triumphantly magnanimous now. But his hand didn't disappear – it reversed direction. Slowly, so slowly her skin had ample time to prickle and heat, his hand traced her back, down over her shoulder blades, over the slight indentation at her waist, then, even more slowly, over the curve of her hips.

Not once did he touch her, yet when his hand dropped away, she was shaking inside – so badly, as she stepped away and, half-turning, inclined her head in his direction, she could barely form the words: 'If you'll excuse me, I should retire.'

She left him without meeting his eyes, quite sure of the male triumph she would see there, unsure of her hold on her temper if she did.

Meg had returned; she was sitting, wan-faced, in an armchair. Catriona stopped before her. 'Come to my room when you go up – I'll have that potion ready.'

'Are you going up now?'

'Yes.' Catriona bit off the word, then forced a smile. 'I fear the journey here was more fatiguing than I'd thought.'

With a regal nod, she swept from the room, conscious, to the very last, of a blue, blue gaze fixed unwaveringly on her back.

# Chapter Three

A few minutes before eleven o'clock the next morning, Catriona made her way to the library, whence they'd been summoned to hear Seamus's last testament. She'd breakfasted in her room – because it was warmer there.

The attempt at self-deception worried her, as did its cause. She'd breakfasted privately so she wouldn't have to face Richard Cynster and the power he wielded. Whatever it was. She knew, of course, but she wasn't game to let herself contemplate it. At all. That way lay confusion.

A footman stood before the library door; he opened it and she glided through. And gave thanks that some sensible soul had given orders for the fire to be built up above its usual meager pile. The cavernous fireplace filled one end of the monstrous room, the largest in the house, stretching the length of one entire wing. As the walls were stone and the narrow windows uncurtained, the room was perpetually chill. She'd dressed appropriately in a dress of blue merino wool with long fitted sleeves, but was still grateful for the fire.

Jamie and Mary sat on the *chaise;* the others sat in armchairs on either side, all the seats arrayed in a semicircle facing the fire and, to one side, the huge old desk behind which Seamus had habitually sat. Now, a Perth solicitor sat in Seamus's chair and shuffled papers.

Subsiding into the one vacant armchair, between Meg and

Malcolm, Catriona returned the solicitor's polite nod, then acknowledged the others present, only at the very last letting her eyes meet Richard Cynster's.

He sat on the other side of the *chaise,* beyond Mary, filling a chair with an indolent grace in stark contrast to the tentative postures of the other males present. He inclined his head, his expression impassive; Catriona inclined her head in return and forced her eyes elsewhere.

One glance had been enough to fill her mind with a vision far more powerful than the one that had brought her here. He was wearing a blue coat of a deeper hue than her dress, superbly tailored to hug his broad shoulders. A blueand-black striped silk waistcoat covered a snowy white shirt topped by a beautifully tied cravat. His breeches, of the finest buckskin, clung to long, powerful thighs far too tightly for her comfort; his boots she already knew.

She wished him anywhere else but here; she had to fight to keep her eyes from him. Malcolm, beside her, was not so restrained; slumped in his chair, he gnawed on one knuckle and stared openly at the lounging elegance opposite. Catriona suppressed a waspish urge to tell him he'd never measure up, not while he slouched like that.

Instead, she breathed deeply, and determinedly settled, drawing calmness to her with every breath. Hands clasped in her lap, she reminded herself that she was here by The Lady's orders; perhaps she'd been sent here to meet Richard Cynster to learn what it was she should avoid.

Masterful men.

Denying the urge to glance at one, she fixed her gaze on the solicitor and willed him to get on with his business. He looked up and blinked, then owlishly peered at the mantel clock. 'Hurrumph! Yes.' He glanced around, clearly counting heads, matching faces against a list before laying it aside. 'Well then, if we're all assembled ...?'

When no one contradicted him, he picked up a long parchment, cleared his throat, and commenced. 'I read the words of our client, Seamus McEnery, Laird of Keltyhead, as dictated to our clerk on the fifth of September this year.'

He cleared his throat again, and changed his voice; all understood that they were now hearing Seamus's words verbatim.

'"This, my last will and testament, will not be what any of you, gathered here at my request, will be expecting. This is my last chance at influencing things on this earth – to put right what I did wrong, to rectify the omissions I made. With the hindsight of age, I've been moved to use this, my will, to that end.'"

Not surprisingly, a nervous flutter did the rounds of the listeners. Catriona was immune, but even she frowned – what was the wily old badger up to now? Even Richard Cynster, she noticed, shifted slightly.

Settling in his chair, Richard inwardly frowned and struggled to shake off the premonition Seamus's opening paragraph had evoked. He was only a minor player in this scene; there was no reason to imagine those words were aimed at him.

Yet, as the solicitor went on, it seemed he was wrong.

'"My first bequest will close a chapter of my life otherwise long completed. I wish to give into her son's hands the necklace my first wife bequeathed to him. As I have stipulated that he, Richard Melville Cynster, must be here to receive it, it has now served its purpose."' The solicitor fumbled on the desk, then rose and crossed to Richard.

'Thank you,' Richard murmured, lifting the delicate strands from the solicitor's gnarled hands. Gently, he untangled the finely wrought gold links, interspersed with opaque rose pink stones. From the center of the necklace hung a long crystal of amethyst, etched with signs too small for him to make out.

'It was quite out of order for Mr. McEnery to keep it from you,' the solicitor whispered. 'Please do believe it was entirely against our advice.'

Studying the pendant, noting the curious warmth of the stones, Richard nodded absentmindedly. As the solicitor returned to the desk, Richard glanced up – from across the circle of seats, Catriona's gaze was fixed on the pendant. Her absorption was complete; deliberately, he let the crystal hang, then moved it – her gaze remained riveted. The solicitor reseated himself; Richard closed his fist about the pendant. Catriona sighed and looked up; she met his gaze, then calmly looked away. Resisting an urge to raise his brows, Richard pocketed the necklace.

'Now, where were we? Ah ... yes.' The solicitor cleared his throat, then warbled: '"As to all the wealth of which I die possessed, property, furniture, and funds, all is to be held in trust for a period of one week from today, the day on which my will is read."' The man paused, drew breath, then went on in a rush: '"If during that one week, Richard Melville Cynster agrees to marry Catriona Mary Hennessy, the estate will be divided amongst my surviving children, as described below. If, however, by the end of that week, Richard Cynster refuses to marry Catriona Hennessy, my entire estate is to be sold and the funds divided equally between the dioceses of Edinburgh and Glasgow."'

Shock – absolute and overpowering – held them all silent. For one minute, only the rustle of parchment and the odd crackle from the fire broke the stillness. Richard recovered, if that was the right word, first; he dragged in a huge breath, conscious of a sense of unreality, as if in a crazy dream. He glanced at Catriona, but she wasn't looking at him. Her gaze was fixed in the distance, her expression one of stunned incredulity.

*'How could he?'* Her vehement question broke the spell;

she focused abruptly on the solicitor.

A cacophany of questions and exclamations poured forth. Seamus's family could not take in what their sire had done to them; most of them were helpless, barely coherent.

Seated beside Richard, Mary turned a stricken face to him. 'My God – *how* will we manage?' Her eyes filled; she grasped Richard's hand, not in supplication, but for support.

Instinctively, he gave it, curling his fingers about hers and pressing reassuringly. He saw her face as she turned to Jamie, saw the hopelessness that swamped her.

'What will we do?' she all but sobbed as Jamie gathered her into his arms.

As stunned as she, Jamie looked at the solicitor over her head. *'Why?'*

It was, Richard felt, the most pertinent question; the solicitor took it as his cue and waved his hands at the others to hush them. 'If I might continue . . .?'

They fell silent, and he picked up the will. He drew breath, then looked up, peering over his pince-nez. 'This is a most irregular will, so I feel no compunction in breaking with tradition and stating that I and all others in my firm argued most strongly against these provisions, but Mr. McEnery would not be moved. As it stands, the will is legal and, in our opinion, uncontestable by law.'

With that, he looked down at the parchment. '"These next words are addressed to my ward, Catriona Mary Hennessy. Regardless of what she might think, it was my duty to see to her future. As in life I was not strong enough to influence her, so in death I am putting her in the way of one who, if half the tales told of him and his clan are true, possesses the requisite talents to deal with her."'

There followed a detailed description of how the estate was to be divided between Seamus's children in the event Richard agreed to marry Catriona, to which no one listened. The

45

family and Catriona were too busy decrying Seamus's perfidy; Richard was too absorbed in noting that not one of them imagined any other outcome than that the estate would pass to the Church.

By the time the solicitor had reached the end of the will, despair, utter and complete, had taken posssession of the McEnerys. Jamie, swallowing his bitter disappointment, rose to shake the solicitor's hand and thank him. Then he turned away to comfort Mary, distraught and weeping.

'It's iniquitous,' she sobbed. 'Not even the barest living! And what about the children?'

'Hush, shussh.' Jamie tried to soothe her, his expression one of abject defeat.

'He was mad.' Malcolm spat the words out. 'He's cheated us of everything we'd a right to expect.'

Meg and Cordelia were sobbing, their meek spouses incoherent.

Sitting quietly in his chair, untouched by the emotion sweeping his hosts, Richard watched, and listened, and considered. Considered the fact that not one of the company expected him to save them.

Considered Catriona, sleek and slender in deep blue, her hair burning even more brightly in the dull and somber room. She was comforting Meg, counselling her away from hysteria, exuding calm in an almost visible stream. Straining his ears, he listened to her words.

'There's nothing to be done, so there's no sense in working yourself into a state and having a miscarriage. You know as well as anyone I didn't get along with Seamus, but I would never have believed him capable of this. I'm as deeply shocked as you.' She continued talking quickly, filling Meg's ears, forcing the woman to listen to her and not descend into excessive tears. 'The solicitor says it's a *fait accompli*, so other than calling down curses on Seamus's dead head, there's no use in having the vapors now. We must all get together and see what can be done, what can be salvaged.'

She continued, moving the direction of her thoughts, and Meg's and Cordelia's and their husbands', into a more positive vein. But that vein followed the line of what to do to cope with this unexpected shock; at no point did she, or anyone, not even Jamie or Mary when they joined the group, allude to any alternative.

Not once did Catriona glance his way; it was almost as if she'd dismissed him from her mind, forgotten his existence. As if they'd all forgotten him – the dark predator, the interloper, the Cynster in their midst. No one thought to appeal to him.

To them all, not only Catriona, the outcome was a *fait accompli*. They didn't even bother to ask for his decision, his answer to Seamus's challenge.

But then, they were the weak and helpless; he was something else again.

'Ah-hem.'

Richard glanced up to see the solicitor, his papers packed, peering at him. His exclamation startled the others to silence.

'If I could have your formal decision, Mr. Cynster, so that we can start finalizing the estate?'

Richard raised his brows. 'I have one week to decide, I believe?'

The solicitor blinked, then straightened. 'Indeed.' He shot a glance at Catriona. 'Seven full days is the time the will stipulates.'

'Very well.' Uncrossing his legs, Richard rose. 'You may call on me here, one week from today' – he smiled slightly at the man – 'and I will give you my answer then.'

Responding to his manner, the solicitor bowed. 'As you wish, sir. In accordance with the will, the estate will remain in trust until that time.'

47

Quickly gathering his papers, the solicitor shook hands with Richard, then with Jamie, stunned anew, then, with a general nod to the rest of them, quit the library.

The door shut behind him; the click of the latch echoed through the huge room, through the unnatural stillness. As one, the family turned to stare, dumbfounded, at Richard, all except Catriona; she was already staring at him, through ominously narrowed eyes.

Richard smiled, smoothly, easily. 'If you'll excuse me, I believe I'll stretch my legs.'

With that, he did so, strolling nonchalantly to the door.

'Don't get your hopes up.' Brutally candid, Catriona all but pushed Jamie into a chair in the parlor, then plopped down on the *chaise* facing him. 'Now, concentrate,' she admonished him, 'and tell me everything you know of Richard Cynster.'

Still dazed, Jamie shrugged. 'He's the son of Da's first wife – hers, and the man the English government sent up here one time. A duke, he was – I've forgotten the title, if I ever heard it.' He screwed up his face. 'I can't remember much – it was all before I was born. I only know what Da' let slip now and then.'

Catriona restrained her temper with an effort. 'Just tell me everything you *can* remember.' She needed to know the enemy. When Jamie looked blank, she blew out a breath. 'All right – questions. Does he live in London?'

'Aye – he came up from there. His valet said so.'

'He has a valet?'

'Aye – a very starchy sort.'

'What's his reputation?' Catriona blinked. 'No – never mind.' She muttered beneath her breath: 'I know more about that than you.' About a man with lips like cool marble, arms that had held her trapped, and a body . . . she blinked again. 'His family – what do you know of them? Do they acknowledge him openly?'

'Seemingly.' Jamie shrugged. 'I recall Da' saying the Cynsters were a damned powerful lot – military, mostly, a verra old family. They sent seven to Waterloo – I remember Da' saying as the ton had labelled them invincible because all seven returned with nary a scratch.'

Catriona humphed. 'Are they wealthy?'

'Aye – I'd say so.'

'Prominent in society?'

'Aye – they're well connected and all tha'. There's this group of them—' Jamie broke off, coloring.

Catriona narrowed her eyes. 'This group of them?'

Jamie shifted. 'It's nothing as . . .' His words trailed away.

'As should concern me?' Catriona held his gaze mercilessly. 'Let me be the judge of that. This group?'

She waited; eventually, Jamie capitulated. 'Six of them – all cousins. The ton calls them the Bar Cynster.'

'And what does this group do?'

Jamie squirmed. 'They have reputations. And nicknames. Like Devil, and Demon, and Lucifer.'

'I see. And what nickname is Richard Cynster known by?'

Jamie's lips compressed mulishly; Catriona levelled her gaze at him.

'Scandal.'

Catriona's lips thinned. 'I might have guessed. And no, you need not explain how he came by the title.'

Jamie looked relieved. 'I dinna recall Da' saying much more – other than they were all right powerful bastards wi' the women, but he would say that, in the circumstances.'

Catriona humphed. Right powerful bastards with women – so, thanks to her late guardian's misbegotten notions, here she was, faced with a right powerful bastard who, on top of it all, was in truth a bastard. Did that make him more or less powerful? Somehow, she didn't think the answer was less. She looked at Jamie. 'Seamus said nothing else?'

Jamie shook his head. 'Other than that it's only fools think they can stand against a Cynster.'

*Right powerful bastards with women* – that, Catriona thought, summed it up. Arms crossed, she paced before the windows of the back parlor, keeping watch over the snowcovered lawn across which Richard Cynster would return to the house.

She could see it all now – what Seamus had intended with his iniquitous will. His final attempt to interfere with her life, from beyond the grave, no less. She wasn't having it, a Cynster or not, powerful bastard or otherwise.

If anything, Richard Cynster's antecedents sounded even worse than she'd imagined. She knew little of the ways of the ton, but the fact that his father's wife, indeed, the whole family, had apparently so readily accepted a bastard into their midst, smacked of male dominance. At the very least, it suggested Cynster wives were weak, mere cyphers to their powerful husbands. Cynster males sounded like tyrants run amok, very likely domestic dictators, accustomed to ruling ruthlessly.

But no man would ever rule her, ruthlessly or otherwise. She would never allow that to happen; the fate of the vale and her people rested on her shoulders. And to fulfill that fate, to achieve her aim on this earth, she needed to remain free, independent, capable of exercising her will as required, capable of acting as her people needed, without the constraint of a conventional marriage. A conventional husband.

A conventional *powerful bastard* of a husband was simply not possible for the lady of the vale.

The distant scrunch of a boot on snow had her peering out the window. It was mid-afternoon; the light was rapidly fading. She saw the dark figure she'd been waiting for emerge from the trees and stroll up the slope, his powerful physique in no way disguised by a heavy, many-caped greatcoat.

Panic clutched her – it had to be panic. It cut off her breathing and left her quivering. Suddenly, the room seemed far too dark. She grabbed a tinderbox and raced around, lighting every candle she could reach. By the time he'd gained the terrace, and she opened the long windows and waved him in, the room was ablaze.

He entered, brushing snowflakes from his black hair, with nothing more than a quirking brow to show he'd noticed her burst of activity. Catriona ignored it. Pressing her hands together, she waited only until he'd shrugged off his coat and turned to lay it aside before stating: 'I don't know *what* is going on in your mind, but I *will not* agree to marry you.'

The statement was as categorical and definite as she could make it. He straightened and turned toward her.

The room shrank.

The walls pressed in on her; she couldn't breathe, she could barely think. The compulsion to flee – to escape – was strong; stronger still was the mesmeric attraction, the impulse to learn what power it was that set her pulse pounding, her skin tingling, her nerves flickering.

Defiantly she held firm and tilted her chin.

His eyes met hers; there was clear consideration in the blue, but beyond that, his expression told her nothing. Then he moved – toward her, toward the fire – abruptly, Catriona scuttled aside to allow him to warm his hands. While he did so, she struggled to breathe, to think – to suppress the skittering sensations that frazzled her nerves, to prise open the vise that had laid seige to her breathing. Why a large male should evoke such a reaction she did not know – or rather, she didn't like to think. The blacksmith at the vale certainly didn't have the same effect.

He straightened, and she decided it was his movements, so smoothly controlled, so reminiscent of leashed power, like a panther not yet ready to pounce, that most unnerved her.

51

Leaning one arm along the mantelpiece, he looked down at her.

'Why?'

She frowned. 'Why what?'

The very ends of his lips twitched. 'Why won't you agree to marry me?'

'Because I have no need of a husband.' *Especially not a husband like you.* She folded her arms beneath her breasts and focused, solely, on his face. 'My role within the vale does not permit the usual relationships a woman of my station might expect to enjoy.' She tilted her chin. 'I am unmarried by choice, not for lack of offers. It's a sacrifice I have made for my people.'

She was rather pleased with that tack; men like the Cynsters understood sacrifice and honor.

His black brows rose; silently he considered her. Then, 'Who will inherit your manor, your position, if you do not marry and beget heirs?'

Inwardly, Catriona cursed; outwardly, she merely raised her brows back. 'In time, I will, of course, marry for heirs, but I need not do so for many years yet.'

'Ah – so you don't have a complete and absolute aversion to marriage?'

Head high, her eyes locked on his, Catriona drew a deep breath and held it. 'No,' she eventually admitted, and started to pace. 'But there are various caveats, conditions, and considerations involved.'

'Such as?'

'Such as my devotions to The Lady. And my duties as a healer. You may not realize it, but . . .'

Propped against the mantelpiece, Richard listened to her excuses – all revolved about the duties she saw as devolving to her through her ownership of the manor. She paced incessantly back and forth; he almost ordered her to sit, so he

52

could sit, too, and not tower over her, forcing her to glance up every time she wanted to check his deliberately uninformative countenance, then he realized who her pacing reminded him of. Honoria, Devil's duchess, also paced, in just the same way, skirts swishing in time with her temper. Catriona's skirts were presently swinging with agitated tension; Richard inwardly sighed and leaned more heavily on the mantelpiece.

'So you see,' she concluded, swinging to face him, 'at present, a husband is simply out of the question.'

'No, I don't see.' He trapped her gaze. 'All you've given me is a litany of your duties, which in no way that I can see preclude a husband.'

She had never in her adult life had to explain herself to anyone; that was clearly written in the astonished, slightly hoity expression that infused her green eyes. Then they flared. 'I don't have *time* for a husband!' Quick as a flash, she added: 'For the arguments, like this one.'

'Why should you argue?'

'Why, indeed – but all men argue, and a husband certainly would. He would want me to do things his way, not my way – not The Lady's way.'

'Ah – so your real concern is that a husband would interfere with your duties.'

'That he'd seek to interfere in *how I perform* my duties.' She paused in her pacing and eyed him narrowly. 'Gentlemen such as you have a habit of expecting to have your own way in all things. I could not possibly marry such a man.'

'Because you want to have your *own* way in *all things?*'

Her eyes flashed. 'Because I need to be free to perform my duties – free of any husbandly interference.'

Calmly, he considered her. 'What if a husband didn't interfere?'

She snorted derisively and resumed her pacing.

53

Richard's lips twitched. 'It is possible, you know.'

'That you would let your wife go her own way?' At the far end of her route, she turned and raked him with a dismissively contemptuous glance. 'Not even in the vale do pigs fly.'

It was no effort not to smile; Richard felt her raking gaze pass over every inch of his body – he had to clamp an immediate hold over his instinctive reaction. Ravishing her wouldn't serve his purpose – he had yet to decide just what his purpose was. Learning more of her would, however, greatly assist in clarifying that point.

'If we married, a man such as I,' his tone parodied her distinction, 'might, given your position, agree to' – he gestured easily – 'accommodate you and your duties.' She shot him a skeptical glance; he trapped her gaze. 'There's no reason some sort of agreement couldn't be reached.'

She considered him, a frown slowly forming in her eyes, then she humphed and turned away.

Richard studied her back, the sweeping line of her spine from her nape to the ripe hemispheres of her bottom. The view was one designed to distract him, attract him – the stiffness of her stance, the sheer challenge of her reluctance, only deepened the magnetic tug.

'You're *not* seriously considering marrying me.'

She made the statement, clear and absolute, to the darkness beyond the window.

Richard lowered his arm and leaned back against the mantlepiece. 'Aren't I?'

She continued to gaze into the gloaming. 'You only claimed the week's grace because we all took it for granted that you would refuse.' She paused, then added: 'You don't like being taken for granted.'

Richard felt his brows rise. 'Actually, it was because *you* took me for granted. The others don't count.'

The swift glance she shot him was scathing. 'I might have

54

known you'd say it was my fault.'

'You might have noticed I haven't. You *were* the reason I so promptly claimed the time, but ... on reflection' – his gesture encompassed the woods through which he'd tramped – 'I would have claimed it anyway.'

She frowned. 'Why?'

He studied her and wondered if he could ever explain to anyone how he felt about family. 'Let's just say that I've a constitutional dislike of making rushed decisions, and Seamus laid his plans very carefully. He knew I wouldn't appreciate being used as a pawn to disenfranchise his family.'

Her frown deepened. 'Because of being a bastard?'

'No. Because of being a Cynster.'

Her frown grew more puzzled. 'I don't understand.'

Richard grimaced. 'Nor do I. I'm not at all clear, for instance, on why Seamus went to such lengths – such machinations – to get me here, into this bizarre situation.'

She humphed and turned back to the window. 'That's because you didn't know Seamus. He was forever plotting and scheming – like many men of wealth and position. Indeed, he often spent so much time making plans he never got around to the execution.'

Richard raised his brows. 'No wonder my father was sent here.' Catriona looked her question; he met her gaze. 'Cynsters are renowned for action. We might plan, just enough, but our talents lie in the execution. Never ones to drag our heels.'

She humphed softly and turned back to the night. After a moment, she raised a hand and started drawing spirals on the cold pane. 'I was thinking ...' She paused; he could hear the grimace in her voice. 'Seamus may have envisioned marriage to me as a penance – a sort of deferred punishment – with you paying the price in place of your father.'

Richard frowned. 'If he thought that, then the joke's on him. It would be no hardship to be married to you.'

She turned her head; their gazes locked – everything else did as well. Time, their breathing, even their heartbeats. Desire shimmered, filling the air, heightening senses, tightening nerves.

She drew breath and looked away. 'Be that as it may, you *aren't* considering it.'

Richard sighed. When would she learn she couldn't sway him with her tone? 'Think what you will. But the solicitor's left and won't be back for a week. I won't make my decision until then.' He wouldn't be rushed, he wasn't impulsive – and he needed to know more. Of her, and *why* Seamus had made such an iniquitous will.

She humphed and muttered something; he thought it might have been 'stubborn as a mule.'

Pushing away from the mantlepiece, he strolled toward her, his footfalls muffled by the carpet. As he neared, she whirled, only just suppressing a gasp. She went to step back – and stopped herself. And tilted her chin instead.

Inwardly, he smiled – she looked deliciously ruffled, and it was he who'd done the ruffling. 'Don't worry, I'm not about to pounce.'

The gold flecks in her eyes flared. 'I didn't imagine—'

'Yes, you did.' He looked down at her, at her too-wide eyes, at the way her breasts rose and fell. Bringing his eyes back to hers, he grimaced. 'If it eases your mind, as my host's ward and a virtuous, unmarried lady, you are effectively removed from my list of potential seductees.'

He could follow her thoughts easily in her vibrant eyes.

'Ah, no,' he murmured, 'that doesn't mean you're safe with me.' He smiled. 'Just that I won't seduce you without marrying you.'

She glared – at this distance, he could feel the heat. It stopped abruptly; an arrested expression filled her eyes. Then she focused on him.

56

'I just realized ... Seamus only required *you* to agree to marry *me,* not that *I* agree to marry *you.* He knew I wouldn't agree; I'm under no compulsion to obey him.' She frowned. 'What *did* he imagine he'd achieve?'

Looking down into her upturned face, at her eyes, wide and puzzled, at her lips, warm and slightly parted, Richard fought down an urge to kiss her. 'I told you – Seamus made a very thorough study of the Cynsters.'

'So?' She searched his face, then his eyes.

'So he knew that, if I publically declare I'll wed you, I will.'

Her eyes flew wide, then narrowed to green shards. 'That's *ridiculous!* You can't simply declare we'll wed – *I* have to agree. And I won't!'

'*If* I decide to have you ...' – he kept his words deliberate, pausing to let the qualification sink in – 'I'll have to change your mind.'

'And just how do you imagine doing that?'

The words were flung at him, a challenge, a taunt. Brows slowly rising, his gaze intent, locked on hers, Richard held her trapped – and raised one hand. And deliberately caressed the curl quivering by one ear.

Her ice shattered – she gasped, shivered, and stepped back. The blood drained from her face, then rushed back as she stiffened.

And threw him a sizzling glare. 'Forget it!'

She whirled, skirts hissing; spine rigid, she stalked out.

And slammed the door behind her.

# Chapter Four

That night, Catriona slept poorly, bedevilled by a vision of a warrior's face. Forced to view that same vision, in the flesh, over the breakfast table, she inwardly sniffed and decided to go for a long ride.

Heading upstairs to change, she met Algaria at the top of the stairs. Algaria's black gaze swept her, then fastened on her face.

'Where are you off to so early?'

'I need some fresh air – how can a place so cold be so stuffy?'

'Hmm.' Looking down into the hall, Algaria sniffed disparagingly. 'The atmosphere is certainly less than convivial' – she shot a shrewd glance at Catriona – 'what with this unnecessary charade.'

'Charade?'

'Aye. It's plain as a pikestaff that bastard from below has no real intention to wed – not you, nor, I'll warrant, any woman.' Algaria's face was set, the lines deeply etched. 'It's clear he's a wastrel and just enjoying himself at our expense. Even Mary holds no hope other than that he'll eventually decline to be a part of Seamus's wild scheme and go back to London. She thinks he's making a show of considering the issue out of politeness.'

Catriona stiffened. 'Indeed?'

Algaria's lips twitched; she patted Catriona's hand. 'No

need to take offense – it's what we want, after all.' She started down the stairs. 'Him to go away and leave you alone.'

Catriona stared at the back of Algaria's head; her answering 'Hmm' was supposed to be approving – somehow, a hint of disappointment crept in. She shut her ears to it; swinging about, she marched purposefully to her room.

It was the work of a few minutes to don her riding habit, a snugly fitting jacket and full skirt in jewel green twill. Serviceable, it was not especially warm; she hunted through the wardrobe for her old-fashioned fur-lined cloak. Her hair was a problem – in the end, she braided it and looped the braids about her head.

'There!' satisfied her hair would not come loose no matter how hard she rode, she swung the cloak about her shoulders and headed for the door.

The stables huddled between the main house and the mountain, sheltered from the incessant winds and, at present, the lightly flurrying snow. The day was overcast, but the clouds were too light to deter her; she was accustomed to riding in all weather, whenever her duties called. The views might be grey, but they were visible; the hovering clouds kept the temperature above freezing. While the snow on the bare fields was hoof-deep, on the paths and tracks, the cover was less, and none of it was dangerously icy.

All in all, a perfectly acceptable winter's day to go riding in The Trossachs. That was Catriona's determined thought as, atop a strong chestnut, she clattered out of the stable yard and headed into the trees. She'd ridden often in the few weeks she'd previously spent here as an escape from the battleground of the house; she remembered the tracks well. The one she took wound its way through stands of birch girding the rocky mountainside, eventually meeting another bridle path leading to the summit. Looking forward to a brisk gallop across the clear top of Keltyhead, she urged her mount upward.

The Highlands spread out before her as she emerged from the trees onto the normally wind-swept mountaintop. The earlier breeze had died to nothing more than a whisper, threading sibilantly through the bare boughs. Even the fall of fine snow had ceased. Catriona's spirits soared; scanning the wide views, she drew in a deep breath. Directly before her, an open area thinly covered with rough mountain grass beckoned – she waited for no more. A smile on her face, a 'Whoop!' on her lips, she set the chestnut to a canter, then shifted fluidly into a gallop.

Cold, bitterly fresh, the air rushed to greet her. It whipped her cheeks and tugged at her braids. She welcomed it joyously – one of The Lady's simple pleasures. Exhilarated, at one with her mount, she journeyed across the empty space, immersed in the wide silence about her.

She was halfway across the treeless expanse when a heavy clop and a whinny broke the stillness. Glancing back, she saw a familiar tall figure, mounted, watching her from the skirts of the forest. As still and dark as the trees behind him, he studied her. Then he moved; the deep-chested black beneath him stepped out powerfully, on a course to intercept her.

Her breath tangled in her throat; abruptly, Catriona looked forward and urged her mount on. Damn the man! Why couldn't he leave her alone? The thought was shrewish, the smile tugging at her lips much less so – *that* was instinctively feminine, a reflection of the *frisson* of excitement that had shot down her nerves.

Had he followed her?

She plunged on, determined to lose him – he rode much heavier than she. And she knew she rode well; as the end of the open area neared, she considered which of the three tracks ahead, each leading in a different direction over different terrain, would best serve her purpose. That depended on how close he was. She glanced over her shoulder, expecting to see him in the distance – and nearly lost her seat. Eyes widening, she gasped and swung forward. He was only two lengths away!

Lunging onto the nearest path, she raced along it, through twists, around turns, over rocky ground screened by tall trees. She burst into the next clearing at a flat gallop, the chestnut eagerly answering the challenge. They flew across the snowy white ground – but she heard, insistent, persistent, inexorably drawing nearer, the heavy thud of the black's hooves gradually gaining ground, moving alongside.

A quick glance revealed her nemesis riding effortlessly, managing one of Seamus's big stallions with ease. He sat the horse like a god – the warrior of her dreams. The sight stole her breath; abruptly, she looked ahead. Why on earth was she running?

And how, once he caught up with her, would she explain her reckless flight? What excuse could she give for fleeing so precipitously?

Catriona blinked, then, dragging in a breath, slowed the chestnut and wheeled away from the approaching trees. In a smooth arc, she curved back into the clearing; the black followed on the chestnut's heels. She slowed to a walk as they neared a section where the trees fell away. Halting, she crossed her hands on the saddlebow; eyes fixed on the white mountains spread before her, she breathed deeply, then exhaled, forcing her shoulders to relax. 'So exhilarating, a quick gallop in these climes.' Her expression one of infinite calmness, she looked over her shoulder. 'Don't you find it so?'

Blue, blue eyes met hers. One of his black brows slowly arched. 'You ride like a hoyden.'

His expression remained impassive; she felt sure he intended the remark as a reprimand. Her giddy senses, however, heard it as a compliment – one from a man who rode well; it was an effort to keep a silly grin from her lips. She met his blue gaze with regal assurance. 'I ride as I wish.'

Her emphasis was subtle, but he heard it; his brow quirked irritatingly higher. 'Hell for leather, without fear for life or limb?'

She shrugged as haughtily as she could and returned to surveying the scenery.

'Hmm,' he murmured. She could feel his gaze on her face. 'I'm beginning to understand Seamus's reasoning.'

'Indeed?' She tried to hold them back, but the words tumbled out. 'And what do you mean by that?'

'That you've run wild for too long, without anyone to ride rein on you. You need someone to watch over you for your own protection.'

'I've been managing my life for the past six years without anyone's help or interference. I haven't needed anyone's protection – why should I need it now?'

'Because ...' And, quite suddenly, Richard saw it all – why, on his death, Seamus had trampled on custom to do all he could to put Catriona into the hands of a strong man, one he knew would protect her. His gaze distant, fixed unseeing on the white peaks before them, he continued: 'As time goes on, you'll face different threats, ones you've not yet encountered.'

Not yet, because while he'd been alive, Seamus had acted as her protector, albeit from a distance. They'd found the letters, but how many more advances had been made directly? And Jamie was no Seamus – he wouldn't be able to withstand the renewed offers, the guileful entreaties. He'd refer them to Catriona, and then *she* would have to deal with ... all the threats from which Seamus had shielded her.

*That* was why he, Richard, was here – why Seamus had couched his will as he had.

Frowning, Richard refocused to discover Catriona studying his face. She humphed, then haughtily turned away, pert nose in the air. 'Don't let me keep you.' With an airy wave, she gestured a dismissal. 'I know this area well – I'm quite capable of finding my own way back.'

Richard swallowed a laugh. 'How reassuring.' She slanted him a frowning glance; he responded with a charming smile. 'I'm lost.'

Her eyes narrowed as she clearly debated whether she dared call him a liar. Deciding against it, she shifted from defense to attack. 'It's truly unconscionable of you to raise the family's hopes.'

'By considering whether it's possible to help them?' He raised his brows haughtily. 'It would be *unconscionable* of me to do otherwise.'

She frowned at him. 'They're not your family.'

'No – but they are *a* family, and as such, command my respect. And my consideration.'

*They do?* She didn't speak them, but the words were clear in her eyes. Richard held her gaze. 'I'd vaguely imagined that families lay at the heart of your doctrine, too.'

She blinked. 'They do.'

'Then shouldn't you be considering what you can do to help them? They're weaker, less able, than you or I. And none of this is their doing.'

It was a scramble to get back behind her defenses; she accomplished it with a frown and a fictitious shiver. 'It's cold to be standing.' She looked up. 'And there's more snow coming. We'd better return to the house.'

Richard made no demur as she turned her horse. He brought the black up alongside the chestnut, then gallantly drew back to amble behind her as she set the chestnut down a steep track. His gaze locked on her hips, swaying deliberately, first this way, then that, he spent the descent, not considering Seamus's family, but the mechanics of releasing them from his iniquitous will.

The behavior of Seamus's family in the drawing room, and over the dinner table, tried Catriona's temper sorely. While clearly of the opinion their cause was hopeless, they nevertheless endeavored to cast her in the most flattering light, to convince a reluctant suitor of her manifold charms. As they were self-effacing, bumbling, and close to helpless, she was forced to rein in her temper – forced to smile tightly rather than annihilate them with a crushing retort, or cut them to ribbons with her saber tongue. Richard noted her simmering – reminiscent of a barely capped volcano – and bided his time.

When they returned to the drawing room, and the tea trolley arrived, no one challenged his suggestion that he take Catriona her cup. As she was, by then, standing stiff and straight, looking out of one of the uncurtained windows, it was doubtful anyone else would have dared. As he strolled up, two cups in his hands, he fixed his gaze, deliberately unreadable, on Algaria O'Rourke's face. Holding fast to her customary position beside Catriona, she returned his stare with a black, unfathomable one of her own.

'Oh, Algaria?'

From behind him, Richard heard Mary call, and saw consternation and indecision infuse Algaria's face.

Halting before her, a pace behind Catriona's back, Richard smiled, all teeth. 'I don't bite – at least, not in drawing rooms.'

The comment, or perhaps its tone, reached Catriona; she stirred and turned and took the situation in in one glance. Reaching for one of the cups, she grimaced at Algaria. 'Oh, go! And you might check on Meg for me.'

With one last, warning glance at Richard, Algaria inclined her head and went. Richard watched her retreat, her spine poker-stiff. 'Does *she* bite?'

Catriona nearly choked on her tea. 'She's a fully fledged disciple – she was my mentor after my mother died. So beware – she might turn you into a toad if you step too far over the line.'

Richard sipped, then turned and studied her. She was still

simmering. 'You can rip up at me, if you like.'

The glance she shot him suggested she was seriously considering it. 'This is all your fault. While they think there's an outside chance – the most distant possibility – they'll feel compelled to make a push to' – she gestured – 'interest you in me.'

'You could always explain they don't need to make the effort.'

Catriona stiffened; she glanced up – and saw the lurking heat in his eyes. She frowned. 'Stop it.'

'Stop what?'

'Stop thinking of that kiss in the graveyard.'

'Why? It was a very enjoyable kiss, even in a graveyard.'

She fought not to wriggle her shoulders, fought not to think of it herself. 'It was a mistake.'

'So you keep insisting.'

'You could end this entire charade, this senseless agony of expectation, by simply stating your mind.'

'How can I do that if I don't know it myself?'

She narrowed her eyes at him. 'You know perfectly well you'll return to London in a week's time, unencumbered by a wife.' He merely raised his brows, with that irritatingly arrogant confidence that never failed to get her goat. She looked away. 'You don't want to marry me, any more than I wish to marry you.'

Turning his head, he looked down at her; she felt the sudden intensity of his gaze.

'Ah – but I do wish, very much, to bed you, as much, if not more, than you wish me to do so, which might well predispose us to wed.'

Stunned, Catriona looked up; politely, he raised his brows, his eyes like blue flame. 'Don't you think?'

She snapped her mouth shut. 'I do *not!*' Her cheeks burned; she dragged in a breath and looked away, adding through clenched teeth: 'I most certainly do *not* wish you to bed me.'

He studied her profile; even without looking, she knew his brows rose higher. '*Now* who's lying?'

She straightened, but couldn't meet his eyes. 'You're only teasing me.'

'Am I?'

The soft words set her nerves skittering. And his fingers settled on the sensitive skin of her nape. She lost her wits, lost her breath. His fingers shifted, in the lightest caress—

She hauled in a breath and whirled to face him. 'Stop that!'

'Why?' His expression unreadable, he studied her frown. 'You like it.'

Biting her tongue against another lie, she forced herself to meet his gaze – to ignore the wild sensations crashing through her. 'Given that you *will not* be bedding me, there will be *no reason* for us to wed, and you will go back to London, and Seamus's fortune will go to the Church. Why won't you admit it?'

He raised his brows. 'I will admit that if I'm involved at all, a wedding will certainly necessitate a bedding. In your case, to my mind, the two are inseparable – the one will beget the other.'

'Very likely.' Catriona spoke through gritted teeth. '*However,* as there will be *no wedding*—'

'What's this?'

Before she could focus, let alone gather her wits, he reached for the fine chain that hung about her throat, visible above the neckline of her gown. Before she could catch his hand, he drew the chain free, lifting the pendant from its sanctuary in the valley between her breasts.

And clasped it in his hand, turned it between his long fingers. Catriona froze.

Squinting at the long crystal, he frowned. 'It's carved, like the one on my mother's necklace, only of the other stone.'

Drawing a shaky breath, Catriona lifted the pendant from

his grasp. 'Rose quartz.' She wondered whether her voice sounded as strained as it felt. She dropped the pendant back into its haven – and nearly gasped in shock at its heat. It had been warm from her flesh, but the heat of his hand had raised its temperature much higher. With a herculean effort, she reassembled her scattered defenses, and retreated behind a haughty wall. 'And now, if you've quite finished teasing me—'

The chuckle he gave was the definition of devilish. 'Sweet witch, I haven't even started.'

His blue eyes held hers; trapped for one instant too long, Catriona felt the hot flames sear her. And felt . . .

'You're a *devil*.' She picked up her skirts. 'And very definitely no gentleman!'

His lips twitched, just a little at the ends. 'Naturally not. I'm a bastard.'


He was that – and much more.

*And he will father your children.*

Catriona awoke with a start, with a gasp that hung, quivering, in the empty dark. About her, the room lay still and silent; the bedcovers lay over her, in tangled disarray. She lay on her back, her heart racing to a beat she did not know, but recognized too well. Her arms lay tensed at her sides, her fingers gripping the sheets.

It took effort to straighten her fingers, to ease her locked muscles. Gradually, the tension holding her decreased; her breathing slowed.

Leaving behind confusion, consternation – and a compulsion that grew stronger by the day, by the hour. And even more by the night.

Night – when she need not – could not – hide from herself, when, in her dreams, her deepest yearnings and unvoiced needs held sway. Overridden, as always, by The Lady's will.

67

But that was not happening now. Instead, The Lady's will and her own deep yearnings were acting in concert, pushing her forward, into the arms of—

'A man I *can't* marry.'

Rolling onto her elbow, Catriona reached for the glass of water on the table by the bed. She sipped; the cool water doused the lingering heat – heat that had flared at the dream of his lips on hers, of the touch of cool marble that incited flame. Heat that had spread through her like forest fire in response to the hot hunger in his eyes, in his soul.

In response to his desire.

Alone in the night, there was no point in denying that, from the first, she had wanted him. Wanted him with a finality, a certainty, an absolute conviction that stunned her. She wanted him in her bed, wanted him to be the one to fill the empty space beside her, to dispel the private loneliness that was a part of her public persona. But from childhood she'd been taught to put her wants below the needs of her people; in this instance, the choice had been clear.

Or so she had thought.

She was no longer so sure. Of anything.

Slumping back in the bed, she focused on the canopy. She had occasionally in the past, in her wild and willful youth, fought The Lady's will; she knew what it felt like. *This* was what it felt like. A draining combination of uncertainty, dissatisfaction, and an overwhelming confusion, from which, no matter how hard she tried, she could not break free.

She was at odds with herself, because she was at odds with fate, with The Lady's will.

Muting a scream of keen frustration, she thumped her pillow, then turned on her side and snuggled down.

It had to be impossible. Had the Lady *seen* him? Did she know what – in this case – she was suggesting? Ordering?

Did she know what she was getting her senior disciple into?

68

Marriage to a masterful bastard.

The thought froze her mind; she stared, unseeing, into the dark, then shook herself, closed her eyes, and willed herself to sleep – without any more dreams.

She woke late the next morning – too late for breakfast. After taking tea and toast on a tray, she dressed warmly, dragged on her pelisse, and, avoiding Algaria's watchful eye, set out for a long walk. She needed to clear her head.

The day was brighter than the one before; only a sprinkling of snow remained on the paths. Pausing on the side steps, Catriona looked around; seeing no one, she walked briskly to the opening of one of the three paths leading downward, and slipped into the shadows beneath the trees.

Under the spreading branches, cool peace held sway. She swung along, the scrunch of her boots on the crisp, dead leaves the only sound she could hear. The air was fresh and clean; she drew it deep into her lungs. And felt better.

The path swung sharply, descending into a hollow; she rounded the bend – and saw him waiting, leaning negligently against the bole of a tall tree, his greatcoat protecting him against the light breeze that ruffled his black hair.

His eyes were on her, his attitude that of a man waiting for his lover at an assignation previously planned.

As she drew level with him, Catriona was tempted to reach out and lay her hand over his heart, to see if it was beating too quickly. He must have left the house behind her; he must have run down the other path to get here – be here – now. But touching him was out of the question. She raised her brows instead. 'Lost again?'

His eyes held hers steadily. 'No.' He paused, then added: 'I was waiting for you.'

She returned his gaze consideringly, then humphed, and waved an acceptance of his escort. He fell in beside her as she strolled on, his stride a long prowl. He was so much larger, stronger, than she, his presence weighed heavily on her senses. Catriona drew a tight breath; she looked up at the patches of sky framed by the bare branches. 'Do the Cynsters live in London?'

'Yes. Some all of the time, others some of the time.'

'And you?'

'All of the time, these days.' He scanned their surroundings. 'But I grew up in Cambridgeshire, at Somersham Place, the ducal seat.'

She threw him a quick glance. 'Jamie said your father was a duke.'

'Sebastian Sylvester Cynster, 5th Duke of St. Ives.'

The affection in his tone was easily heard; she glanced at him again. 'You were brought up within the family?'

'Oh, yes.'

'And you have an older brother?'

'Devil.' When she raised her brows, he grinned and added: 'Sylvester Sebastian to *Maman* – Devil to all others.'

'I see.'

'Devil has the title now. He lives at Somersham with his duchess, Honoria, and his heir.'

'Is it a big family?'

'No, if you mean do I have other brothers and sisters, but yes, if you mean is the clan, as you might call it, large.'

'There are lots of Cynsters?'

'*More* than enough, as any fond mama in the ton will tell you.'

'I see.' She was too interested to sound suitably reproving. 'So you have – what? Lots of cousins?'

With an ease she hadn't expected, he described them – his uncles and aunts, and their children, led by his four male cousins. After a quick listing of the family's major connections, he enumerated his younger cousins. 'Of course,' he concluded, 'about town, I tend to meet only Amanda and Amelia.'

Catriona located them on the mental tree she'd been constructing. 'The twins?'

'Hmm.'

He frowned and looked down. When he said nothing more, she prompted: 'Why are they a worry?'

He glanced at her. 'I was just thinking ... both Devil and Vane, who are recently married gentlemen, are unlikely to spend much time in town. And with me up here ...' His frown deepened. 'There's Demon, of course, but he might have to visit his stud farm, which leaves it all up to Gabriel and Lucifer.' He grimaced. 'I just hope Demon remembers to jog their elbows before he leaves town.'

'But why do they need to be "jogged?" Surely, with all your relatives and connections, the twins will be closely watched over.'

His expression hardened; he threw her another glance. 'There are some dangers extant within the *ton* which are best dealt with by experts.'

She opened her eyes wide. 'I would have thought you rated more as one of the dangers.'

His mask slipped; the warrior showed through. 'That's precisely why I – and the others – are the sort of watchers the twins most need.'

She could tell – from his eyes, his expression – that he was deadly serious. Nevertheless ... looking ahead, she fought to keep her lips straight – and failed. A gurgle of laughter escaped her.

He shot her a narrow-eyed glance.

She waved placatingly. 'It's just the thought of it – the vision of you and your cousins creeping around ballrooms keeping surreptitious watch over two young ladies.'

'*Cynster* young ladies.'

'Indeed.' Tilting her head, she met his gaze. 'But what if the twins don't want to be watched – what if, indeed, they possess the same inclinations as you? You come from the same stock – such inclinations aren't restricted to males.'

He stopped stock-still and stared at her, then humphed, shook his shoulders, and started to pace once more. Frowning again. 'They're too young,' he finally stated.

Lips still not straight, Catriona looked away, across the snowy tops of the foothills. After a moment, she mused: 'So the family's large, and you were brought up within it – and that's why you see family as important.'

She did not look at him, but felt the swift touch of his gaze on her face. Although delivered as a statement, that was, in fact, her principal question: why did a man like him have such strong feelings about family?

They strolled on for a full minute before he replied. 'Actually, I think it's the other way around.'

Puzzled, she looked up; he trapped her gaze. 'The Cynsters are as they are *because* family is important to us.' He looked down and they walked on. She didn't try to disguise her interest; she kept her gaze on his face, her mind on his words.

He grimaced lightly. 'Cynsters are acquisitive by nature – we *need* possessions – the family motto, after all, is *'To Have and To Hold.'* But even long ago, the motto was not – or not only – a material one.' He paused; when he spoke again, he spoke slowly, clearly, his frowning gaze fixed on the snow. 'We were always a warrior breed, but we don't fight solely for lands and material wealth. There's an understanding, drummed into us all from our earliest years, that success – true success – means capturing and holding something more. That something more is the future – to excel is very well, but one needs to excel *and survive*. To seize lands is well and good, but we want to hold them for all time. Which means creating and building a family – defending the family that is,

72

and creating the next generation. Because it's the next generation that's our future. Without securing that future, material success is no real success at all.'

It seemed as if he'd forgotten her; Catriona walked silently, careful not to disturb his mood. Then he looked up, squinting a little in the glare, his face exactly as she had seen it in her dreams – the far-sighted warrior.

'You could say,' he murmured, 'that a Cynster without a family is a Cynster who's failed.'

They'd reached the end of the ridge; the path turned at the rocky point, which formed a small lookout, then wound back up the slope through the trees. They halted on the point; the wind blew fresh and chill from the white mountaintops before them.

As one, they viewed the majestic sight; unprompted, Catriona pointed out various peaks and landmarks, naming them, citing their significance. Richard listened attentively, blue eyes narrowed against the wind and glare. As he studied the landscape, Catriona surreptitiously studied him.

His expression, she had realized, was very rarely spontaneous, even though he sometimes appeared open and easy. He was, in reality, reserved, his feelings kept close behind his mask – that facade he showed to the world. Whatever reactions he displayed were those he wanted to show; even his glib and ready charm was a carefully cultivated skill.

But when he'd spoken of his family – and of family – his mask had slipped, and she'd seen the man behind, and a little of his vulnerability. The insight had touched her, stirred her – and made her clamp a firm hold over her own reactions before they could carry her away. Richard Cynster, she'd already realized, was temptation incarnate – this morning had added another dimension to his attractiveness.

Quite the last thing she needed.

With a half-suppressed sigh, she turned. 'We'd better get back.'

Richard turned, and, scanning the path upward, suppressed a sigh of his own. Tightening his grip on his rakish impulses, he gave Catriona his arm up the first section of path, made hazardous by melting snow. Pacing slowly beside her, aware through every pore of her soft warmth, gliding along beside him, and not making any advance whatsoever, had taken considerable effort; speaking of his family, explaining why he felt as he did, while maintaining the distance between them, had required superhuman resolution. But he wasn't yet sure how far he could push her – and he wasn't yet sure if he should.

As he'd foreseen, she slipped on the path; resigned, he caught her against him, unable to deaden the impact of her soft curves against him, let alone his instant reaction. Luckily, she was engrossed in regaining her footing, but when she tumbled against him again, one ripe breast pressing hard against his chest, one hip and sleek thigh riding against his hip, he had to bite his lip against a groan.

When they finally reached the place where the path leveled out, he'd given up hiding his scowl. She stopped to catch her breath; he stopped to let his body ease. Innocently, she regarded the scenery; annoyed, irritated, and mightily frustrated, he regarded her. And resumed his impassive mask. 'You do understand why Seamus did as he did, don't you?'

She turned to face him. 'Because he was mad?'

Richard let his lips thin. 'No.' He hesitated, studying her clear eyes. 'You're an attractive proposition, both personally and for your lands. You can't be unaware of it. The offers for your hand have apparently been legion, most from men who would sell your vale from under you and treat you with far less respect than is your due. Seamus, more than anyone, was aware of that, so he tried a last throw, a last attempt to see you safe.'

She half smiled, her expression, her eyes, full of a feminine superiority expressly designed to goad him – or any male. 'Seamus was a tyrant in his own family – it would never have occurred to him that I'm well able to take care of myself.'

If she had patted him on the hand and told him not to worry, it would have had the same effect; he didn't bother to suppress his aggravated sigh. 'Catriona, you are *incapable* of defending yourself against one determined callow youth, let alone a determined man.'

Up went her pert nose. 'Rubbish.' Green eyes clashed with his. 'Besides, The Lady protects me.'

'Oh?'

'Indeed – men always think they have the winning hand, simply because they're bigger and stronger.'

'And they're wrong?'

'Completely. The Lady has ways of dealing with importunate suitors – and so do I.'

Richard sighed and looked away – then abruptly swung back and stepped toward her. She half-shrieked and jumped back – plastering herself helpfully against the bole of a tall tree. He splayed one hand on the bole by her side; with his other hand, he trapped and framed her face. The base of the tree was higher than the path, making her relatively taller. Richard tilted her face to his; with her skirts brushing his boots, and a mere inch between them, he looked down into her wide eyes. 'Show me.'

Her eyes grew wider as they searched his. Her breasts rose and fell rapidly, straining the fabric of her coat – and still she was breathless. 'Show you ... what?'

'These ways you and Your Lady have of dealing with importunate suitors.' His gaze dropped to her lips; with his thumb, he brushed the lower.

And felt her quiver. Her heart was racing, and he hadn't even kissed her.

The thought prompted the deed; bending his head, he brushed his lips tantalizingly over hers, not sure who he was teasing the most.

'How had you planned to protect yourself against a man who accosts you and kisses you?' He whispered the taunt against her lips, then raised his head – her lips parted fractionally. He sucked in a breath, and went back for more – for a slow, leisurely exploration of her luscious lips, of the soft, warm cavern of her mouth.

And she melted for him – with no hint of a struggle, she welcomed him in, her tongue tangling tentatively with his.

He drew back only to drag in a breath, and, his voice deep and grating, ask: 'Just how had you planned to stop a man ravishing you?'

He didn't wait for an answer, but ravished her mouth, taking all she offered, and demanding more. Commanding more. Which she gave.

Unstintingly.

*The damned woman had no defenses to speak of.*

Some small part of Catriona's mind knew what he was thinking – the rest of her mind didn't care. She'd never expected to have any defense against *him*; she could normally freeze any man with a mere glance, yet from the first, he'd been immune, both to such overt intimidation and to more subtle manipulations. But she certainly wasn't going to explain that – that with him, her defenses, those The Lady had gifted her with, would not, for some misbegotten reason, work.

Even with her head spinning, her wits reeling, she wasn't that daft. She could normally tie men in mental or verbal knots, make them trip over their toes, stutter, wheeze – a whole host of simple difficulties that would send the most confident fleeing.

But not him.

With him, all she could do was run.

But at present, she couldn't run. All she could do was ...

Enjoy her ravishment.

Not a difficult task. One her senses recommended.

Wholeheartedly.

At some point, she lifted her arms and wrapped them about his neck, and he moved closer, the pressure of his chest easing her aching breasts. She kissed him back with giddy abandon and felt him shift. Then his hand slid behind her, between the tree and her back, and slid down. Her willful senses leapt as he cradled her bottom, tilting her hips away from the tree. Then he pressed one hard thigh between hers.

She would have pulled back from their kiss and gasped, but he wouldn't let her go – their kiss continued with escalating urgency, an urgency she felt to her bones. Their lips fused, eased, then melded again – his were cool marble, hers burned. He leaned into her – she drew him closer. Her thick pelisse muted the sensation of body meeting body, yet heat still swept through her, wave after wave, increasing in intensity – they had to be melting the snow for yards.

But she didn't pull back – didn't struggle to escape – she returned his kisses with increasing fervor, undismayed by the intimacy he pressed on her, eagerly savoring every nuance, every facet – what else could she do? This was experience, one she might never again enjoy.

So she enjoyed – and encouraged, invited, incited.

And he responded. Ardently.

His desire, his fire, set her aflame. When his hand dropped from her face to close firmly about her breast, she gasped and swayed – her knees literally wobbled. His hand firmed beneath her bottom, supporting her as his long fingers closed and caressed, firming about her nipple, squeezing gently. She arched against him, driven by instinct, by a hot need that was the counterpart of his. His prowling hunger had never been so clear, so forcefully imprinted on her senses. She tasted it in his kiss, felt it in his locked muscles, in the ridge of rampant flesh riding against her belly.

He tilted her hips, lifting her slightly – his thigh pressed deeper between hers, shifting suggestively.

The heat took her – a storm of fire and flame raced through her. She clutched his head wildly, threading her fingers through his thick locks as she angled her lips beneath his.

*Crack!*

Mere seconds later, or so it seemed, she was stepping carefully along the path a full five yards past the comfortable tree, one hand on Richard's sleeve, the other holding her skirts as she stepped over a tree root, when firm footsteps approached from behind.

They both turned, with wholly false expressions of polite surprise. Catriona could only be thankful for the dappled shadows that hid her face as Algaria's black gaze found her.

Algaria frowned. 'I thought you might have got lost.'

Refraining from pointing out that she knew these woods better than her mentor, Catriona inclined her head. Carefully – it was still spinning. 'I showed Mr. Cynster the lookout. We were on our way back.' Via a tree.

She could only just summon enough breath to get the words out; Algaria merely humphed and waved them on.

'Don't wait for me – I'll just plod along slowly.'

Catriona flicked a glance at her companion in time to see his lips twitch; she ignored the dangerous light in his eyes. 'Very well.'

Gracefully haughty, as befitted The Lady's senior disciple, she turned and allowed her nemesis to lead her on. She felt his gaze on her face, but kept her eyes fixed on the path and the scenery; she was still giddy, and flushed, with her senses clamoring. Insistently.

Steadfastly, she ignored them – and the question of what

might have happened had Algaria not arrived. Such speculation was not calming, and right now, she needed calm.

Calm to deal with Richard Cynster – and calm to deal with herself. And she wasn't at all sure which would prove more difficult.

His attitude to family had intrigued her, so she'd tried to draw him out, driven by a compulsive need to know more about him, so she could interpret her visions in a more sensible light. Instead, what she'd learned had made her decision harder still – how could she not respond to a man who desired and actively sought to establish a real family?

Yet the rest – all she had learned since they'd left the lookout – had only hardened her resolve to resist him. His facade had slipped long enough to confirm her inner view of him – to confirm his emotional motivation. He was, indeed, a warrior without a cause – the cause he searched for, yearned for, was a family to defend and protect.

Which was all very well, but warriors, especially the hereditary sort, did not hang up their swords in the hall and become simple family men. Far from it. They remained warriors still, to the heart, to the soul.

And warriors ruled.

Inwardly she sighed, and saw the house looming ahead. All she had learned had confirmed her in her resistance, while increasing the temptation to give herself to him – to have him as her lord. But first and last, she was the lady of the vale – she couldn't, simply could not, let him into her life, couldn't let him think of her as part of his cause, no matter how tempting that might be.

And tempting it was. Just how tempting she hadn't understood, not until she'd stood pressed against him under that tree.

They stepped out of the woods and onto the lawn, spotted white with snow; Algaria followed close behind them. Calmer, more determined, Catriona drew a deep breath; she glanced briefly at Richard's face, then looked at the house.

Temptation incarnate was what he was – his attitudes were strongly attractive, his sensuality so compelling he engaged her senses to the exclusion of all else. But his very strength was what stood between them. He was too powerful a personality, too strong a male, to surrender his natural dominance to a wife. A witch-wife at that.

He was a powerfully attractive, family-oriented gentleman, but he was still a warrior to the core.

The house rose before them, cold and grey; she felt his gaze on her face.

'You look pale.'

She glanced up and realized he thought she was still reeling. She let cool haughtiness infuse her eyes. 'I haven't been sleeping well lately.'

She looked ahead; from the corner of her eye, she saw his lips twitch.

'Indeed? Perhaps you should take up the local custom of a dram of whiskey before climbing into bed. Jamie tells me the locals all swear by it.'

Catriona humphed. 'They'd swear by any "custom" that means drinking whiskey.'

He chuckled. 'Understandable – it's good stuff. I hadn't really appreciated it before. I'm a rabid convert to the local custom.'

'Converts are always the most rabid,' Catriona observed. 'But if you really are interested, you should visit the distillery in the valley.'

They'd reached the side steps; describing the distillery, she led the way inside.

# Chapter Five

'Ah – Richard?'

Halfway across the front hall, Richard halted and swiveled – Jamie stood uncertainly in a doorway.

'I . . . ah, wondered if you could spare me a moment of your time?'

As lunch had concluded half an hour ago, and as his witch had haughtily declined his invitation to find another tree and, nose in the air, hips seductively swaying, retired to her room, he'd been on his way to the billiards room to while away the afternoon, Richard saw no reason not to smoothly incline his head and stroll through the doorway through which Jamie waved him.

He knew what was coming.

Jamie didn't disappoint him. Closing the door, Jamie followed him into the room and indicated a large chair angled before a desk. Richard sank into the chair, lounging grace-fully, balancing one boot on his knee.

His host, however, didn't settle in the chair behind the desk, but paced nervously before the hearth – before Richard. Glanc-ing about, Richard noted the ledgers filling the shelves lining one wall, and the maps and diagrams of the area scattered about the room. This was clearly the estate office, equally clearly Jamie's domain. The room was small but comfortable, much more comfortable than the library Seamus had inhabited.

'I wondered,' Jamie eventually began, 'whether you've decided yet how you will answer the solicitor next week.'

The look he bent on Richard was a plea – not to be saved, but to have the worst told to him.

'I'm afraid,' Richard replied in his London drawl, 'that I've not yet decided.'

Jamie frowned and paced on. 'But . . . well, it isn't all that likely, is it?'

'As to that,' Richard answered, 'I really can't say.'

In the hall, hugging the shadows, Algaria pressed her ear to the oak panels of the office door. She'd been traversing the gallery upstairs, on her way to Catriona's room to inquire as to the reason for her unusual withdrawal, when she'd heard Jamie speak to Richard in the hall. His intent had been obvious; what she'd heard thus far confirmed it. She was not averse to a little eavesdropping if it served to ease her mind. And Catriona's.

'But you normally reside in London, I understand. I'm afraid Catriona will never live anywhere else but Casphairn Manor.'

'So I apprehend.'

'And, well, she really is a sort of a witch, you know. Not the sort to change people into toads or eels or whatever she might say, but she really does – can – do strange things – and make other people do strange things.'

'Really?'

The tone of that response had Algaria gritting her teeth.

'And doubtless you're accustomed to balls and parties in London – a constant stream of them, I imagine.'

'Indeed – a never-ending stream of balls and parties.'

The undertone sliding beneath that reply made Algaria frown, but before she could define the emotion, Jamie spoke again.

'And, ah . . .' He coughed. 'I daresay there are many ladies

– very beautiful ladies – gracing the balls and parties.'

Leaning back in the chair, Richard merely inclined his head and kept his face expressionless.

His lack of response made Jamie more nervous. 'I understand life at the manor is very quiet – no balls or parties at all. In fact, according to Catriona, it's even quieter than here.'

'But not colder.' The words left Richard's lips before he'd thought; luckily, Jamie took them only literally.

'True – but it's still very cold.' He threw him a searching look. 'The Lowlands are a lot colder than London.'

'Indubitably.'

As Jamie continued highlighting the stark contrasts between the life he imagined Richard led in London – only a slight exaggeration of the truth – and the life he could expect to lead as the lord of Casphairn Manor, Richard politely held to his noncommittal replies. As Jamie was his host, he felt obliged to humor him thus far, but would not commit himself, one way or the other.

He couldn't. He hadn't yet made up his mind.

Commited by a freakish, witch-induced impulse to seriously consider Seamus's proposal, the more he did – the more he learned of Catriona Hennessey – the more he felt inclined to accept. To take up Seamus's gauntlet, accept his challenge, which, day by day, was looking more like an appeal – an appeal to greater strength – the offer of a commission.

A commission for life, admittedly, but he was developing a serious taste for one of the payments that would accrue. The idea of having a witch in his bed for the rest of his life, his to tease, taunt and enjoy as he – and she – pleased, was shaping as a potent inducement.

But he distrusted the entire situation. Fate and Seamus McEnery had conspired to place him in it – he had no reason to trust either. Not on the question of marriage, not given what marriage meant to him.

So he hedged and said nothing – the gentlemanly course.

'Well!' Jamie exhaled as he ground to a halt and somewhat dampeningly concluded: 'The truth is, I suppose, that life in the Lowlands, married to a wild witch, would not measure on the same scale as the life of a London swell.'

Lids lowered, Richard gravely inclined his head. 'Indeed not.'

Life with a wild witch was infinitely more alluring.


Out of breath, Algaria reached the top of the stairs just as the office door opened. Silently, she slipped into the shadows of the gallery and headed for Catriona's room.

Her brief tap on the door went unanswered; frowning, she tapped again. When no sound came from within, she frowned even harder and opened the door.

And saw Catriona slumped on the floor.

Smothering a cry, Algaria quickly shut the door and rushed forward; the briefest glance at the items on the table beside which Catriona lay was sufficient to tell her all. Her erstwhile pupil had been scrying, and scrying deep, if her swoon was any guide.

Even as Algaria straightened her limbs, Catriona stirred.

A second later, as a wet cloth passed over her face, she regained full consciousness. Peeking through her lashes, she saw that her attendant was Algaria, and relaxed. 'Oh, *hell!*'

Algaria sat back. 'Hell?'

Struggling onto one elbow, Catriona waved. 'Not you – this whole situation.' She'd gone further than mere scrying – she'd literally challenged the powers that be to reconsider, and demanded an unequivocal answer.

The answer she'd received had been more than unequivocal – it had been emphatic.

'Ah, well – the situation has just taken a turn for the better.'

'It has?' Catriona frowned as Algaria helped her to her feet. Her mentor's smug expression rang warning bells. 'How?'

'In a minute.' Algaria steered her to the bed. 'Here – just lie back and rest, and I'll tell you all I heard.'

Still weak from her exertions – facing She Who Knew All was exceedingly draining – Catriona was very willing to lie down. Algaria sat beside her and proceeded to tell her tale – how she'd listened to Jamie's discussion with Richard Cynster in the office.

Algaria's memory, perfected by the demands of her calling, was exceptional; Catriona had no doubt she was hearing exactly the words that had been said. Algaria's veracity was beyond question, as was her devotion to her own welfare – Catriona knew that for fact. However, in this instance, Algaria's tale gave her a headache.

A massive one.

'So!' Algaria triumphantly concluded. 'It's as I said – he's only amusing himself – teasing you, if you like. But he's absolutely certain to go back to London and leave you unwed – he made no attempt to deny it.'

'Hmm.' Frowning direfully, Catriona massaged her temples.

Studying her face, Algaria's triumphant expression faded. 'What is it?'

Catriona glanced at her, then grimaced. 'A complication.' She saw the questions gathering on Algaria's lips; she stayed them with a raised hand. 'I'm too tired to think, just now.' After a moment, she continued: 'I need to rest, and consider – to see how what I've been told fits with the facts, and how the whole might come together.'

Lifting her head, she smiled, a trifle wanly, at Algaria. 'Let me rest for an hour or two – come back and wake me for dinner.'

Algaria hesitated. 'You'll tell me what you learned then?'

With swift understanding of the older woman's fear of being left out, being redundant, Catriona smiled and squeezed her hand. 'Before dinner, I'll tell you all.'

Dinner time came around far too fast; it seemed to Catriona that she'd barely had time to marshal her thoughts before Algaria returned.

Struggling up against the pillows, she waved Algaria forward. 'Come sit and I'll tell you all.'

She did, starting from the first visions she'd had, through all her subsequent communcations with The Lady, culminating in the most recent.

As she restated that last, emphatic dictate, Algaria stared. Then frowned. 'Just that – no qualifications?'

'Not a one. She could hardly put it more simply: *He will father your children.*' The words still rang in Catriona's mind.

Algaria's frown mirrored her own. 'But . . .'

Together, they revisted the problem – concisely; Catriona had been over the same ground on her own so many times her head still hurt.

'But he's *too strong,*' Algaria insisted. 'He's not the sort of man you *can* marry – he'll never be content to sit back in besotted bliss and let you make the decisions.' Bewildered, she shook her head. 'But if The Lady says . . .'

'Precisely.' Catriona waited patiently while Algaria examined the problem from every angle – her mentor's view in large part mirrored her own.

In the end, Algaria simply shook her head. 'I can't make head or tail of it – we'll just have to wait for some sign of how we should proceed.'

Catriona caught her eye. 'I've just had the next sign. You brought it.'

Algaria stared at her, then blinked. 'The news that he'll be leaving?'

'Indeed – and if he leaves, just how is he to father a child on me? I can't go chasing him to London, yet, as you say, he seems certain to leave at the end of the week – in all my discussions with him, I've had no indication otherwise.'

Algaria shot her a quick glance. 'He does seem taken with you, but many men are.'

Catriona inclined her head. 'As you say – physically, I'm attractive enough, but on further reflection . . .' She considered, then stated: 'All he has said and done is consistent with what you overheard – he's considering the possibility because there are various elements in the proposed situation that attract him, but, ultimately, there's nothing I can offer him that he can't, in reality, find in London, with a wife much more suited to his lifestyle.'

She felt proud of that assessment – it had taken some soul-searching, and the exercise of brutal candor, to reach it. Richard Cynster was attracted to her for a number of reasons, but she would not, ultimately, be a suitable wife for him. He was too far-sighted not to see it.

'So, what now?' Algaria asked. 'If he leaves . . .'

Catriona drew in a deep breath. 'If he leaves, he leaves – we can do nothing to stop him. Which means . . .' She looked at Algaria, waiting for her to reach the same conclusion she had.

This time, her mentor failed her. Totally bemused, Algaria stared at her. 'Means what?'

'It means,' Catriona declared, getting off the bed to pace, 'that I'm to beget a child by him, but we won't be married.' She waved aside Algaria's frown. 'That, if you think about it, is possibly the perfect solution for me – to have a child outside wedlock. The Lady, you'll notice, does not mention marriage, only the fact that I'm to have a child by him. And you have to admit, if he'd been a stallion, he'd be a prize.'

'*Prize?* You're going to . . .' Algaria's voice trailed away; aghast, she stared. Then: 'How?'

Catriona paced determinedly. 'Presumably by going to his bed.'

'Yes – but . . .' Clearly dumbfounded, Algaria drew a deep breath. 'It's not that simple.'

Irritated by her lingering uncertainty, *and* her lack of experience, Catriona frowned. 'It can't be that hard. He's a rake – the activity should come naturally. And it's the right time of my cycle – all the signs are propitious.'

Algaria shook her head. 'But what if, after the deed, he changes his mind and decides to stay. You can't be *sure* he'll leave.'

'I've thought of that.' Catriona paced before the fireplace, all that Richard had said of family still fresh in her mind. And although they hadn't discussed it, she could guess what his stance over abandoning a bastard child would be. She felt some qualms over that, but . . . she had always obeyed The Lady, and always would. Besides, Richard's child would not be alone – it would be a much-loved child. Hers. 'He won't know.'

Algaria simply stared. 'He'll father a child on you and he won't know?' She got off the bed and laid a hand on Catriona's forehead.

Irritated, Catriona brushed it aside. 'I've thought it through – it can be done – you know that as well as I. It's tricky, admittedly – he must be asleep enough not to consciously remember, and yet his body and senses must be able to respond and perform. A sleeping potion will dull the brain, an aphrodisiac will prime the body. The doses will have to be perfectly judged, one against the other, but if I gauge the amounts correctly, all should go smoothly.'

Algaria looked ill, but didn't contradict her – she couldn't; she'd taught her most of that lore herself. She could, however, protest. 'You're mad. This will simply not work – too many things can go wrong.'

88

'Nonsense!'

Algaria grew stern, but her underlying fear and concern showed through. 'I'll have no part in it – this scheme is as mad as old Seamus's.'

'It's what The Lady requires. She will guide me.'

Tight-lipped, Algaria shook her head. 'You must have misinterpreted.'

Catriona drew herself up – she knew Algaria didn't believe that; there was no possiblity she could have misinterpreted such a strong and repeated directive. Folding her arms, she returned her mentor's black stare. 'Give me an alternative and I'll consider it – just as long as it results in Richard Melville Cynster being the father of my child.'

Slowly, Algaria shook her head. 'I'm against it – this *can't* be right.'

Aware of her mentor's deep distrust of most men, and ones like Richard Cynster in particular, Catriona didn't argue. 'I have The Lady's orders – I'm determined to obey them.' She paused, then asked, more gently: 'Will you help me?

Algaria met her gaze, and held it for a full minute. Then, slowly, she shook her head. 'No – I cannot. I'll have no part in this – no good will come of it, mark my words.' She spoke slowly; she had no alternative to offer and she knew it.

Catriona sighed. 'Very well. Leave me – I need to work up the mixture.' She had all she needed in her traveling kit, the kit she'd inherited from her mother. She'd religiously replaced each herb and specific as they aged without questioning why each was included in the selection. The aphrodisiac had always been there – it was there now, when she needed it. Along with a powerful sleeping potion.

Algaria trailed to the door; hand on the knob, she paused and looked back.

Sensing her gaze, Catriona looked up, and raised a brow.

Algaria straightened and lifted her chin. 'If you bear any

love for me, I pray you, *do not go* to Richard Cynster.'

Catriona held her black gaze steadily. 'The Lady wills it – so I must.'

The mechanics of drugging her nemesis proved much easier than she'd expected. Late that night, Catriona paced her bedchamber and waited for the moment of truth – when she would go to his room and discover how successful she had been.

Mixing the potion had been merely a matter of making a series of estimations, all based on her extensive experience. She routinely held the health of the more than two hundred souls who inhabited the vale in her hands – she treated them from birth to death; she knew her herbs. Her only uncertainty lay in gauging her mark's weight – in the end, she'd simply added an extra dash of both potions and prayed fervently to The Lady.

As for getting him to down the drug, the vehicle had been ready to hand – she'd remembered his talk of the whiskey; it was perfect for her needs. The strong, smoky taste would disguise the tang of the herbs, at least to one who was not a connoisseur. She had gauged the amount to add to the decanter so that a good dram would hold enough drug to accomplish what she needed.

Introducing the potion to his decanter had been simplicity itself. She was always the last down to dinner; she simply waited until her usual time, then stopped by his room on the way. Her one tense moment had occurred when she was almost at his door. It had opened, and his servant had come out. Standing still as a statue in the shadows, she had watched him depart, then, barely breathing, smoothly continued on and entered the room.

It was one of the largest bedchambers in the house; the decanter stood on a sideboard beneath one window. It had been the work of a moment to gauge the volume in the decanter and add the required amount of her mixture. Then, stoppering the vial, she'd turned and glided out of the room and down to dinner.

And had had the devil's own time dampening her awareness, her consciousness of what she was up to, especially while under Richard's blue gaze. He'd sensed that she was edgy, so she'd put on a haughty act and prayed he'd see her skittishness as a lingering effect of their morning's kiss.

Catriona humphed and swung about, the skirts of her dressing robe flaring about her. Beneath it, she wore a fine lawn nightgown – she supposed, for him, it should have been silk, but she didn't possess any such apparel. The thought of his hands on her body shielded only by the thin gown made her shiver. She glanced up at the clock on the mantelpiece just as it chimed.

Twelve solid bongs.

It was time for her to go.

Dragging in a breath past the vise locked about her lungs, she closed her eyes and uttered a brief prayer, then, clutching her robe about her, determinedly headed for the door.

To keep her appointment with he who was to father her child.

# Chapter Six

Two minutes later, Catriona stood in the shadows before Richard's door and stared at the oak panels. An overwhelming sense of fatality weighed heavily upon her; she stood on the threshold of far more than just a room. In opening the door and stepping inside, she would take an irrevocable step into a future only dimly perceived.

Never before had she faced such a choice – such a crucial, life-changing decision.

Shifting, she drew her dressing robe closer and inwardly chided her hesitant self. Of course stepping over the threshold would change her life – getting with child was definitely irrevocable, but quite clearly part of her future. That future lay beyond the door – why was she hesitating?

Because it wasn't just a child who lay beyond the door.

Exasperated, she straightened and reached for the doorknob, simultaneously opening her senses – to detect any hint of warning, any last-minute premonition that her intent was wrong. All she sensed was peace and silence, a deep, quiet steadiness throughout the house.

Drawing a deep breath, she opened the door. It swung noiselessly wide; beyond, the room lay silent and still, lit only by the glow of the fire still flickering in the hearth.

Stepping quietly inside, Catriona closed the door, easing the lock back so it slid home without a sound. Eyes already adjusted to the dark, she scanned the room. The huge four-poster bed stood shrouded in shadows, its head against the corridor wall. The sight held her eyes, her senses. Slowly, on silent slippered feet, she approached the bed.

She was five paces from it when she realized it was empty, the coverlet flat, undisturbed. Eyes flying wide, her breath caught in her throat, she whirled and scanned the room again.

And, from her new position, saw an arm, clad in a dark coat sleeve, wide white cuff golden in the firelight, hanging over the side of the wing chair facing the fire. The arm hung limply, long, lax fingers almost reaching the floor. Between their tips hung a crystal tumbler, its base balanced on the polished boards.

It was empty.

Drawing a calming breath, Catriona waited for her heart to slow, then, carefully silent, glided forward and rounded the chair.

At least one part of her potion had worked – he was asleep. Asprawl in the chair, his long legs stretched before him, his waistcoat undone, his cravat untied, he still managed to look elegant. Elegantly dissolute, elegantly dangerous. His chest, covered by his fine linen shirt, rose and fell regularly.

Catriona's gaze roamed, then lifted to his face; she studied the lean planes gilded by the firelight – a bronze mask more relaxed than she'd yet seen it. With his eyes shut, it was easier to concentrate on his face, on what it showed. Strength was still there, glaringly apparent even in repose; the hint of not sadness, but a lack of happiness that hung about his well-shaped mouth was not something she'd noticed before.

Inwardly frowning, she committed the sight to memory, then shook herself, and turned her mind to her task. Step one had been accomplished – he was asleep.

Fully dressed.

In the chair before the fire.

A good ten paces from the bed.

Catriona frowned in earnest. 'What now?' she muttered under her breath. Hands rising to her hips, she studied him – and considered – and studied him some more. Her head was shaking even before she reached her conclusion: with him asleep, *she'd* have to provide the lead in the upcoming proceedings, and for that, she definitely needed him on the bed. A chair might be possible, but her imagination boggled at the thought.

She glared at her sleeping victim. 'I might have known you'd find some way to be difficult,' she informed him in a hissed whisper. Bending, she retrieved the tumbler from his fingers before it fell, and turned to set it on a side table. The glass clicked on the polished table top.

Catriona swung back, her eyes flying to Richard's face. The black crescents of his lashes flickered. Then rose.

He looked directly at her.

She froze. Her mind seized; she stopped breathing.

His lips curved, kicking up at the ends first, then curving fully into a beguiling smile. 'I might have known you'd turn up in my dreams.'

Daring to breathe – just a little – Catriona slowly straightened and finished turning to stand before him. His eyes followed her; as his lids lifted farther, it was clear he was drugged. Ringed by deep blue, his pupils were huge, his gaze unfocused, not sharp and intent as it usually was.

His beguiling smile, both inviting and evocative, deepened. 'Only fair, I suppose – the witch of my dreams haunting my dreams.'

He was awake, but thought he was dreaming. Catriona blessed The Lady – this way, she could get him to the bed. Letting her features, which had blanked with shock, ease, she smiled back. 'I've come to spend the night with you.'

His smile changed to a wicked grin. 'That's usually my

94

line, but in the circumstances, I'll let you borrow it.'

He seemed in no hurry to rise from the chair; smiling still, Catriona held out one hand.

Retrieving his right arm from over the side of the chair, he reached out and grasped her fingers; before she could urge him up, he drew her closer. His gaze swept her, far hotter than the fire at her back.

'You need to get rid of that robe.'

Catriona hesitated for only a second; any argument might bring him to his senses. Drawing her fingers from his, still smiling, she raised her hands and lifted the loose robe from her shoulders, then let it slide down her arms.

His dazed blue gaze followed it to the floor, then slowly, very slowly, as if he had all the time in the world, rose, caressing her legs, her thighs, her hips, her breasts – by the time he reached her face her cheeks were flaming.

A situation not helped by the wicked glint in his eyes or his openly lustful smile.

'Good enough to eat.'

He made the pronouncement as if he was contemplating doing just that. His gaze slid from her face to rove hungrily again – and Catriona realized that with the fire behind her, her fine nightgown would be translucent.

'Ahh . . . come to the bed.' She held out both hands.

His gaze still on her body, he lifted his hands, every movement slow and heavy, as if his limbs were leaden. His fingers closed about hers – then he lifted his blue gaze to her face, to her eyes, and she saw the wicked laughter flare.

'Not yet.'

He pulled her into his lap.

Catriona went to shriek – and had to swallow the sound. She tensed to struggle – and had to suppress the impulse. Sharp sound, or a fight, could wake him. She wriggled in his lap and managed to face him. His thighs felt like solid oak beneath hers, his chest, when she placed both palms against it, felt like warm rock. About her, his arms lay heavy and relaxed – they might as well have been steel bands holding her trapped.

They shifted; she felt his fingers slide up the back of her neck, splaying into her thick hair. He angled her head – his lips closed over hers.

Hungrily.

She was kissing him back, exchanging breath for breath, caress for fiery caress, before she had a chance to think. Heat rose, pooling within her, radiating from him. As her wits whirled and desire danced in the air, she didn't think she'd have much trouble carrying out her plan. Provided she could get him to the bed.

With an effort, she drew back from the kiss. He let her go; her head tipped back – and back – as he trailed fire down her throat. 'The bed,' she gasped. 'We have to get to the bed.'

'Later.'

Catriona's temper kicked in. She opened her mouth – and lost her breath on a gasp as his hands closed possessively about her breasts, protected only by thin lawn. His thumbs circled, then finger and thumb closed tightly. She bit her lip hard, denying her instinctive shriek.

His hands left her breasts and she breathed again. Only to feel long fingers, hard palms, tracing her body, investigating every curve, subtly caressing yet with a deeper purpose – as if he was learning her.

Licking lips suddenly dry, she managed to gasp: 'Richard – the bed.'

His hands stopped; she sensed his attention – and held her breath. Would he wake? What had she said to focus him so?

Slow and sure, his hands resumed their meandering, imparting heat through her thin gown.

'That's the first time you've said my name.' He breathed

the words against her jaw, then feathered a kiss across her already swollen lips. 'Say it again.'

Catriona dragged in a breath too shallow to steady her head; she lifted a hand and brushed back the heavy lock of hair falling across his forehead. 'Richard?'

He kissed his name from her lips, then drank deep while his hands continued to roam, tracing breasts, hips, the long muscles of her back, the backs of her thighs, the globes of her bottom. Slowly arousing her – and him. When next he lifted his head, she was quivering. 'Richard – take me to your bed.' She had no difficulty investing the plea with believable feeling.

His reply was a wicked chuckle – a sound that played havoc with her overstretched nerves.

'Not yet. What's the hurry?' He tipped her chin up and nibbled his way down her throat. 'We've all night – and time stands still in dreams, anyway.'

*Not this one.* Catriona struggled to harness her wits. 'Just think how much more confortable we'll be in your bed.'

'I'm perfectly comfortable here – and so are you. And we're about to be even more comfortable yet.'

Catriona righted her head, registering as she did that one large hand was presently cradling her bottom, fondling far too knowingly, leaving her flesh heated, fevered. She looked down – and saw long fingers, dark against the white of her nightgown, artfully slipping the tiny buttons free.

Her eyes flew wide; she sucked in a desperate breath – and lost it in a shuddering, achingly desperate sigh as his hand flicked back the open bodice and his fingers brushed the peak of her swollen breast.

His artful fingers returned, caressing, tracing, teasing, then possessing.

She let her lids fall, felt her bones melt, felt her will evaporate like mist before the sun. But ... '*The bed,*' she whispered.

97

'Later,' he insisted. Cool air caressed her heated breasts as he pressed back her gown and bared them fully. One hand closed firmly, gently kneading. 'This is *my* dream. I intend to enjoy it – and you – to the full.'

Catriona bit back a groan. Cracking open her lids, she studied his face, lit by the fire's glow. Saw the sleepy smile of lustful anticipation on his lips, felt the heat of desire in his gaze, fixed on her breast, on the throbbing, aching nipple his wicked fingers teased and taunted.

He sensed her gaze, and glanced at her – then smiled, oddly confiding, and returned his attention to her breast. 'There are ladies in London who imagine they're cold.' His smile deepened – for an instant distinctly predatory. 'Some like to believe their flesh is chilled, that their passion is locked in ice.' His knowing fingers played over her aching flesh – never forceful, always teasing. His lips twisted, wryly triumphant. 'I've melted quite a few of them. There's a knack to it.'

As if to demonstrate, he shifted her in his arms, exposing her other breast, simultaneously letting her feel how intimate was his hold on her bottom.

'You, however, are going to be no trouble – you're like that mountain in whose shadow you were born.'

Dazed, Catriona blinked. 'Merrick?'

'Hmm.' He turned his head and looked into her eyes. 'Snow and ice on the peak ...' Looking down, he lifted his hand from her bare breast and trailed his fingers down, over the curve of her stomach, into the hollow at the apex of her thighs. 'But fires burn beneath.'

Catriona sucked in a breath as his fingers lightly traced the line between her thighs. She couldn't suppress the impulse to squirm, and felt his fingers firm about her bottom. He held her still and continued to play, tracing the long lines of her legs through her fine gown. His touch was tantalizing; she was breathing rapidly – her heart thudding in her throat – when he reached down and caught the gown's hem.

He lifted it slowly, then slid his hand beneath; the gown rose on the back of his hand as he traced, caressed, assessed her ankle, calf, knee, and thigh. He pushed the gown up over her hip, then, with complete and utter absorption, fell to caressing the expanse of thigh thus exposed. Beneath his fingers, a thousand fires sprang up, heating her, dewing her skin.

Caught in his play, as absorbed as he, Catriona knew he was right. She didn't need him to shift her again, so he could study the copper-bright curls at the junction of her thighs, didn't need to feel his fingers stroke them, then part them, then slide past, into her softness.

Didn't need him to look at her with unfocused eyes lit by blue flame and say: 'You're just like that mountain – you're a volcano inside.' He looked down again. 'A dormant one, perhaps.' Very gently, he stroked the soft flesh between her thighs, which had parted of their own accord. 'I'm going to stir you to life. Until passion pours like lava through your veins. Until you're hot and aching and wet. Until you're so slick and needy, you spread your lovely thighs wide and let me enter you. Fill you. Until I bathe in your heat.'

Catriona closed her eyes and felt her body surrender – felt the slickness he drew forth. Felt his fingers slide and glide, over and between the throbbing folds. Then his lips brushed hers. On a gasp, she kissed him back, sliding her hands from where they'd lain passive against his chest, around and about, holding him to her.

The kiss reached deep, then he drew back and chuckled – a wickedly devilish sound. 'You're not like those ladies in London at all. The most intriguing thing about you is that you *know* you've fire in your soul.'

Eyes closed, her body so heated she felt liquid, Catriona

felt him open her, felt him press gently, then slowly, deliberately, slide one long finger into her.

She felt the invasion keenly, felt it in her soul.

Welcomed it in her heart.

He shifted within her, gently stroking; the sudden tension that gripped her eased. She softened about him, about his probing finger, relaxing against him, sinking into his embrace.

'You're not a woman of ice and snow.'

She heard his words, and felt them, a breath across her temple, a deep reverberation in his chest. She tightened her hold on him, spreading her hands across his back, hanging on for dear life as if he was a rock anchoring her against the waves of heat beating through her.

Waves he incited with every smooth slick stroke, every subtle twist of his finger, every probing caress.

'You're heat – pure heat. Elemental heat. The heat of the earth, the purest fire.'

He was right – she was burning now with a flame hotter than the blue of his eyes. She'd always known this was how it would be – that passion for her would be hot and heated, steamy and searing. How she'd known, she didn't know, but the knowledge had always been there. And it had been so hard to hold the fire in, to quench it, tame it, hide it through all the years she'd waited.

Waited for this.

She was long past asking him to stop and adjourn to the bed. That would necessitate him taking his hands from her, and she couldn't bear that. His hands were pure magic, wicked fingers made to tease her, to light her fires.

And there was a tidal wave of flame bearing down on her.

She cracked open her lids just enough to find his head – to drag his lips to hers. She kissed him deeply, urgently, wantonly. Let her thighs part farther, urged him to reach deeper.

100

Instead, he drew back. And chuckled wickedly again. 'Oh, no. Not yet, sweet witch.' He withdrew his hand from between her thighs.

Breasts heaving, Catriona lay back in his arms and stared at him. 'What do you mean?' she finally managed to gasp. 'Not yet?'

He grinned. 'This is my dream, remember. You have to wait until you're frantic.'

Lips parted, she stared at him. 'I *am* frantic.'

The look he bent on her was patronizingly dismissive. 'Not *nearly* frantic enough.'

With that, he lifted her and set her on her feet between his thighs. Her legs quaked; his hands steadied her. Her gown slithered down to cover her legs; the bodice gaped.

Catriona yanked the two halves together and ignored the teasing quirk of his brow.

Once she'd steadied, he rose – and immediately tottered; *she* had to steady *him*.

His frown was only fleeting; another chuckle banished it. 'I must have had more of that whiskey than I'd thought.'

All but collapsing under his weight, Catriona, suddenly suspicious, looked up into his face. His eyes met hers, still dark as the night, his gaze still vague and unfocused; his lips were still set in that boyishly open smile.

He was still . . . dreaming.

Shifting her feet so she could better support his weight as he slumped, unrestrainedly heavy, against her, Catriona muttered a curse and struggled to ease him around the chair.

'The bed,' she stated.

'Oh, indeed,' he averred. 'It's definitely time for the bed.'

His devilish chuckle ensued; she shut her ears against it. If she hadn't known she'd drugged him, she would have thought him drunk – he could barely set one foot before the other. Certainly not in a straight line.

'Keep looking at the bed,' she instructed as they lurched heavily toward the door. 'Look – it's over there.' Exerting all her strength, she managed to turn him and get them back on course.

'Never had such trouble in my life,' he said, not sounding terribly concerned. 'Usually know precisely where the bed is.' After two more heavy steps, he added: 'Must be that whiskey. Hope I'm not too drunk to accommodate you.'

Gritting her teeth with the effort of holding him steady, Catriona didn't reassure him. And then wished she had.

'Never mind,' he murmured, and threw her a lecherous leer. 'If I am too debilitated, I'll just tease you until the effect wears off.'

Catriona closed her eyes fleetingly and stifled a groan. What had she done? She'd willingly taken the principal role in the dreams of a rake. She must have been mad.

But it was too late to draw back. Far too late. Aside from anything else, no matter how frantic she had to get, she wanted to reach the end of the hot, steamy, heated road he'd started her upon.

She definitely wanted to be hot and needy, and to feel him enter her.

Three more lurching steps and they reached the side of the bed – the opposite side to the one they'd started out for. Catriona was simply relieved. 'There!'

Swinging him around so his back was to the bed, she placed both palms against his chest and shoved. He obligingly toppled back across the bed – but took her with him.

Landing half-across him, Catriona couldn't manage even a squeak. She immediately wriggled, fighting free of his arms but not of his hands – they were everywhere. She tried to ignore them. 'We have to get you undressed.' At least undressed enough.

Predictably, he chuckled. 'Be my guest.' Flinging both

arms wide, he lay back. And grinned.

Catriona narrowed her eyes at him and tugged his cravat free. She flung it over the end of the bed, then, kneeling beside him, grabbed the lapel of his coat. No matter how she tugged, she couldn't get it even close to his shoulder. Exasperated she sat back, and noticed that his chest was quaking, even though his expression remained guileless.

She glared at him. 'If you don't help me undress you, I'll leave.'

Laughing softly, he rolled onto one shoulder, then sat up. 'It's impossible to get a well-cut coat off me without my help.'

Catriona humphed. She watched as he shrugged the coat off and sent it to join his cravat. Impelled by she knew not what, she reached out and ran her hands over his chest, pressing aside his waistcoat to explore the wide expanse. Beneath her questing hands, muscles shifted, rippled, then set. He caught her wrists and yanked her to him, then bent his head and kissed her.

She sank into his embrace, felt the heat surround her, rise within her, lick tantalizingly up her spine as he gathered her closer. With a mind of their own, her fingers quickly undid the buttons of his shirt, then slid inside, spreading wide over warm tight skin, over ridged muscles, hard bands of hair-dusted flesh.

He broke from the kiss with a soft curse. From beneath her lashes, she saw him fight free of both waistcoat and shirt and fling them aside. She also saw one hand drop to his waist-band, undoing the buttons there. Closing her eyes quickly, she reached for him, relieved when he captured her lips with his and kissed her witless.

He shifted, coming up on his knees and guiding her back, down onto the bed. She sank back obediently, eyes closed, silently willing him to be quick.

His weight shifted on the bed; she heard the dull thwacks as his shoes, then his trousers hit the floor. She kept her eyes tight shut – she definitely wasn't going to look. Then she felt him beside her; he leaned over her, and his lips covered hers.

He kissed her deeply, commandingly – more intimately than before. He took her mouth as if she'd offered herself; in a way, she supposed she had. The claiming was complete, unrestrained – as if even asleep he knew she was his. His for the taking.

And he took.

Somewhere along the line, she opened her senses, let them reach and tell her what her eyes could not. She set her hands exploring, over the smooth acres of his chest, tight and hard under her hands and roughened by crinkly hair, then over the rounded curves of his shoulders. Flexing her fingers into the steel of his upper arms, she lifted against him, driven by his kiss – he was leaning far over her, his body, hot and hard, a mere inch from hers.

He was lying beside her, his hip against hers, his body radiating heat and a sensuality that wrapped about her, about them, and shielded them from the world.

And still he kissed her, reaching deep, asking for more and taking it. Emboldened, she met his demands – and let her hands stray lower.

To his hip. Fingers reaching, she traced the wide bone, sensed the slightly different texture of his skin. And sensed the sudden hiatus in their kiss – the abrupt refocusing of his senses.

Deliberately, she let her hand fall, fingers languidly trailing over his lower stomach.

His breath hitched – he pulled back from the kiss.

Just as she found him.

Eyes still closed, she touched tentatively, surprised to find such delicate skin. And felt him quiver, then tense. Intrigued, she slowly reached farther, and wrapped her fingers around the heavy length. Every muscle he possessed locked.

The one in her hands throbbed.

Lips curving in a wicked smile, she stroked, and caressed, closed her hands and weighed, then explored farther still.

He broke and caught her hands. 'Sweet witch, you're killing me.'

The words sounded as if they'd been said through clenched teeth; she gave a wicked chuckle of her own.

Only to have him kiss her voraciously, ravenously, until her wits whirled and she lost touch with reality. Then he drew back.

'Now it's my turn.'

He swung over her, kneeling, his knees on either side of hers. Catching the hem of her nightgown, he raised it.

Eyes closed, expectation hammering in her veins, Catriona lay still and waited.

He pulled her gown up to her waist – then straight up to her shoulders, drawing her arms up, clearly intending to wrestle it from her.

Catriona gasped and came alive. Grabbing folds of the gown, she tried to wrestle it back down. He didn't need her naked to—

He chuckled, the sound even more evocative with her head wrapped in her gown, her body fully exposed. To the night, to him.

'Actually,' he drawled, 'that's an even better idea.'

The gown shifted, twisted; Catriona waited half a second, then tried to move her arms, only to find them stuck. Her head, arms and shoulders were wrapped, trapped, in her gown.

'Hmm. *Excellent.*'

The purring drawl had her biting her lip, had her tensing with expectation. An expectation fully borne out when she felt him lower his naked body upon hers. He shifted, sliding lower, his legs outside hers.

'Positively succulent.'

She felt his breath against the soft skin of her breasts and wondered what he meant.

The next instant, she arched wildly and nearly screamed as his mouth closed hotly about one nipple. He pressed open-mouthed kisses over her quivering flesh, then lovingly licked each peak to a tight bud – before torturing it with his tongue.

Catriona fought wildly – just to catch her breath. When she finally thought she'd become used to the new sensations, he suckled one nipple fiercely – she screamed and melted anew.

Luckily, the folds of her gown got into her mouth and muffled her shriek. As sanity returned, she realized his attentions hadn't faltered – she hadn't jarred him fully awake. When he suckled her other breast, she was prepared for the lightning bolt – the shocking strike of pure sensation. Her body arched, but she contained her scream.

Panting, gasping, her body afire, she waited, desperately trying to imagine what he would do next.

His lips drifted lower, leaving trails of fire down her body, over her waist. He pressed hot kisses to her stomach; she tensed, then relaxed as the trails continued down her thighs, first one, then the other.

Then he shifted, moving back and away. Senses searching, Catriona placed him kneeling astride her calves. Then she felt his hands close about her knees and lift them, parting her thighs.

After the slightest hesitation, she let him open her; catching her breath, she waited for him to cover her.

Instead, she felt a feathery touch, then feathery kisses dotting along her inner thigh. First one, then the other.

As what he *might* intend broke on her mind, she gasped and tried to clamp her thighs shut, only to find his broad shoulders between.

He chuckled wickedly.

And pressed a long, hot kiss to her damp curls.

'Not yet, sweet witch.'

Then he kissed her.

And licked her. And sucked so gently she thought she would die.

Mindless, she threshed, trying to fight her way free of her nightgown; defeated, she tried to sit up – only to feel the heavy weight of his forearm across her waist press her down. Only to feel his other hand slide beneath her bottom and tilt her up. So he could savor her softness more thoroughly.

And savor her he did. Long and slow, languid and devastating, his lips and tongue wove their magic, until fires burned under every inch of her skin, until her bones had melted and her nerves shrivelled and her wits had reduced to ashes. Until she was panting, almost crying in her need.

She was hot, she was needy – she was ready.

She was frantic.

*Then* he pulled back.

'*Richard!*'

Her cry was weak – a demand and a plea.

He shifted back onto his knees with a satisfied groan; the next instant, he smoothed aside the folds of her gown, searching for her hands. Their fingers touched, and locked; he drew her up so she was sitting.

Catriona swung her legs under her so she was kneeling, too – but before she could push her gown down, he whisked it off over her head. Aghast, she watched it float over the end of the bed.

She looked at her tormentor.

Which was a big mistake.

Fully dressed, he was intimidating. Naked, he was mesmerizing. Fascinatingly, mind-numbingly male – a potent, powerful presence just waiting to claim her.

107

In all that had led to this moment, she had steadfastly refused to let her mind form any picture – to imagine how he would look naked, without the civilized cloak he wore when he stalked the world. Dragging in a tight breath, she wondered if imagining might have been better – might have better prepared her to face this.

To her mind, to all her senses, he was magnificent, his long, lean frame covered with taut muscle. The sight of him stirred her powerfully, unfurled some primitive emotion in her.

She gulped, and forced her gaze upward, relieved to see his boyish grin still in place.

'That's better.'

While her eyes had been roaming, so had his, with very evident results. He reached for her; she tried to hold back but her knees slid across the sheets. To her surprise, he didn't gather her into his arms, but, sinking back on his ankles, stopped her with her knees against his and eased her back so she was sitting as he was, on her ankles, knees wide.

He grinned, his expression the very essence of male sexual expectation. 'Next installment.'

Her wits long gone, her senses reeling, she couldn't even summon a frown. 'Installment?'

His hands closed over her breasts, confident and firm. His thumbs rubbed her tightly budded nipples; her body came instantly alive. Her lids fell of their own accord as she arched lightly, pressing her breasts into his palms. 'What do you mean?'

'I want to see how high you can go – how high I can take you before you shatter.'

She struggled to frown, struggled to make sense of his words, and couldn't. Not with his hands on her breasts, then roaming her body, her sides, her thighs, quiveringly tight.

Then he stroked her soft curls, then slid long fingers past

to stroke her there, where she was hot and molten. Two fingers pressed in and filled her, then retreated; he circled her entrance, then pressed – and she gasped. His fingers slid away, and played, then returned to the same excruciatingly sensitive spot, and pressed again.

White light flared behind her lids. And suddenly, Catriona understood. She grabbed his wrist – and felt, beneath her fingers, the seductive shift of tendon and muscle as he probed her – slowly, deliberately, evocatively.

She snapped open her eyes and looked at his face. Harshedged with passion, the planes were set. Fully aroused, his gaze was locked on where his hand worked between her thighs.

She couldn't believe her senses. 'You're teasing me? Like *this?*'

He looked up and met her gaze. His was still clouded, his eyes like black pools; if anything, the hold of the drugs was deepening. Then he smiled – the same boyish smile. 'I've been itching to sink into you since first I set eyes on you – I've been aroused virtually every minute I've spent in your sight. Being around you, especially every time you put your pert nose in the air, has been torture. I thought I'd give you a dose of your own magic before I ease my pain.' His smile grew soft, distinctly dreamy. 'And as for this' – he pressed again; Catriona gasped and swayed – 'I plan on teasing you a lot more yet.'

'A lot *more?*' Aghast, she stared at him and tried to think of what he hadn't yet done.

His grin widened. 'When I'm inside you. It'll be long and slow – the most perfect torture for a sexy witch.'

Catriona simply stared – what had she done? What had she set in train? He was dreaming. He really *was* dreaming – reality fluidly merging with fantasy. He didn't know what he was doing. He didn't realize he was frightening her, pushing her too far. Making her feel far too much. He didn't know she was real.

She was going to lose her mind if he didn't fill her soon. Simply lay her on her back and take her. Quickly. She could feel the passion mounting, bubbling through her veins, exactly as he had predicted. Her inner fires were raging, she was molten with liquid heat. And she needed to release it.

She wanted him – now, immediately, ten minutes ago. It was her own need that was scaring her, not his.

But he didn't know that – and she couldn't explain. She didn't want to beg. Unexpected panic flared within her.

It must have shown in her face, for he frowned. His fingers slowed, and he cocked his head slightly, studying her. He blinked once, twice – confusion was writ plain in his face. 'What is it?'

Catriona opened her lips – but no words came out. What should she say? What should she admit to? He was clearly dazed, increasingly hazy – he was operating on instinct. What sort of instinct did a rake have?

Her gaze locked with his, she moistened her lips, suddenly aware of the huge risk she'd taken. Algaria had tried to warn her, but she hadn't understood. She wasn't in control of this situation – and neither was he.

Which meant she'd thrown herself on the mercy of a rake's true soul, his real, inner self, his true character – and she didn't know what that was.

She was about to find out.

Acting on instinct, she held out her arms to him. 'I want you now.'

She didn't try to hide the genuineness of her need – her vulnerability. Her only guarantee that she would be safe in so doing was The Lady's insistence that he was the one. Placing her trust in The Lady's judgment, with her arms, with her eyes, she reached for him. '*Please.*'

110

She didn't see him move, only felt his arms close about her as he gathered her close.

'Sshhh.' He held her against him, hot skin to hot skin, and pressed his face into her hair. 'I didn't mean to frighten you.' His hands stroked her back, soothingly, comfortingly. Cupping her bottom lightly, he shifted against her, his erection riding against her belly. 'Put it down to too much imagining. I've been fantasizing for so long about you – how you'd feel' – he slid his hands over her back and hips – 'how you'd taste.' With his shoulder, he nudged her head up and kissed her – gently, lingeringly – the hunger in him held back, the tangy taste of her still there on his lips and tongue.

Then he raised his head and looked into her face. 'I want you in the worst possible way' – he grinned ruefully, boyishness overlaid by passion – 'in every way known to man. I want to see you flower for me – spread your legs for me and hold out your arms for me. I want to be inside you more than I want to breathe – I want to feel you rising beneath me as I ride you. And I want to wake and find you beside me – I want to hold you forever.' He pressed a kiss to her lips. 'I want to *care* for you forever.' Lifting his head, he looked into her eyes. 'I want to be your lover in all ways – in every sense of the word, and the deed.'

Locked in his dark, cloudy gaze, Catriona could only quiver. He'd seduced her all over again. 'Come.'

It was she who took his hand, she who lay down upon the bed, spread her thighs wide and held out her arms to him.

And he came to her – the invincible warrior without a cause – devoid, because of her scheming, of his mask, the shield he held up to the world. In that instant, when he'd looked into her eyes and made his declaration, he hadn't been capable of lying. He wanted to love her – and to have her love him. Not just physically but in all ways. He wanted her as part of his life – and wanted to be part of hers. She'd needed no higher powers to read the truth – it had been there, trans-parent in his unshielded eyes.

It was there, written on his soul – and in that moment she'd been able to read the words. The truth. The reality of what he yearned for.

So she welcomed him to her, wrapping her arms about him as he covered her. Nudging her thighs wider, he settled between and fitted himself to her slick sheath. Turning his head, he took one pebbled nipple into his mouth and suckled fiercely; she arched, and he pressed inside her, stretching her.

She tensed and tried to force her muscles to ease. He reached down, between their bodies, and caressed the nubbin he'd earlier teased.

Sensation streaked – jagged lightning striking deep. It broke the banks and set the floodtide raging, molten passion, lava hot, surging, racing through her. And she was caught in the tide, swept up and whirled away, into the pure heat of the moment. She felt him retreat, then powerfully surge, and fill her.

Felt him ride deep to her core.

She melted about him and welcomed him in – into her body, into her heart. She knew it was dangerous – she saw the gaping hole yawning at her feet, but the desire that drove him, the raw need that now filled him, driving him into her again and again – as surely as it had caught him, it caught her. She jumped into the hole without a second thought.

And gave herself to him, opened her body and her senses, and let him fill both. Exquisitely vulnerable, spread beneath his hard strength, held immobile by it, impaled by it, she kissed him wildly, and urged him on.

But not even she could warp his true character; despite the force of the energy flowing so strongly between them, he harnessed it and set himself to please her. Pleasure her.

In a wild and wonderful way.

His surging rhythm became hers, became her very heart-beat. He used his body to love her – she learned to use hers to love him back. He was no gentle teacher, yet he forced nothing but pleasure on her. She raised her knees and gripped his hips, and gave herself up to his loving.

To the joy, the heat, and the escalating pleasure. To the moment that came upon her unawares, and stole her mind, her senses, her very being from her.

And left her floating in a void of delight, anchored only by his heartbeat.

She only just managed to smother her scream; she wasn't even sure she succeeded. She wasn't even sure that she cared.

Richard felt her melt beneath him, felt the last of her contractions fade, sensed her final surrender. With a gasp and a groan, he thrust deep and shut his eyes, blocking out the sight of her, the blazing mane of her hair a frame for her ecstasy, for the expression of pure peace that filled her face.

Racking shudders swamped him; he felt her grip him tight.

He gasped again and surrendered, and followed her into the void.

Later, much later, he lifted from her and drew her into his arms. She turned and snuggled closer, warming him inside and out. He felt his lips lift – he couldn't understand why he felt so pleased. Why he felt so at ease. So complete.

Then he remembered.

But it was just a dream.

With a soft sigh, he closed his eyes and wished dreams could last forever.

113

# Chapter Seven

Richard woke the next morning, very slowly. An age seemed to pass before he felt certain he was in this world, and not some other. He felt disoriented, lethargic. Drained.

If he hadn't known better, he would have said he felt sated.

The thought made him frown. The thoughts that followed made him frown even more.

'Rubbish.' He looked at the bed beside him. The covers were straight, the pillow still plump. No hint of a bedmate. To prove the point, he lifted the covers and peered down. Beside him, the sheet was not rumpled in the least; it was, in fact, very neat.

Instead of lightning, his frown grew blacker. He shifted his gaze to that part of his anatomy that featured most prominently in his disturbing dream. He gazed at it as if it could answer the wild question in his mind; it simply lay there, in its customary semi-aroused morning state, and told him nothing. He checked, but there was no discernible evidence that it had engaged in any wild nocturnal coupling.

Dropping the covers, Richard lay back on the pillows; crossing his arms above his head, he gazed at the canopy. But the more he let his mind dwell on his dream, the more vivid it became, refusing to fade in the cold morning light. The more he thought of it, the more definite details became, the more intense the sensual memories.

'Ridiculous.' Flinging back the covers, he sat up.

He washed and shaved, attended by Worboys, then dressed, shrugged into his coat and headed downstairs. Throughout his ablutions, his dream had refused to get out of his mind, had only grown more vivid. More detailed.

Lips compressed, he stepped off the stairs. Given his recent abstinence, given the witch presently under the same roof, given the fantasies he'd been consciously and unconsciously concocting about her, it probably *wasn't* surprising she'd started inhabiting his dreams.

He strolled into the breakfast parlor, knowing he was late. Exchanging mild nods with the rest of Seamus's dull household, he filled his plate and carried it to the table. The object of his lustful dreams was not present, but she'd proved to be an early riser.

At McEnery House, bright morning chatter was unheard of, which suited his mood. He ate in silence. He was devilishly hungry. He'd cleared half his plate when rushing footsteps sounded in the corridor. Everyone looked up.

Catriona hurried in.

Her gaze collided with his; she stopped as if she'd run into a wall. For one instant, she stared, her expression unreadable.

'Well! I wondered when you'd rouse.'

Algaria's dry, disapproving comment broke the spell; Richard couldn't tell who'd thrown it – Catriona or him. Or some other force entirely.

Catriona glanced at Algaria, then approached the table. 'I . . . ah, overslept.'

'You were dead to the world when I looked in.'

'Hmm.' Without meeting anyone's eye, Catriona served herself a large portion of the kedgeree the butler offered. Instead of her customary tea and toast.

Richard frowned – first at her plate, then at his. And wondered if it was possible for people to share dreams.

It was a horridly dull day, with sleet and snow lashing the house. Denied any chance of a walk to clear her head, Catriona set herself to review the stillroom. Which appeared not to have been reviewed since last she'd visited. The task proved so consuming, she got no chance to devote any sensible thought to the problem she'd seen looming on her horizon.

She hadn't seen it until that morning, when she'd rushed into the breakfast parlor. Not that she could have foreseen it, given she hadn't foreseen the depth of her involvement with Richard.

He who was to father her child.

But she got no chance to think on that, to dwell on how her view of him had changed, and on whether that meant she could, or should, change her plan, or even whether her plan was now safer, or more dangerous.

He'd been confused this morning – and that she hadn't expected. She'd seen it in his eyes as he'd looked at her – a remembrance of the night. Given what had happened, she wasn't surprised; she hadn't expected him to be even partially awake, much less in that peculiar state of a waking dream.

It wasn't, therefore, surprising that he remembered something; his confusion told her he hadn't remembered enough. Enough to be sure it hadn't been a dream.

She was safe, but he was disturbed. She needed to think about that.

'Tie all these up in bunches and hang them properly. And when you've finished with that, you can throw all this away.' 'All this' was a pile of ancient herbs that had long ago lost their efficacy. Hands on hips, Catriona surveyed the much-improved stillroom, then nodded briskly. 'We'll make a start on the oils in the morning.'

'Yes, ma'am,' the housekeeper and two maids chorused.

Catriona left them to their labors and headed back to the

116

family parlor. Her route lay through a labyrinth of corridors giving onto a narrow gallery overlooking the side drive.

The gallery led to the main wing of the house. She'd started along it before she looked up and saw the large figure standing before one of the long windows looking out at the wintry day. He heard her and turned his head, then turned fully, not precisely blocking her path, but giving the impression he would like to.

Head high, Catriona's steps did not falter. But she slowed as she neared him, suddenly aware of a changed presence in the air, of some blatantly sexual reaction. On his part – and on hers.

She stopped a full yard away, not daring to venture closer, unsure just what the sudden searing impulse to touch him might lead her to do. Keeping her expression mild and uninformative, she lifted her chin and raised a questioning brow.

He looked down at her, his expression as unreadable as hers.

And the hot attraction between them grew stronger, more intense.

It stole her breath and fanned heat over her body. Her nipples crinkled tight; she held her ground and prayed he wouldn't notice.

'I wondered,' he eventually said, 'if you'd like to stroll.' His tone made it clear he wanted her alone, somewhere private so he could investigate what he was feeling. 'The conservatory as we have no other choice.'

The fact that – even knowing the truth – she actually considered the possibility truly scared her. 'Ahh ... I think not.' Prudence reasserted itself in a rush; Catriona softened her refusal with a smile. 'I must tend to Meg – she's unwell.'

'Can't Algaria tend Meg?'

His irritation nearly made her grin; his mask was slipping – the warrior was showing. 'No – Meg prefers me.'

His lips thinned. 'So do I.'

Catriona couldn't stop her grin. 'She's ill – you're not.'

'Much you know.' Thrusting his hands in his trouser pockets, he turned and sauntered beside her as she resumed her progress into the main wing.

Catriona shot him a careful glance. 'You're not sick.'

He raised an arrogant brow. 'You can tell just by looking?'

'Generally, yes.' She trapped his gaze. 'In your case, your aura is very strong, and there's no hint of any illness.'

He searched her eyes, then humphed. 'When you've finished with Meg, you can come and examine my strength in greater detail.'

Catriona fought to keep her lips straight enough to frown. 'You're just feeling a trifle under the weather. Perfectly understandable.' They'd reached the bottom of the main stairs; with a nod, she indicated the bleak scene beyond the hall windows.

He looked, but didn't seem to see. He stopped before the stairs; she halted on the bottom step and faced him.

'I'd be perfectly all right,' he said, meeting her eyes, 'if I could just . . .'

His words died; desire swept over them, tangible and hot as a desert wind. He stared at her; Catriona held tight to the banister and struggled not to respond, to keep her own mask in place as his wavered.

Then he blinked, frowned, and shook his head. 'Never mind.'

More shaken than she could allow him to see, Catriona smiled weakly. 'Later, perhaps.'

He looked at her again, then nodded. 'Later.'

There was to be no later – not that day. Despite her best intentions, Catriona found herself in constant demand, with Meg, with the children, even with Mary, who was usually as hale as a horse. The tensions in the house, generated by Seamus's iniquitous will, were taking their toll.

The only time she had to herself was the half-hour while she dressed for dinner. Hardly enough time to consider the implications of the unexpected turn her straightforward plan had taken. As she scrambled into her gown, then shook out her hair, brushed it and rebraided it, she swiftly reevaluated her position.

If things had gone as she'd planned, she would have steadfastly avoided Richard during the days, done nothing to give him the slightest reason to change his mind. She had planned to hold aloof until he'd refused Seamus's edict, seen him on the road to London, then headed for the vale. Carrying his child.

Such had been her plan.

Now, however, one small element had gone awry. She needed to adjust. He'd remembered enough of the night to be seriously disturbed. The idea that he might be affected in some way as a result of her machinations was not one she could accept.

She'd have to do something about it.

The first thing she did, on her way down to dinner, last as ever, was to add to his fateful decanter a few drops of another potion, one that would prevent him from remembering any further 'dreams.'

The second thing she did was stand, rather than flee, when he reentered the drawing room after dinner and stalked straight to her side.

Algaria, beside her, stiffened. Catriona waved her away – she went, reluctantly. Richard barely nodded at her as he took her place.

'Where the devil have you been?'

Catriona opened her eyes wide. 'Calming Meg, dosing the children – all six of them – then mixing Mary a potion, then checking the children, then helping Meg get up, then checking the children, then ...' She waved. 'My day flew, I'm afraid.'

He eyed her narrowly. 'I'd hoped to catch up with you after lunch.'

Catriona threw him a helpless, apologetic look.

Richard inwardly snorted, and all but glowered at the rest of the company. He'd filled in what probably ranked as the dullest day of his life in the library and in the billiard room, praying that his sudden susceptibility would fade.

It hadn't.

Even now, just standing beside her, his body was literally remembering what hers had felt like pressed against him. Naked – skin to skin. The thought made him hot – hotter than he already was. If she'd been a problem yesterday, with her ability to arouse him, after last night's dream, she qualified as a full blown crisis. 'I wanted to speak with you.'

About what, he wasn't sure. But he definitely wanted to know if she felt what he did – if she could sense the sheer lust that scorched the air between them. He'd watched her carefully but had detected no especial awareness; he slanted a glance at her now, as, with less than a foot between them, she calmly considered his words. Not a glimmer of consciousness showed.

While all he could think of was how it had felt to slide inside her.

He bit back a groan; it was no use hardening his muscles against the remembered sensations – they were hard enough as it was. 'We need to talk.'

The glance she threw him was searching. 'You're not sick – you don't need my professional advice.'

She sounded positive – Richard wasn't so sure. He might not be physically ill, but ... he knew his 'dream' was a dream for the simple reason it could not have really happened. The chances of her turning up in his room like that, smiling and saying she'd come to go to bed with him, were, in his estimation, less than nil.

And if that hadn't happened, then the rest certainly hadn't.

But he'd never had memories like this, not even of real events. Real women – ones with whom he *had* shared a bed. Much as he hated to think it, he wasn't at all sure that all the long nights of his lenthy and lustfully successful rakish career weren't coming back to haunt him.

Because he was sure – to his bones – that he knew her in the biblical sense.

He drew in a deep breath and let it out through clenched teeth. 'Do you know much about dreams?' He glanced at her. 'Can you read them?'

She looked up and met his eyes; he sensed her hesitation. 'Sometimes,' she eventually replied. 'Dreams often mean something, but that something often isn't clear.' She considered, then quickly added: 'And it's often not the thing it appears as in the dream.'

He threw her an exasperated look. 'That's a lot of help.'

She blinked and considered him. Rather carefully, he thought.

'If you're troubled by some dream, then the best thing to do is set it aside for the moment, because if it *is* supposed to mean something, then that something will become apparent, usually in a few days. Or the dream will disappear.'

'Indeed?' Richard raised a brow, then reluctantly nodded. That was probably sound advice – he might as well put it into practice. But first, he needed to stop her from deserting him. He nodded to the tea trolley being stationed before Mary. 'I'll get our cups.'

Catriona graciously inclined her head and watched him cross the room. And swore she'd start carrying a fan. She was so hot, she was surprised she hadn't spontaneously combusted – gone

121

up in flames right here in Mary's drawing room. The flushes that washed through her came in two forms – hot and hotter. Hot when he wasn't looking directly at her, hotter when he was. The only reason she was still standing here, using every ounce of her will and experience to appear unaffected, was because she'd convinced herself this was the penance she had to pay for the way her plan had affected him – to bear with the countereffect and bring him what ease she could. But . . .

She was desperately in need of her tea.

He returned and handed her her cup; she accepted it and sipped gratefully.

Richard sipped, too, for much the same reason, then set his cup back on its saucer. 'Tell me about this role of yours – being the lady of the vale.'

Catriona blinked and looked up at him. 'The lady of the vale?' When he simply waited, she asked: 'You want to know what I do?'

Richard nodded. And saw wariness seep into her eyes.
'Why?'

'Because . . .' He paused, then continued, 'I want to know what I'm turning down.' If she thought he was considering falling in with Seamus's plan, she'd tell him nothing. He capped the words with one of his teasing smiles, and was rewarded with one of her humphs.

'You don't need to know.'

'Where's the harm?' He slanted her a glance – she'd tossed her pert nose in the air again and he was wretchedly uncomfortable. 'You're the local healer, but that can't be the summation of your duties, not if you own the vale.'

'Of course not.'

'I assume you keep control over the rents and sales of produce, but what about the other areas? The livestock, for instance. Do you supervise the breeding yourself, or does someone else help?'

The glance she shot him was part irritation, part resignation. 'There are others, of course. Most of the husbandry is dealt with by one of my staff, but the dairy is separate.'

'Do you make your own cheese?' By dint of a succession of careful questions, he dragged a reasonable outline of her holdings, and how she managed them, from her. As he'd expected, there were gaps in her management – important areas in which she relied on people who themselves had no real qualifications. She trusted too easily, despite, or perhaps because of, her beliefs.

He'd already proved that.

Catriona answered his questions because she couldn't see any reason not to. And he surprised her – with his insight, his understanding, his experience. In the end, she asked: 'How do you know to ask all this?' She frowned at him, grateful the heat between them had ebbed. Not disappeared, but eased. 'Do you manage large estates in your spare time?'

He looked mildly bemused. 'Spare time?'

'I gathered your conquests in London take up *most* of your time.'

'Ahh.' Her tart reply amused him. 'You forget – I'm a Cynster.'

'So?'

His smile started off as teasing, but somewhere along the way turned intent. 'You've forgotten,' he murmured, 'the family motto.'

Catriona felt the air about her stir; she was surprised it didn't crackle. She held his gaze and lifted a haughty brow. 'Which is?'

*'To have . . . and to hold.'*

The words hung between them, layered with meaning; holding his gaze, Catriona prayed he couldn't see through her mask as easily as she could see through his. She didn't need to be told those words were not just a motto – they were a *raison d'être*. For them all, perhaps, but especially for him.

The bastard – the warrior without a cause.

Barely able to breathe, she reached for his empty cup. 'If you'll excuse me, I must check on Meg.'

He let her go without a word, which was just as well. How much longer she could have withstood the temptation to reach out to him – to let him have her as his cause – she didn't like to think.

Nevertheless, later that night, when the last of the midnight chimes died, she once more stood before his closed door – and stared at it. While telling herself, in very plain terms, precisely why she was there.

First and foremost there were The Lady's orders, orders she could not defy. And it was indisputable fact that three nights was the minimum she should spend with him – that was what she would advise any other woman in her place.

And lastly, but, she had to admit, very far from least, there was the simple fact she wanted him. Wanted to lie in his arms again, wanted to miss none of the short time fate had granted them. She wanted to hold him again, the vulnerable warrior, and give herself to him completely – give herself to fill the void in his soul. She couldn't marry him, but that didn't mean that he – and she – couldn't have that.

Even if only in his dreams.

She drew a deep breath and reached for the door handle.

Lying back in his bed, wide awake, Richard stared moodily at the whiskey decanter. He'd gone without his usual night-cap. It had occurred to him that the whiskey – not his normal drop – might be to blame for his over-vivid dreams.

If it was, he'd avoid it. He couldn't handle another day like this, with his body clamoring – reacting – as if something that hadn't happened had. He'd go mad. Some held that the Scots

124

were all insane – witness Seamus. Maybe whiskey was to blame.

The soft swoosh of air as the door opened had him turning his head. The door swung open – not tentatively – and Catriona walked in. She closed the door quietly, then scanned the room – and saw him. The fire had burned low, but he still saw her soft, peculiarly witchy smile.

Every muscle in his body locked; he couldn't breathe. A condition that worsened as, her smile still playing over her face, she walked toward the bed, slipping off her robe – a robe he remembered – as she came. She let the robe fall as she reached the side of the bed. Head on one side, she studied him – still smiling softly.

Absolutely rigid, he watched her, then realized she was searching his face. The light from the fire didn't reach the head of the bed; she might be able to see his eyes were open, but she couldn't possibly read them. If she did, she'd flee.

Instead, her smile deepened. She reached for the covers, then hesitated. Then she shrugged and straightened – and calmly unbuttoned the bodice of her nightgown, grasped the skirt, and drew it off over her head.

Richard sucked in a tortured breath; if he could have moved he'd have pinched himself. But he *knew* he wasn't asleep.

He wasn't dreaming. This was real.

Totally naked, her long tresses hanging free about her shoulders, over her back, her skin – smooth breasts, sleek flanks – gleaming like ivory in the weak light, she lifted the covers and slid in. The dipping of the mattress as she settled beside him triggered an instinctive, almost violent response. He only just managed to suppress it – the primitive urge to roll over, cover her, take her.

His mind was reeling, his wits in disarray, struggling to

grasp the fact that this was *real* – that she was, in solid fact, here, in his bed – blissfully naked.

*What in all hell was she up to?*

He hadn't moved – he didn't dare; if he did, the reins would slip from his grasp, and God alone knew what would happen then. Every muscle quivering with restraint, he looked at her.

And she touched him.

Spread one small, warm hand over his chest, then swept it down to boldy cup him.

After that, hell, God – even her Lady – didn't matter.

He closed his eyes on a long groan. Her fingers tightened; his reins snapped. He caught her hands, first one, then the other, locking them above her head in one of his. In the same movement, he lifted over her, found her lips, and plundered.

One thought burned in his fevered brain – to confirm, beyond all doubt, that *she* had been the woman in his dream. That she'd been the woman he'd brought to life the night before, the woman who'd begged him to take her, then writhed like a wanton in his arms.

He closed his hand over one firm breast and recognized it. Felt it swell, found the tight pebble of her nipple. And recognized that, too. He swept his hand down, tracing curve after curve, of breast, waist, hip and thigh; the globes of her bottom, smooth and perfect, filled his hand. As they had last night.

And she was with him, as she had been last night – hot and urgent, her mouth, her lips, melding with his, her tongue dueling with his. With her arms still anchored above her head, her body arched beneath him, caressing him as he caressed her.

Caught in her heat, driven by wild compulsion, he wedged her thighs wide. And touched her. She was wet, scorchingly hot – she rose to his touch, mutely begging for more. He slid one finger deep and she gasped.

126

His name.

He drank it from her lips as he pushed her thighs wide, positioned himself between. And slid home.

Braced above her, he let his head fall back as she closed, scalding velvet, about him. He moved within her and she answered, matching him stroke for stroke, taking him deep into her heat, and holding him.

Freed, her hands rose to caress his chest, then strayed to his flexing flanks. She held him lightly, then repositioned her hips and guided him deeper.

He gasped, and came down on his elbows, framed her face and kissed her. Voraciously. The friction between their bodies was driving them both insane – demented with desire.

But he kept them there, held them there, in the heat of the furnace, in the eye of the storm. He prolonged their joining for as long as he could, addicted to the sheer joy of filling her.

Beneath him, Catriona gloried in the exquisite intimacy, in the clear, shining knowledge that this was how it was meant to be. Their bodies moved in a dance older than time, his hard, driving, hers soft, accepting.

Both loving.

The thought came to her on a fractured sigh and a guttural groan; bodies locked, they climbed higher, and higher, both focused totally on sensation – on sensation that went further than the physical, that breached some other plane.

Some plane where each touch became laden with meaning, with feeling, with emotion, where they asked and answered through each caress, through each deep thrust that linked them.

It was a plane where their heartbeats joined and swelled, where bodies ceased to exist and souls, freed, could touch. And be touched.

It was a plane of unlimited joy, unlimited ecstasy. Freed,

together, they explored – and lived for every precious moment.

Their fusion, when it came, was all heat, glorious heat, molten rivers pouring through their bodies, down their veins. Bodies locked, they climaxed together, melted together, fused, then, as one, slowly cooled.

Richard returned from the dead first, but was too deeply sated, too shaken, to move. His mind was still in limbo, reeling between truth, reality, and an even greater truth. Her body beneath him, around him, was his anchor; her arms tight about him, she seemed as disinclined to move as he.

It seemed like hours before they could bear to part, slowly, reluctantly, disengaging their limbs. Even then, she turned to him, slipping into his arms as if she belonged there.

Richard held her – and tried to hold back his thoughts, tried not to recognize that greater truth. Tried instead to focus on the far less unnerving fact that it had indeed been she last night – it hadn't been a dream. He wasn't going insane. At least, not in the way he'd thought.

The clock on the stairs struck one. He glanced down at her face and realized she was awake. He hesitated, then said: 'Sometimes, dreams don't turn out as you expect.'

He felt her exhale slowly, then she whispered, 'No.' Lifting her head, she stretched up and kissed him, long and lingeringly, then sank back, settling in his arms. 'No.'

She fell asleep with her head on his shoulder, leaving him frowning into the dark.

# Chapter Eight

She had the touch of a goddess. He could feel her hands on him, on his back, on his flanks. On his—

Richard awoke with a start. He glanced at the bed beside him and realized he'd been dreaming. 'Or rather,' he murmured, lips thinning, 'remembering.'

He noted the bed's state – as neat and tidy as the morning before. Scanning the room, he saw not one sign of his witch's presence. Lying back on the pillows, he frowned. He wasn't a particularly heavy sleeper, but clearly she could slide from his arms, even straighten the sheet beside him, without awakening him. She moved smoothly – gliding rather than walking; her hands were used to soothing, her gestures always graceful.

He didn't want to think about her hands.

With an oath, he flung back the covers and stalked across the room to the bellpull. He was in hunter mode again; all he needed to do now was locate his prey.


He found her in the breakfast parlor, sunnily eating a boiled egg. She greeted him with a breezy smile.

And such transparent happiness he was momentarily thrown off-balance.

He hesitated, then nodded back and headed for the buffet. After making a selection of the various meats on offer, he returned to the table, to the chair opposite hers. Malcolm, morosely munching toast at the table's other end, and Algaria O'Rourke were the only others down yet.

Catriona's watchdog sat beside her, regarding him with her usual disapproval; Richard ignored her and ate – while watching Catriona do the same. Watched her lick egg-yolk from her lower lip, then lick her spoon. Saw her lips sheening pink when she sipped her tea.

He shifted in his seat, looked down at his plate, and tried to remember how to fashion a trap.

'Did you have any disturbing dreams last night?'

He looked up; Catriona smiled at him, her green eyes openly studying him. He waited until her gaze reached his eyes. 'No.' He held her gaze steadily. 'In fact, I don't believe I dreamed *anything* last night.'

Her smile was glorious, as warming as the sun. 'Good.'

Richard blinked and inwardly shook himself. 'I was wondering—'

'Catriona?'

All looked up; Mary hovered in the doorway, wringing her hands. 'If you've finished, could you see to the children? They're so *fractious.*'

'Of course.' Laying her napkin by her plate, Catriona stood. 'Are they still feverish?'

She bustled out, with not even a last look for him; Richard eyed her departing rear through narrowing eyes.

Turning back to his plate, he returned to his plans – the first item on his agenda was a very long ride.


He rode late into the afternoon, until the light was almost gone. Returning to the house, he ordered a late tea to be eaten in his rooms. Worboys arrived with the tray.

And remained to shake out his greatcoat and put away his gloves. And interrogate him.

130

'Am I right in assuming we'll be departing on the heels of the solicitor, sir?'

'Hmm,' Richard answered around a portion of roast beef.

'I must say,' Worboys persisted, 'that it's been a most *instructive* stay. Makes one appreciate the little joys of London.'

Sunk in the armchair before the fire, Richard didn't reply.

'I take it we'll be returning to the capital directly? Or do you intend visiting in Leicestershire?'

'I haven't the faintest notion.'

Worboys sniffed, clearly disapproving of such aimlessness. He opened the wardrobe door. While he shuffled coats and straightened sleeves, Richard munched steadily, his gaze on the flames.

And pondered the fate of one witch.

Some part of his mind – the Cynster part of his mind – had, from the first moment he'd set eyes on her, been considering making her his. Ever since the reading of the will, he'd been toying with the prospect. Trying to decide, one way or the other, whether he should seize the opportunity Seamus had created, bow to fate and take a wife – or drive away and leave her behind.

Such had been his state before she'd come to his bed.

Now ... long fingers tightening about the chased goblet, Richard stared at the leaping flames.

'Are you ready to dress for dinner, sir?'

Richard looked up, his features set. 'I am indeed.'


Motive. She had to have some reason for coming to his bed.

Crossing the threshold of the drawing room, Richard instantly located Catriona, and strolled, apparently languid, in reality with fell intent, toward her.

She welcomed him with an open smile; he returned it with a wholly deceptive smile of his own.

His memories of their first night were incomplete, yet he was prepared to swear she'd been a virgin. An enthusiastic, eager, ready-to-be-wanton virgin, but a virgin nonetheless. She'd never lain with any man before him.

Which raised one very large question: Why him?

Or was that: Why now?

'I was wondering,' he said, as he claimed his now customary place beside her, 'where you intend going after we settle this business of the will.'

She turned and met his eyes. 'Why, to the vale, of course. I never stay away for long – usually not for more than a day.'

'You never travel to Edinburgh or Glasgow?'

'Not even Carlisle, and that's closer.'

'But you order things – you mentioned you did.'

'I have agents call at the vale.' She shrugged. 'It seems wiser not to flaunt my existence – or that of the vale. We do very well in our anonymity.'

'Hmmm.' Richard studied her face. 'Are there many other families of standing in the vale?'

'Standing?'

'Independent. Not your tenants.'

She shook her head. 'No – I own the whole vale.' Fleetingly, she raised her brows. 'We don't even have a curate, because there's no church, of course.'

Richard humphed. 'How did you escape that? Or did the initial incumbents simply disappear?'

She tried to straighten her lips, but didn't succeed. 'The Lady doesn't approve of violence. But the answer to your question is geography. The vale is isolated – indeed, if you don't know it's there, it's not easy to find.'

'You must at least have neighbors – the surrounding landowners.'

She nodded. 'But in the Hills the population is widely scattered.' She looked up at him. 'It's a lonely existence.'

132

He had the impression she'd intended that last sentence one way, but it had come out another. She held his gaze for an instant, then seemed to draw back. She blinked and looked away, smiling quickly as she reached for one of the cups Mary carried.

Richard perforce smiled at Mary, too, and relieved her of the second cup.

'My dear, I can't thank you enough.' Mary looked at Catriona with gratitude in her eyes. 'I don't know *how* we would have coped if you hadn't been here – the children would have driven us all insane. Instead, they listened to your stories for the whole afternoon – I don't know how you do it. You're so good with them, even the little ones.'

Catriona smiled one of her 'lady of the vale' smiles. 'It's just part of the healer's art.'

Behind his teacup, Richard raised a skeptical brow. The healers he knew often took delight in scaring children, and treated them as patients only grudgingly. Not all healers, any more than all adults, had the patience to bear with children's capriciousness.

'Whatever,' Mary said, 'we most sincerely appreciate your efforts.' She looked hopefully at Catriona. 'Are you sure you won't stay?' A shadow passed over her face, then she grimaced. 'I don't know where we'll be, after next week' – she shot an apologetic glance at Richard – 'but you'll always be welcome wherever we are.'

Catriona squeezed her hand. 'I know – and don't worry. Things will sort themselves out. But I must return to the vale – I've already been away far longer than I'd expected.'

A slight frown, a shadow of concern, momentarily clouded her eyes. Richard noted it. Draining his cup, he inwardly reflected that, whatever else, Catriona Hennessey took her role as lady of the vale seriously.

Perhaps too seriously.

\*

He wanted to know why she'd done it – put some potion in his whiskey, then climbed into his bed. And given herself to him.

Was it simply for experience – or was there more to it than that?

Lying in his bed with the bed curtains drawn, Richard stared into the blackness and listened to the clock on the stairs announce the quarter hours.

And waited for her to come to him.

He didn't know what he felt – his reactions, even after a whole day on horseback in an empty world, were still too violently tangled for him to be sure of them, much less consider them. On the one hand, he felt honored she'd chosen him for whatever reason; on the other, he was furious that she'd dared. And there were other feelings that surged through him whenever he thought of her – and their nocturnal couplings – that went far beyond any rational response. Any response he could understand.

He wanted to know – needed to know – why.

He could, of course, ask – simply wait for her to appear, then put a simple question. If he did, he doubted he'd get an answer. He doubted she'd stay to spend the rest of the night in his arms, either.

On both the previous nights, she'd thought him asleep – drugged. Capable physically, but not *compos mentis*. On the first night, that had indeed been the case. He still couldn't remember all of it – snippets were crystal clear, while other parts were a phantasmagoria of remembered sensation, drowning out all other recollections. He knew he'd spoken, and she'd replied – which was why she hadn't reacted last night, when he'd spoken again. She'd thought he was speaking in his dreams.

And that, after a whole day of planning, was the only avenue he could see that might get him the answer he wanted.

If he put the question to her while she was in his arms, and thought him asleep, she would be far less inhibited in answering. She might even tell him the truth.

Not straight away, perhaps, but ...

One thing he did remember from that first night was the way he'd teased her – parts of that burned, beacon bright, in his brain. She'd crumpled very quickly. Which, now he knew her in the biblical sense, wasn't a surprise. She'd bottled up all her hot heat for too long – new to the game, she didn't have the ability to stave off completion for long, to hold back all that suppressed energy.

He'd only just started to torture her – there was a lot more he could do in that vein. And he'd enjoy the doing. As long as she thought him asleep, she'd talk – eventually; he was sure of that. And the longer she resisted, the more he'd enjoy it. And so would she.

Tonight, he'd have his answer. Which was why the bed curtains were drawn.

And why he didn't hear her enter, why he didn't know she was there until the curtains parted. He'd left a gap at the foot of the bed, admitting a weak beam from the fire, just enough so he, with excellent night vision, could see her clearly.

She checked that he was there, lying relaxed beneath the covers, then she looked wonderingly at the curtains all but enclosing the bed.

Her lips lifted in a soft, distinctly witchy smile that had him stiffening. Lifting her hands to her shoulders, she slid her robe off and let it fall. Beneath it, she was naked, all ivory limbs and flaming red hair.

Richard fought the urge to reach for her; he couldn't stop his gaze from devouring her. She sensed it, and looked at him, and smiled.

And, lifting the covers, slid in beside him.

He turned and drew her into his arms before she could touch him. She sighed softly and sank against him, then lifted her face to his.

He kissed her gently, unhurriedly, content to savor the soft warmth of her body pressed freely against his, content to explore the soft warmth of her mouth, his to claim as he willed.

As was she. He held the thought back, channeled his aggression into anticipation, and kept every touch languid. He was supposed to be asleep, making love to her in his dreams.

So he held himself back and let her urgency build, let her grow hot, her skin fevered, her kisses increasingly demanding. He sank back on the pillows and let her take the lead – or at least, let her think she did. Half atop him, she kissed him wildly, and squirmed – heated, silk-encased flesh pressing caress after intimate caress upon him.

He gritted his teeth – and enjoyed every minute.

But he kept her hands high, lacing his fingers through hers to prevent her precipitating events – events he intended orchestrating to the full.

Wrapped in the warm dark, Catriona surrendered to the night, to her deepest desires, and gave herself to him. This was the last night they would share – she was determined to fill it with pleasure, on both the emotional and physical planes. The physical sensations were pure bliss, but for the emotional joy she found in their union, she would sell her very soul.

All but blind in the dense darkness, she could see him only as a deep shadow – closing her eyes, she could sense him more clearly. Dispensing with sight, she explored – by touch, by tactile impression as she lay on top of him. With her hands locked in his, she was acutely aware of the sensations felt through the soft skin of her breasts, midriff and belly. Drinking in the fascinating contrasts – of textures – hot, taut

136

skin roughened by crisp hair – of the innate, readily discernible strength lying so lax, so amenable beneath her – she wriggled, slowly, sensuously. Filling her mind, her memories.

Between them, heat welled, swelled, and hot became hotter.

He seemed content to wallow in the heatwave; with a mental snort, she tugged her fingers from his, framed his face, and kissed him voraciously. Rapaciously.

She sank into the kiss, caught in a sudden flare like a sunspot; her limbs heated still more until she melted against him. Wanted to melt beneath him – have him fuse with her. Sliding her fingers into his hair, she let her lips, her tongue, taunt him, challenge him. Incite him.

Despite responding ardently, he remained supine beneath her. Inwardly cursing the effects of her potion, she avoided his hands and set hers to trace the ridges and hollows of his chest, the heavy bones of his shoulders, the tensed muscles of his upper arms.

His arms locked around her, heavy and warm across her waist – denying her quest to reach lower.

Not that she needed to touch him there – he was already fully aroused. The steely length of him rode against her hip, hot and urgent. That much of him, at least, was cooperating. The rest of him was not.

Shifting, she lay fully atop him, settling his erection between her thighs. She rolled her hips, experimenting until she found the particular shifting slide that most evocatively stroked him.

And felt the muscles in his arms shift, tensing, relaxing, then tensing again, as if he couldn't make up his mind.

Swallowing a curse, she trapped his lips with hers – and put her heart and soul into a slow, deliberate undulation, breasts, hips and thighs – even the curls at the base of her belly – coming into play. Deliberately evocative, she called to

137

him.

And he answered. She felt the wave of response building in his body, felt the need she baited flare and swell. Felt hard become harder, felt tense muscles turn taut.

With a gasp – of relief, of anticipation – she dragged her lips from his and half wriggled, half slid to the side. Puppetlike, his body followed; as she turned on her back, she grasped his upper arm, tugging him over her.

The reins of his lust locked in a grip of iron, Richard followed her lead – let her shift, let her tug – let her believe he was dazedly following her directions as she urged him over her. He complied, moving heavily, unhurriedly.

While she panted, in heat.

Consumed by heat. At his touch, her thighs parted. He swung heavily over her, then let himself down between, then took his time settling himself – and her. Impatient, she arched, and he felt her heat scald him, touch and cling to that most exquisitely sensitive part of him.

He caught his breath – and felt, in his chest, something shift, something lock. With a soft, desperate gasp, she arched again – and he eased into her.

Slowly. Savoring every inch of her hot softness as she stretched to accommodate him, savoring the subtle easing of her body as she accepted him.

She sighed as he sank home, then her hands, tensed on his arms, relaxed. And skimmed down his sides.

He caught them – first one, then the other – letting his weight down on her as he trapped them. And gently but firmly removed the reins from her grasp. Beneath him, she shifted, sinking deeper into the soft mattress, angling her hips to cradle him more effectively.

Tentatively, she lifted her legs, sliding them over his flanks.

'Yes.' He breathed the word against her lips as he settled

fully upon her. He found her lips with his and took them, took her mouth, then pressed deeper into her.

He drank her instinctive gasp – a gasp of pure pleasure. Inwardly smiling, he drew back, then sank deep again, and felt her flaring response. He set himself to feed it.

To stoke her fires, to drive her frantic. More frantic than she'd ever been.

With each slow, controlled thrust, the flames within her rose higher; he held to a steady, rolling rhythm until she was burning. Until, hot and heated, awash with desire, she rose beneath him, meeting every thrust, her body caressing him, clinging to him, cleaving to him. Until she was aflame, urgent in her wanting, desperate in her need.

Frantic.

Trapped in the heat, Catriona flexed her fingers, trying to slip them from his grasp, frantic to hold him, desperate to draw him to her – to reach the bright pinnacle of physical bliss that hovered on her horizon. Sunk deep in the mattress, she squirmed and panted, trying to get that last inch closer, trying to get him that last fraction of an inch deeper. His fingers, clamped about hers, didn't give, but, to her surging relief, surging expectation, he raised his chest slightly, just enough so her nipples, excruciatingly tight, brushed his chest.

So they were brushed by his chest.

A scream welled in her throat; struggling to lift her heavy lids, she swallowed it as he lifted higher, breaking their kiss. He was a dense shadow looming over her, shoulders and chest surging in a slow, powerful rhythm, a rhythm she could feel in her marrow. In her womb.

With her hands still anchored, one on either side of her head, she gripped his flanks with her thighs, gasping, arching, as he thrust harder, deeper.

Then he drew back farther; lips parted, senses whirling, she waited, quivering, for the next impaling stroke. Only to feel him rock lightly, penetrating her with just the tip of the hard length she wanted buried inside her.

She opened her lips on a protest – instead, she gasped anew as, bending his head, he took one ruched nipple into his mouth. Hips rocking gently, teasingly, he feasted on her swollen breasts, until she was awash on an endless sea. A sea of pure pleasure.

After laving her hot flesh, his lips burned when they again brushed hers.

'Why are you here?'

She wasn't, at first, sure whether he had spoken, or she'd simply heard the words in her head. But his hips stopped rocking; he lay, hot and hard as a brand, just parting the swollen folds about her entrance.

Leaving her empty.

'Because I want you.'

After an instant's pause, he started rocking again, once, twice – then he slid into her anew. She sighed, then lost what breath she had left as he pushed deep, then nudged deeper, and let his weight down on her once more.

Richard rode her, just a little deeper, just a little harder, just a fraction more intimately. He was having a hard time clinging to his reins – only rock-hard determination, and his Cynster strength of will – of endurance – allowed him to do it – to see her panting beneath him, her hair a burning veil spread across the pillows, her thighs gripping him urgently as he loved her. She responded without guile, without reticence, without hesitation – with a complete lack of reserve, the strongest feminine spell he'd ever encountered.

Her welcome, every time he sank into her, was bone deep. The temptation to lose himself in her arms, in her body, grew with every passing second.

But he needed to know her reasons, as well as her.

Gradually, he slowed, letting the rhythm stretch – not die,

but slow to the point where her frantic need – a need he knew well how to manage – rose to the fore again.

When she whimpered, and squirmed, trying to urge him on, he brushed a kiss to her temple. 'Why do you want me? Why me? Why now?'

A frown passed across her face like a breeze rippling corn, then she shook her head and it was gone. She lifted beneath him, wriggling more urgently; swallowing a curse, he impaled her fully again, then kissed her breathless.

And gave her a little more – rode her a little higher up the mountain of desire. Despite his weight, she undulated beneath him, hips rising, meeting him more fully. Letting go of her hands, he grabbed a pillow; releasing her from their kiss, he eased back, lifted her hips and stuffed the pillow beneath them.

Tilting her up so he could sink deeper – without stimulating her to completion. Her breath fractured when he thrust deep – an urgently evocative sound. He shut his ears to it. 'Wrap your legs about me.'

She did, immediately; arms braced, he held himself over her and drove her up, up, and on to the next level, the next plane of passion. Eagerly, she clung to him, her hands, now free, trailing over his chest and arms, then gripping tight as he delved deeper and pushed her on.

Fingers sinking into flexing sinews, Catriona let her head fall back, lips parted as she struggled to breathe. Senses aswirl, her wits long gone, she surrendered to the whirlpool of sensations he commanded, surrendered to the power she could feel in every thrust that joined them, in every synchronous beat of their hearts. A sense of beauty, of delight, of joy unimaginable hovered – just out of reach.

'Why are you here, with your legs spread wide, locked about my waist – with me buried to the hilt inside you?'

The question floated down to her, a whisper in the night.

It was beyond her – eyes closed, she shook her head. And concentrated on the steely flex of his body as it melded with hers.

Powerfully, yet still slowly. In some dim corner of her mind, a hazy, rather acid thought formed: If this was his performance when asleep, what would he be like awake?

A soft moan surprised her – she bit her lip, determined to be quiet. Then gasped as he surged more powerfully, faster, deeper . . .

She caught her breath on a strangled gasp – then cried out, in shocked disbelief, when he pulled back and left her. Fighting to raise her lids, she saw him lift fully away from her. Stunned she reached for him, half-sitting—?

Large hands caught her and flipped her over, then locked about her hips and pulled her back onto her knees.

And they were everywhere, those large, hard hands – kneading, stroking, squeezing, probing. Until her breasts ached, until her skin glowed, until her nerves were taut and tingling. Until the heat within her was a raging furnace and pure molten need filled her veins. And her loins.

Kneeling behind her, reaching over and around her, a dark, rampantly aroused presence in the night, he bent his head and nipped her ear lobe, then soothed it with his lips. 'Lean farther forward.'

His hands clamped about her hips as she did, steadying her. Then he nudged her thighs wider, and caressed her – stroked her slick, swollen flesh until it was throbbing anew, until she sobbed his name.

He slid into her – smoothly, easily – filling her deeply, until she was so full of him she could sense him throughout her body. Eyes closed in rapturous delight, she pressed back and took him all.

Richard felt her clamp tight about him; features set, etched with passion, he couldn't smile, not even smugly. She needed

142

him inside her now – if he was not there, she'd feel empty, hot and aching. This way, he could fill her without risking her willfullness getting the upper hand. She couldn't reach heaven this way, not without his active cooperation. Taking her from behind, with her on her knees, he could keep her locked for just a little longer in the web he'd woven – and try again to get the answer to his question.

But first . . .

He was going to love her until she couldn't think, until she had no will left to deny him.

So he caressed her, inside and out, using his body, hands, and lips in concert, consciously bringing the full force of his expertise and experience to bear.

He intended to be ruthless.

He filled his hands with her swollen breasts and kneaded, and she whimpered with desire; he shut his ears to the sound, and dotted kisses along her exposed nape. Locating her nipples, he teased and tweaked, until she moaned and sobbed. Nuzzling aside the heavy fall of her hair, he pressed hot open-mouthed kisses along her shoulder, then down her spine.

And all the while he filled her, to a slow, steady rhythm guaranteed to leave her both satisfied and wanting – glorying in what was, and ready to sell her soul – tell the truth – in order to get more.

He was going to be ruthless.

He had already studied her curves – he knew them well. Now, with her on her knees before him, he took in other aspects of her beauty – her delicate bones, the sleek, supple strength of her, the very feminine curve of her spine. The sweet hollow between shoulder and throat, the long sweep of her neck.

Letting his gaze roam, he straightened, hands drifting back to close about her hips. The smooth planes of her back were exquisite, perfect ivory, unblemished, unmarred. Hands trailing farther, he traced the long muscles of her thighs, braced, lightly quivering, flexing slightly as he rode her. His gaze, however, had fixed – on the firm globes of her bottom, ivory hemispheres meeting his body with satisfying force every time he thrust into her, on his staff, rigid and engorged, gleaming with her slickness, sliding effortlessly into her, deep into the embrace of her waiting, willing sheath.

The sight held him entranced. She moaned softly, then rotated her hips, clinging to him, closing like a burning glove about him as he pressed deep.

Richard gasped; he closed his eyes and tightened his death grip on his impulses.

Opening his eyes again, he drew a ragged breath – and leaned forward. And reminded himself to be ruthless.

But the instant his hands curved about her shoulders, then trailed down to cup her breasts, he knew the best he could hope to be – with her – was ruthlessly gentle.

Not even she could worship her Lady with the same devotion with which he worshipped her – felt compelled to worship her. She was his temple, he her priest, serving her. Lavishing attention on her. Helplessly in thrall, drawn deeper with every heated thrust, every caress he pressed on her – and she pressed on him – he was a victim of emotion that bound him to her through this act and yet more deeply, reaching to his soul. Demanding his obedience, his acceptance, his surrender. It was as if some deeply buried part of him recognized her as his mate – and his salvation.

When next he straightened, his breathing was beyond ragged, his control badly frayed. He knew he had a question – it took a moment to recall what it was. With her on her knees before him, with his staff buried in her sweet heat, it was difficult to imagine anything else mattered.

But one thing did. Chest swelling, he set himself to take her up the last stretch of their road. Fingers tightening about

144

her hips, he looked down – and noticed a birthmark, just by his thumb on her right buttock – a strawberry mark in the shape of a butterfly in flight. The size of his thumbnail, the mark showed clearly against her pale skin.

Richard dragged in a deep breath; fingers sinking into her hips, he anchored her, and thrust deep. Again, and again – pushing her high, then higher, swiftly taking her toward the shattering climax that he'd deliberately designed for her. On and on, higher and higher – she panted, then sobbed in her need.

He took her to the last but one step—

And withdrew from her, drawing her up against him, his hands full of her breasts, his throbbing erection riding between the globes of her bottom. He held her upright on her knees against him, and delicately kissed one ear.

The change was so swift, Catriona could barely take it in, barely heard, over the desperate thudding of her heart, his gravelly whisper.

'Why do you want me inside you?'

She couldn't see his face; she was so heated and urgent and needy she couldn't think – yet she heard the warrior's demand in his voice; she answered truthfully.

'Because I need you.' The words came out on a sob – a sob of pure need. Raising one hand, she reached back and traced his lean cheek. '*Please,* Richard. *Now.*'

His face was beside hers; she heard a soft hiss, then a smothered curse.

Then he reached around her, grabbing first one pillow, then another, piling them before her, even as his other hand pressed on her back and guided her down. Swiftly, he drew her knees back, and she was lying on her stomach, the piled pillows beneath her hips.

And he was behind her, between her spread thighs, his hips pressing against her bottom. Against skin flickering with heightened nerves, her inner thighs excruciatingly sensitive to the brush of his hair-dusted limbs.

With one thrust, he surged into her.

She screamed with sheer delight. Horrified, she grabbed handfuls of the twisted sheets and held them to her face. And heard him groan – braced above her, his hands planted on either side of her, he drew back, and surged deep – so deep – again.

In bliss – and knowing there was more to come – Catriona closed her eyes, buried her face in the bedclothes, and surrendered – her wits, her senses, her body – to the glory that beckoned. Surrendered to the desire to take him deep and love him, hold him tight and caress him.

He rode her hard, filling her completely, driving her on – straight over a precipice and into the sun.

She screamed as it shattered about her.

Eyes closed tight, braced above her, Richard drank in the lovely sound. Half muffled by the sheets, it was still pure magic; the sound of her ecstasy was pure ecstasy to him. Sunk to the hilt inside her, he held still, rigid, tense as a coiled spring, and savored her contractions, the rippling caress of her body as release swept through her.

He waited, not patiently, but with steely determination, until she eased beneath him, then, gritting his teeth, he leaned forward, grabbed two more pillows, lifted her, and raised her hips still higher.

So he could ride her on, up the next peak – the one she hadn't even guessed existed. When she realized it was there, she joined him – eagerly, wantonly – as focused as he. Heated once more, flushed, her skin dewed, she writhed beneath him, urging him on not with words but with deeds, with the flagrant encouragement of her lush body.

And when he sent her tumbling through the stars again, the effect was cataclysmic. He heard it in her unrestrained scream. The sound caught him up – tugged at his heart, his loins, his soul. Closing his eyes, he filled her completely and swiftly followed her beyond the end of the world.

Catriona awoke, disoriented, not entirely sure she *was* awake. Sweet peace held her; warmth surrounded her – she didn't want to move, to disturb the spell.

But presentiment nagged her – reluctantly, she lifted her lids. And looked into gloomy darkness. Blinking rapidly improved her vision marginally, enough to realize where she still was – where she shouldn't be.

In Richard's bed.

The warmth around her was him. The fact she could see at all warned her that deepest night had passed – morning was not far away.

Wielding a mental whip, she drew a shallow breath – all she could manage with his arm over her waist – and started the process of carefully untangling her limbs from his. This was the third morning she'd had to ease from his arms, but the task wasn't getting any easier with practice.

Eventually, she managed to slide from the bed. Quickly donning her robe, she fastened it, then swiftly straightened the sheet, settled the covers and silently plumped the pillow.

Pausing, she looked down at her companion of the night. He slept sprawled on his stomach, the arm and leg that had been thrown over her now relaxed on the bed. She studied his face, what she could see of it. The harsh planes had eased, but still retained their hardness, the promise of strength; his lashes lay, black crescents on his cheekbones, his lips still firm, purposeful. Even in repose, his face told her little – beyond the fact that here lay a warrior without a cause.

She had to leave him.

Drawing in a deep breath, she reached out to brush back the errant lock of hair that made a habit of falling over his forehead – and stopped herself. For one instant, her hand hovered over the neatened covers, then she sighed and, with a sad grimace, drew it back.

She couldn't risk waking him.

And she could sense the house stirring, tweenies waking in the attics, doors banging in the far distance.

Hugging her robe about her against the morning chill, she took one last, long look – at the husband she couldn't have – then slipped out through the bed curtains.

The instant the curtains closed, Richard opened his eyes. He listened – and heard the faintest of clicks as the door closed. For an instant, he simply stared at the closed curtains, at the empty space beside him, then he drew a huge breath and turned on his back. Crossing his arms behind his head, he stared at the canopy.

He still didn't have his answer – at least, not all of it. But he had learned something through the night. Whatever it was that drove his lust for her – she felt it, too. When they were together, her feelings for him were the counterpart of his feelings for her.

What his feelings for her were, however, was beyond his ability to describe. There was a sensual connection between them, something that invested their lovemaking with a deeper, stronger, more vibrant energy than the norm. He knew all about the norm – he'd had so many women, the difference was stark. Even in her innocence, she must be aware of it – that power that flared between them every time they touched, every time they kissed.

In his case, it was now with him constantly, ready to rear its head every time he set eyes on her. He was even, heaven help him, getting used to it. It had very quickly become a part of him.

Grimacing, he threw back the covers, sat up, and ran his hands over his face. He knew himself too well not to know, not to accept, that he wouldn't readily give it up – cut himself off from that power, from the addictive surge of possessiveness that swept him every time he saw her.

He still didn't know why she'd given herself to him. In the depths of the night, when they'd stirred and untangled their limbs, and she'd wordlessly slid into his arms, he hadn't had the heart to further interrogate her – he'd kissed her, soothed her into sleep, then tightened his arms about her and fallen into blissfully sated slumber himself.

Standing, he stretched, then grimaced. He'd have it out with her tonight. Once she was in his arms. Today, especially after last night, there were other things he needed to do.

The solicitor would return tomorrow.

He waited at the breakfast table until Jamie appeared. His host passed Algaria in the doorway. After waiting, and waiting, for Catriona to appear, Algaria had thrown him a black look that should have flayed him, then risen and gone to search out her erstwhile pupil.

Richard watched her go – Algaria clearly knew where her erstwhile pupil had been spending her nights – then turned to Jamie.

Who looked worried and drawn, obviously exercised by the difficulties of where the family would remove to, how they would cope after tomorrow. Jamie smiled wanly. 'Not a particularly fine day, I fear.'

Richard hadn't noticed. 'Actually, I was wondering if you might appease my curiosity.' Before Jamie could ask how, Richard waved languidly at Jamie's plate and picked up his coffee mug. 'Once you've finished breakfast.'

Malcolm and one of Jamie's nondescript brothers-in-law was present; Richard did not want his plans broadcast, especially not to the ears of his witch. He intended to inform her of his decision in person. Tonight. He was looking forward to

149

it; he would allow no one to spoil his plans.

Jamie ate quickly; together they left the breakfast parlor and strolled into the hall. Jamie paused and looked inquiringly at him. Richard waved toward Jamie's office, and they strolled on, into the corridor.

'I was curious,' Richard murmured, 'about those letters you mentioned. The ones Seamus received about Catriona and her lands. I've been trying to fathom just why your father wanted me to marry Catriona – if I could see what he'd been handling in relation to her, it might clarify the matter.'

Jamie's brows rose. He blinked at Richard, rather owlishly. 'I see.' He halted outside his office door; Richard halted, too. Jamie cleared his throat. 'Are you ... ah ... *considering* ...?'

Richard grimaced lightly. 'Considering, yes. But ...' He met Jamie's eyes. 'If even that gets to Catriona's ears, life for all of us will be that much harder.'

Jamie blinked and straightened. 'Indeed.' As Richard watched, Jamie's face lost some of its unnatural pallor, as hope, however faint, replaced despondency.

'Those letters?'

'Oh! Yes.' Jamie shook himself. 'I left them in the library.'

The afternoon was dying beyond the library windows before he'd read them all. When Jamie had spoken of a pile of letters, Richard hadn't imagined a pile literally two feet high. And in no order to speak of. He'd spent hours sorting them, then even more hours deciphering the scripts and the demands.

For demands there'd been. Many of them.

Of Seamus's replies there was no record, but from the continuing correspondence, his attitude was clear. He'd done a stalwart job of defending Catriona and her vale.

Heaving a sigh, Richard set the last of the letters back on

the stack, then pushed back his chair, opened the large bottom drawer of the desk and set the stack, in two halves, back where Jamie had stored it. Then he sat back in the chair and stared at the three piles he'd separated from the stack and lined up on the blotter.

Each little pile derived from one of Catriona's nearest neighbors. He had earlier taken a break and wandered down the hall to Jamie's office to check the maps. Her neighbors wanted her land. However, contrary to Jamie's recollections, all three still offered marriage – Sir Olwyn Glean to himself, Sir Thomas Jenner to his son, Matthew, while Dougal Douglas had not specified.

All three sets of correspondence were current – all three were at the stage of veiled threats on both sides. Seamus was less than subtle, Glean was patronizing, Jenner pompous, and Douglas the most disturbing, the most pointed.

Richard lit the desk lamp, and reread the letters, every one, then stacked them together. His expression set, his lips a thin line, he considered the pile, then folded it and slipped it into his coat pocket.

In the distance, the dinner gong boomed. Pushing back his chair, Richard rose and headed upstairs to change.

That night, Catriona tossed and turned. Wide awake, she stared at the canopy of her bed, then turned – and tossed – again.

She couldn't get to sleep.

Some devil inside her informed her why – and prodded her. Pointed out it was only a short distance to Richard's room. Richard's bed. Richard's arms.

And all the rest of him.

With a frustrated groan, Catriona shut her ears to the temptation. She had to – she couldn't give into it.

She'd known how it would be – that she would be tempted

151

to go to him, that she would try to tell herself one more night wouldn't matter. But her only justification for going to him as she had was The Lady's orders – and they didn't include extra nights purely for her own indulgence. At this time of her cycle, three nights were enough. The way he'd loved her, that should be *more* than enough. She couldn't justify more.

But she'd known she'd be tempted, so while, in the full light of day, her resolution had held firm, and he'd been ensconced in the library, she'd gone to his room and replaced the drugged brandy with untainted stock. So she couldn't go to him, even if she weakened.

She'd weakened long before the clock struck twelve.

Now it was striking four, and she still hadn't fallen asleep. She hadn't settled in the least. First, she felt hot, then not hot enough. Her body was restless, her emotions disturbed. As for her thoughts . . . she would much rather be asleep.

In the forefront of her mind hung the fact that, after tomorrow, when the solitcitor left, she would never see Richard again.

And he would never see his child.

She didn't know which thought made her feel worse.

# Chapter Nine

Morning eventually dawned. Weary, wrung-out, Catriona dragged herself from her uncomfortable bed. She washed and dressed, then paused before the door – and plastered on a bright, breezy smile before opening it.

As had been her previous habit, she was early to the breakfast table. As the others appeared, she poured tea and helped herself to toast, all the while maintaining her glamor of morning cheer.

Richard saw her smile, her bright eyes, the instant he stalked in. Sweetly sunny, her expression stated she did not have a care in the world.

Little did she know.

Her gaze flew to his face – he saw her eyes widen. Richard suppressed an impulse to snarl. He met her gaze – pinned her for one brief instant – then turned and stalked to the sideboard.

And piled his plate high. He would rather have followed up the threat in that one glance, but there were others present. There was a need for civility – for the cloak of sophisticated behavior he habitually wore. He reminded himself of that – even while he itched to throw the cloak aside.

He was frustrated to the point of violence.

Never in his life had he had to cope with this degree of sexual frustration. Of frustrated intent. As for the emotional side of the coin – he couldn't even think of that. Not without a swirling haze of anger clouding his mind.

His response was not rational – the realization didn't help in the least. When it came to Catriona Hennessey, witch, his thoughts – his feelings – definitely didn't qualify as rational. They were powerful. Strong. And very close to slipping their leash.

Plunking his plate down at the place opposite hers, Richard sat. He met her wide gaze with a hard stare and saw her cheery smile waver. Belatedly remembering what the morning held, he gritted his teeth and looked down at his plate. And kept his gaze lowered as he ate.

She'd fled from him before – he didn't want to look out of the library window and see her carriage rolling down the drive. His plans were otherwise.

'Miss? They be a-waiting ye in the lib'ry.'

Catriona whirled, straightening, her attention flying from the child she'd been tucking in. 'Already?'

Head poked around the nursery door, the maid nodded, wide-eyed. 'Did hear as the s'licitor came early.'

Catriona inwardly cursed. 'Very well.' Turning to the children's nurse, she gave brisk instructions, patted heads all around, then hurried down the long, cold corridors.

She stopped in the front hall to check her reflection in the mirror – what she saw did not reassure her. Her hair was neat, but not as lustrous as usual; the curls at her nape hung limp. As for her eyes, they were overlarge and faded. Washed-out – just like she felt. Her morning gown of rich brown, normally a good color for her, did nothing to disguise her pallor. She was tired; she still felt drained. Not, in all honesty, up to handling the inevitable grief when the final blow *finally* fell and Seamus's maltreated family learned they would have to quit the house. She'd intended to leave this afternoon, but had already revised her plans – she would be needed here for another day at least, to calm Meg and the children most of all.

With a sigh, she braced herself and headed for the library.

The butler opened the door for her; she glided through – and was instantly aware of a presence in the air. An unexpected presence. The hair on her nape lifted; she paused just inside the long room and took stock.

The family – *all of them*! – she inwardly sighed – were gathered before the fireplace as before. Seated at the desk, the solicitor shuffled papers; he glanced at her fleetingly, then looked away.

To where Richard stood, looking out one long window, his back to the room.

Together with the solicitor, Catriona studied that back, elegantly clad in deep blue. Her earlier uneasiness returned – that edgy, nervous feeling that had overtaken her in the breakfast parlor when he'd looked at her so accusingly. As if he had a very large bone to pick with her.

She didn't know – couldn't guess – what it was.

Neither his back, straight and tall, nor his hands, clasped behind him, offered any clues.

And now, on top of that uneasiness, came this other presentiment. A swirling, building sense of impending . . . something. Something momentous. The energy was strong, all-pervasive in the room; she couldn't discern its focus. On guard, she glided forward and took the empty seat beside Mary.

In that instant, Richard turned – and looked at her.

She met his gaze – and instantly understood who was the source of that energy. And who its focus. Suddenly breathless, she glanced at the door, then back at him.

Prowling forward to stand by the mantelpiece, he gazed at her steadily, his message transparent. He was now ten feet away, the door was thirty. No escape.

His intention, however, remained unclear.

Catriona dragged in a breath past the now familiar vise locked about her lungs and let haughtiness infuse her expression. Tilting her chin, she returned his regard, then pointedly switched her gaze to the solicitor. And willed him to get on with his business. To get this over and done with, so Richard Cynster could leave, and she could breathe again.

The solicitor coughed, sent a shaggy browed look around the room, then peered at the papers in his hand. 'As you are all aware . . .'

His preamble outlined the situation as they knew it; everyone shifted and shuffled and waited for him to get to the point. Eventually, he cleared his throat and looked directly at Richard. 'My purpose here today is to ask you, Richard Melville Cynster, if you accept and agree to fulfill the terms of our client Seamus McEnery's will.'

'I do so accept and agree.'

The words, so unexpected, were uttered so calmly Catriona did not – could not – take them in. Her mind refused to believe her ears.

Apparently similarly afflicted, the solicitor blinked. He peered at his papers, adjusted his spectacles, drew breath, and looked again at Richard. 'You declare that you will marry the late Mr. McEnery's ward?'

Richard met his gaze levelly, then looked at Catriona. Trapping her gaze, he spoke evenly, deliberately. 'Yes. I will wed Catriona Mary Hennessey, ward of the late Seamus McEnery.'

'Good-*oh!*'

Malcolm's gleeful shout led the cacophany; the room erupted with exclamations, heartfelt thanks, outpourings of profound relief.

Catriona barely heard them – her gaze locked with

Richard's, she let the tide wash over her and sensed a none-too-subtle shift in the energy around her. Some trap was closing on her – and she couldn't even see what it was.

Despite Jamie thumping him on the back and pumping his hand, despite the questions of the solicitor, Richard's blue gaze didn't waver. Trapped in that steady beam, Catriona slowly rose, much less steadily, to her feet. Putting out one hand, she gripped the chairback and straightened to her full height, so much less than his; unable to help herself, she tilted her chin defiantly.

Gradually, the clamor about them died, as the family belatedly sensed the clash of wills occurring beneath their noses.

Catriona waited until silence reigned, then, in a cool, clear voice, stated: '*I*, however, will not marry you.'

A shadow passed through his eyes; the planes of his face set. He shifted – the others stepped quickly from between them. He strolled toward her, his stride his customary prowl. While subtly intimidating, there was no overt threat in his approach. He stopped directly before her, looking down at her, still holding her gaze, then he glanced over his shoulder at the others. 'If you'll excuse us?'

He waited for no yea or nay, not from them or her; he grasped her hand – before she could blink he was striding down the long room, towing her with him.

Catriona stifled a vitriolic curse; she had to pace quickly to keep up. But she reined in her temper – there was a definite advantage in putting distance between themselves and the rest of the company.

He didn't stop until they reached the other end of the room, hard up against the wall of bookshelves and flanked by two heavy armchairs and a small table. The instant he released her, she swung to face him. 'I will *not* marry you. I've told you why.'

'Indeed.'

The word was a lethal purr. She blinked and found herself pinned by a stare so hard she literally felt stunned.

'But that was *before* you came to my bed.'

Her world tilted. She could hear her heart thudding in her throat. She blinked again, slowly. And opened her lips on a denial – the look in his eyes, burning blue, changed her mind. She lifted her chin. 'You'll never get anyone to believe that.'

His brows rose. 'Oh?'

To her surprise, he glanced around – Meg's sketchbook and pencil lay on the small table. He picked both up; before her puzzled eyes, he opened the book to a blank page and sketched rapidly, then handed the book to her.

'And just how do you plan explaining how I know about this?'

She stared. He'd sketched her birthmark. Her world had already tipped; now it reeled.

He shifted, leaning closer, simultaneously protective and threatening. 'I'm sure you can recall the circumstances in which I saw it. You were in my bed, on your knees, totally naked, before me – and I was buried to the hilt in you.'

The words, uttered low, forcefully and succinctly, from less than a foot away, battered at her defenses. Catriona felt them weaken, then crack – and felt the emotion, the sensations, all she'd felt at that moment when she'd been in his bed, seep through. And touch her.

It took all her will to shut them out and seal up the break in her shields. She stared, unseeing, at the drawing until she'd regained some degree of calm, then, very slowly, lifted her gaze to his face. 'You were awake.'

'I was.' His face was a mask of hard angles and planes – determination incarnate.

Catriona mentally girded her loins. 'Completely awake?'

'*Wide* awake. I didn't touch the whiskey the second night. Or the third.'

She studied his face, his eyes, then grimaced, and looked down.

He waited. When she said nothing more, he straightened, and took the sketch book from her hands. 'So' – he nodded toward the others – 'shall we go and tell them the news.'

She lifted her head. 'I haven't changed my mind.'

He looked down at her – then stepped closer, towering over her. 'Well, *change it.*'

He took another step; eyes locked on his, Catriona backed. She glanced up the room and saw the others watching. Immediately, she stiffened her spine; switching her gaze back to her tormentor, she halted, raised her hands and pushed against his chest. 'Stop that! You're deliberately trying to frighten me.'

'I'm *not* trying to frighten you,' he growled through clenched teeth. 'I'm trying to *intimidate* you – there's a difference.'

Catriona glowered. 'You don't need to intimidate me – just stop and *think!* You don't want to marry me – you don't want to marry at all. I'm just a woman – just like all the others.' She gestured, as if encompassing hordes. 'If you just leave, you'll discover I'm like all of the rest of them – you'll forget me within a week.'

'Much you know about it.'

His tone was contemptuous; his eyes bored into hers. He slapped one hand on the bookshelf by her shoulder, half caging her. Catriona felt the shelves at her back; she stiffened her spine and tilted her chin higher. And kept her eyes locked on his.

Lips compressed, he looked down at her. 'Just so you know ... I generally insist that the ladies I consort with have the good sense not to get under my skin. Some try, I admit, but none succeed. They all stay precisely where I want them – at a safe distance. They don't get into my dreams, interfere

159

with my aspirations, challenge my hopes – or my fears.' His eyes narrowed. '*You*, however, are different. *You* succeeded in getting under my skin without even trying – before I even knew how witchy you were going to be. Now you're there, you're there to stay.' His gaze hardened. 'I suggest you accustom yourself to your new position.'

Catriona held his gaze. 'It sounds as if you'd rather I *wasn't* there – under your skin, as you put it.'

He hesitated; a long moment passed before he said, 'I'll admit that I'm not certain I approve of our particular closeness – and I definitely don't approve of your initiative. However, the plain truth is, having had you beneath me,

I'm not about to let you go.' He held her gaze steadily. 'It's as simple as that.'

Catriona read the truth in his eyes – she frowned and shook her head. 'It *can't* be.'

'It can.' Blue eyes held hers. 'Fate's offered you to me on a silver platter – I'm not about to pass.'

A fraught moment ensued. Catriona could feel the sensuality that lay between them, a living, vital thing. It radiated heat, almost seemed to have a will of its own – a dangerously compulsive thing. Her eyes locked with his, she drew in a slow, much-needed breath – and tried another tack. 'You agreed because you're in a temper.'

That, too, she could sense – suppressed rage locked behind his mask. Her own temper flared; she glared at him. 'How typically male – you've agreed to marry me, and created goodness knows what legal muddle, all because you're in a foul mood with me over something I've done.' She frowned. 'I can't imagine what, but it's hardly sufficient reason for creating this much fuss.'

He stiffened. 'I'm not angry – I'm frustrated. A result, *not* of something you *have* done, but of something you've *neglected* to do.'

160

The words, bitten off, issuing through clenched teeth, held enough force – enough intimidation – to make her step back. The look in his eyes had her pressed against the bookshelves. But she refused to cower – she stared belligerently back at him. 'What?'

'You neglected to come to my bed.'

The smile he bent upon her reminded her forcibly of Red Riding Hood's wolf. She studied him in growing bewilderment. 'You agreed to marry me just because I didn't succumb to your all but legendary charms? Because I wasn't so mindless that I couldn't resist—'

'*No!*' Richard used the tone he'd most recently used to troops at Waterloo. Thankfully, it worked – it cut her off in mid-tirade; he could see where the tirade was headed. His eyes locked warningly on hers, his lips compressed, jaw set, he gripped the bookshelf tightly – and waited. Until he could say, in more reasonable tones: 'I meant *I* was sexually frustrated because *I* wanted *you*. *I'm* the one who can't resist. And no, I don't like it that you can.'

She blinked at him, studying his eyes, his face. 'Oh.'

Richard held her wide, slightly wary gaze – and hung on to his temper, to the illusion of civility that was all that stood between her and an effective demonstration of the strongest argument impelling him to marriage. If he gave into the urge to demonstrate, he'd shock Jamie and company to their toes. 'I do hope,' he said, and despite the polite form, his tone was savage, 'that we're now clear on that point. I want to marry you because I want you as my wife.'

Catriona nodded; she didn't need any further explanation of that. His feelings – his need – was reaching her in waves. And helping her cause not at all. Clasping her hands before her, she drew a deep breath – and tried desperately to find a chink, some gap, in the wall he was building around her. 'But why have you *decided* to marry me? You wanted me from the first,

161

but you decided on marriage only recently.'

'Because—' Richard stopped and considered her – then shrugged aside caution and continued: 'Because you're a damned witch who walks alone. Rides alone. A sweet, help-less witch who has a touching but thoroughly misplaced confidence in the protective capacity of mystical powers.' His face hardened. 'But you live in a world of men – and with Seamus's death, your protection from them has gone. Evaporated – and, most telling, you don't even realize it. You haven't even recognized the danger.'

She frowned. 'What danger?'

'The danger posed by your neighbors.' Briefly, succinctly, he elaborated – drew the folded letters from his pocket and showed her the demands, and the threats, Seamus had received. 'Look at the last one from Dougal Douglas.' He waited while she found it. 'You need to read between the lines, but his message is clear enough.'

Catriona read the single sheet, crossed and recrossed, then drew in a tight breath. 'He'll bring me to the attention of the authorities – church and state – if I don't marry him?'

She looked up, something close to fear in her eyes.

Richard frowned and reclaimed the letters. 'Don't worry. There's a simple way to spike his guns.'

'There is?'

'Marry me.'

'How will that help?'

'If you marry me, your lands legally become mine, so there's no point pursuing you.'

Catriona glanced at the letters in his hand. 'What if he does anyway – out of spite?'

'If he does, I can guarantee nothing will come of it.'

She looked at his face. 'Because you're a Cynster?'

'Precisely.' Richard hesitated, then added: 'Seamus knew he needed a certain type of man for you – one of the right sort, with the right degree of power.' He considered, then grimaced. 'A Cynster fitted the bill to perfection, and he had one – me – on a chain. To wit, my mother's necklace. Above all he knew that if you give land to a Cynster, he'll never let it go – *"To Have and to Hold"* still rules us. Which meant you'd be safe – if it were mine, I could never bring myself to sell the vale.'

He looked into Catriona's eyes and stated what now seemed obvious. 'Through all this farce of his will, Seamus had only one true aim: to ensure your continued safety.'

'Hmm.' She frowned, then grimaced and looked away.

When she said no more, Richard ruthlessly pressed his point. 'By making it widely known he was your guardian, Seamus drew all the approaches to him, leaving you undisturbed. But Jamie is no Seamus – he won't be able to deflect those three from their goal. While Seamus was alive, you were shielded – now he's gone, it'll be open season – on you, and your vale.'

She glanced at the letters. 'I didn't realize. I didn't know.'

'You do know.' She looked up; Richard tucked the letters back in his pocket and trapped her gaze. 'You said it the night before last. *You need me.* You may choose not to acknowledge it consciously, but you do know it. You may not accept it, but that doesn't alter the reality.'

Her eyes flared, spitting gold sparks. '*You* are not my keeper!'

He looked down at her; he couldn't help his growl. 'Where you're concerned, if the cap fits, I'll wear it.'

She glared at him – he gave not an inch. Slowly, her glare faded – she frowned as she studied his eyes.

He studied hers. 'Why did you come to my bed?'

Her eyes locked with his, Catriona drew a deep breath. He'd been totally honest – totally open – with her. 'Because The Lady willed it.'

163

For one long instant, he stared into her eyes, then his brow rose. 'Your Lady told you to come to my bed?'

'Yes.' Briefly, she explained.

Richard heard her out in silence. In genuine surprise. He'd expected the answer to be loneliness – something he understood, something he'd instinctively recognized in her. Divine intervention was a little harder to assimilate. As was the possessive lust that roared through him at the thought of her heavy with his child.

He was not at all sure how he felt about her reason, but the opportunity was too good not to seize.

'In that case' – he straightened away from the bookcase – 'there's obviously no impediment to our marriage on your side.'

She frowned at him. 'Why do you imagine that?'

Brows high, he met her gaze. 'Children. The Lady told you I was to father your children.' She stared at him blankly; he elaborated: 'Children. Plural. More than one.'

She blinked, then her features blanked completely.

'It's a little hard to imagine how you could have a brood of children by me, without the benefit of marriage.'

'Twins.' She refocused abruptly on his face. 'There's twins in your family – Amanda and Amelia.'

Richard shook his head. 'Their father's a twin, and their mother has twin brothers. Not at all the same as us.'

'But ...' Catriona stared at him. 'The Lady made no mention of marriage.'

'The gods don't have such ceremonies – marriage is an institution created by man.'

'But ...' She'd run out of buts.

He sensed it; he studied her, then said, his voice lower, less forceful – more beguiling: 'I meant what I said before – that, if we marry, I won't interfere with your role.' He searched her eyes, then his gaze steadied. 'I swear always to

164

support you in your position, to defer to you as lady of the vale.'

He meant it; it was there in his eyes – a promise of fealty only a warrior could make – and then only to his queen. Catriona felt her will swaying, bending . . . she was losing the battle to remain beyond his reach. And losing it on far too many fronts. More than one part of her mind was urging her to rethink – to accept all he offered.

As perhaps The Lady had intended her to.

Her head, mind and senses were whirling. With an effort, she regrouped – looked down and forced herself to strip aside all the complications of his motives and hers. And get to the heart of the matter.

After a quiet moment, she raised her head and looked him in the eye. 'You're not going to let me go, are you?'

He looked straight at her – through blue, blue eyes. 'No.' She considered him. His face hardened. His gaze locked with hers, he softly added: 'And you might like to ponder the fact that if you refuse me and bear my child, I'll have an unassailable legal right to that child.'

Catriona heard the depth of his commitment, not to her but to their unborn child. 'You'd take our child from me?'

His gaze didn't waver; she'd read his answer in his eyes before he stated: 'I'd claim any child of mine from the arms of The Lady herself, if she sought to keep it from me.'

Dragging in an unsteady breath, Catriona straightened – and felt the trap close firmly, tenderly, but tight.

The warrior had secured his cause.


'It won't be as bad as I feared.' Catriona dragged her brush through her hair and glanced at Algaria in the mirror. Her erstwhile mentor was agitated to the point of panic. 'He's promised to support my position, my role, not undermine it. He didn't have to do that.'

165

'Humph! That's what he says now – just wait until he gets you back to the vale. Once you're big with his child, he'll take over!' Pacing, Algaria swung about. 'Do you realize he'll have the power to sell the vale?'

'He won't.' In stating it, she was sure of it. 'He's landless – a bastard – *and* a Cynster. He's more likely than any other to *keep* the vale – keep it for his children.' Protect it for his children. Inwardly smiling, Catriona wielded her brush vigorously.

Algaria had not been present in the library; expecting to leave within a day, she'd been shocked to learn of the impending wedding. And convinced that Richard must have, using some unspecified and utterly inconceivable power, forced Catriona into accepting.

The only power he'd used was simply who he was – who he really was behind his mask; Catriona had tried to explain that, but Algaria wasn't ready to listen.

'I can't believe you've simply acquiesced!' Halting, Algaria stared at her.

'Believe me, there was nothing simple about it. Our discussions ranged over a gamut of issues.'

'Did you discuss his character? The fact he'll want to rule – that he'll *need* to rule just as much as he'll need to breathe?'

Sighing, Catriona laid down her brush. 'I didn't say it would be easy.'

'*Easy?* It's going to be impossible!'

'Algaria.' Turning on the stool, Catriona faced her mentor, her second-in-command. 'I didn't make the decision lightly. When it came to the point, there were too many convincing reasons why this marriage should be – and few, if any, reasons against.' Algaria opened her mouth; Catriona silenced her with an upraised hand. 'No – I know about his strength – and so does he. He's vowed to contain it, to use it to support me, not wield it against me.' She met Algaria's black gaze

166

steadily. 'I intend giving him a chance to fulfill that vow. That's a right he's claimed – and one I cannot justifiably deny him. Until such time as he fails – until he breaks that vow – I do not wish to hear any more on the subject.'

She waited, but Algaria, pinch-lipped, said nothing – she started to pace again. 'You could have suggested handfasting – at least until he shows his true colors.'

'I doubt he'd accept it, and you know that's never been our way.'

'Marrying men like him has never been our way, either!'

Catriona sighed and let Algaria's agitation slide past her. She didn't share it, but could understand Algaria's state. In common with all disciples of The Lady, Algaria possessed a deep-seated distrust of dominant men – for good and obvious reasons. It was a distrust she had shared, until she'd met Richard Cynster and felt the attraction a strong man could pose, and seen behind his mask to his vulnerabilty. Algaria possessed the talent to see behind his mask, too, but it was pointless to suggest that now. Her erstwhile mentor was too repelled by the vision of strength and dominance to stop and look beyond it.

Considering Algaria, she sighed again. 'Times change, and we must change, too. I'm too wise in life's ways to try to resist its flow – the currents carrying me to his arms are considerable. Many more than one, and powerful – The Lady's will and more.' Algaria slowed; Catriona caught her eye. 'I won't fight fate – I won't fight life. That's not why The Lady put me here.'

She held Algaria's black gaze for a moment, then calmly turned back to the mirror and picked up her brush. 'I've agreed to marry Richard Cynster before witnesses – we'll be wed as soon as may be.' She stroked the brush through her heavy hair; the rhythmic tug on her scalp was soothing. 'And then,' she murmured, eyes closing, 'then, we'll return to the vale.'

167

Tight-lipped, Algaria left her; in a state of unusual mental weariness, Catriona climbed into her bed. The thought of visiting Richard occurred only to be dismissed – she would be his soon enough, and he knew it. Triumphant, he'd been magnanimous in victory – in the drawing room, he'd frowned at her over the teacups and told her to get to bed and get some sleep.

Halfway there, Catriona felt her lips lift. Luckily, no one had been near enough to hear – all the rest of the family had been distracted, struggling to assimilate their 'new' state. It was, in fact, their old state – that, perhaps, was one of the positives of the case – that being given their inheritance back, they now viewed it as truly theirs.

Now, hopefully, Mary would get new curtains.

The thought made her smile; she drifted deeper into sleep. More peacefully, more serenely, more reassured than she'd expected.

Things, somehow, would turn out right – so The Lady whispered.

# Chapter Ten

They were married by special license, granted by the Bishop of Perth. Three days later, in the kirk in the village, Catriona stood beside Richard Cynster and listened as he vowed to love, honor and protect her. If he did all three, she would be safe; she made her responding vows – to love, honor and obey him – with an open heart.

And felt The Lady's blessing in the shaft of sunshine that broke through the heavy clouds and beamed through the small rose window set high above the altar to bathe them in Her glow.

Richard gathered her in his arms and kissed her – lingeringly. Only when he lifted his head and they turned to walk up the short nave did the sunbeam fade.

By the time they signed the register, then strolled out to the small porch, winter had reclaimed the ascendancy. Clouds laden with snow, grey and churning, stretched from horizon to horizon. A carpet of snow already covered the ground; light flurries whirled on the bitter breeze.

The family followed them to the door, excited and garrulous. Because of Seamus's death, the small private ceremony in the old kirk – all that either she or Richard had wanted – had been agreed to by all. Both the weather and Seamus's death had mitigated against any further revelry. The snows had started in earnest; the passes were slowly filling. Richard

169

and she had been in perfect accord that they should leave immediately after the ceremony, to ensure they weren't snowed in for weeks.

Pausing in the porch, Catriona saw the steamy breaths of their carriage horses rising beyond the lych-gate. She looked up at Richard; he was looking across the graveyard. She followed his gaze – and guessed his thoughts.

'Go!' Lightly, she pushed him. He looked down at her, his mask in place; she ignored it. 'Go and say good-bye.' She looked inward and afar, then refocused on him. 'I don't think either of us will be here again.'

He hesitated for an instant more, then nodded and stepped off the porch. She watched him head for a simple grave by the wall, then swung around and gave her attention to Jamie, Meg and the rest.

Halting before his mother's grave, Richard wondered what she would have thought of him marrying Catriona Hennessy. His mother had been from the Lowlands, too; perhaps she would approve. He gazed at the headstone, studied it carefully, letting the vision sink into his mind.

And recalled his thought, when he'd stood here in the moonlight just before he'd first met his witchy wife.

His wife. The words, even unuttered, sent a streak of unnerving sensation through him, powerful enough to shift the very bedrock of his foundations. Sensation and recollection mingled; eyes narrowing, he gazed at his mother's grave and silently made another vow.

To live life fully.

Straightening, he drew a deep breath and turned. And discovered Catriona waiting a yard behind him. She met his eyes, then looked at the grave. Richard gestured her forward; she came to his side.

For a moment, side by side, they looked at the headstone; inwardly, Richard said good-bye. Then he took Catriona's gloved hand. 'Come. It's freezing.'

He drew her away. It was she who, halfway down the path, glanced back, then looked at his face, before shifting her gaze forward to where their party waited in the protection of the lych-gate.

They had two carriages – his and hers. Their leave-taking was foreshortened by the increasing snow; within minutes, Richard handed Catriona into his carriage, then followed her in. Jamie shut the door and stepped back. Through the glass, Richard met Jamie's eyes, and, smiling, raised his hand in brief salute. Jamie grinned and saluted back.

'Good-bye!'

'Good luck!'

The carriage lurched; the wedding party, waving madly, fell behind. Sitting back, wrapped in his greatcoat, Richard stretched his legs out and settled his shoulders against the leather seat. Beside him, Catriona flicked out her skirts, then drew her cloak about her. Boots propped on a hot brick wrapped in flannel, she settled her head against the squabs and closed her eyes.

Silence, tinged with expectation, filled the carriage as it rumbled out of the Highlands.

Richard saw no reason to break it – as each mile of white landscape was replaced with the next, his mind was busy listing the various letters he needed to write. The first – a short note to Devil – had already been dispatched, along with Worboys, sent ahead to ensure the comfort of their first night. Informing Devil of his change of status had been easy; informing Helena, Dowager Duchess of St. Ives, would be much less so. Aside from anything else, he would need to break his news in such a way that his stepmother did not immediately appear on the manor's doorstep, seeking to welcome Catriona into the Cynster family in the time-honored way. Oh, no – he wanted time – wanted them to have time –

to find their own equilibrium.

To learn how to get on – for him to learn how to manage a witchy wife.

That definitely came first. Helena would have to wait.

'I hope we get to The Boar before nightfall.'

Catriona was peering into the whirling white outside.

Richard studied her profile; his lips quirked. Straightening them, he looked ahead. 'We'll be staying at The Angel.'

'Oh?' Catriona turned. 'But . . .' Her words died away.

Turning his head, Richard met her eyes, clear question in his.

'Well' – she gestured – 'it's simply that The Angel is a very *superior* house.'

'I know. That's why I sent Worboys to secure rooms for us there.'

'You did?' She stared at him, then grimaced.

Richard kept his expression mild. 'Don't you like The Angel?'

'It's not that. It's just that *superior* also means expensive.'

'A fact you need not concern yourself over.'

She humphed. 'That's all very well, but—'

Richard knew the instant the penny dropped, saw her eyes widen as she finally noticed the luxurious appointments of his carriage – the fine, supple leather, the gleaming brass – finally remembered the lines and deep chests of the four greys between the shafts. Finally considered what she should have long before.

Her eyes, wide and startled, swung to his, her gaze arrested. She opened her lips on hasty words and nearly choked. Clearing her throat, she sat back against the seat and gestured airily. 'Are you . . .?'

'Very.' Enjoying himself, Richard leaned his head back and closed his eyes.

And felt the increasing intensity of her gaze. 'How much is very?'

172

He considered, then said: 'Enough to keep me, and you . . . and your vale if need be.'

She searched his face, then humphed and sank back. 'I didn't realize.'

'I know.'

'Are the Cynsters *exceedingly* wealthy?'

'Yes.' After a moment, he continued, his eyes still closed: 'Within the family, my bastardry counts for nothing – my father made provision for me as his second son, which, to all intents and purposes, I am.'

She was silent for so long, he wondered what she was thinking.

'Jamie mentioned that you're accepted socially.'

The murmured statement held no element of question; opening his eyes, Richard turned his head and looked at her – she was staring out at the snow.

'I expect that means you could have had your choice of all the young ladies from the very best families.'

Compelled by the ensuing silence, he replied: 'Yes.'

'So . . .' She sighed, and turned to meet his eyes. 'What will your family think when they learn you've married a Scottish witch?'

He would have quipped that they'd either think he'd lost his senses, or that it served him right, but the shadows in her eyes held him. Compelled him to reach out, slowly, and slide one arm about her. And lift her, with an ease that sent a very definite shiver through her, onto his lap.

'The only thing they'll care about,' he murmured, juggling her, 'is that I've chosen you.'

He would have kissed her, but she stayed him, small hands braced against his chest. 'But you haven't.' Gratifyingly breathless, she searched his eyes, then blushed lightly. 'Chosen me, I mean.'

He'd chosen her in the instant he'd first closed his arms

173

about her, in the moonlight near his mother's grave, but he wasn't bewitched enough to admit it; his witch had enough powers as it was. Ignoring her hands, he bent his head and brushed his lips across hers. 'You're mine.' Breaths mingling, driven, their gazes locked – then, simultaneously, dropped to each other's lips. Searching, hungry, their lips touched again – achingly gentle – then parted. 'That's all that matters.'

Her lashes fluttered up; for one instant, green eyes met blue, and the air about them shimmered.

She sucked in a quick, shallow breath; in the same instant, he tightened his arms about her, then lowered his head and kissed her.

And she kissed him. With a devastating sweetness, an innocence – as if this were the first time. Which, in some ways, for her, it was. The first time she'd knowingly welcomed him as her lover – a lover fully conscious, wide awake. Richard realized and inwardly groaned, and harnessed his raging desires, savagely hungry after four days' starvation.

He deepened the kiss by gradual degrees, letting them both sink into the caress, into the warmth and heat, into that pleasurable sea. Letting their embers slowly glow stronger, then flicker into flame; with an expert's touch, he fanned the flames until they burned steadily.

She followed his lead readily, openly, without guile. As was her wont, she freely gave all he asked, accepting each intimacy as he offered it, surrendering her mouth to his conquest. He savored her thoroughly, then teased her into making her own demands, into meeting him and matching him, into returning the slow, languid thrusting of his tongue with clinging caresses equally evocative.

But their nerves remained curiously taut, their play curiously charged, as if their first encounter as a married couple was somehow different. Richard sensed it in her, in the tension that invested her slight frame, in the tightness of her

174

breathing – sensed it in himself – an alertness, an awareness, heightened to exquisite sensitivity.

As if their nerves, their bodies, their very beings, thrummed to some magic in the air.

Gently, he lifted her, rearranging her on his lap so that she sat across his legs facing him, one knee on either side of his hips. Locked in their kiss, she barely seemed to notice; pushing her hands up, over his shoulders, she slid her fingers into his hair and angled her lips beneath his.

She moaned when he closed his hands about her breasts. He kneaded and, through the thick fabric of her pelisse, felt the mounds firm and fill his hands. Even with the benefit of a number of hot bricks, even with the heat rising between them, it was too cold to contemplate baring her. Instead, he glided his hands over her in long, sweeping caresses – caresses designed to stir her to life. To love.

When she wriggled impatiently on his thighs, Richard reached between them, found the hem of her skirt, and slid his hand beneath.

He found her – startlingly hot in the cold air in the carriage. She would have pulled back from their kiss but he refused to let her; he kept her lips trapped, filled her mouth with slow, languid thrusts as he stroked her, parted her, penetrated her.

She melted about his fingers; he probed deeper, then stroked gently. She was hot and very ready.

He had to draw back from their kiss to deal with his own clothing. Her questing fingers had already pushed his great-coat aside and undone both coat and waistcoat. Fingers splayed across the fine linen of his shirt, breasts rising and falling dramatically, her lips swollen and parted, eyes jewel green under heavy lids, she stared dazedly down as he flicked his trouser buttons undone.

They slipped free – abruptly, she lifted her head and stared at him. 'What ...?'

The half-squeaked question was eloquent; Richard raised a suggestive brow.

'Here?'

He raised his brow higher. 'Where else?'

'But ...' Aghast, she stared at him. Then she looked up at the carriage roof. 'Your coachman ...'

'Is paid enough to feign deafness.' Ready, Richard reached for her.

She looked back at him and licked her lips, glanced at the seat beside them, then shook her head in disbelief. 'How ...?'

He showed her, drawing her fully to him, then easing into her softness. As she fathomed his intention and felt him enter her, she spread her thighs, slid her knees along the cushions, and, with a soft sigh, sank down, impaling herself fully upon him.

As she closed, scalding hot, around him, Richard, watching her face and seeing the expression of sheer relief that washed over her fine features, got the distinct impression that she was as thankful to have him inside her again as he was to be there.

Wrapping his arms about her, one beneath her hips, he took her lips in a searing kiss, then lifted her. Rocked her.

She caught the rhythm quickly. Rising on her knees, she tried to increase the tempo.

'No.' Anchoring her hips, he drew her fully down, held her there for a moment, then picked up the rhythm again. 'Keep in time with the horses.'

She blinked at him, but did; gradually, the steady, rolling rocking became so instinctive they no longer needed to think of it – but could think, instead, solely of the indescribable pleasure of their bodies merging intimately, again and again, in a journey of infinite delight.

Held firmly, closely, Catriona shuddered – with pure pleasure, with sharp excitement. With an unfurling sense of the

176

illicit – of the wild, the unconventional – in her soul and his. Eyes closed, held close in his embrace, their fully dressed state contradicted, contrasted – focused her senses on – the area of their naked engagement. Along the bare inner face of her thighs, all she could feel was the fabric of his trousers, the smooth leather of the seat. Over her flanks and legs, over the curves of her bottom, all she could feel was the shift and glide of her lawn chemise and petticoats.

Only at the core of her, in the soft, swollen, heated flesh between her widespread thighs – only there could she feel him, only there did they touch with no barriers between.

Only there did they merge, sweetly slick, powerfully smooth.

With heightened senses, she reveled in the power inherent in their joining, in the deeply compulsive repetition, in the burgeoning energy rising within them.

Senses wide open, awareness complete, she was deeply conscious that outside the carriage, the world, ice cold and blanketed in white, went on, committed to its own steady rhythm, the unquenchable rhythm of life. Under the snow, life still glowed, seeds warm, fecundity waiting to flower. Just as, beneath their heavy clothes, they – their bodies and their lives – were melding, seeds sown in darkness to flower later – in summer, when the sun returned.

With their own rhythm, the rhythm of their breathing, of their heartbeats, of the constant flexing of their bodies, locked to the rolling gait of the horses plodding through that wintry scene, they, too, became part of it. A natural part of the landscape, the act of their joining invested with the same, intrinsic force that breathed life into the world.

As the snow swirled and the light slowly faded and the horses plodded on, locked in each others arms, their bodies slowly tensing, straining toward shimmering release, they were a piece of the jigsaw of the world at that moment. An essential, necessary piece.

With that certainty investing her mind, her soul, Catriona dragged her lips from his. Laying her head on his shoulder, her forehead by his jaw, she breathed rapidly, raggedly. Her body moved incessantly without her direction, driven by a need she no longer needed to conceal. Didn't know how to conceal.

Caught in the moment, she clung to him, conscious to her toes of the steely strength of him, the hot hard length of him, sliding so effortlessly deep into her core, nudging her womb, soon to fill it, to provide the seed for her fruit.

Need built, then flooded her; she heard herself moan. He shifted and brushed a hot kiss to her temple, then tightened his arms about her and urged her on. Urged her deeper upon him.

She dragged in a desperate breath, and tightened about him, and drew him in – into her body, into her soul.

Into her heart.

She could feel her protective distance dissolving – feel her shields slide away – leaving her defenseless. At her feet, the hole she'd jumped into that first night yawned and beckoned anew – tempting her to recommit to it, to jump in as she had when she'd first given herself to him, when she'd first welcomed him – the warrior – into her body. The second night she'd gone to him had dug the hole deeper, the third night had sealed her fate.

Now, compelled by that same fate, drawn on by a force more powerful than any she'd known, she stepped forward gladly and slid into the dark.

And she was falling.

Through darkness hot with passion, sparking with desire, heated by their yearning bodies. The rush of need rose up and caught her, swept her up and on, a wave lifting her to blessed oblivion. She rode it, rode him, urgently – he met her, reflected her energy and pushed her on. Ever on.

To culmination, to the peak of joy that swelled and welled, then crashed about her, showering her body, her mind with wonder, with release so fragilely beautiful it shimmered in her veins and glowed beneath her skin.

Eyes shut, fingers clenched in his shirt, she muffled her scream against his warm chest. She clung, blissfully buoyed, to the peak for one long instant, then let go.

And floated, at peace.

He gathered her to him, pressed a kiss to her cheek, and filled her even more deeply, even more forcefully. Fully open, she received him joyfully, softly smiling at his deep groan of completion, at the warmth that flooded her womb.

She'd made her decision and stepped into the unknown, and there was nowhere to land but in his arms.

They closed about her, holding her tight.

Shutting her eyes against a sharp rush of emotion, Catriona surrendered and sank into his embrace.


'I take it,' Richard drawled, 'that that's Merrick looming ahead?'

'Yes.' Nose all but pressed to the window, Catriona spared no more than a swift glance for the majestic peak towering over the head of the vale. The carriage rocked and raced on, swiftly pulled by Richard's powerful horses; they were almost home, and she had so many things to think of. 'That's the Melchetts' farm.' She nodded to a huddle of low-roofed buildings hugging the protection of a rise. 'The woods beyond yield most of our firelogs.'

She sensed Richard's nod; she kept her eyes glued to the scene beyond the window, as if cataloging all she saw. In reality, her mind was in an unaccustomed, but oddly pleasant whirl – due, of course, to him. They'd crossed into the vale ten minutes before, having left Ayr, on the coast, at first light, after only two nights on the road.

179

The first, spent at The Angel in Stirling, had opened her eyes to the benefits of traveling with a gentleman – a rich, powerful, protective one. Through Worboys, Richard made his wishes – their requirements – known; all had happened as he'd decreed. Even Algaria, traveling behind them in the vale's carriage, had muted her unspoken disapproval. Even she had had to appreciate the ease of a private parlor and the quality of an excellent dinner.

Algaria had fallen silent; as the days passed, she'd become withdrawn. Inwardly sighing, Catriona accepted it and waited for her mentor to see the light.

For herself, revelation had already come.

As husband and wife, she and Richard had shared a room, shared a bed, for the past two nights. Time enough, opportunity enough, for her to see what the future might hold. Falling asleep in his arms had been heaven. Waking up there had proved a new delight.

Feeling heat in her cheeks, Catriona inwardly grinned. She avoided looking at the cause and kept her gaze on the white fields, her hot cheeks close to the cold window.

While her mind remembered all the details, and her wayward senses reveled in recollected sensation.

She'd woken that morning to find him wrapped around her, woken to the sensation of him sliding into her. She'd gasped and clutched the arm wrapped about her waist, only to have him tip her hips back so he could enter her more deeply.

He'd loved her as he always did – slowly, languorously, powerfully. Indefatigably. That seemed to be his style. It was one she found addictive. There was a depth to their intimacy, both physical and emotional, that she hadn't expected.

She'd closed her eyes and drunk it in, let it seep through her and nourish her soul.

Now, she was all but hanging out of the window in her excitement, her eagerness to be home. To start her new life –

to have him there, a part of it.

'There!' Like a child, she pointed through the birches, a forest of trunks and bare branches. She glanced over her shoulder at Richard. 'That's Casphairn Manor.'

He shifted and drew near to peer over her shoulder. 'Grey stone?'

Catriona nodded as a turret flashed into view.

'The park looks extensive.'

'It is.' She glanced at him. 'It's necessary to protect the manor from the winds and snows driving off Merrick.'

He nodded and sat back again; Catriona turned back to the window. 'Another ten minutes and we'll be there.' Worry tinged her voice – directly attributable to the sudden, disconcerting thought of whether there was any potential problem she'd failed to foresee, any action she ought to be prepared to take to smooth his entry into the vale, into her life. Inwardly frowning, she stared out the window.

Richard noted her concern, as he'd noted her earlier absorption with her holdings. Her mind was clearly on her fields, on the vale – on her responsibilities, not on him.

His gaze on her profile, he inwardly grimaced. The last two days had gone his way – all his way. She was his on one level at least. But once they gained Casphairn Manor, he'd face new challenges – ones he'd never faced before.

Like keeping his promise not to interfere with her role, with how she ran the vale. Like learning to accept what he meant to her – whatever that was.

That last grated, on his temper, on his Cynster soul. He was not at all sure he appreciated the hand Her Lady had had in bringing about their marriage. Admittedly, if it hadn't been for such divine intervention, Catriona might not now be his – not on any level. Witch that she was, she was stubborn, willful, and not easily swayed, particularly when it came to matters affecting her calling.

His gaze locked on her face, he felt his features harden, felt determination swell.

It must, he reflected, be his week for making vows.

In this case – her case – he didn't even have to think of the wording, the statement simply rang in his mind. She would, he swore, come to want him on her own account, not because Her Lady had ordained it. She'd want him, all of him, for herself – for what he gave her.

That wasn't, he felt sure, how she felt about him now, how she saw him in relation to herself, but he was a hunter to his soul – he was perfectly prepared to play a waiting game. Prepared to lay snares, carefully camouflaged traps, to persist until she was his.

His in body, as she already was, and his in her mind as well.

His – freely. That was, he suddenly realized, the only way he'd truly have her – the only way he'd know that she truly was his.

As the carriage slowed, rocked, then rumbled through a pair of gateposts and on down a long avenue through the park, Richard watched his new bride – and idly speculated on just how she would tell him – how she would show him – when the time came, and she truly was his.


'Good morning, m'lady! And a good morning it is that brings you home safe and sound.'

'Thank you, Mrs. Broom.' Taking Richard's hand, Catriona descended the steps of his carriage, and, to her surprise, couldn't exactly place what her housekeeper was thinking. Mrs. Broom was usually easy to read, but the huge grin on her homely face as she beamed up at Richard, all handsomely elegant as usual, defied interpretation.

The sight of an unknown carriage leading her own up the long drive had brought the manor's people running. Maids and stablelads, grooms and workmen, all piled into the court-yard, gathering in a loose crowd about the main steps before which Richard's coachman had pulled up.

Richard had descended first; from the shadows of the carriage, Catriona had watched her people's eyes widen, seen the surprise, the speculation. She'd waited for the distrust, the defensiveness, ready to combat it – but it hadn't yet appeared.

Leaving one hand in Richard's, she gestured with the other, smiling as, with a wave, she gathered her people's attention, then directed it to Richard. 'This is my husband, Mr. Richard Cynster. We were married two days ago.'

A wave of excitement, a murmur of clear approval, swept the crowd. Catriona smiled at Richard, then smoothly turned to the old man leaning heavily on a stick beside Mrs. Broom. 'Allow me to present McArdle.'

The old man bowed, slow and deep; when he straightened, a smile wider than any Catriona could recall wreathed his face.

''Tis a pleasure to welcome you to Casphairn Manor, sir.'

Smiling back, Richard inclined his head urbanely. 'It's a pleasure to be here, McArdle.'

As if some ritual – one *she* was unaware of – had been successfully completed, everyone – all those who had served her since birth, all those who were in her care – relaxed and welcomed Richard Cynster into their midst. Utterly bemused, Catriona felt their warm welcome enfold him. He responded; placing her hand on his sleeve, he turned her. With her at his side, he slowly circled the gathering, so he could meet all her household.

While making the introductions, Catriona studied her staff – one and all, their response to Richard was genuine. They were, indeed, very pleased to see him, to welcome him as her husband. The more he spoke, the more they smiled and grinned. The more she inwardly frowned.

183

When they were free to go inside, Richard led her up the steps. They passed Algaria, standing silent and withdrawn at the top. Catriona met her black gaze – and instantly knew what she, at least, was thinking.

But Richard's reaction was not feigned, nor part of any plan; as she'd introduced him to a welcome she hadn't fore-seen, she'd sensed – known beyond question – that he hadn't foreseen it, either. He'd been as surprised as she, but quick to respond to her people's invitation.

What had her puzzled was what, precisely, that invitation was – and why it had been issued so readily.

Those questions plagued her all day.

By the time the household gathered for dinner, she was seriously disturbed. There was something happening in her small world that she didn't understand, some force stirring over which she had no control. Which was definitely not how it had been, nor how she liked it.

Made uneasy by something she could not name, she glided into the dining hall. Richard prowled at her heels, as he had for most of the afternoon, as she'd shown him about her home. Now his home.

Glancing over her shoulder, Catriona inwardly frowned. The matter of where they would live was something they hadn't actually discussed – she'd simply assumed they would live here. Together. Lady and consort. But she'd assumed wrong on one point – she could be wrong on that issue, too. The thought did not calm her – right now, she needed calm.

Drawing that emotion to her, she smiled at Mrs. Broom and stepped up to the dais. Going to her place at the center of the long table, she graciously waved Richard to the carved chair beside hers. The chair that had stood against the wall, unneeded since her parents' deaths.

Richard held her chair as she sat, then took the chair beside her. Catriona nodded to Mrs. Broom, who clapped her hands for the first course to be served. Maids hurried in, carting piled platters. Unlike the household of gentry elsewhere, at the manor, all the household ate together, as they had for centuries.

Lounging in the chair beside Catriona, Richard studied her people, studied the open and easy manners that pertained between mistress and staff. There was a warmth, a camaraderie present that he previously had encountered only among soldiers; given the vale's isolation, the trials of long winters and wild weather, it was perhaps a good thing – a necessary cohesiveness.

All in all, he approved.

Not so Worboys.

Seated at the table directly below the main one, poor Worboys looked stunned. Inwardly grimacing, Richard made a mental note to expect his resignation. Used to the strict observances pertaining among the best households in the ton, the situation at Casphairn Manor would not meet Worboys's high standards.

And God only knew what the blacking was like.

'Do you care for some wine?'

Turning his head, Richard saw Catriona lift a decanter. Reaching out, he took it from her and studied the golden liquid within. 'What is it?'

'Dandelion wine. We make it ourselves.'

'Oh.' Richard hesitated, then, inwardly grimacing, poured himself a half glass. He passed the decanter to Mrs. Broom, who had slipped into the seat beside him.

'You must tell me,' she said, 'what your favorite dishes are.' She flashed him a wide smile. 'So we can see what we can do to accommodate your tastes.'

Richard smiled his slow Cynster smile. 'How kind of you. I'll give the matter some thought.'

She beamed, then turned aside.

Richard turned back to Catriona, but she was absorbed in her meal. Lifting his wineglass, he sipped. Then blinked. Then sipped again, more slowly, savoring the tart taste, the complexities of the bouquet.

Liquid ambrosia.

Straightening, he set his glass down and picked up his soup spoon. 'How much of that wine do you have?'

Catriona shot him a glance. 'We make as many casks as we can every summer. But we always have some left year to year.'

'What do you do with it? The stuff left over?'

Laying down her spoon, she shrugged. 'I expect the old casks are still there, in the cellars. I told you they're extensive – they run all the way beneath the main building.'

'You can show me tomorrow.' When she looked at him suspiciously, he smiled. 'Your cellars sound quite fascinating.'

She humphed.

A clanging sounded throughout the large room. All turned to where McArdle stood at the end of the main table. When all had quieted, he raised his goblet high. 'I propose a toast – to Casphairn Manor. Long may it thrive. To our lady of the vale – long may she reign. And to our lady's new consort, Mister Richard Cynster – a warm welcome to the vale, Sassenach though he might be.'

Laughter greeted that last; McArdle grinned and turned to address Catriona and Richard directly. 'To you, my lady – and the consort The Lady has sent you.'

Wild cheering and clapping rose throughout the hall, echoing from the stone walls and high rafters. Smiling easily, fingers crooked about the stem of his glass, Richard turned his head and cocked a brow at Catriona.

His question was clear; Catriona hesitated, then nodded.

186

She watched as, with nonchalant grace, Richard rose; cradling his goblet, he lifted it high and said, very simply: 'To Casphairn Manor.'

All drank, as did he. Lowering his glass, he scanned the room, but did not sit down. After a moment, when all attention was again focused on him, on his commanding figure dominating the main table, he said, his voice low but carrying readily through the room: 'I make the same pledge to you, and the vale, that I have already made to your lady.' A glance directed their attention to her, then he lifted his head and raised his glass. 'As consort to your lady, I will honor the ways of the vale and protect you and the vale from all threats.'

He drank off his wine, then lowered his glass as clapping erupted from all sides. Heartfelt, the sound rose and rolled over the room. Richard sat – instinctively, Catriona put out a hand to his sleeve. He looked at her – she met his gaze fleetingly, then smiled and looked away.

And wondered at herself – at what he'd made her feel – all of them feel – in those few brief moments, with those few simple words. Magnetic words – she'd felt the tug herself, seen the effect it had had on her household. Her people were very much his already, and he'd only crossed the threshold mere hours ago.

Through the rest of the meal, Catriona pondered that fact. She steadfastly avoided looking at Algaria, but could feel her black glare. And sense her thoughts.

Nevertheless . . . she knew, to her bones, that this was how it was meant to be. Quite how their marriage would work out was what she couldn't, at present, see. She'd known Richard for a potent force even before she had met him, which was why she'd believed he was no suitable consort for her. The Lady had deemed otherwise.

Which was all very well but it was *she* who had to cope

with his unsettling presence.

Off-balance, uncertain – in severe need of some quiet and calm – she waited until dessert was being cleared, then set aside her napkin. 'I'm afraid the journey must have been more tiring than I thought.' She smiled at McArdle. 'I'm for bed.'

'Of course, of course.' He started to rise to draw out her chair, then smiled over her head and subsided.

Catriona felt the chair shift and looked around. Richard stood behind her. She smiled at him, then smiled at Mrs. Broom and the rest of the table. 'Goodnight.'

The others all nodded and smiled. Richard drew her chair farther back; she slipped past, then glided along behind the other chairs, stepped off the dais, and turned through an archway into the corridor leading to the stairs.

The instant she was out of sight of the dining hall, she frowned and looked down. Pondering her state – the uneasiness, the sense of being off-center that had gripped her the moment she'd stepped over her own threshold, Richard by her side – she absentmindedly trailed through the corridors, through the front hall, and climbed the stairs to the gallery and crossed it to her chamber.

Halting before her chamber door, she focused – to find herself standing in deep shadow. She'd forgotten to pick up a candle from the hall table. Luckily, born in this house, she didn't need to see to find her room. She reached for the door latch—

And very nearly screamed when a dark shadow reached past her, gripped the latch, and lifted it.

Hand to her throat, she whirled – even before she saw him, denser than night at her side, she realized who it must be. *'Richard!'*

He stilled; she could feel his frown. 'What's the matter?'

The door swung wide, revealing her familiar room, lit by flames leaping in the grate. Catriona gazed in and tried to calm her racing heart. 'I didn't realize you were there.' She stepped over the threshold.

'I'll always be here.' He followed her in.

Catriona whirled – her heart raced again as she faced him. And realized what he meant. 'Ah ... yes. Well ...' Airily gesturing, she turned and walked further into the room. 'I'm just not used to it – having someone there.'

Truer words she'd never spoken. That was borne in on her as she walked to the fire, scanning the oh-so-familiar, oh-so-comforting furniture, and behind her, heard the latch click. Stopping by the fire, she half turned and glanced at him from beneath her lashes – he was standing just inside the door, studying her.

This was her own private sanctuary. A place he now had the right to enter whenever he chose. Yet another change marriage had wrought – yet another change she would have to accept.

'I ... was tired.'

He tilted his head, still studying her. 'So you said.' With that, he started to stroll, prowling about the room. Like some wild male animal assessing his new home.

Pushing the vison from her, Catriona straightened and jettisoned all thoughts of spending a quiet hour or two considering her state. Considering her husband.

She could hardly do that with him prowling so close.

She could barely *think* with him prowling so close.

His 'I'll always be here' was not reassuring.

'Ah ...' Eyeing him as he neared, she forced herself to meet his eyes. 'We didn't discuss our sleeping arrangements here.'

One black brow rose. 'What's to discuss?' Reaching her side, he looked down at her, then crouched to tend the blaze.

Looking down at his head, Catriona felt her temper stir. 'We could discuss where you'll sleep, for instance.'

189

'I'll sleep with you.'

She bit her tongue – and warned herself of the unwisdom of biting off her nose. 'Yes, but what I wondered was whether you would like a chamber of your own.'

He seemed to consider that; he remained silent as he piled on logs, building a massive blaze. Then he stood; Catriona only just stopped herself from taking a step back.

Richard looked down at her, then scanned the large room. Despite containing a bureau, dresser, dressing table and chairs, wardrobe and two chests, as well as the reassuringly massive four poster bed, the room was sparsely furnished. They could share it comfortably and still have room to spare. His traveling case, set against one wall, was barely noticeable.

He looked down, into Catriona's eyes. 'Will it bother you if I say no?'

The puzzlement that filled her eyes was impossible to mistake. 'No, of course ...'

He raised a brow.

'Well ...' Abruptly, she glared. 'I don't know!'

Unwisely, he grinned.

She slapped him across the chest. 'Don't laugh! I've never felt so at sea in my life!'

His grin turned wry. 'Why?' Catching her hand, he headed for the bed, towing her, unresisting, behind him.

'I don't know. Well ... yes, I do. It's you.'

Reaching the bed, he turned and sat, pulling her to stand between his thighs. 'What about me?'

She frowned at him; holding her gaze, his expression mild and questioning, he set his fingers to the buttons of her carriage dress.

After a long moment, she grimaced. 'No – that's not it either.'

Frowning absently, she reached for the pin securing his

cravat, slipped it free, then slid it into the lapel of his coat. 'I'm not sure what it is – just something unsettling – something not quite in its right place.' Frowning still, she flicked the ends of his cravat undone, then fell to untwisting the folds.

Richard held his tongue and let her tug his cravat free, then obediently shrugged out of his coat and waistcoat before helping her from her dress. Sitting again, he drew her to him; trapping her between his knees, he started unpicking the laces of her petticoat.

She was still frowning.

'Did my reception surprise you?'

She looked up. He pushed her petticoats down.

'Yes.' She met his gaze squarely. 'I don't understand it.' One hand in his, she stepped from the pile of her skirts. 'It was as if you were' – she gestured – 'someone they'd been waiting for.'

Closing his hands about her waist, Richard drew her back, locking her between his thighs. 'That's how they see me, I think.'

'But . . . *why?*'

For one minute, he kept his gaze on the tiny buttons of her chemise as he slipped them from their moorings. Then he lifted his gaze and met her eyes. 'Because I think they fear for you – and thus, indirectly, for themselves. I showed you the letters. I imagine, if you asked, you would discover many of your household have their own suspicions of your neighbors and the threat they pose to the vale.'

Looking down, he separated the two halves of her chemise, now open to her waist, and drew the sleeves down. She shivered as the cool air touched her flesh, but lowered her arms and slid them free.

Raising his head, he trapped her gaze. 'They see me as a protector – for you, the vale, and them.'

Her frown wavered, then she grimaced. 'I suppose that's

what the consort is supposed to be.'

'Indeed.' Richard closed his hands over her bare breasts and felt her tremble, heard her indrawn breath. Her lids drifted low; he brushed his thumbs over her nipples, and she shuddered.

'The Lady chose me for you, remember.' Drawing her closer, he kissed her, then whispered against her lips: 'She chose me to be the one to wed you, bed you and get you with child. Chose me to defend and protect you. That's how your people see me – as the one The Lady sent for you.'

'Hmmm.' Her hands rising to his shoulders, Catriona leaned into the next kiss.

A minute later, he pulled back and urged her on to the bed, divesting himself of his clothes as she slipped between the sheets. Then he joined her, moving immediately over her, spreading her thighs wide and settling between. He fitted himself to her, then, settling heavily upon her, framed her face with both hands and kissed her deeply – as he pressed into her.

He slid fully home, then stopped and lifted his head, breaking their kiss. 'I told you I won't undermine your authority.' He pressed deeper still, then lowered his head. 'Just trust me – it'll all settle into place.' In the instant before his lips reclaimed hers, he whispered: 'Just like this has.'

She couldn't argue with that; as she instinctively eased beneath him, supple and soft as he rode her slowly, deeply, Catriona relaxed, and did as he asked, and put her trust in him.

It wasn't, of course, how she'd imagined things would be. She'd thought to be the assured one, the one to do the reassuring, secure in her position as she eased him into his new role. Instead, the shoe seemed to be on the other foot, with him sliding effortlessly into a role she hadn't known was waiting for him – and having to reassure her of her own.

192

But here, in their bed, she didn't need reassurance. He'd taught her well, taught her all she needed to know to love him. So she clung to him and gave to him, uncaring of how the future might unfurl.

The future was the province of The Lady; the night – this night – was for them.

Later, much later, in the depths of the night, Richard lay on his back and studied his sleeping wife. His exhausted, sated wife – who had exhausted and sated him. The minutes ticked by as he studied her face, the flawless ivory skin, the wild mane of fire-gold hair.

She was a witch who had bewitched him; he would walk through fire for her, sell his soul and more for her.

And if she couldn't understand that, it didn't really matter, because he couldn't understand it, either.

Sliding deeper into the bed, he gathered her into his arms and felt her warmth sink to his bones. Felt her turn to him in her sleep and curl into his arms.

As his body relaxed, and he drifted into dreams, it occurred to him that few men such as he – strong enough, powerful enough to act as her protector – would agree to wed a witch and then give her free rein.

He had.

He didn't like to think why.

It was almost as if it *had* been preordained – that The Lady had indeed chosen him for her.

# Chapter Eleven

Richard woke the next morning as he had the past two – at dawn, reaching for his wife.

This morning, all he found was cold sheets.

'What . . .?' Lifting his lids, and his head, he confirmed that the bed beside him was indeed empty. Stifling a curse, he half sat and scanned the room.

There was no sign of Catriona.

Cursing freely, he flung back the covers and stalked to the window. Opening the pane, he pushed back the shutters. Dawn was a glimmer on the distant horizon. Abruptly shutting the window on the morning's chill, he turned back into the room. Scowling ferociously.

'Where the devil has she gone?'

Determined to get an answer, he hauled on buckskin breeches and boots, a warm shirt and a hacking jacket. Tying a kerchief about his throat, his greatcoat over one arm, he strode out of the room.

The front hall and the dining hall were empty; no one was about. Not even a scullery maid clearing the ashes from the huge fireplace in the kitchen. It took him three tries to find the right corridor leading to the back door; finally there, he needed both hands to haul open the heavy oak door – Catriona certainly hadn't gone that way.

Richard paused on the threshold and looked across the

cobbled yard, joined to the front courtyard by a wide drive circling the main house. The sun was just rising, streaking-light across the world, striking fire from ice crystals dotted like diamonds over the snow. It was cold and chill, but clear, the air invigorating, his breath condensing in gentle puffs before his face. The stables stood directly opposite, on the other side of the yard, a conglomeration of buildings in stone and wood. The manor house itself was of dark grey stone, with steep gables edging the slate roofs and three turrets growing out of the angles of the walls. Irregularly shaped, the main building was large, but surprisingly unified – not the hodge-podge the outbuildings appeared to be.

Everything, however, was neat and tidy, everything in its place.

Except his wife.

Gritting his teeth, Richard shrugged on his greatcoat, then tugged the back door shut. He couldn't see any reason why Catriona would have gone riding, but if he didn't find her soon, he might do the same.

His short tour yesterday with her as his guide had been confined to the reception rooms and gallery, the library, billiard room – a welcome surprise – and her estate office. Punctuated by introductions to a constant stream of staff who had found occasion to pop up in their path, he hadn't seen all that much.

As he strode across the cobbles, the clack of his bootheels echoed weakly, thrown back by the stone. In the center of the yard, he halted – arrested by sheer beauty. The yard was large; from this position, he had an unimpeded view of the fields leading up to the head of the vale. Directly ahead of him, rising majestically into the sky, stood Merrick, the vale embraced within its foothills. Slowly, he pivoted, until he faced the house; on either side of its bulk, he could see the fields beyond, white-flecked ground stretching away beyond the brown of the park.

195

The manor was sited on a rise roughly at the center of the vale. To one side, the river that bisected the vale curved about the base of the rise; even under the snow and ice, Richard could hear it murmuring. Between the house and the river lay carefully tended gardens, stone paths wending between what he assumed would be beds of herbs and healing plants. It wasn't hard, in his mind's eye, to see it without snow, to see green instead of brown, to imagine the richness that in summer would be there. Even now, dormant, hibernating under winter's blanket, the sense of vibrant life was strong.

To a Cynster, it was a breathtaking scene. All the land he could see was – if not, in his mind, his – then under his protection.

Drawing in a deep breath, feeling the cold singing through his veins, Richard slowly swung around and resumed his trek to the stables. In the distance, he saw dots ambling across the snowy fields – cattle drifting in and out of crude shelters. He frowned, then reached for the latch of the stable door.

It opened noiselessly – it hadn't, in fact, been fully latched. His frown deepening, Richard drew the door wide. He was about to step through, when hoofbeats came pounding up the slope beyond the stables.

The next instant, a rough-coated chestnut mare swung around the corner and into the yard, Catriona in the saddle. She saw him instantly. Her cheeks were flushed, her wayward curls dancing – her bright eyes grew wary the instant they met his.

'What's the matter?' Drawing rein a few feet away, she asked the question breathlessly.

Richard fought down an urge to roar. 'I was looking for you.' The words were clipped and steely. 'Where the devil have you been?'

'Praying, of course.'

Taking in her heavy cloak and the thick leggings she wore

beneath her skirts, rucked up as she was riding astride, he caught her mount's bridle as she kicked free of the stirrups. 'You pray outside? In this weather?'

'In *all* weathers.' Lifting one leg over the chestnut's neck, she prepared to slide down – stifling a curse, he reached up and lifted her to the ground.

And held her before him, trapped between his hands. 'Where?'

Her gaze locked on his, she hesitated, then tilted her chin. 'There's a circle at the head of the vale.'

'A circle?'

Whisking free of his grasp, she nodded and caught the mare's reins.

Suppressing a curse, he reached out and tugged them from her, then gestured for her to precede him. She did – nose in the air, hips swaying provocatively.

For her sake, Richard prayed there were no convenient piles of hay lying loose about the stable. Teeth gritted, he followed her into the warm dark. 'Do you go to pray often? Disappear like this, before dawn?' Before he'd woken?

'At least once every week – sometimes more often. But not every day.'

Richard gave thanks for small mercies. Her Lady obviously had some understanding of the needs of mortal men. Securing the mare in the stall Cartriona had led him to, he turned to find her tugging the girths free. Then she reached for the saddle.

'Here – let me.' He grasped the saddle and lifted it from her and set it atop the stall wall. Turning back, he found her with a currying brush in her hand – he took that, too. And fell to brushing the mare's thick coat.

By the light of a sharp green glare.

'I'm perfectly capable of caring for my own horse.'

'I daresay. You might not, however, care for the alternative to letting *me* care for your horse in this instance.'

Wariness muted her glare. 'Alternative?'

Richard kept his eyes on the mare's hairy hide. 'As there's no loose straw about, it'll have to be the wall.' Without looking, he gestured with his head. 'The corner by the trough might be wise – you could balance with one foot on the edge.'

She actually looked – the expression on her face nearly had him throwing the brush aside.

'Then again' – he gripped the brush tightly and put all his pent-up energy into every stroke – 'this mangy beast looks like she bites – which doesn't bear thinking of.'

Drawing herself up to her full, less-than-adequate height, she stalked around the mare so she could glare at him directly, with the horse a safe bolster between them.

'Why are you so . . .' – she gestured wildly – 'whatever it is you are?'

Lips compressed, Richard flicked her a hard stare and brushed on.

Catriona folded her arms and tilted her chin. 'Because I went to pray and didn't ask your permission?'

She waited; gradually, the violence behind his brushing abated. His face like stone, he glanced at her over the mare's back. 'Not permission – but I need to know where you are, where you go. I can hardly protect you if I don't know where you are.'

'I don't need protection while praying – no one in the vale would dare go into the circle. It's hallowed ground.'

'Do people from outside the vale know that?'

'I'm as safe within the circle as an archbishop in his cathedral.'

'Thomas a` Becket was slain before the altar at Canterbury.'

She hesitated, then shrugged. And tipped her nose in the air. 'That was different.'

With a frustrated growl, Richard tossed the currying brush

aside, stepped around the mare – and trapped her against the stall wall. Eyes wide, locked on his, all fiery blue, Catriona heroically denied a crazed impulse to glance at the nearby trough.

'Just *tell* me where you're going in future. *Don't* disappear.'

Lips thinning, she gave him back glare for glare. 'If I wake you in the morning to tell you where I'm going, I won't get there.'

His eyes bored into hers while she inwardly dared him to deny it.

Instead, after a fraught moment, he nodded curtly and drew back. 'Tell me your plans the night before.'

With that, he grasped her elbow and steered her, much less gently than was his wont, out of the stall. Forced to pace quickly by his side, Catriona stared up at him, struggling to make out his features in the stable's dim light.

'Very well,' she agreed, as they reached the stable door. 'But I don't need any protection while at the circle.'

They stepped into the yard; the morning light found his face – illuminating a grim mask. 'I'll think about it.'

He continued to march her across the cobbles, heading for the house. The tension gripping him, shimmering about her, was beyond Catriona's comprehension.

'What is the matter with you?' Reaching the back doorstep, she swung to face him. 'I've agreed to tell you where I go – so what's *this*?' With one finger, she prodded one bicep – locked and as hard as iron.

His chest swelled. 'That,' he said, his voice very low, issuing through clenched teeth, 'is because I'm hungry.'

'Well, breakfast should nearly be ready—'

'*Wrong* appetite.'

She blinked – and looked into his eyes. And saw the truth simmering. 'Great heavens! But ...' She frowned at him.

199

'You *can't* be. What about last night?'

'That was last night. Because you disappeared, I missed my morning snack.'

'Morning ...?' She felt her features blank, heard her incredulity ring in her weak: *'Every* morning?'

He grinned – a distinctly feral expression. 'Let's just say that for the foreseeable future, it would help. But for now' – hauling open the door, he waved her inside – 'why don't we see if I can be distracted with breakfast? Unless, of course, you're in favor of snacking throughout the day?'

For one instant, Catriona simply stared at him, then she glared and tossed her head – and ignored the shivery tendrils of excitement slithering down her spine. 'Breakfast,' she declared, and swept into the house.

His features like stone, Richard followed her in.

They breakfasted together; in passing pikelets and jam, sharing toast, pouring coffee, the tension between them eased. They were the first to take their seats of those who sat at the main table. Mrs. Broom was fussing, overseeing the serving of the trays; McArdle hobbled in late. Algaria, arriving relatively early, took a seat at the far end and kept her black thoughts to herself.

Sitting back in the carved chair that was now his, Richard idly sipped coffee and watched to see how his wife started her day. Algaria's continued disapproval surprised him; he hoped she'd eventually get over it and accept their marriage, not for his sake, but Catriona's. He saw the hopeful glance Catriona threw the woman and sensed her sigh when it wasn't returned. If he'd thought it would help, he would have spoken to Algaria, but her defensiveness where he was concerned remained marked.

'Have there been any replies to those letters I sent about the grain?'

200

Catriona's question drew Richard's attention; it was addressed to McArdle.

'Hmm ... yes, actually, I believe there were.' McArdle frowned. 'One or two, at least.'

'Well, I'll see those first, then we really must make some headway on the plans for next season's plantings.'

'Ahh ... Jem's not brought in his figures yet. Nor's Melchett.'

'They haven't?' Catriona stared at McArdle. 'But we need them to make any sense of it.'

McArdle raised brows and shoulders in a comprehensive shrug. 'You know how it is – they don't understand what you want, so they hope you'll forget – and so they forget.'

Heaving an exasperated sigh, Catriona stood. 'I'll see to that later then. But if you've finished, we may as well get started.'

As McArdle heaved himself up, Richard reached out and caught Catriona's hand. She turned and raised a brow.

'Don't forget,' he murmured, his eyes on hers, his thumb brushing over the back of her hand.

For one instant, she stared at him – and he could see she couldn't decide what he was reminding her of – her agreement to tell him her whereabouts, or his invitation to midday snacks. Then she blinked. And looked at him again. 'I'll be in the office for most of the day.'

And it was his turn to be uncertain – unsure – just what she meant. She gently tugged and he eased his grip and let her fingers slide from his. She inclined her head, then turned away.

As he watched her glide to the door, he still wasn't sure which she meant.

He'd decided on the library as his own domain – according to Catriona, only she, and Algaria occasionally, used it.

There was a huge, old desk, lovingly polished, and a well-padded chair that accommodated his large frame surprisingly well.

Through the combined efforts of Mrs. Broom and Henderson, a large morose man who filled the position of general factotum, he was supplied with paper, pen and ink. Worboys, looking in on him, departed and returned bearing his seal and a stub of wax. After dispatching a maid to fetch a candle, Worboys cast a haughty, barely approving glance over the leatherbound tomes, then sniffed.

'If you need me, sir, I'll be in your room. Henderson – a nice enough chap if one can cope with his brogue – is organizing to have a second wardrobe moved in. I'll be tending your coats.'

Lovingly, Richard had not a doubt. 'Very well – I doubt I'll need you much in the coming days.' He looked up at Worboys. 'We won't be entertaining.'

Worboys only just avoided a snort. 'It does seem unlikely, sir.' With that comment on his new home, Worboys took himself off.

Raising his brows, secretly surprised not to have been presented with Worboys' resignation, Richard turned back to his letters.

He considered, then settled to write a fuller account of his marriage to Devil – the easiest task facing him. He filled in the details he'd omitted in his earlier brief note, but saw no reason to elaborate on his feelings, on the reasons he'd taken the plunge. He was quite sure Devil, having already succumbed, and having lived with the outcome for a year, could fill in the blanks for himself.

And heaven knew Honoria, Devil's duchess, and Helena, Richard's stepmother, certainly would.

Sealing Devil's letter, Richard grimaced and set another blank sheet before him.

He stared at it for half an hour. In the end, he wrote a very careful, exquisitely guarded account, rather shorter on actual facts than the first note he'd sent Devil, but filled instead with the sort of information he knew his stepmother would want to know. That yes, he'd found his mother's grave. A description of the necklace his mother had left him. The fact Catriona had long red hair and green eyes. That it had snowed on the day they had married.

Those sort of things.

He penned them carefully and hoped, without much hope, that she'd be satisfied with that. At least for a while.

With a sigh, he signed his name. He'd told Devil they wouldn't be attending the Christmas celebrations at Somersham this year. He knew without asking that Catriona would prefer to remain here, and even after only one night under this roof, he agreed. Maybe, in years to come, when their life here was more established, they would journey south for those few, family-filled days – he, she and their children.

The thought held him for long moments, then he stirred, sealed his missive to Helena, and turned to his last letter – to Heathcote Montague, man of business, on permanent retainer to all the Cynsters.

That letter was more to his liking – making decisions, dealing with his varied interests, giving directions to enable him to manage them all from the vale – these were positive actions reinforcing his new position, his new role.

He signed that letter with a flourish. Impressing his seal on the melted wax, he waved the letter to cool it, then gathered up all three packets and rose. And set out to discover who collected the mail.

There was no butler as such. Old McArdle retained the title of steward, but from all he'd heard, Richard strongly suspected that Catriona did the bulk of the work herself. Henderson, as factotum, was the most likely to oversee the delivery of letters and parcels. Richard wandered through the corridors toward the back of the house, looking in on small workrooms, finding the butler's pantry – but no Henderson.

Deciding to place the matter – along with his letters – in Worboys's ever efficient hands and only then remembering Henderson's appointment with his henchman in the main bedchamber, Richard headed back toward the stairs.

Somewhere in the depths of the house, a bell clanged.

He was in the corridor heading for the front hall when he heard footsteps cross the tiles, then a heavy creak as the front doors were opened.

'Good morning, Henderson! And where is your mistress? Pray tell her I wish to see her right away. A matter of some seriousness, I fear.'

The hearty, emphatically genial tones carried clearly; slowing, Richard halted in the shadows of the archway giving onto the front hall. From there, he could see the large, heavily built gentleman handing his hat to Henderson – and the reluctance with which Henderson accepted it.

'I'll see if the mistress is free, sir.'

Piggy eyes in a round, reddened face narrowed slightly. 'Now you just tell her it's me, and she'll be free, I'll warrant. Now get a move on, sirrah – don't keep me standing—'

'Sir Olwyn.' Catriona's quiet, dignified tones carried clearly down the hall. Richard watched as, having glided from the office, she took up a stance directly before the main stairs. And faced Sir Olwyn calmly.

'Miss Hennessey!' Sir Olwyn's impending scowl was banished by a beaming smile. With over-hearty eagerness, he strode up the hall. 'A *pleasure* to see you returned, my dear.' Catriona smiled coolly and inclined her head, but offered no hand in greeting; Sir Olwyn only beamed brighter. 'I trust your little sojourn in the Highlands passed without mishap?' As if only then recalling what had occasioned her absence, his smile evaporated, to be replaced with an expression of patently false sympathy. 'A great loss, I'm sure, your guardian.'

'Indeed.' Her voice as cold as the snows outside, Catriona inclined her head again. 'But—' 'His son has inherited, I understand?'

Catriona drew a patient breath. 'Yes. His son Jamie was, indeed, my late guardian's heir. But—'

'Aye, well – he'll want to pay attention to things down here, and that right quickly, I make no doubt.' Bluffy earnest again, Sir Olwyn looked at Catriona and shook his head. 'I fear, my dear, that I must again lodge a protest – vale cattle have been found wandering *miles* into my fields.'

'Indeed?' Brows rising, Catriona turned and looked at McArdle, who had followed her into the hall. He looked steadily back, then gave one of his exaggerated, disclaiming shrugs – this one expressing subtle contempt for the suggestion. Catriona turned back to Sir Olwyn. 'I fear, sir, that you must be mistaken. None of our cattle are missing.'

'No, no, my dear – of *course* they aren't.' Braving the prevailing chill, Sir Olwyn boldly took Catriona's hand and patted it. 'My men have strict orders to return them. Many other landowners would not be so lenient, my dear – I do hope you appreciate my concern for you.' Cloyingly paternalistic, he smiled into her eyes. 'No, no – you losing beasts is not the *point*, sweet lady. The point is that they should *not* have wandered in the first place and should certainly *not* have caused damage to *my fields*.

Not thawed in the least, Catriona, very deliberately, withdrew her hand. 'What—'

'No, no! Never fear.' With a hearty laugh, Sir Olwyn held up one hand. 'We'll say no more of it this time. But you really need to pay attention to your stock management, my dear. Of course, being a female, you shouldn't need to worry your pretty head over

205

such matters. A man is what you need, m'dear—'

'I doubt that.' With languid ease, Richard strolled into the hall. 'At least, not another one.'

Sir Olwyn stared, then he bristled. 'Who are you?'

Richard raised one brow and looked at Catriona.

With unimpaired calm, she returned her gaze to Sir Olwyn. 'Allow me to present Richard Cynster – my husband.'

Sir Olwyn blinked, then he goggled. *'Husband?'*

'As I was *trying* to tell you, Sir Olwyn, while in the Highlands, I married.'

'Me.' Richard smiled – a distinctly Cynster smile.

Sir Olwyn eyed it dubiously. He mouthed a silent 'Oh,' then flushed and turned to Catriona. 'Felicitations, my dear – well! It's quite a surprise.' His piggy eyes sharpened; he looked intently at her. '*Quite* a surprise.'

'Indeed,' Richard drawled, 'a surprise all around, I fancy.' Smoothly moving forward, he interposed himself between Catriona and Sir Olwyn, ineffably gathering Sir Olwyn within one outstretched arm, turning him and steering him back down the hall. 'Glean – it is Sir Olwyn Glean, is it not? – perhaps . . . you understand I haven't yet had time to fully acquaint myself with the situation here – we've only just arrived, you see . . . where was I? Ah, yes – perhaps you'd be so good as to explain to me how you identified these wandering cattle as originating from the vale. I gather you didn't see them?'

Discovering himself back at the front door, which Henderson had helpfully set wide, Sir Olwyn blinked, then shook himself. And flushed. 'Well, no – but—'

'Ah! Your men verified their identities, then. I'm so glad – they'll be able to tell me the farm from which the cattle escaped.'

Sir Olwyn flustered. 'Well – as to that—'

Catching his eye, Richard dispensed with his drawl. 'I will, of course, be taking steps to ensure no similar situation occurs again.' He smiled, very slightly, very intently. 'I do hope you take my meaning.'

Sir Olwyn flushed to the roots of his hair. He threw a stunned look back at Catriona, then grabbed the hat Henderson held out, crammed it on his crown, swung on his heel and clattered down the steps.

Richard watched him go – watched him scramble atop his showy bay and canter out of the courtyard.

At Richard's shoulder, the taciturn Henderson nodded at Glean's departing back. 'Good job, that.'

Richard thought so. He smiled and handed Henderson his letters, then turned back into the hall. Behind him, Henderson pulled the heavy doors shut.

Catriona hadn't moved from her position before the stairs; Richard strolled up the hall and stopped directly before her.

She met his gaze directly. 'Our cattle don't stray beyond the vale – I'd know if they did.'

Richard studied her eyes, then nodded. 'I'd assumed after reading Glean's letters to Seasmus that all that was so much hot air.' He took her hand and turned her toward the stairs.

'Sir Olwyn's always trying to create situations out of nothing.'

'Hmmm.' Placing her hand on his sleeve, Richard started up the stairs.

Catriona frowned. 'Where are we going?'

'To our room.' Richard waved ahead. 'Henderson and Worboys have been doing a little reorganizing – I think we should see if you approve.' He smiled at her, effortlessly charming. 'And there's one or two other things I'd like you to consider.'

Like the appetite he'd worked up dispensing with Sir Olwyn.

It was time for a midday snack.

*

207

Four days later, when Catriona again tried to slip from her husband's arms before dawn, he grunted, held her close for an instant, then let her go – and rolled out of bed as well.

'This is really not necessary,' Catriona stated as, ten minutes later, she stood in the dimness of the stable and watched Richard saddle her mare. 'I'm perfectly capable of doing it myself.'

'Hmm.'

Catriona glared. She knew it was useless, but it eased her temper, confused as it was. 'You could have stayed nicely warm in bed.'

Cinching the girths, he looked up and met her eyes. 'There's no point in staying nicely warm in bed if you're not in it.'

It was her turn to humph. Gathering the reins, she put her hands to the saddle, intending to scramble up. He was around beside her in a blink; lifting her, he dropped her onto her perch.

Glaring, she reminded herself, was wasted effort. She settled her feet in the stirrups. 'I'll be back in less than two hours.'

Tight-lipped, he nodded and led the way up the long main corridor of the stable to open the door for her.

Halfway along, he abruptly ducked – avoiding a huge horsy head that suddenly appeared over the top of one stall. The head bobbed and danced, huge eyes rolling at the mare, who promptly skittered and shied. Catriona cursed and drew the mare back.

Richard stared at the huge horse, its head considerably higher than his. 'Where the devil did you come from?'

'That's Thunderer.' Holding the mare still, Catriona looked at the troublemaker. 'He's not usually in this section of the stables. Higgins is making repairs in the other building – perhaps that's why he's moved Thunderer here.'

208

The big horse shifted, then snorted and kicked restlessly. Catriona sighed. 'I wish he'd calm down. He half demolishes his stall every month.'

'He probably just needs more exercise.' Climbing up on the gate of the next stall, Richard looked down on the massive beast. The sleek, dappled grey coat had obviously given him his name – that, and the noise he made with his huge hooves, constantly stamping, shifting, kicking. Richard frowned. 'Is he a stallion?'

'Yes – he's stallion to the vale's herd. In winter, all the mares are quartered around the other side.'

With a snort, Richard dropped back to the ground. 'Poor animal.' He shot a glance at Catriona. 'I know just how he feels.' She sniffed; he looked back at the stallion. 'You need to give orders for him to be ridden more – at least once a day. Or you'll be paying for it in timber and tending bitten grooms.'

'Unfortunately, with Thunderer, we have to pay and tend. He's unridable.'

Richard frowned at her, then back at the horse.

'He's a superb horse, a thoroughbred with excellent blood-lines. We needed a stallion like him to improve the herd, and he was a bargain because the gentleman who owned him couldn't ride him.'

'Hmm. That doesn't necessarily mean he's unridable.'

Catriona shrugged. 'He's thrown every groom in the vale. So now, in winter, he just mooches around in a foul temper.'

Richard shot her a sharp glance. 'That, I can appreciate.'

Sticking her nose in the air, Catriona waved at the door. 'I have to reach the circle before dawn.'

She couldn't hear what Richard grumbled, but he turned and strode on. Keeping to the far side of the corridor, she walked the mare past Thunderer, who whinnied pitifully. 'Males!' she muttered under her breath.

Her own male was waiting, holding the door wide; she rode through and turned – and met his eye. And heard herself assure him: 'I'll be back soon.'

For all the world as if she was promising on her return to engage in their habitual morning activities. As if her prayers were merely an interruption. A quirk of his brow told her how he'd interpreted her impulsive words; mentally cursing, Catriona turned, touched her heels to the mare's flanks – and escaped.

For now. Later, she was obviously destined to provide another of his midday snacks.

The fact that the tingling in her veins owed nothing to the exhilaration of her ride she studiously ignored.

His arms draped over the top rail of the yard fence, Richard watched her fly across the winter landscape. When she was halfway to where he would lose sight of her, he slid his hand into his greatcoat pocket and drew out the spyglass he'd found in the library. Extending the glass to its full length, he put it to his eye, adjusted the focus, then scanned the snow-covered ground ahead of Catriona.

Not a single hoofprint – or footprint – marred the snow carpet.

Lips curving in grim satisfaction, Richard lowered the glass and put it away. There were more ways than one to keep a witch safe.

He'd ridden out to her circle two days before. Even he, unsusceptible to local superstitions, had felt the power that protected the grove of yews, elms and alders – trees not common in these parts. He'd circled it on foot and had confirmed to his own satisfaction that there was no possible approach to the circle other than by crossing the expanse of ground he'd just scanned.

While he'd much rather be with her – was, indeed, conscious of a strong desire to ride there at her side – without

210

an invitation from her, watching over her from afar was the best he could do.

At least, he thought, as the flying figure that was his witch rounded a small hillock and disappeared from sight, this way, the possessive protectiveness that was now a constant part of him was at least partly assuaged.

Turning from the now empty landscape, he started back to the house. Then stopped. Slowly, frowning, he looked back at the stable, then swung about and strode back to the door.

'Where *is* he?' Tugging her day gown over her head, Catriona heard the waspishness in her tone, and humphed. 'That, I suppose, is what comes of consorting with rakes.' Having a rake for a consort.

With another disgusted humph, she scooped her discarded riding clothes into a pile and dumped them on a chair.

She'd returned from her prayers, from her wild ride through the snow-kissed countryside, excited and exhilarated, bubblingly eager to set eyes on her handsome husband again. He who she'd left waiting.

Ridiculously eager to soothe his frustrations.

She'd expected to find him in the warmth of the kitchen, or perhaps in the dining hall, or even brooding – darkly sensual – in the library.

He hadn't been anywhere, brooding or otherwise. She'd looked, but hadn't been able to locate him.

Now, she was disappointed.

Now, *she* was frustrated.

With a smothered growl, Catriona stalked to the window and threw back the curtains, then opened the pane and set the shutters wide.

And saw him.

Her room was in one of the turrets set into the angles at the front of the house; its windows revealed a vista stretching

211

over her lands to the mouth of the vale. Nearer at hand, the gardens rolled down to the river, now visible only as a snow ribbon edged by banks of brown.

It was there that she saw him, riding like the wind along the path that followed the river. The horse under him was dappled grey, a flash of silver in the crisp morning light.

Her heart in her throat, Catriona watched, waiting for the inevitable balk, the scream, the rearing and bucking – the inevitable fall.

It didn't happen. Like kindred souls, man and beast flew over the white ground in perfect harmony, every movement a testimony to their innate strength, every line a testimony to their breeding.

She watched until they disappeared into the glare of the morning sun, rising like a silver disc over the mouth of the vale.

She was waiting for him in the stable when he clattered in. He saw her – his brows quirked, then he dismounted. Hands on hips, she watched as he led Thunderer back to his stall and unsaddled the huge grey. Both he and the horse were breathing fast; they were both smiling the same, thoroughly male smile.

Suppressing a humph, she leaned against the open stall door and folded her arms. 'How did you manage it?'

Busy brushing the now peaceable stallion, he glanced at her. 'It was easy. Thunderer here had simply never had the option put to him.'

'What option?'

'The option of staying cooped up in here, or of going for a long run with me on his back.'

'I see. And so you simply put this option to him and he agreed?'

'As you saw.' Tossing the brush aside, Richard checked the stallion's provisions, then joined her by the stall door.

212

Arms still crossed, she eyed him broodingly. He was still breathing more rapidly than usual, his chest rising and falling – and he still wore that same, ridiculously pleased-with-himself smile.

He glanced back at Thunderer. 'I'll take him for a run every now and then.' He looked down at her. 'Just to keep him in shape.'

His eyes trapped hers – Catriona sucked in a quick breath. They were blue – burning blue – hot with passion and desire. As she stared into their heat, wariness – and expectation – washed over her. No one else was around; all the stable hands were at breakfast.

'Ah ...' Eyes locked on his, she slid sideways, along the open door. He followed, slowly, as if stalking her. But the threat didn't come from him; the knowing lilt to his lips said he knew it. She should, she knew, draw herself up, find her haughty cloak and put it on without delay. Instead, his burning gaze drew forth the exhilaration she'd felt earlier, and sent it singing through her veins. 'Breakfast?' she managed, her voice faint.

His eyes held hers; his lips lifted in a slow, slight, very intent smile. 'Later.'

She'd slid away from the door; reaching out, he swung it shut without looking and continued to follow her, herd her, into the next stall. Which was empty.

Wide-eyed, still backing up, Catriona glanced wildly about. And came up against the wall. She put up her hands, far too weak to hold him back. Even had that been her intent. 'Richard?'

It was clearly a question. He answered with actions. And she discovered how useful a feed trough could be.

# Chapter Twelve

December rolled on, and winter tightened its grip on the vale. Richard's boxes and trunks arrived, sent north by Devil, delivered by a carter anxious to turn his horses about and get home for Christmas.

Along with the boxes came letters – a whole sack of them. Letters for Richard from Devil, Vane and the Dowager, as well as a host of pithy billets from his aunts and female cousins, not amused by his distant wedding, and notes of commiseration from his uncles and ones of sympathy from his unmarried male cousins.

For Catriona came a long letter from Honoria, Devil's duchess, which Richard would have liked to read, but he was never offered the opportunity. After spending a full hour perusing the letter, Catriona folded it up and put it away. In her desk. In a locked drawer. Richard was tempted to pick the lock, but couldn't quite bring himself to do it. What could Honoria have said anyway?

As well as Honoria's letter, Catriona received scented notes from all the Cynster ladies welcoming her into the family. She did not, however, receive any communication from the Dowager, a fact she seemed not to notice, but which Richard noted with some concern.

The only reason Helena would not to write to Catriona was because she was planning on talking to her instead.

It was, he supposed, fair warning.

But fate and the season were on his side; the snows blew hard – the passes were blocked, the highways impassable.

He was safe until the thaw.

Then Christmas was upon them, and he had too much on his plate with the here and now – with absorbing traditions somewhat different from those he knew, with learning how the vale and all the manor celebrated yuletide – to worry about what the future held.

And over and above, through all the merriment and laughter, all the joys and small sorrows, there remained what he considered his principal duty – his principal focus. Learning everything he could about his witchy wife.

Having her in his arms every morning and every night, and in between learning all her strengths, her weaknesses, her foibles, her needs. Learning how he could best support her, as he had vowed to do. Learning how to fit into her life. And how she fitted into his.

It was, he discovered, an absorbing task.

A temporary easing in the weather between Christmas and the New Year saw three travellers appear at the manor's gate. They proved to be a father and his two adult sons, agents for various produce, come to see the lady of the vale.

Catriona received them as old acquaintances. Introduced, Richard smiled politely, then lounged in a chair set back against the office wall and watched how his witchy wife conducted the vale's business.

She was, he learned, no easy mark.

'My dear Mr. Potts, your offer simply will not do. If, as you say, the market is so well supplied, perhaps we should store all our grain for the next year.' Catriona glanced at McArdle, sitting at the end of her desk. 'Could we do that, do you think?'

'Oh, aye, m'lady.' Like a benighted gnome, McArdle

nodded sagely. 'There's space in the cellars, and we're high and dry here, so there's no fear of it going damp.'

'Perhaps that would be best.' Catriona turned back to Mr. Potts. 'If that's the best offer you can manage?'

'Ah. Well.' Mr. Potts all but squirmed. 'It's possible we *might* – considering the quality of the vale's grain, you understand – manage some concession on the price.'

'Indeed?'

Fifteen minutes of haggling ensued, during which Potts made more than one concession.

'Done,' Catriona finally declared. She smiled benignly on all three Pottses. 'Perhaps you'd like a glass of our dandelion wine?'

'I don't mind if I do,' Mr. Potts agreed. 'Very partial to your dandelion wine.'

Richard inwardly humphed and made a mental note to take a piece of chalk down to the cellars and inscribe all the remaining barrels of dandelion wine with an instruction that they were not to be broached without his express permission. Then he recalled that he really should gain his wife's approval for such an edict – which led to thoughts of taking her down to the cellars, which led to thoughts . . .

He frowned, and shifted in his seat. Accepting the wine one of the maids served, he directed his attention once more to the Pottses.

'Now, about those cattle you wanted.' Potts the elder leaned forward. 'I think I can get some young heifers from up Montrose way.'

Catriona raised her brows. 'None from any nearer? I don't like to have them transported so far.'

'Aye, well. Cattle – good breeding stock – are in rare demand these days. Have to take what you can get.'

Richard inwardly frowned. As he listened to the discussion – of sources of breeding stock, of prices, of the best breeds for

216

the changing market – he shifted and inwardly frowned harder.

From all he'd heard, all he'd already noted, he knew more about livestock than his witch. Not that she lacked knowledge in general, or an understanding of the vale's present needs – it was more that she lacked experience of what was available in the wider world – a world she, for good reason, eschewed.

The temptation to speak – to butt in and take over – grew; Richard ruthlessly squelched it. If he so much as said a word, all three Pottses would turn to him. From the first, the younger ones had eyed him expectantly – from the looks on their faces now, they would be much more comfortable continuing their discussion of the performance characteristics of breeding stock with him. Man to man.

Richard cared nothing for their sensitivities – he cared much more about his witch, and hers.

He'd sworn not to take the lead, not to take her role, not to interfere with how she ran the vale. He couldn't speak publically, not without her invitation. He couldn't even bring the matter up privately – even there, she might construe it as indicating somewhat less than complete commitment to adhering to his vow.

A vow that, indeed, required complete commitment, required real and constant effort from him to keep it. It was not, after all, a vow a man like him could easily abide by. But he would abide by it – for her.

So he couldn't say anything – not unless she asked. Not unless she invited his comment or sought his views.

And so he sat there, mum, and listened, and itched to set her – and the Pottses – right. To explain that there were other options they ought to consider. Should consider.

But his witch didn't look his way – not once.

He had never felt the constraint of his vow more than he did that day.

*

217

The year turned; the weather continued bitter and bleak. Within the manor's stone walls, the lamps burned throughout the dull days, and the fires leapt in every hearth. It was a quiet time, a peaceful time. The men gathered in the dining hall, whiling away the hours with chess and backgammon. The women still had chores – cooking, cleaning, mending – but there was no sense of urgency.

Early in the new year, Catriona took advantage of the quiet and compiled an inventory of the curtains. Which resulted in a list of those she wanted mended or replaced. In search of a seamstress, she wandered into the maze of smaller rooms at the back of the ground floor, her attention focused on the list in her hand.

'Hee, hee, hee!'

The childish giggle stopped her; it was followed by a high-pitched trill of laughter. Curious, she turned from her path and followed the sound of continuing chortles. As she neared the source, she heard a deeper, intermittent rumble.

They were in the old games room. The manor children, of whom there were many, used it as their playroom, the place they spent most of the hard winter. Today, Catriona saw, as she paused in the shadows just outside the open door, that they had a visitor.

Then again, he might just be a hostage.

Trapped in the huge old armchair before the fire, Richard was surrounded by children. The two youngest had clambered onto his lap and cuddled close, one on either side, two others perched on his knees, while still others balanced on the wide arms of the chair. One was even sprawled across the chair-back, almost draped over Richard's shoulders. The rest surrounded him, their faces upturned, alight as they hung on his words. His stories.

Folding her arms, Catriona leaned against the door frame and listened.

Listened to tales of boys running wild – a veritable tribe of them, it seemed. Listened to tales of youthful derringdo, of cheeky larks, of dangerous dragons vanquished, of genuine adventures that fate had sent to shape their lives.

The stories were of him and his cousins, she had not a doubt, although he never identified the heroes. The culprits. The demons in disguise.

Catriona wondered how many of his tales were true. She looked at him, so impressively large, his strength still apparent even relaxed as he was, and was tempted to think they all were. His stories were the adventures that had made him what he was.

For long moments, she stood still in the shadows, unremarked as she watched. Watched him, so large and strong, so deeply masculine, open the jewel box of his childhood memories and take them out, one by one, like delicate necklaces of bright gold and beaten silver, to awe, to entertain, to amuse the children.

They were enthralled – they were his. Just as their parents were. She'd noticed that from his first day here – his intrinsic ability to give of himself, and thus inspire devotion, loyalty – his ability to lead. She wasn't sure he recognized it in himself; it was simply an inherent part of him.

As she watched, one of the littlest two, thumb in mouth and almost asleep, started to tip. Without faltering in his recitation, without, apparently, even noticing what he did, Richard cradled the tot in one hand and resettled him more securely against his side.

Catriona stood in the shadows, her gaze on him, on them, her mind full of his stories, her heart full of him, for as long as she dared, then, misty-eyed, retreated without disturbing them.

'Well! I thought I might find you here.'

Catriona looked up as Algaria entered the stillroom, and blinked at the expression of joyful confidence that lit her erstwhile mentor's face. 'Are you all right?'

'Me?' Algaria smiled. 'I'm very well. But I came to ask you the same question.'

Catriona straightened. 'I'm well, too.'

Algaria eyed her straitly. Pointedly. When Catriona remained stubbornly silent, she elucidated: 'I wanted to ask if that' – she gestured back into the house; Catriona narrowed her eyes – '*husband* of yours,' Algaria sweetly amended, 'has succeeded in getting you with child.'

Catriona looked down at the herbs she was pounding. 'I can't tell yet, can I?'

'Can't you?'

'Not for certain, no.'

She did know, of course, but the sheer power of the feelings that surged through her whenever she thought of Richard's child – a tiny speck of life slowly growing within her – shook her so much she couldn't yet bring herself to speak of it. Not until she was absolutely, beyond any doubt or early mishap, sure. And then the first person she would speak to was Richard. Lips firming, she ground up her herbs. 'I'll tell you when I am.'

'Humph! Well, whatever, it seems as if The Lady's prophesy will, despite all, come to pass. As it always does. I have to admit I didn't think you could be right in deciding you should go to him as you did – it's so transparently obvious that he must never rule here. But The Lady has her ways.' With a graceful, devotional gesture, Algaria moved to peer out of the high window. 'It all looks like turning out much as you planned.'

Grinding the pestle into the mortar, Catriona frowned. 'What do you mean – as I'd planned?'

'Why, that he'll get you with child, then leave.' Algaria turned from the window and met Catriona's puzzled gaze. 'The only thing you didn't foresee correctly is that he'd marry you as well. Really, it's all worked out for the best. This way, you not only get the child, but the formal protection of being a married lady. And all without the bother of a husband – a resident one, anyway.'

'But ...' It took a full minute before Catriona fathomed Algaria's direction. When she did, the knowledge chilled her. 'Why do you imagine he's leaving?'

Algaria smiled and patted her hand reassuringly. 'You needn't think I have it wrong this time. His man has been with him for more than eight years and he's speaking very openly of their plans to return to London.'

'He is?' Catriona gave thanks for the dim light in the still-room – because of the fumes, only one small lamp was burning. Carefully resting the heavy pestle in the mortar, she gripped the edge of the table. And forced herself to ask: 'What is he saying?'

'Oh, no specific details yet. Just that it's apparently their way to spend winter visiting the homes of friends and acquaintances, but that sometime in February, they always return to the capital. For the Season, I understand. Worboys has been regaling the staff with stories of the balls and parties, and all the other entertainments Mr. Cynster customarily enjoys. Without expressly *stating* it, he's given the clear impression that marriage has not changed his master's style. He's expecting they'll be in London before March.'

'I see.' Wiping her hands, suddenly cold, on her apron, Catriona picked up the pestle again. She kept her gaze on her preparation, avoiding Algaria's bright eyes. 'I'm sure The Lady will ensure all goes as it should.'

And arrangements that had not been expressly *stated* might not come to pass at all.

That night, Catriona sat before her dressing table brushing her long hair for far longer than was her wont. Long enough for

221

Richard to come in and, after throwing her a lustful smile, start to undress.

Calmly, Catriona brushed and watched him in her mirror. 'Your aunts, in their letters, spoke a lot of London. They seem to expect that we'll join them shortly – once the snows melt.' Serenely brushing, she watched his brows rise. 'For the balls, the parties – the Season.'

He grimaced. And dropped his trousers. And stepped out of them.

Then he turned and, stark naked, prowled toward her.

'You don't need to imagine I'll insist that we go.'

'You won't?'

'No.'

He stopped behind her – all she could see was his bare chest, crisp black hair adorning the heavy muscles. He lifted her hair, spreading it, fanning it over her shoulders, over her breasts. 'I'll never force you to leave the vale.'

His features had assumed an intent expression she now knew well; reaching out, he took the brush from her hand and laid it on the table.

Her heart thudding in her throat, and throbbing in her loins, she abruptly stood. His hands closed about her waist and held her still; his eyes locked on hers in the mirror.

'Open your nightgown.'

The nightgown she wore reached only to her knees; it was fastened down the front with tiny buttons. Barely able to breathe, incapable of taking her eyes from the vision before her, Catriona slowly obeyed.

One by one, the buttons slid free, all the way to her knees. She straightened, and the gown gaped. Revealing the ripe swells of her breasts, the smooth slope of her belly, the long lines of her thighs, the flaming curls between. She stared at the sight, then looked at his face.

And saw the hard planes shift, saw passion lock tight.

Hands tightening about her waist, he lifted her.

'Kneel on the stool.'

She did; he straddled her calves. And drew the nightgown from her.

Catriona's eyes flew wide; she couldn't help her shocked gasp.

Immediately he held her, his chest warm against her shoulders and back, his thighs hard, abrasive, against the sensitive skin of her bottom. 'Sssh.' Head bent, he nuzzled her ear, one dark hand splayed across her midriff, a powerful contrast against her ivory skin.

Shocked to her toes, Catriona felt her senses reel. They were bathed in light – as well as the two candlesticks burning on the dressing table, two candlestands stood on either side, both holding large candles, both lit. She could see the width of his shoulders, clearly visible above and beyond her own, could see the dark, hair-dusted columns of his legs on either side of hers.

Could feel the thick, ridged rod, so flagrantly male, pressed against the cleft between her buttocks.

And felt – and saw – his other hand slide from her hip, under the shimmering veil of her hair, to close firmly about one breast, long fingers curling about her soft flesh.

She moaned softly and let her head fall back against his shoulder. From beneath heavy lids, she watched his fingers flex. Swallowing, she moistened her lips, saw them already parted, already sheening. 'The bed?'

'No.' He breathed the word against the soft skin of her throat – he was watching his hand on her. 'Here.'

She shuddered, one small part of her mind desperate to protest, the rest awash with tingling anticipation. Anticipation that steadily built, then silvered into excitement. Into arousal that escalated with each slow sweep of his hands over her flickering skin, with each knowing caress, each expert touch.

He did nothing else but caress her bare body, worshipped

it until her skin was flushed rose in the golden candle-glow, and she was quivering with need.

'Lean forward.' His voice was a deep, gravelly whisper in her ear. 'Place your hands palms down on the table.'

She did; he shifted behind her. From under weighted lids, she saw him steady her before him, then reach around her. Splaying one hand across her stomach, he angled her hips back; looking down, he fitted himself to her.

Then, with one slow thrust that threatened to lift her from her knees, he filled her. Stretched her. Completed her.

Fully embedded within her, he leaned forward; his lips brushing her nape, he filled his hands with her breasts. And fondled her swollen flesh as he rocked her. Rocked her slowly, languorously, to heaven.

Until she panted, and moaned, and tried to wriggle her hips – tried to urge him on. His slow rhythm was driving her insane – she wanted him deep, wanted him filling her more forcefully. More rapidly.

She wanted to rush on to the stars.

He straightened; his hands drifted from her breasts to lock about her hips. He anchored her before him, so she couldn't move – and pressed more deeply into her. But he still kept the rhythm slow – slower than she wanted.

So she could feel every inch of his repeated penetrations, was aware to her fingertips of the reined strength of his invasions. Was intimately conscious of the hard, hot rod with which he claimed her, of the slick softness with which she accepted him.

She shuddered and closed her eyes and clamped tightly about him. And sensed his chest swell, sensed his tension tighten. Felt his grip about her hips lock like iron and felt the brush of his thumb over her birthmark. It would be clearly visible in the light, contrasting against the ivory of her buttock, so taut, so tight.

Compulsion forced her to look, to crack open her lids and look at him behind her, his hard body flexing as he loved her. Forced her to study his face, to see the concentration and passion and sheer devotion etched therein, delineating the hard angles gilded by the candles' glow. Forced her to notice her own body, lushly wanton, her skin flushed, her hair wild fire spread over her shoulders and arms, her breasts swollen and tipped with deep rose, her thighs clamped together, her hips rocking only slightly as he filled her. Forced her, at the last, to look at her face, at the expression of sensual abandon stamped on her features, her heavy-lidded eyes, her panting, parted lips.

With a soft moan, she closed her eyes tightly and felt him lift the tempo, felt him start the long crescendo that would carry her to the stars.

And when she reached them, he held her there for long, immeasurable minutes, caught on the cusp of delight – then he joined her, and her heaven was complete.

A week later, Catriona pulled on her heavy cloak, picked up a basket lined with scraps of flannel, and headed out to the large barn. It was three o'clock; the light would soon fade. As she trudged across the yard whipped by lightly flurrying snow, the sun, hidden behind banks of grey cloud, cast the scene in a smoky, pale gold haze.

Struggling against the flurries, she hauled open the single door set in the barn's main doors, then slipped inside. Setting her basket down, she latched the door, then turned, paused to let her eyes adjust to the dimness, then scooped up her basket and headed for the loft ladder.

To find the kitchen cat, who, entirely out of synchrony with the seasons, had given birth somewhere up in the hay.

Gaining the top of the ladder, Catriona swung her basket up, then surveyed the scene – the expanse of hay bales stacked almost to the roof all the way along the loft which stretched

225

down one side of the long barn.

She knew the cat and kittens were in the hay somewhere. She didn't know how she knew – she just did. She also knew that the kittens would die by morning if she didn't find them and take them into the warm kitchen.

With a sigh, she clambered up onto the hay-strewn loft boards and started to search.

The loft extended over the entire barn, over the three separate sections the large building housed. Mentally tossing a coin, she elected to start searching the section nearest, the one over the carriages, carts and ploughs.

Methodically pushing through hay stacks, pressing apart bales, sliding her hand, oh-so-trustingly, into possible dens, she tried to keep her mind on her search and away from its principal preoccupation.

As usual, she failed.

Her husband exerted an almost hypnotic attraction over her thoughts. Over her senses, he wielded absolute control – that, she accepted. But the degree to which she found herself dwelling on him – on his plans – on what his intentions really were – was disconcerting. She'd never before been that linked to anyone, never before felt her happiness dependent on someone else.

She'd been her own mistress for years – being his was changing her in ways she hadn't expected.

In ways she didn't entirely like – in ways she couldn't control.

In moments of weakness, like the present, as she absentmindedly crooned for the cat, when her mind was caught, trapped, in senseless speculation, raising visions that were unnervingly depressing, she'd fallen back on her old habit of lecturing herself. Telling herself, sternly, that what would be, would be.

It only made her feel more helpless, more in the grip of some force beyond her control, as if her life was now tuned to some unknown piper.

226

Reaching the end of the first section without any sign of the cat, she straightened, pressed out the kinks in her spine, then trailed back to the ladder to fetch her basket. And doggedly glided into the next section – the one over the quartered dairy herd.

She was halfway through that section when she heard voices. Rocking back on her heels, she listened – and heard them again, low, almost murmuring. Curious, she rose and quietly walked into the last section of the loft.

In the back of her mind ran the thought that she might stumble on some illicit assignation – such was her interpretation of the tone of those murmurs. Ready to retreat silently if that proved the case, she inched closer to the loft's edge.

And heard Richard say: 'Gently. Easy, sweetheart. Now – let's take it very slowly.'

An assenting murmur in a light female tone answered him.

Catriona froze. She turned cold, then burned as temper seared her. What she felt in that instant was beyond her description – but betrayal was there, certainly, as was a furious force she'd never before felt – every bit as green as her eyes. It was that force that fanned the flames of anger into a righteous blaze. Fists clenched, quivering with rage, she marched to the top of the ladder leading down into the last section of the barn.

They heard her footsteps – and looked up.

For one fractured instant, Catriona stared down at her husband and the maid within his arms.

The eight-year-old maid he held balanced on the back of a shaggy coated pony.

Catriona's eyes widened from their angry slits; even while she mentally scrambled to keep her features unrevealing, her lips formed a telltale 'Oh.' Relief swept her; she teetered and had to take a quick step back from the loft's edge.

Richard's gaze, locked on her face, intensified. He straightened, fluidly swinging the girl down. Only then did Catriona notice the others surrounding the improvised ring, all waiting, obediently silent, for their turn.

'I, ah ...' Weakly, she gestured to the hay-filled loft behind her. 'The cat's had kittens.'

'Tabitha?' One of the boys broke from the circle and raced to the ladder. 'Where?'

'Well, ...' Flustered, Catriona stepped back as the whole riding school swarmed up the ladder. 'That's the problem, you see.'

The pupils were followed by their teacher who, as was his wont, made the loft shrink as he stepped onto the boards. Catriona backed against the wall of hay and waved down the loft. 'She's somewhere up here. We have to find her and take the kittens into the kitchen to keep warm, or they'll die.'

The children didn't wait for more. They enthusiastically clambered over the hay, calling the cat, a favorite of theirs.

Leaving her with their teacher. Catriona flicked him a quick glance. 'I've searched the first section.'

Head tilted, he studied her. 'They'll find her.' A ferocious sneeze was echoed by two more. He raised his brows. 'That, or die trying.' He continued to study her; after a moment, he asked: 'Have you been up here long?'

Catriona shrugged as nonchalantly as she could and avoided his gaze. 'A few minutes.' She waved along the loft. 'I was at the other end.'

'Ah.' Straightening, he strolled toward her. He stopped by her side, then, without warning, gathered her into his arms. And kissed her. Very warmly.

Emerging, breathless, some moments later, Catriona blinked at him. 'What was that for?'

'Reassurance.' He'd lifted his head only to change his hold; as he lowered his lips to hers again, she tried to hold him back.

'The children,' she hissed.

'Are busy,' he replied – and kissed her again.

'Tabby! Tabby!'

The shrill call had all the children running to one corner of the middle section. None looked back; none saw their lady, flustered and flushed, win free of her consort's arms. And none saw the knowing smile that lifted his lips.

Catriona tried not to notice it either; blotting the sight from her mind, she hurried after the children.

They found five tiny kittens, pathetically shivering, huddling close to their weakened mother's flank. There were ready hands enough to lift the whole family together into the lined basket, which was then carried in procession along the loft, taken down the ladder by Richard as his contribution to the rescue, then entrusted to the care of the eightyear-old maid. Surrounded by her absorbed fellows, she crossed the yard carefully, all the children huddling to protect the cat and her brood from the swirling snow.

The light had all but gone. Catriona stepped out of the barn into a twilight world. Richard pulled the door shut and fastened it, then tugged her cloak around her and anchored her against him, within one arm.

They followed in the children's wake.

'I hope the kittens will recover – they felt very cold. I suppose a little warm milk wouldn't hurt them. I'll have to ask Cook ...'

She blathered on, not once looking up – not once meeting his eyes. Richard held her fast against the wind's tug and, smiling into the swirling snow, steered her toward the kitchen.

He didn't know what woke him – certainly not her footfalls, for she was as silent as a ghost. Perhaps it was the bone-deep knowledge that she was not there, in their bed beside him, where she was supposed to be.

Warm beneath the covers, his limbs heavy with satiation, he lifted his head and saw her, arms crossed tightly over her robe, pacing before the hearth.

The fire had died, leaving only embers to shed their glow upon the room; about them, the house lay silent, asleep.

She was frowning. He watched her pace and gnaw her lower lip, something he'd never seen her do.

'What's the matter?'

She halted; her eyes, widening, flew to his face.

And in that instant, that infinitesimal pause before she replied, he knew she wouldn't tell him.

'I'm sorry. I didn't mean to wake you.' She hesitated. When he remained propped on one elbow, watching her, she drifted back to the bed. 'Go back to sleep.'

He waited until she halted by the side of the bed. 'I can't – not with you pacing.' Not with her worrying. He could sense it strongly, now; some deep concern that was ruffling her normally unruffleable serenity. 'What is it?'

Catriona sighed and shrugged out of her robe. 'It's nothing.' It was the breeding stock, or lack thereof. But ...

She shouldn't involve him.

When she'd heard his voice, heard him ask, her instinctive impulse had been to tell him, to lay her growing problem on shoulders broader than hers – to share her burden with him. But ... in the back of her mind lurked an unwelcome notion that appealing to him was not the right thing to do. On a number of counts.

Asking him, inviting him to become more deeply involved with running the vale, might not, in the long run, be fair, either to him, or to her. There was a subtle line between offering advice and sage counsel, and making the decisions, determining the final outcome. She had always been taught that strong men, powerful men, had difficulty with that distinction.

Forcing him to face it might not be wise.

And, even if he hadn't said so yet, if he was considering leaving her and journeying to London for the Season, she would be wise to keep her own counsel. Wise to hold him at a distance, in that arena at least. She couldn't afford to start to rely on him only to find him bidding her adieu.

It hadn't escaped her that while he'd promised repeatedly not to force her to leave the vale, he'd never promised to stay. To remain by her side, to face the problems of the vale by her side.

Much as she might now feel a need for a strong shoulder to lean on, a strong arm to rely on, she couldn't afford to let herself develop that sort of vulnerability. Ultimately the vale was her responsibility.

So she summoned a smile and hoped it was reassuring. 'It's just a minor vale problem.' Dropping her robe, she slid under the covers. He hesitated, then drew her into his arms, settling her against him.

Snuggling her head on his chest, she forced herself to relax against him – forced herself to let her problems lie.

Until she could deal with them alone.

She was being silly. Overly sensitive.

The next morning, pacing before her office window, Catriona berated herself sternly. She still didn't know what she could, or should, do about the breeding stock – it was time she asked Richard for advice.

When viewed in the sane light of morning, the concerns that had prevented her from asking last night no longer seemed sufficient to stop her, excuse her, from taking the sensible course. Such silly sensitivity was unlike her.

She needed help – and she was reasonably sure he could give it. She recalled quite clearly how, at McEnery House, she'd been impressed with his knowledge of farming practices and estate management. It was senseless, in her time of need, not to avail herself of his expertise.

Frowning at the floor, she swung about and paced on.

He'd said nothing about leaving. It therefore behooved her to have faith, rather than credit him with making plans – plans he hadn't discussed with her. There was no reason at all for her to imagine he was leaving; she should assume that he was staying, that he would remain to support her as her consort, and not hie off to enjoy himself – alone – in London. He'd always behaved with consideration – she should recognize that fact.

And if asking him for advice, inviting him to take a more direct interest in the running of the vale, served to bind him to it – and to her – so be it.

Straightening, she drew in a deep breath, drew herself up that last inch, then glided to the door.

He was in the library; from her office, she took a minor corridor, rather than go around through the front hall. The corridor led to a secondary door set into the wall beside the library fireplace.

She reached it, confidence growing with every step, her heart lifting at the thought of asking him what she'd shied away from asking last night, of inviting him that next step deeper into her life. Grasping the doorknob, she turned it – as the door opened noiselessly, she heard voices.

Halting, the door open only a crack, she hesitated, then recognized Richard's deep 'humph.'

'I imagine I'll start packing in a few days, sir. I don't like to rush things and it is very close to the end of January.'

A pause ensued, then Worboys spoke again. 'According to Henderson, and Huggins, the thaw should set in any day now. I daresay it may take a week to clear the roads sufficiently, but, of course, the farther south we travel, the more the highways will improve.'

'Hmm.'

Frozen outside the door, her heart chilling, sinking, Catriona listened as Worboys continued: 'The rooms in Jermyn Street will need freshening, of course. I wondered . . . perhaps you're thinking of looking in on the Dowager and the duke and duchess? If that were so, I could continue on to town and open up the rooms, ready for your return.'

'Hmm.'

'You'll want to be well settled before the Richmonds' ball, naturally. If I might suggest ... afew new coats might be in order. And your boots, of course – we'll need to make sure Hoby remembers not to attach those tassles. As for linen ...'

Deep in a letter from Heathcote Montague, Richard let Worboys's monologue drift past him. After eight years, Worboys knew perfectly well when he wasn't attending to him – and *he* knew perfectly well when his henchman was in a quandary.

In Worboys's case, the quandary was simple. He liked it here – and couldn't believe it. He was presently dusting the books on the shelves – in itself a most revealing act – and putting on a good show, trying to convince them both that they were shortly to up stakes and depart, when, in reality, he knew Richard had no such thoughts, and he, himself, did not want to go.

In what he viewed as a primitive backwater, Worboys had discovered heaven.

Not an inamorata in his case, but a household where he fitted in perfectly, like a missing link in a chain. The manor's household was unusual, without the lines of precedence Worboys had lived with all his professional life. Instead, it was a place that operated on friendship – a sort of kinship in serving their lady. It was a household where people had to rely on each other – have faith and confidence in each other – just to get through the yearly round of harsh weather and the short growing season, made even more difficult by their isolation.

It was a place where people felt valued for themselves; the household, in its rustic innocence, had welcomed Worboys to its bosom – and Worboys had fallen in love.

He was presently in deep denial – Richard recognized the signs. So he let Worboys ramble – he was really only talking to himself and convincing no one. Whenever Worboys paused and insisted on some response, he humphed or hmm'd and let it go at that. He saw no benefit in getting drawn into a discussion of things that were not going to happen.

His letter was far more interesting. Spurred by the Pottses' visit, he'd written to Montague, inquiring as to the current state of breeding stock, both in the southern and northern counties. He'd also asked Montague to locate the most highly regarded breeder in the Ridings, just south of the border, not too far from the vale.

'So, sir.' Pausing, Worboys drew in a deep breath. 'If you just let me know when you've decided on the date, I'll proceed as we've discussed.'

Looking up, Richard met Worboys's gaze. 'Indeed. When I decide to leave, you'll be the first to know.'

Inclining his head gravely, doubtless feeling much better after having got all his useless plans off his chest, Worboys picked up his duster and a pot of wilting flowers, and headed for the door.

Richard waited until it closed before letting his lips curve. Returning to his letter, he read to its end, then, smiling even more, laid it down, and stretched.

And noticed a draft. He glanced around and saw a door, so well fitted in the paneling he hadn't noticed it before, left ajar. Rising, he rounded the desk and crossed to the panel. Opening it farther, he found a dim secondary corridor. Empty. Inwardly shrugging, Richard closed the door – it could have been ajar for a week for all he knew.

Recrossing to the desk, he sat and pulled out a map of the surrounding counties. A Mister Owen Scroggs, cattle breeder extraordinaire, lived at Hexham. How far, Richard wondered, was Hexham from the vale?

If – *when* – his wife finally trusted him enough to ask for his assistance, his support, he wanted to have all the answers. All the right answers, at his fingertips.

# Chapter Thirteen

He wasn't, in fact, a patient man.

Ever since receiving the information from Montague, he'd been watching for – waiting for – an opportunity to discuss the matter with his wife. To banish the shadows that seemed to grow, day by day, in her eyes.

Instead, four days later, he'd yet to discover a suitable moment to speak to her. Lounging in an archway not far from her office door, Richard, brooding darkly, kept his gaze on the oak panel and waited some more.

He had a bone-deep aversion to discussing business in their bed. There she remained her usual self, warmly wanton, sweetly taking him in and holding him tight, still insisting on trying to muffle her pleasured screams – he was conscious of a deep reluctance to do anything that might alter the openness that had grown between them there.

But her days were busy; she seemed constantly involved in meetings, or discussions, or in overseeing the household. And if she wasn't actually engaged in the above, she was surrounded by others – by McArdle, Mrs. Broom, or, worse still, Algaria. Even in the odd moments when he would come upon her alone, she was always rushing to be somewhere else.

Worse yet, he was starting to become seriously worried about her health. He was too well attuned to her not to sense the tension, the fragility, she hid beneath her cloak of serenity. He couldn't help but wonder if her pregnancy, which she'd yet to mention to him, was the cause of it – the sudden breathlessness that came upon her, and an emotional brittleness she tried hard to hide.

Those symptoms weren't there when she slid into his arms every night. He couldn't help wonder if, during the days, she was working herself too hard, rather than letting him ease the load so she could take better care of herself – and their child.

The office door opened; McArdle stumped out.

Richard straightened; he waited until McArdle disappeared down the corridor, then swiftly strolled to the office door. He hesitated for a moment, reminding himself that he couldn't demand, then opened the door – and strolled languidly in.

Seated behind her desk, Catriona looked up – Richard smiled easily, charmingly. And tried not to notice the clouds dimming her green eyes. 'Are you busy?'

Catriona drew in a deep breath and looked down at the papers before her. 'I am, actually. Henderson and Huggins—'

'I won't keep you above a moment.'

The words were drawled, nonchalant – unthreatening. Acutely conscious of him, Catriona forced herself to sit back in her chair and wait while he strolled, all idle elegance, to the window.

'Actually, I wondered if I might help you out, as you seem so rushed these days.'

Drawing a slow, steadying breath, Catriona turned her head and met his gaze. Swiftly – with a hope she could only just bear to acknowledge – she studied his face. It was an indolent mask of polite indifference; there was no hint of real commitment, real passion – of really wanting to help. No hint that the vale – and she – were seriously important to him.

He smiled, charming as ever, although she noticed the gesture didn't reach his eyes. A languid wave underscored his words: 'There's nothing much for me to do here, so I've plenty of time free.'

236

Catriona fought to keep her expression blank, and succeeded. He was bored and could see she was busy, so he'd done the gentlemanly thing and offered to help. She had no trouble shaking her head brusquely and looking back at her letters. 'There's really no need. I'm quite capable of handling the vale's business on my own.'

The words, uttered in a hard tone, were as much to convince herself of that fact as to decline his *gentlemanly* offer.

He hesitated, then said, a trace of steel in his tones: 'As you wish.' With a graceful inclination of his head, he strolled out and left her to it.


The thaw arrived.

Two mornings later, Richard lay late in bed, listening to the steady drip of water from the eaves. Catriona had slipped from his arms early, whispering about a confinement, assuring him that she wasn't going out but that the mother-to-be was safe inside the manor.

Staring up at the dark red canopy, Richard tried to keep his thoughts from her, from the leaden feeling that, two days ago, had settled in his gut.

And failed.

Inwardly grimacing, he irritably reminded himself that failure was not something Cynsters indulged in – much less on the scale he was presently wallowing in.

He was failing on all fronts.

The new life he'd envisaged for himself at Catriona's side, once so full of promise and possibilities, had turned into a disappointment. A deep, deadening disappointment – he'd never felt so disillusioned with life as he felt now.

There was nothing for him here – nothing for him to do, nothing for him to be. Boredom now haunted him; his old restlessness – something he'd hoped he'd lost for all time in the kirk at Keltyburn – was growing.

Along with a dark, compelling sense of worthlessness – at least, in this place. In this vale – her vale.

He couldn't understand her.

From night to cockcrow, they were as close as a man and woman could be, but when morning came and she slipped from his arms, it was as if, along with her clothes, she donned some invisible mantle and became 'the lady of the vale' – a woman with a calling, a position and a purpose in life, from all of which he was excluded.

While gentlemen of his station did not customarily share their wives' lives, he, very definitely, had expected to share hers. Still wanted to share hers. The prospect of sharing her responsibilities, of sharing it all as a mutual endeavor, and thus having a strong and abiding connection on a daily basis – that was certainly a large part of the attraction he felt for her. She was, he had thought, a woman he could share goals with, share achievements with.

Their marriage hadn't, so far, turned out that way.

He'd been careful of her, careful of pressuring her – he'd given her every chance to ask him for help, for assistance. He'd tried hard not to force her hand – and got nowhere.

For long moments, his gaze locked on the dark red above him, he considered the obvious alternative – the action his Cynster self strongly urged. He could, very easily, take over the reins and steer their marriage into the paths he wanted it to follow. He was not a naturally passive person; he wouldn't normally endure a situation he didn't like. Normally, he'd simply change it.

But . . .

He could forsee two difficulties. The first was that, in taking the reins, he would risk damaging the very thing he most wanted to preserve. He wanted Catriona as a willing life-partner, not as one resenting his dominance.

That, however, while quite bad enough, ranked as the more minor of his difficulties.

The larger, most insurmountable problem, was his vow. The vow he'd made to her – twice – that he would not impinge on her independence, would never seek to override her authority. She'd taken him on trust – she trusted him to keep that vow no matter what. To wrest control from her would betray that trust, in the most damning and damaging way.

There were few things he was sure of in this marriage of theirs, but he knew to his soul that he could never endure the look in her green eyes if he ever betrayed her on that front.

Which meant ...

He was on a narrow track, high up a mountainside, with unbroken rock to one side and a sheer precipice on the other. He could go forward, or retreat.

Heaving a deep sigh, Richard threw back the covers and got up.

Cynsters *never* retreated.

The concept was totally alien to him – the very thought offended him at some deep level. So he waited, and trapped her once more in her office, at a time when he knew he could wrest at least two minutes from her busy schedule.

After ambling idly in and exchanging a mild comment about the weather, he looked down at her and asked: 'Tell me, my dear, do you have any need of me here?'

He wanted to ask the question brutally – wanted to show her how much she was hurting him by shutting him out of her life, by denying him the chance to give what he felt he could – but he couldn't do it, couldn't let her see how pathetically vulnerable he'd become. So he kept his social mask intact and asked the question lightly, coolly. As if the answer was of no great moment.

Which was how Catriona heard it – that and rather more. To her, it rang as the prelude to his informing her that he was leaving – the polite patter of the executioner before the axe fell.

So she held her own calm like a shield over her weeping heart and smiled, a little weakly, back up at him. 'No. There's really nothing for you to do.'

Looking down, she forced herself to go on, forced herself to play the role she'd spent hours rehearsing – the role of acquiescent wife. 'I daresay you'll be heading to London soon – Huggins heard this morning that the roads to the south are all open, at least as far as Carlisle.'

Her head throbbed, her stomach churned, but she continued in the same, lightly distant, tone: 'You'll be anxious to see your family, I expect. Your stepmother must be waiting . . .' She nearly choked, but swallowed just in time. 'And, of course, there'll be the balls and parties.'

She continued to enter the figures she'd been transferring from scraps of paper into a ledger – and didn't look up. She didn't dare – if she did, the tears she was holding back would spill over, and then he would know.

Know what he mustn't. Know that she didn't want him to go – that she wanted him here, forever by her side.

But she'd thought it all through very carefully; she had to – absolutely had to – leave him free to leave her. There was no point in binding him to her – to the vale – with ties that would only be resented.

If she could have, she would have stopped herself from falling in love with him, from being in love with him, but it was far too late for that. Even knowing he was leaving, she still couldn't help but wish that she had been the one to change him – the one to focus all his inherent, unconscious qualities – his innate care, his protectiveness, his absentminded kindness – so he became the man he could be.

Her consort.

The Lady had been right – he was made for the position – the real position – but no one could force him to take it. That was a decision he had to make himself, and she couldn't interfere. She had to let him go.

And hope, and pray, that one day he might want what she could give him.

'It must be quite grand,' she said, determined to make it easy for him, and easier, therefore, for her, 'being in London with all the swells, going to all the balls and parties.'

She felt his gaze leave her; a moment of silence ensued. Then he shifted. 'Indeed.'

She looked up, but he merely inclined his head, his lips lightly curving, and didn't meet her eyes. 'I daresay I'll enjoy the balls and parties.'

He turned from her and strolled, languid as ever, from the room. Catriona stared at his back, then stared at the door when he closed it behind him. And wondered at his tone, wondered whether her own sensitivity had made her imagine a deep bleakness behind his words.

He'd tried a last throw of the dice – and lost. More than he'd known he had bet.

She had told him there was nothing for him here – and he had to accept her decision. And if he'd needed any urging to leave the field of his defeat, her lightly distant tone as she'd dismissed him and all but wished him on his way had provided it.

Richard didn't know how they had come to this – to this brittle state where it took effort to remain in each other's company. He didn't know – he couldn't imagine – he couldn't even think straight. He couldn't even breathe freely; there was an iron vise locked about his lower chest – every breath was a battle.

How they would get through the night, he hadn't any idea. For the first time since they had married, she was later to bed than he. He waited in the dimness, lit only by the dying fire, and wondered if she really was tending the recently born child and its mother or . . . avoiding him.

It was nearly midnight before the door opened; she glanced at the bed only fleetingly, then went to the fire. Richard nearly spoke – nearly called to her – but couldn't think of what to say.

Then he realized she didn't intend sleeping in the armchair; she was simply undressing before the fire.

He watched her – hungrily. Let his eyes feast on her neatly rounded limbs, her skin pearlescent in the fire's flickering light. Drank in the sight of her back, the sleek planes achingly familiar, the globes of her bottom a remembered delight. He stared at her long fire-gold mane as she shook it out, spreading it over her shoulders, as if he could burn the sight into his mind.

Then lost what little breath he had when she turned and, naked – with that glorious unconsciousness she'd displayed from the first – walked to the bed. To where he lay waiting in the dark.

He tensed – expecting her to be tense, too – expecting her to hold herself distantly as she had all day. Instead, she lifted the covers, slid beneath – and slid farther, straight into his arms.

For one moment, his heart stood still, then his arms closed about her. She lifted her lips – he hesitated for only a second before he took them.

Took her – took her mouth as she offered it, took her body as she freely gave it.

If he could have thought, he might have seized the opportunity to ruthlessly, calculatingly, tie her to him with passion – to make her burn so achingly long, so excruciatingly hot, that she would never be able to bid him adieu. Or if she did, would suffer tortures every night without him.

He didn't think – but yet he did. Loved her with such passion, such distilled, poignant force, that she cried. Cried tears of sheer delight, of bliss too great to contain.

All he wanted was to fill his mind, his senses, his heart and soul with her – so inside, she would always be with him.

As he, wherever he was, would, in his mind, always – ever more – be with her.

Beneath him, Catriona clung to him, opened her body and heart to him, knowing full well this might be the last time. If she could have held him with sheer lust she would have – she burned with her need of him and was too desperate to hide it. Desire, unleashed, gave her strength – strength to challenge him on a field that had hitherto been his. Stroked and caressed and loved to flashpoint, still she urged him on – pushed him back and pressed her own wild caresses on him, placed hot, open-mouthed kisses all over his hard body, then, driven by her wildness, took him into her mouth.

And felt the shudder that racked him, the bone deep groan she drew from him.

She loved him with abandon, with her heart, with her soul. Until he, his hands sunk in her hair, helplessly guiding her, suddenly clutched and drew her away. Suddenly sat up, suddenly swung behind her.

And entered her from behind.

Her gasp hung like spun silver in the dark; she arched, clamping tightly about him – he pushed her down, and thrust deeper.

Ultimately, he was stronger – much stronger – than she.

He held her down and raced her straight up the mountain and into earth-shattering delight. Then waited only until her senses were hers again before pressing her on, up the next slope.

Through the dark hours he loved her as he would, and she was his willing slave. She wanted to be everything to him, so she gave all he asked, and offered more.

And he took. He drank from her until she thought she would die, then filled her relentlessly until she did. Until her senses were consumed in a blaze of glory, and she shattered beneath him.

They came together again and again, until there was nothing between them. No space, no feeling, no sense of separate existence. They became, in the dead of that night, one soul melded from the fusion of two.

The final end, when it came, shattered them both, but not even the force of that implosion could undo what the night had wrought.


Richard's return to life – to reality – was a slow, bitter journey.

He couldn't conceive how she could be as she was – so totally abandoned in his arms, yet quite prepared, come the time, to smile sweetly and wave him good-bye.

Lips twisting in bitter self-deprecation, he accepted that he had to have been wrong – that despite his expertise in this theatre, she was an exception. A woman who could love with her heart and soul, without, in fact, loving at all.

He was, it seemed, just like Thunderer – a stud whose physical attributes she appreciated.

She was wrapped half-about him, lying in his arms; he lifted his head and looked at her face, only barely discernible in the dark. She was still on her way back from heaven – he could tell by the lack of tension in her limbs. Lying back again, he waited for her to return to the living. And him.

When she did, however, she simply murmured sleepily and snuggled down, her head on his shoulder, her arm over his chest, one thigh intimately wedged between his.

244

Richard frowned. 'I'll be leaving in the morning.'

Catriona heard the words – words she'd been expecting – and felt them in her heart. She'd already heard from her staff of the packing and carriage arrangements. She hesitated for as long as she dared, while frantically wondering what he expected her to say. 'I know,' she eventually murmured.

The hard body beneath her stiffened fractionally, then, after a second, eased. His chest swelled.

'Well,' he said, his tone light but grating, 'I suppose there really isn't anything more you need from me, now – at least, not for some time.'

He paused; when, bewildered, she said nothing, he continued: 'Now you have the child The Lady told you to get from me.'

His bitterness rang clearly; bowing her head, biting her lower lip, Catriona accepted it.

She should have told him.

'I . . .' How to tell him it had slipped her mind? 'Forgot.' She rushed on. 'It's just that I've been so . . .'

'Busy?'

So caught up with *him*. Her temper flashed – a weak flame, but enough to sour her. She'd been so focused on him, she'd totally forgotten the one thing, the one being, that should have been at the center of her consciousness. If she'd needed any proof of how totally obsessed with him she was, how he completely overshadowed everything else in her life, she had it now.

She couldn't think of any response to his rejoinder, so she let it pass. Slowly, she drew her limbs from his and turned away.

Only to be swept by a desolate bleakness, a bone-deep sense of loss. They'd been cheated. A moment that should have been so special, so joyful and filled with love, had instead been soured by hurt and bitterness.

She closed her eyes and tried to sleep; beside her, Richard did the same.

Disillusionment followed them into troubled dreams.

The next day dawned clear, with a brisk breeze scudding clouds over a pale blue sky – a morning bright with the promise of a new season. Perfect for traveling.

Catriona noted the signs from the top of the manor steps and struggled to reconcile them with the heaviness in her heart.

She would normally have gone to pray this morning, but had changed her mind. It was the first time in her life she'd put something else higher than her devotions to The Lady, but she couldn't deny herself her last sight of Richard. It would have to tide her over, probably for months. Possibly until their child was born. And maybe even longer.

Before her, her people scurried to secure the last of Richard's trunks to the carriage roof – he'd left some things behind, for which she was more pathetically grateful than she would ever let anyone know. They would be her only physical link with him in the coming months.

Blinking back the prickling heat behind her lids, she watched the horses – Richard's handsome greys – led up. Her people, unaware of any undercurrents – not, indeed, the sort of folk who were at all susceptible to such subtleties – threw themselves into the final preparations with innocent energy. They simply imagined this was how it was supposed to be; their trust in The Lady – and in her – was complete. The only member of staff who seemed at all put out was, of all people, Worboys. Catriona studied his long face, and wondered, but could reach no conclusion.

Then Richard appeared from the direction of the stables, where he'd gone to bid Thunderer good-bye. He strode across the cobbles, his greatcoat flapping about his gleaming

Hessians. He was immaculately dressed as always; as he paused to give orders to the grooms harnessing his greys, Catriona drank in the sight.

Drank in the faintly bored, distant expression on his face, the easy air of ineffable superiority that was so innate a part of him.

He turned and saw her, hesitated, then strode toward her; Catriona looked her fill. To her, he was, quite simply, gorgeous – the most fascinating man she'd ever met.

He was also the eptiome of a bored and restless rake shaking the dust of a too-quiet backwater and an unwanted wife from his highly polished boots. That fact was declared in the hard planes of his face as his eyes met hers, in the cynical set of his lips. Bravely, desperately, holding her cloak of regal assurance in place, Catriona smiled distantly.

'I'll bid you adieu, then. I hope you reach London without mishap.'

She lifted her head and met his hard blue gaze directly; that had been the most difficult speech she'd ever made.

Richard studied her eyes, searched them, for some sign all this was a dream. It felt unreal to him – couldn't she sense it? But even more strong than the sense of unreality was the feeling – the compulsion – of inevitability.

It had seemed inevitable they would marry – he'd accepted that and hoped, in his heart, that from their marriage he would gain the stability he'd sought – he'd needed – for so long. Instead, now, it seemed inevitable he would be disappointed in their union, and would, once again, be footless, unanchored, drifting in life's stream. Unconnected to anyone.

He'd thought – hoped – that their marriage would be his salvation. It appeared he'd been wrong; it was therefore inevitable that he would leave.

Would walk away from his wife and leave her to manage on her own.

247

Uncharacteristic rancor filled him when her eyes gave him no hope, no sign, no encouragement to change his mind and stay. 'I'll leave you then.'

The words echoed with the bitterness he couldn't hide.

She smiled and held out her hand. 'Farewell.'

He looked down, into her eyes, trying to fathom, at the last, what shimmered in the vibrant green depths; he took her hand – and felt her fingers slide into his. Felt the touch of her palm, felt her fingertips quiver. And felt – sensed—

'Here you are, sir!'

They both turned to find Mrs. Broom standing beaming just behind them, virtually between them. She held up a packed basket. 'Cook and me thought as how you'd be grateful of some real sustenance on the road. Better'n that terrible inn food.'

Richard knew for a fact that neither Mrs. Broom nor Cook had ever been to an inn in their lives. It was a measure of how his mind was functioning that that was the only thought he could muster. He felt shaken – and torn – and turned inside out. Taking the basket from Mrs. Broom and summoning a weak smile for her from somewhere, he passed the basket straight to a groom and looked back at Catriona.

Only to see her smile evenly. 'Good-bye.'

For one instant, he hovered on the brink – of refusing to accept her dismissal, of hauling her into his arms and refusing to let her go, of telling her straitly how things would henceforth be between them—

Her steady smile, her steady eyes – and the black cloud of inevitability – stopped him.

Faultlessly correct, he inclined his head, then turned and strolled nonchalantly down the steps.

Catriona watched him go and felt her heart go with him. Knew to the depths of her soul that she would never be the same – be as strong – without him. He paused to speak to his

248

coachman, then entered the carriage without a backward glance. He sat back and Worboys shut the door; the carriage lurched into motion and headed, gathering speed as it went, down the drive and into the park.

Raising a hand in farewell, one he couldn't see, Catriona murmured a benediction. She watched, silent and still at the top of the steps, ignoring the people trooping past her, until the carriage disappeared into the trees.

Then she went inside, but didn't join her household at breakfast. Instead, she climbed to her turret room, opened the window wide – and watched the carriage carrying her husband from her, until it had passed from the vale.

# Chapter Fourteen

'Oh, no!' Catriona focused on the curtains shielding her window through which she could see light seeping, and groaned. It was morning – *late* morning.

Falling back on her pillows, she stared at the canopy; she had meant to go to the circle this morning, to atone for yesterday's absence, but it was too late now. Drawing in a tight breath, she glanced at the bed beside her. It was a disaster of tangled sheets and rumpled covers – just as it had been the morning before. The cause, however, was quite different.

She hadn't been able to sleep; only as night was fading had she fallen into a restless doze. Which hadn't refreshed her in the least, hadn't prepared her for the day ahead.

Yesterday had dragged; nothing had gone right. She was still as far from finding good breeding cattle as she had been two weeks ago. Two months ago, and more. She needed to find some reasonable stock soon, or miss the chance of improving the herd through the coming season's breeding – an opportunity the vale could ill afford to miss.

But that wasn't what had kept her awake.

The empty space beside her had done that.

Forced her into a neverending round of thinking if, perhaps, she'd done something different, he might still be here, a warm weight beside her – the comfort of her heart.

Senseless, useless repetition of their words, her thoughts, her conclusions.

It changed nothing – he was gone.

She sighed, then grimaced, recalling the transparent joy that had transformed Algaria. Ever since Richard had appeared on their horizon, Algaria had been worried, then withdrawn. His departure had more than pleased her – yesterday, she'd been reborn. Yet Catriona was sure he had done nothing to deserve Algaria's censure, or even to rattle her, or confirm her in her views. Other than to be himself.

That, apparently, was enough. Hardly a rational response. Algaria's attitude to Richard now worried her even more than it had. Perhaps there was some deeper purpose behind his leaving, one only The Lady could know.

The possibility didn't make his absence any easier to bear.

The emptiness around her weighed heavily on her heart, making breathing difficult. Dragging in some air, she sat up – and wished she hadn't. For one long instant the room spun, then slowly settled.

Forcing herself to breathe evenly, to concentrate on that, she waited, absolutely still, for the queasiness to pass. She had, it seemed, more misery in store for her than a simple broken heart. When the room had steadied and the hot flush had died, she slowly, carefully stood.

'Wonderful,' she muttered, as she crossed to the washstand. 'Morning sickness as well.'

But she was still the lady of the vale – she had a role to fill, decisions to make, orders to give. She dressed with as much speed as she could muster, then, detouring via the stillroom for some soothing herbs, headed for the dining hall.

Herbal tea and plain toast was the most she could manage – the aromas rising from the plates of others nearly made her gag. She nibbled and sipped, grateful for the warmth of the tea, and tried to ignore, blot out, the smells and sounds around her.

Algaria, of course, noticed. 'You're pale,' she said, beaming brightly.

'I'm *wretched,*' Catriona replied through clenched teeth.

'It's only to be expected.'

Catriona turned and met Algaria's black gaze, then realized Algaria was referring, solely, to the consequences of her pregnancy. Algaria wouldn't accept – or even recognize – that Richard's departure was her principal woe. Looking back at her cup, Catriona gritted her teeth. 'Don't tell anyone – not until I make the announcement.'

'Good heavens – why?' Algaria gestured about them. 'It's important news for the vale and the manor – everyone will be delighted.'

'Everyone will be *unbearable.*' Catriona pressed her lips together, waited for three heartbeats, then, in a more reasonable but still cold tone stated: 'The news is important to me, too. I'll make the announcement when I'm ready. I don't want people fussing over me for any longer than necessary.' In her present state, her temper wouldn't stand it. 'I just want to be left alone to get on with the vale's business.'

Algaria raised a shoulder. 'As you wish. Now, about those decoctions . . .'


She hadn't thought it possible to miss him more than she had last night – but she was wrong.

By the end of the day, as the light faded from the world, Catriona huddled at her desk, fretfully tugging two shawls about her shoulders.

She was cold to her bones – a cold that came from inside and spread insidiously through her. It was the cold of loneliness, a bone-deep chill. Throughout the day, she'd been rubbing her arms; at lunchtime she'd fetched the extra shawl. Nothing helped.

252

Worse, she was finding it hard to concentrate, finding it hard to keep her usual serene mask – the face she habitually wore in public as the lady of the vale – in place. Summoning the brightness to put into her smile when she greeted McArdle and the others was very nearly beyond her. Energy was something she no longer had, not in any quantity.

And she needed energy to make her lips curve, to disguise the deadness inside, but supporting her usual sunny disposition was more than she could do. Unfortunately, being the lady of the vale, she couldn't even invent a fictitious malady to account for her state – she was never ill, not in the general way.

Pushing aside the ledgers she'd been studying – the breeding records for the past three years – she sighed. Leaning back in her chair, she closed her eyes. How was she going to cope?

She lay in the chair in the darkened room and opened her senses. But no help came – no suggestion of how she might manage popped into her tired mind.

When she finally opened her eyes and sat up, the one thing she did feel sure of was that the situation was going to get worse.

Dragging herself to her feet, feeling as if the child she carried was seven months older than it was, she straightened, stacked the ledgers neatly, then, setting her shoulders back, lifting her head high, she headed for the door.


While washing and changing for dinner, she grasped the opportunity to lie down – just for a minute.

One minute turned into thirty; by the time she reached the table, it was late. Out of breath, wanting nothing more than to crawl back into her bed, she smiled serenely about the hall and helped herself to lamb collops.

Then pushed them around and around on her plate.

She felt like slumping; only by maintaining a continuous

253

inner lecture did she manage to preserve her facade. But she couldn't eat – she'd lost her appetite. In an effort to conceal her disinterest in the food, she caught Henderson's eye. 'What have the children been up to today?' In spite of his dour demeanor, Henderson had a soft spot for the manor's brats.

'Seems like the master'd been teaching some of them to ride, so I took them out to the barn.' He grimaced, a depressing sight. 'I'm no great horseman, though. I'm thinking they'll have to wait on his return to polish up their skills.'

'Hmm.' Not wanting to dwell on how long the children might have to wait, Catriona looked along the table at Mrs. Broom and gestured to the steaming apple pie just placed before her, the fruity, spicy aroma much more to her liking than the cold collops a maid had whisked away. 'I congratulate you on your new receipe – the spices add a pleasing tang.'

Mrs. Broom beamed. 'Twas the master suggested it – seems they cook it that way in London town, but it was easy enough to do. Pity he isn't here to enjoy it – he said it was one of his favorites. But we've apples aplenty in the store – I'll make it again when he gets back.'

The smile on her face felt tight; Catriona inclined her head gracefully and turned to McArdle. 'Has Melchett—'

'*Mistress!*'

'Mister Henderson!'

'Come *quickly!*'

With those and other cries, the manor children burst into the hall. They were led, as always, by Tom, Cook's redheaded son. He rushed straight to the main table, his gaze locked on Catriona's face. 'It's the blacksmith's house, mistress. It's burning!'

'Burning?' Rising, Catriona stared down at Tom. 'But . . .' She frowned. 'It can't be.'

Tom bobbed his head urgently. 'It *is,* mistress! Flames leaping into the sky, an' all.'

254

Everyone rushed to see. Wide-eyed, Catriona halted on the back step and saw that Tom hadn't lied. The blacksmith's small house, wedged between the forge and the granary, was alight. Angry red flames licked over the wood and stone building, engulfing it from the rear. Beyond, out of sight behind the house, lay open pigpens, presently empty.

As they watched, the flames caught better hold and roared, throwing red sparks high.

Within seconds, the stable yard was a scene of confusion. Pandemonium reigned. People ran this way, then that, bumping into each other and cursing, some running to fetch pails others had already grabbed.

Dragging in a breath, Catriona lifted her head. 'Henderson – you and the stablelads to the pump. Huggins, check the stable. Irons, where are you?'

The big blacksmith, a dripping pail in his hand, raised his arm. 'Here, ma'am.'

'You and all the men start dousing the fire.'

'Aye, ma'am.'

'All the women – into the kitchens. Grab whatever will hold most water.'

They streamed past her; she heard the clatter as the huge pots and pans were collected. They all helped, even Algaria – a deep jam pot gripped tightly, she flung water onto the burning building.

Down on the cobbles, her face lit by the garish glow, Catriona monitored their frantic efforts. Huggins came puffing up. 'The horses and animals are well enough – I've left two lads with them.'

Her eyes on the flames rising above the cottage, then fanning over to embrace it from behind, Catriona grabbed his arm; she had to scream for him to hear. 'Take half the men and start throwing water onto the back. That's where the source is.'

Huggins nodded and went. Catriona coughed as billowing smoke gripped her throat. Turning, she surveyed the yard – there was a large crowd waiting, buckets, pails, pots and pans in hand, around the pump. It wasn't hard to guess the problem. The roads had cleared, but it was a long way from spring – the main snows on Merrick had yet to melt, so the river was still at its winter ebb. Only a gentle gush came up through the pump, enough for daily needs, but not enough to fight a fire.

A hot roar at her back had Catriona whirling; she backed as heat hit her like a surging wave.

Sparks and cinders rained down – a real danger for those running close to throw their precious water on the fire. Then came a loud *crack!* – a beam exploded; flaming debris showered down, driving everyone back.

Gasping, Catriona found herself cowering protectively over Tom. 'Blankets!' Tom looked up at her – she shook his shoulder. 'We need blankets to beat out the sparks. Get the others and fetch the horse blankets from the tack room.'

Tom nodded and fled, shrieking through the din for his cohorts to follow him. They did, an unruly band streaking for the stables. They returned in double time, staggering under the weight of the heavy blankets balanced across their arms. Catriona grabbed one and started beating out the flaming cinders. Other women saw and did the same.

Huggins and his band had reached the back of the house; Catriona heard them bellowing for more help. Brushing the back of her hand over her flushed forehead, she looked around. 'Jem, Joshua! – take your pails to the back.'

They nodded and changed course around the side of the forge.

In the yard, everyone redoubled their efforts, trying to fill the gaps left by those who'd gone to the other front. But the pump would yield only so much. Glancing back through the swirling smoke, Catriona saw Irons had stripped off his shirt and was now bending his back to the pump handle. Henderson was slumped, wheezing, on the water trough – now empty.

'Lady!'

Catriona turned at the tug on her sleeve. Huggins, doubled over and panting, struggling to catch his breath, grimaced up at her.

''Twas the woodpile behind the house – that's where it started.' He paused to drag in another breath, his eyes going to the fiercely burning cottage. 'We can douse the pile, but it's almost ashes now. But that won't stop it. The flames have got a good hold on the back wall, particularly on those big lintel beams across the back.'

Following his nod, Catriona stared at the huge wooden beams that crossed the cottage, one above the door and window, separating the ground floor from the first, and the other above the first floor, supporting the roof timbers. Matching beams spanned the back.

'It's going to go.' Huggins shook his head and slumped forward again. 'We can't reach those big beams, and we haven't got enough water even if we could. It's an inferno, up there.'

Catriona stared at the greedy flames, then dragged in a huge breath. She coughed and took a firm grip on her wits. And ignored the fright licking at her nerves. 'All right.' She squeezed Huggins's arm, sending him a little of her hard-won calm. 'Tell your men to concentrate on saving the granary and the forge.' She hesitated, then added: 'The granary first if a choice has to be made.'

They couldn't afford to lose the grain and other foodstuffs stored in the granary, their larder for the rest of the winter.

Huggins nodded his understanding and stumbled away to issue her orders. Catriona took one last look at the fiercely burning cottage and went to find Irons. She found him slumped by the pump; Henderson was manning it again. Grim-faced, his gaze on his burning home, Irons heard her out, then, with a pain-filled grimace, nodded.

'Aye.' With an effort, he hauled himself to his feet. 'You be right. Cottage can be replaced – granary, and what's in it, can't.'

He started bellowing orders himself; Catriona rushed forward once more to take charge close to the house, instructing the waterbearers where to fling their loads.

Her voice hoarse and fading, she grabbed a pot from a maid hard of hearing and showed her where to throw it – at the junction between the walls of the cottage and the granary. Handing the empty pot back to the woman, she paused, wiping the sweat from her brow, trying not to notice the heat washing over her—

She heard a cry.

Not from the yard, but from the cottage.

She stared at the building, the rough stone between the burning beams glowing pink – and told herself she'd imagined it. Prayed she'd imagined it.

But it came again, a whimpering wail that died beneath the flames' roar.

'Oh, *Lady!*' Hand to her mouth, Catriona whirled and searched the host of scurrying women for the blacksmith's wife. And found her, frantically grabbing the older manor children, having to peer through the soot and grime covering their faces to recognize her own. As Catriona watched, the woman grabbed one girl close, hand gripping the slender shoulder like a claw – she saw the woman scream her question, saw the girl shake her head, her own features changing into a mirror of her mother's horror. Then both mother and daughter looked straight at the burning house.

Catriona didn't hesitate. She grabbed a horse blanket from one of the weary beaters and flung it over her head and shoul-

258

ders. Then she lunged for the closed door of the cottage.

She forced it open, and stepped through—

The flames roared – a wall of heat beat her back.

She staggered and nearly fell; cries and screams from all around filled her ears. Sure of the whimper she'd heard under the roar, she tightened her grip on the blanket and gathered her courage to step forward once more.

Before she could, she was bodily lifted and unceremoniously dumped on her feet ten feet back from where she'd stood. *'Damn, stupid woman!'* was the mildest of the oaths that rang in her ears.

To her stunned amazement, Richard grabbed the singed blanket from her. Then threw it about his head and shoulders and plunged into the cottage himself.

*'Richard!'* Catriona heard her own scream, saw her hands reach out, grasping, trying to catch him to hold him back – but he was already gone.

Into the flames.

Others ran to her and gathered about, their eyes, like hers, glued to the open doorway. They waited, tense, on their toes, ready to dash closer at the slightest sign.

The heat held them were they were. Waiting. Hoping. Praying.

Catriona prayed the hardest – she'd seen the inside of the cottage. Raging inferno didn't come close to describing it – the whole back wall and the ceiling were a mass of hot, searing flames.

Everyone in the yard fell silent, all gripped by the drama. Into the sudden, unnatural silence came a loud, prolonged creak.

Then the main beam beneath the front of the roof exploded.

Before their horrified eyes, it cracked, once, then again, flames spitting victoriously through the gaps.

A second later, the lower beam, between the ground and

upper floor, groaned mightily.

Then, in a vicious splurge, flames spat around the lintel of the door itself. In split seconds, the wood started to glow.

Richard lunged through the door, staggering – a wrapped bundle in his arms, clinging, crying weakly.

Everyone rushed forward – the blacksmith's wife grabbed her child, Irons grabbed both of them in his huge arms and lifted them away. Catriona, Henderson and two of the grooms grabbed Richard, gasping, coughing, struggling to breathe, and hauled him away from the cottage.

On that instant, with a deep, guttural groan like the dying gasp of a tortured animal, the cottage collapsed. Flames shot high; there was a deafening roar. Then the fire settled to crack and consume its prey.

Bare hands smothering the flames flickering in Richard's hair and along his collar and shoulders, Catriona had no time for the cottage.

Richard was not so distracted.

Staring at the furnace growing beside the forge, he finally managed to catch his breath – finally noticed what she was doing. With an oath, he spun and caught her hands – and saw the telltale burns.

'Damn it, woman – don't you have the sense you were born with!'

Stung, Catriona tried to tug her hands free. 'You were alight!' She glared at him. 'What happened to the blanket?'

'The child needed the protection more than me.' Grabbing a full saucepan from a passing waterbearer, Richard plunged Catriona's hands, gripped in one of his, into the cold water. His face like thunder, he dragged her, her wrists locked in one hand, the other holding the water-filled pan, across to the back doorstep.

He forced her to sit. 'Stay here.' Dumping the pan in her lap, he trapped her gaze. 'Stay the hell out of this – leave it to me.'

'But—'

He swore through his teeth. 'Dammit – which do you think your people – or I – would rather lose – the granary, or you?' He held her gaze, then straightened. 'Just *stay here.*'

Without waiting for an answer, he strode away. Into the directionless melee about the pump.

Within seconds, the women were drifting away, pans and pots in hand, uncertain expressions on their faces, all headed to join Catriona. Among them was Algaria. In answer to Catriona's questioning glance, she coldly lifted a shoulder. 'He said we were more distraction than help – that the men would do better fighting the fire without worrying if their women and children were safe.'

Catriona grimaced; she'd seen more than one of the men stop and hunt through the crowd, or leave their post for a moment to shout orders at their children. The women, as they neared, collected their children as they came. The men, now all gathered about the pump, about Richard, taller than them all, were staring at the burning building, listening intently while Richard pointed and rapidly issued orders.

With a sigh, Catriona lifted her hands from the icy water and studied them. Then she grimaced and put them back into the pot. She looked up at Algaria. 'Can you check the baby for me?'

Algaria raised a brow. 'Of course.' She paused, looking down at Catriona. 'That was a foolish thing to do. A few minor burns could hardly harm his black soul.'

With that, she turned away and glided, like a black crow, into the house; stunned, her wits too shaken to respond quickly, Catriona stared, open-mouthed, after her.

Then she snapped her lips shut, glared briefly, and swung her gaze back to more important things.

As she looked, the group of men dispersed, breaking into teams which rapidly deployed as bucket lines, one to each side of the cottage, and another streaming into the barren gardens, ultimately linking the river with the back of the cottage. Peering through the dark, Catriona could see men filling buckets with snow, still piled in drifts through the gardens, and passing the buckets up the line, accepting empty buckets back. Some of the field workers came hurrying with shovels, the better to shift the snow.

In the yard, two pairs of grooms staggered along, each pair carrying one of the huge loft ladders. Others rushed to help steady the ladders against the walls of the forge and the granary; they were long enough to reach the roofs.

By the time the ladders were in place, the first filled bucket arrived and was quickly carried up the ladder to be poured down the wall between the granary and the cottage.

At the center of the yard, his face set, Richard viewed their combined efforts. He hoped his witch was praying to Her Lady – they were going to need all the help they could get. The main thrust of the flames through the cottage had been via the central beam running forward to back through the roof, supporting secondary beams which in turn had supported the roof struts. They'd all burned, but now the flames were spreading outward from the center of the cottage, in both directions, licking along the timbers and beams ultimately abutting the walls of the granary and forge.

Luckily, both granary and forge were significantly taller than the cottage wedged between; if that hadn't been so, both would have caught alight by now. They had a chance, a slim one, of saving both buildings, each, in different ways, essential to life at the manor.

Richard strode into the action before the cottage, now all but pulsing with flames. Time and again, he swore at grooms or laborers who sent their bucket loads too far from the vital walls. 'We need it where it counts!' he roared up the ladder.

Grasping one bucket, he used his height to send its contents

262

washing over one of the exposed beams in the granary wall. 'That,' he yelled, pointing to the area, 'is where the danger lies.'

One of the dangers.

He kept a sharp eye on the men on the ladders, stepping in to rotate them as they, most exposed to the heat rising from the fire, wilted. And when it seemed they were losing the battle for the forge, he went into the garden, grabbed a spade, strode down to the riverbank, and hacked through the softened ice to the water below, uncaring of the iced slush freezing his boots.

Within seconds, Henderson and one of the older grooms were beside him, helping to widen the hole. Then they were bucketing as fast as human hands could manage, sending pails filled with icy slurry up the gardens. Once the faster rate was established, chest heaving, Richard ran back up the slope, grabbing men as he went, positioning them bodily, too out of breath to speak.

As tired as he, but equally determined, they understood; nodding, they formed another bucketline from the river to the front of the forge.

Running back to the yard, Richard paused before the cottage only to rotate the men on the ladders again, then strode quickly to the pump. 'Faster,' he ordered, as he fetched up beside it. 'We need more.'

Two wilting farmhands looked at him in dismay. 'The river's low – we can't,' one of them stammered.

'Low or not,' Richard growled, physically displacing them, 'faster will still yield more.'

He set a new pump rhythm, half again what it had been. 'Here' – he passed the pump handle back to the farmhands – 'keep it going like that.'

They both looked at his face and didn't dare argue. They pumped. Faster. Richard waited to make sure it was fast enough, then nodded, and glanced at the other four men recovering from their shifts. 'If you need to, rotate more often. But if you value your hides, *don't slow down.*'

Quite what he meant by that, he neither knew nor cared, but the threat had the desired effect. The group manning the pump lifted their effort and sustained it – long enough to make the vital difference.

On the back step, leaning against the wall, her hands still in the pot of water, Catriona watched it all – the fight to save the manor's buildings. Watched Richard exhort the men to greater efforts, watched him instill his own determination into them. Watched him form them into a coherent force, then direct it at the enemy in the most effective way. Watched him whip them up when they were flagging, when the flames seemed poised to gain the upper hand. Saw them respond, meeting every demand he made of them.

She'd sent the other women and all the children inside, given orders for food to be prepared, for water to be heated. Done all she could to support the effort he was making for her – for them.

Eventually, they won. The flames, denied any hold on the neighboring buildings, spluttered, faded, then died, leaving the cottage a smoldering ruin of glowing embers and charred wood.

They were exhausted.

Richard started sending the men in, the oldest and weakest first, keeping the strongest with him to finish damping down the scene. At the last, when only wisps of smoke and an acrid stench rose from the building, he and Irons hefted grappling hooks, swung them about the ends of the big beams – and brought the whole structure crashing down.

Henderson, Huggins and the handful of grooms still standing used pitchforks to drag, poke and prod the smoldering remains about the yard, spreading them to minimize any chance of fresh fire.

With heavy axes, Richard and Irons weighed into what was left of the cottage, one from either side. By the time they'd finished, there were no contacts remaining between what had been the cottage and either the forge or the granary.

The buildings were secure.

Heaving a huge sigh, Richard leaned on the axe and cast a long look over the scene. Irons came to stand beside him, his axe on his shoulder. Richard glanced at his face. 'We'll build it again, although not, I think, just there.'

'Aye.' Irons scratched his chin. ''Twasn't wise, seemingly. The woodpile at the back didn't help, neither.'

'Indeed not.' Richard sighed as he straightened. And made a mental note to check where the manor's main woodpile was located. He couldn't remember seeing it; it might well be against the back of the granary. Or the stables. 'Seasoned wood should be stored away from farm buildings – we'll need to build another shelter farther back.'

'Aye, 'twould be silly not to learn the lessons The Lady sends us.' Irons straightened and looked directly at Richard as he held out his hamlike hand for the axe. 'I'm in your debt.'

Richard smiled wearily; he clapped Iron's broad shoulder as he handed over the axe. 'Thank The Lady.' He turned away. Lifting his head, he saw Catriona waiting – and murmured, 'This is what I'm here for.'

They gathered in the aftermath in the dining hall. All were weary, but too keyed up to rest; the effect of what they'd faced had yet to leave them.

Richard took his seat by Catriona's side at the main table and gratefully helped himself to the thick stew and fresh bread Cook and her helpers had labored to provide. A thirty-six-course meal at Prinny's Brighton monstrosity could not possibly have tasted better. Or been more appreciated. Conversation was minimal as both men and women ate, children – all safe – balanced in their laps.

It was Henderson who, as empty plates were cleared and maids hurried to place round cheeses on the tables, voiced the common thought.

'Odd thing, that fire.'

Huggins, at the near end of one of the other tables, nodded. 'Can't see how it started, myself.'

They all looked at Richard. Lounging in his chair, pushed back from the table, with one hand idly resting, unconsciously possessive, on the back of Catriona's chair, he returned their gazes steadily. Then he looked around the room. 'Does anyone know of any possible cause?'

Heads shook on all sides.

'Never seen anything like it in all my years,' McArdle huffed.

'It was all well-seasoned wood – once lit, it *would* burn. What I can't understand,' Richard said, 'is how and why it caught alight.'

'Aye, there's the mystery.' Henderson nodded dourly.

'Midwinter – admittedly it's been dry. And that wood was all under shelter. But ...'

Richard met his eye. 'Precisely. *But* ... something must have touched spark to the tinder.'

'Aye, but what?'

It was a question no one could answer. They batted it back and forth, until Richard, glancing at Catriona, caught her straightening, caught her in the act of drawing on her reserves to preserve her outward facade. Noting the dark shadows beneath her eyes, the incipient haggardness in her face, he swore beneath his breath and turned back to the others. 'Enough. We're merely speculating. Let's sleep on it and see what tomorrow reveals.'

All nodded. Many of the household had already dragged their weary bodies from the hall. Without waiting for the others, Richard placed a hand beneath Catriona's elbow and rose, lifting her to her feet beside him.

She blinked, dazed and weary, up at him; jaw setting, Richard denied the impulse to sweep her up in his arms and instead calmly supported her from the dais and into the front hall. Once out of sight of the others, he slid one arm around her; supporting her against him, he steered her up the stairs.

To their bedchamber. He halted before the door, for the first time in his life, not entirely certain of his footing. His welcome. He glanced down at Catriona; she met his gaze – when he didn't open the door, she frowned.

'What is it?'

The same question he'd asked her – the one she'd refused to answer. Richard held her gaze and fought against the compulsion to make the same mistake. 'I . . .' He paused, then went on: 'Perhaps I'd better find a bed elsewhere.'

The frown in her eyes grew. 'Why? This is our room.' Her tone was entirely uncomprehending. Before he could say more, she set the door wide, then glided through; fingers clutching his sooty sleeve, she towed him, unresisting, behind her.

He shut the door. 'Catriona—'

'Our clothes are ruined.' She looked down at her filthy gown, then turned and looked at him. 'And we both need a bath. And your hair needs cutting – it's badly singed at the back. Come on.'

She tugged; inwardly sighing, Richard acquiesced. Her eyes were still wide, their expression dazed – he knew shock when he saw it, heard it.

He followed her into the small bathing chamber that gave off their room. A welcome surprise awaited them – some kind souls had slipped upstairs while they were discussing the fire and half-filled the large tub with hot water, now cooled to warm, and set metal pails of steaming water in the hearth where the blaze, stoked high, kept them hot.

'Oh.' Catriona stopped and stared.

Richard glanced at her face, then drew up a bathing stool to one side of the fire and sat her upon it. Then he picked up a towel, wrapped it around the handle of one pail, and added it to the tub. After adding all the pails but two, he tested the water; it was perfect, hot but not scorching, just right for easing chilled and tired muscles.

Returning to Catriona, he took her hands and drew her to her feet. She immediately started to unbutton his waistcoat. He sighed and shrugged out of his ruined coats. Once she was absorbed with the buttons on his shirt, he reached around her and tugged her laces free. She didn't notice until he loosened the neckline and started to draw her gown down over her arms.

'No.' She tried to tug it up again. 'You first.'

'No,' Richard said, calmly, soothingly. 'Both together.'

She paused, then looked at the tub; he quickly drew her gown down and freed her hands. She sighed and stepped out of the puddled cambric and kicked it to join his coats. 'I suppose we'll fit.'

They did, very comfortably. Just before she joined him in the blissfully hot water, Catriona went to a shelf and selected a jar, then returned to sprinkle its contents into the tub. Richard, surfacing from rinsing his hair, tensed as crystals hissed in the water, then relaxed as a delicious herbal scent filled the room.

After returning the jar to the shelf, Catriona stepped into the tub and sank down opposite him, then picked up the flannel. 'Turn around.' She gestured with her hand. 'I'll scrub your back.'

Richard complied; he closed his eyes in bliss as she scrubbed and kneaded the stiff muscles. She worked over his shoulders and upper back, then reached below the water.

He heard her hiss – an indrawn hiss of pain. Swinging around, he saw her shake her hand; he caught it – and saw the burned palm. What he said made her wince more.

'Lie back! Rest your hands on the edge.' He took the flannel from her and quickly finished his own ablutions, then found the bar of soap she preferred – a tantalizing mix of summer flowers, the scent she always bore – and lathered the flannel.

And proceeded, ignoring her weak complaints, to wash her.

Catriona tried to struggle, then surrendered. She was in shock and she knew it – the shock of the fire – the shock of his totally unexpected return. The shock of seeing him plunge into the burning building, relief at his safe return. The horror of seeing flames licking his hair, the pain of her burned palms. She didn't know what she thought – she didn't know how she should respond, how she should react to any of it.

All she could do was flow with the tide, close her eyes and accept his ministrations, the steady, unhurried sweep of the flannel over her skin.

He was very thorough. Setting her legs wide apart, he sat between; he started with her face, caressing it gently, then laved her neck, then moved on to her shoulders, then extended each arm to lovingly cleanse it, all the way to her fingertips, carefully avoiding her raw palms. Leaving her hands propped on the tub's edge, he reached around her and stroked her shoulders, then the long planes of her back, the curves of her hips, the globes of her bottom in long lazy sweeps, lifting her easily in the water. Setting her down again, he reached for the soap.

From under heavy lids, she studied his face; his expression was deeply calm, like the surface of a fathomless pool. Calm was usually her province, but in the fright and flurry of the evening, she'd misplaced her inherent serenity. She'd lost her calm – but he'd found his. Or, she silently amended, could show his. He wasn't wearing any mask, any social cloak – this was as he was. The warrior who was most at home on the battlefield, in the heart of the fury – that was where he was most at ease. Where he was calmest.

Opening her weary senses, she closed her eyes and shamelessly drank in his calm, and felt it ease her. Let him press calm on her with every smooth caress of the soapy flannel as he gently, lovingly, washed her breasts, her waist, her gently rounded stomach. He moved steadily down, slowly, soothingly, washing every inch of her; by the time he reached her toes, she was floating on a warm tide.

She felt the water shift as he discarded the flannel, then he gripped her wrists and drew her up. Drew her toward him, lifted her so she sat on his thighs, her legs instinctively wrapping around his waist. Her forearms sliding over his shoulders, she blinked her eyes wide as his arms closed around her and his lips found hers.

He kissed her gently, her wet breasts pressed to his wet chest, a thin layer of water sliding between their warmed bodies. Despite their aroused state, it was a soothing kiss. She kissed him back, in the same vein, simply grateful to feel his achingly familiar lips on hers.

Then he rose, lifting her with him; her legs slid down and she was standing beside him. He reached for one of the pails left waiting and rinsed her, then repeated the performance on himself, using the last pail. She went to clamber out, but he was before her. He closed his hands about her waist and lifted her clear, setting her feet on the thick towel laid before the hearth. She accepted the towel he handed her gratefully, and ignored, as best she could, the flush that turned her skin a delicate rose, and the more pointed evidence of his arousal.

Revived, she quickly dried herself, then helped him mop his broad back. Standing behind him, she considered, then swiftly looped the towel around his hips and anchored it. 'Sit,' she said, prodding him toward the stool. 'I want to neaten your hair.'

He turned and looked at her with that unfathomable calm in his eyes, but consented to sit. She found a comb and scissors, and started snipping, removing the burnt and singed locks. Then she reached to brush the clipping from his shoulders, stopped, and peered. 'You've got burns across your shoulders!'

He wriggled them. 'Only minor ones.'

'Humph! Well you can sit there a minute more while I salve them.' She fetched the right pot from her supplies on the shelf; luckily, her fingers weren't burned, only her palms. She could grip things, could spread and knead; she carefully worked the salve into his burns. Then she stood back and surveyed his back more carefully.

'If you've finished soothing those burns, I have another burning part of my anatomy awaiting your attention.'

The gravelly comment jerked her upright. 'Yes, well.' Quickly, she replaced the pot on the shelf. Half turning, she gestured to the bedchamber. 'Come to bed, then.'

His gaze fastened on her hand as he stood. 'One moment.'

He caught her hand, and inspected the raw redness. He swore, glared at her, then towed her back to the shelf. 'Where's that salve?'

'My hands will be all right.'

'Ah-ha!'

Catriona frowned as he lifted the pot down. 'What happened to your burning anatomy?'

'I can suffer a few minutes more. Hold out your hands.'

Trapped between him and the door, she had to comply. 'This is quite unnecessary.'

He glanced at her briefly. 'All healers are supposed to be terrible patients.'

271

She humphed, but held her tongue, surprised to find how cool and soothing the salve felt on her scorched flesh. She studied her palms while he returned the pot to the shelf. His left hand appeared; he grasped her right wrist and tugged forward. She stepped forward and looked up – and stubbed her nose on his back. 'What ...?'

For answer, he clamped her right forearm beneath his right arm – tight as a vise. She pushed against his back; it was like pushing a mountain. 'What are you doing?'

On the words, she felt the soft touch of gauze; she whipped her head around and scanned the shelf – the roll of gauze bandage she kept there was missing.

'Richard!' She tried to wriggle and accomplished nothing. The gauze wound steadily about her hand. She glared at his back. 'Stop it!'

He didn't. He was surprisingly deft; when he released her hand, she found herself staring at a perfectly neat bandage, secured by a tight knot. He reached for her other hand—

'No!' She danced back, hiding it behind her.

'Yes!' He stepped forward.

'*I'm* the healer!'

'You're a stubborn witch.'

*He* was unstoppable; despite her protests, despite her active resistance, her left hand, too, was carefully wrapped in gauze, so her fingers were locked together with only her fingertips protruding. Defeated, she stared, first at one mittened hand, then the other. 'What ...? How ...?

'There's nothing you need do until morning – that'll give the salve a chance to sink in.'

She narrowed her eyes at him.

'Come here. You have ashes in your hair.'

He pulled her to the stool; resigned, she sank down and stared at the flames as, standing behind her, he pulled out her pins, searching through the wild mass her hair had become to find them. He shook the long tresses out, then fetched her brush from her dressing table and proceeded to brush out her hair.

'Thank God – or The Lady – there are no burned or singed locks. No thanks, however, to you.'

Catriona wisely kept mum and concentrated on the tug of the brush through her long hair, on the soothing, repetitive rhythm. The flames in the hearth burned strongly; she closed her eyes and felt their warmth on her lids, on her naked breasts. With him behind her and the fire before her, she felt secure and warm. Her senses spread, sure and calm; about her, her world had steadied.

'I didn't expect you back – I thought I was dreaming when you appeared in the yard.' She made the statement calmly, leaving it to him to respond if he would.

His eyes on the burnished flame of her hair, rippling and glowing beneath each stroke of the brush, Richard drew in a slow breath, then replied: 'I got as far as Carlisle. We spent the night there, and I decided I'd made a mistake. I didn't want to go to London – I never did.' There was nothing south of the border for him now. He paused, then brushed on. 'And if I'd needed any prompting, discovering this morning that, after my arrival at the inn last night, Dougal Douglas had been inquiring after who I was and where I was headed, clari?ed the position nicely.'

'Douglas?'

'Hmm. He lives near there and was in the town when I drove in. He quizzed the ostlers, then made the mistake of approaching Jessup late that night in the tap. Jessup reported his questioning to me this morning.'

'And that brought you back?'

Lips compressing, Richard held back the impulse to agree. After three long strokes, he managed to get the truth out. 'I'd already decided to return, but the notion that Douglas knew

273

I'd left the vale, leaving you, in his terms, alone, made me hire a horse and ride. I left Worboys and Jessup to follow with the carriage.'

'I didn't hear or see you ride in.'

'No one did. You were all engrossed with the fire.' He gave the lock he was holding an extra tug. 'With running into a burning building.'

She didn't respond. He brushed on, steadily removing flecks of ash from her bright mane. Under the brush, her hair came alive in his hands, like living fire. Warm, fragrant, gentle fire.

'Will you be staying?'

There were times, Richard decided, when he definitely did not appreciate being married to a witch. To a woman who could hold her demeanor to the calm and serene regardless of her true feelings. He never could tell what she really felt. Her question – surely one of the most vital facing them – had been couched as the most politely distant, totally innocent, query. Which, he decided, after all they'd shared, was too much to accept.

Frowning, he stared at the back of her glossy head. '*That* depends on you.'

She clearly expected him to sleep with her – while in this house, he was still, quite obviously, to her, her husband. But what were the boundaries of his role in her eyes? – *that* was something he didn't know, something he needed to find out. Something they needed to discuss.

Abruptly, he stopped brushing. Grasping her shoulders, he drew her around on the stool, then hunkered down before her, so his eyes were level with hers. 'Do you want me to stay?'

Catriona searched his eyes – desperately. They viewed her steadily, but told her nothing. 'Yes – if you wish to. I mean ...' Dragging in a breath, her gaze locked with his, she rattled on: 'If you wished to stay I would be pleased, but I

274

don't want you to think that you must – that I'd be *expecting* you to remain here always ... or, or ... *resenting* ...' She gestured vaguely.

Impatiently, lips thinning, Richard shook his head. 'That's not what I asked.' He trapped her gaze and held it ruthlessly. 'Do you *want* me to stay?'

Wide-eyed, Catriona tried another gesture. 'Well! We're man and wife ... I thought ... that is, I imagined it was customary—'

'No!' He closed his eyes; his jaw set. Through set teeth he said: 'Catriona, please tell me – do you wish me to stay?'

He opened his eyes – his irate gaze pinned her.

Catriona glared. 'Well, of *course,* I want you to stay!' Wildly, she waved her bandaged hands. 'I can't even sleep when you're not here! I feel utterly wretched when you're not by. And how on earth I'm supposed to get on if you're not here I don't know—' She broke off as tears filled her eyes.

Richard saw them; the breath trapped in his chest abruptly released in a huge sigh of relief – he reached out, grabbed her, wrapped his arms about her, and buried his face in her hair. And breathed deeply, inhaling the scent he'd so missed the previous night. 'Then I'll stay.'

After a long, silent moment, she sniffed, and softened in his arms. 'You will?'

'Forever.' Lifting his head, he brushed her hair from her face and kissed her. Long and lingeringly. 'Come to bed.'

Her lids lifted; she met his gaze. 'Bed?'

Richard grimaced. 'Your hands are hurt, remember.' He stood, simultaneously lifting her into his arms. He lost his towel in the process; neither of them cared. He carried her to the bed, laid her down gently, freeing her hair, spreading it over the pillows, then, holding her wrists so she wouldn't forget in her passion and harm them, he covered her.

She'd cooled, but when he pressed into her she arched,

then arched again and took him in. He settled within her, then drank her soft gasp when he drew back and thrust deep. Three thrusts later, she wriggled beneath him, tilting her hips to better receive him, lifting her legs and clasping his flanks – welcoming him in, holding him to her. Loving him.

Richard slowed, wallowing in the glory, in the intimate caresses she pressed on him. He bent his head and kissed her – she drew him deep there as well.

And so they loved – now slow, then faster, then slow again when the compulsion to savor the moment came upon them. Their bodies shifted and flexed in a dance older than time, hard pressing soft, rough rasping smooth. They lost track of time, of the world about them, of the night beyond their bed. The only things that mattered were each other's pleasure and the soft murmurs of contentment they shared.

And when the spinning stars finally crashed down upon them and took them from the world, they were together, as one, much more deeply than before.

Much more wedded than before.

Sunk deep in her softness, collapsed upon her, Richard's last thought was: At long last, he'd found his home.

Later, in the untrammeled depths of the night, held securely in Richard's arms yet still drifting in a sated sea, Catriona recalled her first sensing of him, recalled his hot hunger – his lustful desire – and his restless longing. She remembered very well that restlessness in his soul, his deep-seated need to belong. She could, she now knew, satisfy his lustful hunger – she could fulfill his other need, too. And thus anchor him here, by her side, satisfied with what she could give him.

She could be his cause, become his life's purpose.

Her initial reading of him, that, quite aside from his strengths, he bore a wound which needed her healer's touch, had been accurate. He did have a deep need for something she could give him – herself, but not just physically; he needed much more than that. He needed her specifically, and that need, even once satisfied, would never die; it would always be a part of him. And if that was so, then if she gave freely, she had no reason to fear losing him.

The only question that remained was how much he understood – whether he would still fight fate – The Lady's will – or accept what she offered him.

She knew he was still awake, still floating in the warm afterglow. She drew in a slow breath, and took her courage in both hands. 'Why did you decide to come back?'

The quiet question hung in the dark, a sweetly tolling bell exhorting the truth.

Richard heard and considered the many answers. He'd returned because of the loneliness that had wracked his soul when, last night, he'd slept without her. Tried to sleep without her – without her warmth beside him, without her silken limbs alongside his, the sound of her breathing, soft and low, echoing in his heart. Tried to sleep without the fragrance of her hair sinking through his senses, anchoring him through the night. He hadn't slept at all.

He'd returned even faster after learning of Dougal Douglas, because of the feeling that had churned in his gut, spurring him back from Carlisle. Because of the dread certainty that he should never have left her.

A certainty transmogrified to fact in that horror-filled moment when, clattering wildly into the yard having seen the flames and smoke through the trees, he'd seen his worst nightmare enacted before him – seen her rush into a burning building.

He wasn't about to deny what he felt for her – the depth of what he felt for her – not ever again. He would have to learn to deal with it, learn how to live with it – and so would she.

Not, however, tonight. They were both far too tired to face such a task.

So he searched for a way to answer, some phrase that encompassed the truth. 'I came back because this is my place.' Turning his head, he pressed a soft kiss to her forehead. 'This is where I belong. With you. By your side.'

Catriona closed her eyes tight – against tears of relief, of joy, and something more besides. That last welled through her, poured through her, glowing brighter than spun gold.

This was where he belonged – here – by her side. She knew it – thank The Lady, he knew it, too.

# Chapter Fifteen

Despite the fire and its aftermath, or, perhaps, because of it, they both slept deeply and awoke early, still in each other's arms. The temptation to celebrate the night and its revelations was strong, but . . .

'I have to go to the circle.' Her head resting on Richard's chest, Catriona pushed at the heavy arm lying possessively over her waist. 'I should have gone two mornings ago - I really must go today.'

'I'll go with you.' The words were out before Richard thought; he quickly amended: 'I'll escort you there - if that's permitted?'

Still trapped under his arm, Catriona wriggled around so she could look into his face. 'You'll ride there with me?'

Somewhat warily - was he committing some witchy solecism? - Richard nodded. 'I'll wait, and ride back with you.'

She searched his eyes, searched his face, then her face transformed, lit by a glorious smile. 'Yes - come. I'd like that.'

It was all she said before scrambling from the bed; Richard followed, bemused. The smiles she kept beaming his way, even when - especially when - she thought he wasn't watching, tugged at his heart and made him smile, too. By the time they clattered out of the yard, she on her mare, he on Thunderer, she was radiant with delight.

He shook his head at her. 'Anyone would think I'd offered to buy you diamonds, not just ride with you to your prayers.'

She laughed – a sound so glorious it shook him – touched her heels to her mare's flanks, and headed across the melting snow.

Richard followed, easing Thunderer up alongside her mare. There was no point racing; the mare's short strides were no match for Thunderer's might. So they raced the wind instead, streaking up the vale in the chill of neardawn, hoofbeats thudding in time with their hearts, breaths steaming as exhilaration overtook them.

Reaching the head of the vale, they slowed; Catriona led the way to an outcropping of rock that formed a natural shelf beside the circle. Sliding from her saddle, she glanced down the vale. The sun was rising in the purple mists beyond the mouth of the vale; the line marking the boundary between night and day, fuzzed by the clouds, advanced, unstoppable, toward them.

'I have to hurry.' Breathless, she glanced up at him as he took her reins, then she threw her arms about him, hugged him wildly, then ran for the entrance to the circle.

It was not a simple circle of trees, but a circular grove, grown dense with the centuries. The shadows within swallowed her up as she ran down the dimly lit path. Richard watched until the flickering light of her hair disappeared, then tethered the horses and found a comfortable rock on which to perch.

He was sitting on a lichen-covered boulder appreciating the sunrise when she came running out of the trees, with such joy suffusing her face that just knowing that he, quite aside from The Lady, had played a part in putting it there, warmed his heart. Smiling, he rose, and caught her as she ran full-tilt into his arms. He hugged her, stole a swift kiss, then tossed her to the mare's saddle.

They rode back through the sun-kissed morning, birdcall ringing about them, the chill lifting as the sun struck through the clouds and brought the landscape alive. Snow still stood in drifts across the fields, but brown now showed as well. Behind them, Merrick was still completely mantled, but below the snows, the earth was stirring. Warming. Returning to life.

As they rode side by side into the morning, Richard couldn't suppress the feeling that he, too, had lived through a dark season and was now emerging into the light.

No longer in any hurry, they ambled about the low hummock that hid the manor from sight. Squinting into the silver disc of the sun, they couldn't see the buildings, but knew they were there.

'Hrroooo.'

Richard reined in, blinking to clear his vision. Before them stood two of the vale's steers, in less than perfect condition. The cattle blinked sad brown eyes at them, then turned and ambled away. Frowning, Richard watched them go.

He had to start somewhere.

'Catriona—'

'I was just thinking—'

She broke off and looked at him; Richard quelled a grimace and gestured for her to go on.

Hands crossed on her saddlebow, she stared toward the manor. 'I was just wondering . . .' She paused; he saw her lips tighten. 'If you stay, will you miss the balls and parties?' Swiftly, she glanced at him. 'We don't have any, you know.'

'Thank heaven – and The Lady, I suspect – for that. I don't give a damn about balls and parties.' Considering the statement, Richard raised his brows. 'In fact, I haven't cared for them for years.' He met Catriona's wide – definitely wondering – gaze and narrowed his eyes. 'And I don't give a damn about the incredibly beautiful ladies who attend such events, either.'

Her eyes searched his, then her lips formed a silent 'Oh' before curving, just a little, at the ends.

Richard fought down an urge to kiss them. 'I'm staying – and you can forget any idea that I'll grow bored. There's plenty to keep me busy here – which brings me to what I wanted to discuss with you. The breeding stock.'

She grimaced and set the mare plodding slowly on. 'I haven't been able to find any source that I consider suitable. Mr. Potts is waiting for – *urging* – my final authority to purchase from his contact at Montrose, but I know it's not right – not what the vale needs.'

Richard drew in a long breath. 'I have a suggestion.' When she looked quickly around at him, he held up a staying hand. 'I know I vowed I wouldn't interfere with how you ran things – with how you managed the vale – so if you want to do something different . . .' Frowning, he paused, then caught her eye, and drew in a deep breath. 'The truth is, your whole situation with livestock badly needs an overhaul. The cattle herd is the most desperate case – they need an immediate injection of good quality stock. But your rams and ewes need weeding out, too, and the dairy herd is only just meeting your needs. You should think of diversifying, too – goats should do well here, and geese. The vale's a reasonably sized holding and while you've managed the crops well, the live-stock could do better.' Deciding he may as well be hanged for a wolf as a lamb, he added: 'And your buildings, fences and shel-ters need repair and in some cases resiting.'

She stared at him, then looked ahead, drew a huge breath and turned back to him.

'I know,' Richard said, before she could speak, 'I prom-ised no interference, so I can work on each problem with you, behind the scenes.'

Catriona frowned and reined in her mare. 'That's not—'

'If you prefer, I can just list my suggestions, and you can take it from there.' Richard halted Thunderer beside her. 'Or if you'd rather, I can talk each matter through with McArdle and the others, and then write to the various dealers in your name and set up the meetings, then you could—'

'Richard!'

He looked at her stonily. 'What?'

'Your vow!' Catriona glared at him. 'I've already *realized* it's senseless to refuse your help with the business side of the vale. While the *spiritual* side of things' – she flung out a hand, encompassing the vale and the circle behind them – 'and all healing matters must be left in my hands, I *need* you to help me with the rest.'

He stared at her unblinkingly. 'You need me?'

Catriona met his gaze directly. 'After last night, you need to ask?'

A long moment passed. 'But you *didn't* want me to help – I asked, and you said you didn't need my assistance.'

Catriona blushed; the mare sidled. 'I thought,' she confessed, holding his gaze, 'that you didn't mean to stay – that you were preparing to leave.' She frowned, recalling. 'In fact, I came to the library one morning to ask you for help with the breeding stock and heard you talking to Worboys, making plans to leave. That was *before* you offered to help.'

Richard frowned. 'You were behind that other door in the library?' Catriona nodded; Richard grimaced. 'Worboys and his plans.' Briefly, he explained.

Catriona sat back in her saddle. 'So you never intended to leave at all?'

'Not until you made it impossible to stay.' Remembering how she'd made him feel, Richard narrowed his eyes at her. 'Do you think that in future, you could just tell me what is really in your witchy mind *without* trying to guess my thoughts first?'

Catriona narrowed her eyes back. 'I wouldn't need to guess if you just told me how you felt.' She considered his face.

'You're very good at hiding your feelings – even from me.'

'Humph. I'll take that as a compliment.'

'Don't – it's going to have to change.'

'Oh?' Brows rising, he looked down at her, arrogantly challenging.

'Indeed.' Catriona met his gaze, sheer determination in hers. The horses sidled and stamped – sending them swaying closer. She raised her brows. 'I'll make a deal with you. Another set of vows.'

Richard's brows quirked, then he grimaced. 'Let's make them a little clearer than the last.'

'Assuredly – in fact, these vows are designed to ensure future understanding.'

Richard eyed her with increasing unease. 'What are they?'

Catriona smiled into his eyes and held up her hand. 'I vow before The Lady that I will henceforth always speak my mind directly to you – 'if you will reciprocate in like vein.'

Richard studied her eyes, her face, then drew breath, raised his hand, placed it palm to palm with hers, and linked their fingers. 'Before Your Lady, I swear I'll ...' – he hesitated, then grimaced—' try.'

Catriona blinked at him, then her lips twitched, then curved, then she threw back her head and laughed. Peal after peal of her glorious laughter rang out; mockdisgruntled, Richard reached for her. 'It's not funny, being naturally reticent.'

She stopped laughing on a gasp as she landed in his saddle, facing him. 'Reticent? *You?*' As his hands ran over her body, then slid beneath her hems, her eyes widened even more. 'You don't know the meaning of the word.'

Over the next few minutes, he gave her justification and more for that assessment, until she finally gasped, as categorically as she could: *'Richard!* It is *not* possible on a horse.'

It was, of course; he demonstrated with an e´lan that left her shuddering.

Neither of them noticed, on the sun-glazed horizon, a flashing pinprick of light – a reflection off the manor's spyglass as it was lowered and snapped shut.

From the fence near the stables, Algaria stood, watching the two figures locked together on the back of the grey stallion, for two more minutes, then, her face colder than ice, she turned and reentered the house.

That afternoon, Richard penned a detailed inquiry to Mr. Scroggs of Hexham, describing the breed, age, gender and number of cattle he wished to purchase on behalf of his client, unnamed. That letter was easy – he knew exactly how his father, or Devil, would have worded such a missive. By leaving the identity of the ultimate purchaser unspecified, he left the breeder no facts on which to speculate, and no reason to inflate his prices.

Enclosing the letter with a note instructing Heathcote Montague to forward the letter on, Richard sealed the packet and set it aside. Drawing forth a fresh sheet, he settled to write a more challenging missive – a letter to Mr. Potts.

That letter took him two hours and five sheets, resulting in a brief, single-page epistle. Rereading it, he smiled. After laboring to find the correct tone, the precise colors in which he wished to paint himself, he'd finally taken it into his head to approach the exercise as if he was Catriona's champion, her protector, her right arm. To wit, her consort. *She* was the lady, but he was the one who dealt with beef.

Proud of his handiwork, he rose and went to show her.

He found her, as always, in her office, poring over a collection of lists and detailed maps. She looked up as he entered, and smiled – warmly, welcomingly. Richard grinned. He waved the letter at her. 'For your approval.'

'Approval?' Her eyes flicking to his face, she took the letter, then glanced at it. 'Who . . .? Oh – Potts.'

Scanning the letter, her expression softened from unreadable, to amused, to one step away from joyful. Reaching the end, she giggled and looked up at Richard. 'That's perfect!' She handed the sheet back. 'Here – I received this in today's packet.'

Richard took the letter she held out and swiftly read it – it was from Potts.

'He's becoming more and more insistent.' Catriona heaved a relieved sigh. 'I'd laid it aside to talk to you about later, but the truth is, I need to deal with Potts for our grain. He's always been our most active and reliable buyer, so putting him off over the breeding stock, especially when they're so expensive and will bring him a good commission, had started to give me a headache.'

'Stop worrying.' His gaze on her face, Richard heard the order in his tone, but made no effort to soften it. Maybe it was because she wasn't trying to conceal her feelings from him anymore, but he could now see – and sense – how deeply concerned she'd become over the breeding stock. He knew he was reserved, but with her witchy cloak of seeming serenity, she was every bit as bad.

She smiled up at him; he was relieved to see the clouds gone from her eyes. 'I have – now I can leave all that to you.' Tilting her head, she asked: 'Do you have any sources or definite buys in mind?'

Richard hesitated, then grinned charmingly. 'Not yet,' he lied.

He'd surprise her – it had suddenly occurred to him that she'd been carrying the problems of the vale on her slight shoulders for more than six years. She was due a pleasant surprise or two. Like an unusual wedding gift – one she couldn't ask the price of, and so couldn't worry how the vale would pay for it.

Still grinning, he twitched his missive to Mr. Potts from her fingers. 'I'll get this in the post.'

He ambled from the room, leaving her to rotate her crops, perfectly sure that Her Lady would, if not precisely approve, then at least turn a blind eye to lies born of good intent.

The next day saw him outdoors, marking out positions for large shelters for the cattle, both those presently in the vale and those he intended to add to the herd. Together with Irons, Henderson and McAlvie, the herdsman – excited to the point of garrulousness – he hammered short stakes into the ice-hard ground, outlining the buildings, then moved on to mark out a series of yards, pens and races, all linked to the buildings.

'I see, I see.' McAlvie nodded briskly. 'We can move them in, then move them out, at will and without mixing the groups.'

'And we won't need to get them all 'round to the one side, neither,' observed Irons.

'That's the idea.' Taking a brief rest on the rising slope leading to the house, Richard looked down on their handiwork. 'This will let us get the herd in quickly – they won't lose condition as badly as they do at present if they're properly protected. And we'll also be able to get them back out as soon as the snow melts. We can keep them in the yards until there's enough new growth in the pastures.'

'Which means they'll be easier to feed, and it'll protect the pastures from too-early grazing.' Henderson nodded in dour approval. 'Sensible.'

'We'll put gates inside, too,' Richard said, leading the way back down the slope to the field of their endeavor, 'so that once in, you'll be able to bring them out into whatever yard gives access to the fields you want to run them on.'

They tramped eagerly after him, McAlvie's expression one of bliss.

In the ensuing days, the new cattle barn became the focus

of vale interest. All the farmhands and laborers at the manor threw themselves into its construction with an enthusiasm that grew with it – as its realization revealed its possibilities. Others from the farms dropped by – and stayed to help.

The children, of course, swarmed everywhere, fetching nails and tools, providing unsolicited opinions. Despite the hard ground and the difficulty of sinking foundations, the barn grew apace.

'Oooh!' McAlvie's eyes gleamed as he surveyed the long loft running the length of the barn. 'We'll be able to feed by simply pushing half bales over the edge and into the stalls below.'

'Not this year,' Richard answered caustically, handing him a hammer and directing him to a brace waiting to be secured. 'Let's get this up, and the herd under cover, *before* you start to dream.'

The end walls of the main barn went up slowly, rock and stone filling the wooden frames. Meanwhile, the long side walls, wooden slats over a complex wooden frame allowing for doors, gates, shutters and runs, took shape. The sound of hammering rang over the vale; with every day the sense of shared purpose grew. Eventually, every man had contributed something – hammered in at least one nail – even old McArdle, who had hobbled down to view the enterprise and hadn't been able to resist.

As a shared distraction in a season usually marked by doing nothing, the men, used to outdoor work, welcomed the chance of activity wholeheartedly, and happily immersed themselves in it. 'Better 'n chess,' was the general opinion.

Eventually, the women came to see what was afoot.

'Mercy be!' exclaimed Mrs. Broom. 'The cattle won't know themselves.'

Cook humphed. 'Get ideas above their station, I shouldn't be surprised.'

Catriona came down late in the afternoon, just before the light started to fade. Algaria, dressed, as usual, in unrelieved black, glided in her wake.

'This way, mistress.' With a flourish, McAlvie conducted her around his charges' new quarters. 'I'm thinking, if they spend winters like this, they'll regain their summer weight in weeks, rather than months.'

Nodding, Catriona slowly pivoted, taking in the size of the structure – rather larger than she had supposed. 'How many will it hold?'

'Oh, it'll take our present numbers easily.'

'Hmm.' Discovering a gate before her, Catriona opened it. 'What are these for?'

'They,' Richard answered, strolling up, 'are for channeling the occupants.' Taking Catriona's hand, he led her to a ladder left leaning against the loft's edge. 'Go up a few steps and you'll see the pattern more easily.'

Catriona climbed up, and he explained the flow of traffic through the barn.

'How very useful.' Looking down, she smiled at him.

Richard reached up and lifted her down. 'Useful is what I do best.'

She smiled and pressed his hand; together they strolled to the main doors. Leaving him there with a lingering smile and a promise in her eyes, Catriona started back to the house.

Algaria trudged behind her.

Catriona stopped at the stable yard fence and looked back – at the useful structure her consort had fashioned from the materials and energy lying dormant in the vale. A soft smile curved her lips as she turned away and started across the cobbles.

Algaria, behind her, humphed disgustedly. 'Newfangled nonsense!'

As often happened, winter refused to cede its authority

289

without one last freeze. It came literally overnight, a storm that dumped feet of snow over the vale, followed by a cold snap, which froze it all in place.

The cattle barn, while far from finished, was complete enough to house the present herd. McAlvie, warned the day before by both Catriona and Cook's aching joints, had sent his farmhands to all corners of the vale to bring the herd in.

Everyone, both from the manor and the farms, had been there to see the herd, shaggy and gaunt, come plodding and swaying, lowing and mooing, up to the manor. Then McAlvie and his lads turned them down the slope to their new quarters; they'd gone readily, filing in through the main doors, heads up, eyes wide. Those watching had waited, listening for any hint of problems; instead, all they heard was a murmur of contented moos.

That had been yesterday; now, standing by the stable yard fence, Catriona looked down on the snow-shrouded barn. The contented sound still rose from the building. The herd was safe and warm; she could see footsteps sunk deep in the snow leading to the barn and guessed McAlvie's lads had already been out to feed them.

Turning, she surveyed the scene in the yard behind her. Irons was in charge of the team set to clear the pump of snow and ice. Richard was about somewhere; she could hear him issuing orders about sweeping some of the snow from the roofs of the forge and two of the smaller barns. The fall had been heavy; from what she could gather, certain eaves were in danger of snapping under the weight.

All the children had been sternly confined to the house; Catriona could see noses pressed to the window panes of the games room. But she agreed with the edict – every now and then, as the men worked to clear the eaves, a minor avalanche would ensue.

Even she was only there on sufferance. That much was

obvious from the frown on Richard's face as he rounded the barn and saw her. He strode up. 'I'm sure you must have better things to do than freeze your witchy arse out here.'

Catriona grinned. 'I'll go inside in a minute. I was just wondering' – she glanced at the games room – 'how to best to reward the children. They've been so very good, helping with the barn, among other things.'

Richard frowned at the fogged windows. 'Why don't you tell them that if they manage to *remain* good until after luncheon, I'll give them another riding lesson?'

Catriona opened her eyes wide. 'You will?'

Richard narrowed his eyes at her. 'Any further orders, ma'am?'

Catriona giggled. Gripping his coat, she stretched up, kissed his cheek, then his lips fleetingly; then, smiling serenely, keeping her eyes on his to the very last, she drew her shawls about her, and headed back to the house.

Richard watched her go – watched her hips sway provocatively as she crossed the snow. Then he drew a deep breath, wrenched his mind back from where it had wandered, and returned to his task – that of being her right arm.

He had it all done – the eaves all checked, those in danger swept, all the stock checked and safe, paths to the buildings cleared – by lunchtime. Crossing the front hall on his way upstairs to change, he heard Catriona call his name.

She was in her office, seated at her desk with McArdle and a dour man he identified as the recalcitrant Melchett in attendance. Catriona looked up as he entered, and smiled, but a frown lurked in her eyes.

'We've been discussing the crop schedules.' With a wave, she indicated the papers and maps spread over her desk. 'We were wondering if you had any suggestions to make?'

*We who?* Aware of a certain tension in the air, Richard frowned and looked down at the lists and field placements. 'I

291

suspect,' he said, 'you'd know better than I.'

'We were thinking as how you'd done so much with the cattle, that you might have a few pointers, like, about the crops.' Melchett studied Richard unblinkingly.

Richard returned his stare, then glanced at McArdle, then looked back at the maps. 'If you asked me about crops and rotation patterns in Cambridgeshire I could give you chapter and verse. But here? There's too many variables in different parts of the country to make facile comparisons. What we grow in the south won't grow so well here. Livestock are different – the principles of sound stock managment are the same anywhere.'

'But you must have some ideas,' Melchett pressed. 'Some principles, like you said.'

Resisting the urge to narrow his eyes and put the man firmly in his place, on Catriona's behalf, Richard switched from his instinctive role as Catriona's protector, to that of her champion. 'The only real measure of effectiveness in crop farming is the yield per acre. If you had those figures' – he looked at McArdle and raised his brows – 'I could tell you if you were doing well, or needed to do more.'

'Yields, yields.' McArdle flicked pages in a huge worn ledger sitting on the table before him. 'Here they are.' He turned the ledger around so Richard could read it. 'For the last five years.'

Richard looked, and looked again. He'd expected to see good figures – Jamie had told him the vale was fertile and did well. But what danced before his widening eyes were yields consistently more than fifty percent above the accepted best. And he'd been raised in some of the highest yielding country in England. He said as much – in tones edged with awe. 'These are without doubt the best figures I've ever seen.' He returned the tome to McArdle, now grinning widely. Richard glanced at Melchett. 'Whatever you've been doing, I'd strongly advise you to keep doing it.'

'Oh! Aye—' The big man straightened. 'If that's the way of things ...'

Richard straightened and smiled down at Catriona. 'I'll leave you to get on with it.' Turning away, he added: 'Incidentally, remind me to make sure my brother and my cousin Vane have a chance to quiz you when we meet.' From the door, Richard caught Catriona's eye. 'They'll be very keen to learn the secrets of your agricultural success.'

With that, he left them, Catriona with her eyes wide,

McArdle still grinning, and Melchett in a much more humble mood.


'Catriona.'

On her way through the kitchen to the barn to oversee the children's riding lesson, currently in progress, Catriona halted and swung back to face Algaria, who had followed her down the corridor.

'Corby's just come in.' With a graceful gesture, Algaria indicated the front hall. 'He says the snow has snapped branches from at least five trees in the orchard. Do you want me to tell him to lop the branches off and seal the scars as usual?'

Catriona opened her mouth to agree, then hesitated. 'Corby will be staying the night, won't he?'

'Yes.'

'Good.' Catriona smiled. 'I'll discuss the matter with Richard – tell Corby we'll speak to him this evening.'

With her customary regal nod, she whirled; eager to join the fun in the big barn, she hurried on through the kitchens, her smile radiant, happiness lighting her eyes.

Behind her, Algaria stood, silently contained, her black gaze fixed on Catriona as she hurried away. Her suppressed fury vibrated around her, an anger others could sense; the kitchen staff warily gave her a wide berth. Finally drawing in a slow breath, Algaria drew herself up, drew her anger in, and, lips tightly compressed, turned and quit the kitchens.

Leaving Cook, kneading dough, sighing and shaking her head.


'Thank you.' Catriona pressed a warm kiss to Richard's lips the instant he settled beside her in their big bed.

'What was that for?'

'For your kind words on the crop yields.'

'Kind?' Richard snorted, and wrestled her atop him, sitting her upright, straddling his hips. 'Cynsters do not know any kind words when it comes to land. That was the truth. Your yields are absolutely staggering.' He started to unbutton her nightgown. 'And I was perfectly serious about Devil and Vane wanting to talk to you. They will. They'll be excessively glad I've married you.'

'Will they?'

'Hmm.' Frowning, Richard struggled with the tiny button at her throat. 'They both manage lots of acres. In Devil's case, being Cambridgeshire, it's mostly crops, but Vane farms in Kent – hops, fruit and nuts, mainly.'

'Mmm.'

The odd sound, one of surprised discovery, had Richard looking into her face. 'Mmm what?'

She refocused on him. 'Mmm, I'd envisaged your brother and cousins as "gentlemen about town," more interested in assessing ladies' contours than the contours of land.'

'Ah, well . . .' Richard popped the button located between her breasts. 'I wouldn't say Cynsters ever totally lose their interest in ladies' contours.' He popped the next button and couldn't imagine that being otherwise. 'Land, however, is our other obsession – an equally abiding one.'

Her gaze abstracted, Catriona considered that. She opened

her lips on a question – Richard distracted her by opening her gown. Lifting the sides wide, baring her to his gaze, but leaving it draped on her shoulders. Her hands resting for balance on his arms, she glanced down – a wild sensation of nakedness swept her, stronger, more titillating than if she'd been completely bare. Her skin flushed and prickled, all over. Even over her back and bottom, the backs of her thighs, all still cloaked in the soft lawn of her gown.

But she was naked to him, totally wantonly naked, bathed in the light of the two candles he'd left burning, one on each bedside table. His gaze feasted; she felt it sweep over her – down from her throat, over the full swells of her breasts, growing heavier by the day. Her nipples crinkled tight; his lips curved, too knowingly, then he continued his leisurely perusal, scanning her stomach, taut and quivering, to the bright curls between her widespread thighs – which quivered even more as the heat of his gaze touched her.

Closing his hands about her waist, Richard held her there, delectably displayed before him, while he pondered his next move. He was in no hurry to make it; he knew, very well, what her present position – sitting astride him, displayed, exposed to him – was doing to his sweet witch. She was melting, heating – just behind her flaming curls, she was open and vulnerable, her knees held wide.

He was hardly immune himself. He could feel the silky pressure of her naked inner thighs pressing on either side of his hips, could feel the warm, heating weight of her across his lower stomach. Half an inch behind the taut globes of her bottom, he was achingly rigid.

Then he remembered. Turning, he looked at the beside table; reaching out, he snagged the knob of the drawer, tugged the drawer open, then dipped his fingers inside. 'Worboys found this in the pocket of one of my coats.'

He drew out his mother's necklace, the finely wrought gold

chain interspersed with round, rose pink stones. The amethyst pendant slid from the drawer last, swinging heavily on the chain. Richard held the necklace in both hands, gently shaking the pendant free – and for one wild minute, considered using it to love her. Considered placing it – the heavy, slightly bulbous crystal with its edges smoothed, the numerous round, tumbled stones, each one carrying a certain weight – inside her, sliding it into her warm sheath, stone by stone, each pushing the wider, heavier crystal deeper, each pressing against her soft inner surfaces, drawing the necklace out, pushing it in, until she cried out, until she convulsed.

It was an attractive vision; with a mental sigh, he set it aside – for later. After he'd thought through all the possibilties, developed the idea to its fullest, made plans to extract every last ounce of sensuality from it. *Then* he'd break the news to her. But there was no need to rush, to miss anything. He had all his life to tease her.

With his Cynster smile curving his lips, he looked up and met Catriona's wide gaze. 'For you.' Raising his arms, he slipped the necklace over her head, then gently lifted her hair free. 'A belated bridal gift.'

He'd teased her about giving her diamonds – he was rich enough to give her them and more, but ... in his heart, he knew diamonds would mean nothing to her, not at the moment. But she'd been fascinated by the one sight she'd had of his mother's necklace – she would, he felt, appreciate it far more than other jewelry.

He was perfectly right. Wide-eyed, lips parted, Catriona stared down at the necklace as it settled against the soft skin of her chest, the heavy pendant sliding into the valley between her breasts as if it belonged there.

Perhaps it did.

There were times when even she was stunned to silence by The Lady's ways.

She knew her eyes were shining, knew her face glowed as she carefully took the pendant between her fingers and raised it to scan the tiny engravings.

'Do you know what this is?' Her words were hushed, tinged with awe.

She felt Richard's gaze on her face, sensed he was intrigued by her reaction. Eventually, drawing the last lock of her hair free, he answered: 'It's my mother's necklace – now yours.'

Catriona sucked in a huge breath – truer words he could not have spoken; it was as if The Lady had used him to voice her decision. 'It's a disciple's necklace – the engravings say that. They're the same as those on my crystal, committing the wearer to allegiance to The Lady and her teachings. But *this* necklace is from a very senior disciple – more senior than me, or any of the past ladies of the vale.' She had to stop, to fight for calm; her heart felt like it might burst with sheer joy. She moistened her lips. 'This necklace is much older than mine.'

'I knew it was different but similar.' Reaching to the other table, Richard drew her necklace, which she left there every night, to him, then held it up between them. 'I thought it was the same but with the stones inverted.'

Catriona looked at him, then drew in a deep breath and nodded; he was involved in this, he was her consort. She could tell him the facts. 'On the surface, of course, it is. But there's a deeper meaning.' She caught the pendant of her own necklace. 'This is rose quartz, which signifies love, and these' – she pointed to the round purple stones embedded in the chain – 'are amethyst, which signi?es intelligence. So in this arrangement, the stones mean intelligence driving love, the rose quartz being the focus. However' – pausing, she licked her lips and looked back at the necklace now lying against her skin – '*this* is the way it was supposed to be – used to be – before the supplies of amethyst crystals large enough and fine

297

enough to make the focus crystals ran out.'

'So,' frowning slightly, Richard followed her thoughts, 'this necklace' – he placed his fingers on the necklace lying on her flesh and was surprised at how warm it felt – 'signifies intelligence driven by love?'

Catriona nodded. 'That was the original meaning. That's The Lady's message, the one every disciple must understand and learn to live by. Love is the principal force – the driving force – behind all; all intelligent acts should be governed by, directed by, love.'

After a moment's pause, Richard shifted, and laid Catriona's own necklace aside, then settled back beneath her, studying her rapt expression. Quite obviously, he could not possibly have given her a more meaningful gift. But ... 'How did my mother come to have such a necklace?'

Catriona lifted her head and met his gaze. 'She must have been a disciple, too.' When Richard raised his brows, she nodded. 'That's possible. She came from the Lowlands, where there were once many followers of The Lady. It's possible that she was descended from one of the oldest lines of disciples – that's what the necklace suggests – but that she wasn't trained, or, even if trained, had been forced to marry Seamus.'

Richard lay back on the pillows and stared at his witchy wife, stared deep into her green eyes. And wondered ...

Her eyes widened slightly. 'The ways of The Lady are often complex, far-sighted – too intricate for us to understand.' Slowly, her gaze locked mesmerizingly on his, she leaned forward. 'Stop thinking about it.'

The soft command, enforced by an underlying compulsion, fell from her lips; the next instant they touched his in an achingly sweet kiss. Richard inwardly shuddered and decided, for once, to obey.

Decided to follow her lead as she wove her witchy wiles

and drew them both deeper into desire, deeper into the heat spiralling upward between them.

Followed her as she shifted, lifted, and drew him deep into the shocking heat of her body, into the furnace of her need. He rose with her as she rode him, sweetly urgent, without guile, in undisguised abandon. Brushing aside her gown, he clamped his hands about her hips, then leaned forward and drew one turgid nipple into his mouth. He laved it – a muted cry was his reward.

He settled to feast on her bounty, pausing now and then to watch their bodies merge, to wonder, sensually dazed, as he gazed at his mother's necklace, now gracing his wife's flushed skin.

Then her heat reached flashpoint and exploded; she clung to the peak, her face awash with sensation, then, with a long, soft, sob of joy, crumpled against him.

Burying his face in her hair, he held her close, anchored her hips against him, and drove into her molten softness, once, twice, and again, savoring to his marrow the sense of completeness that was always his when he was buried within her.

Between them, locked in the valley between her breasts, crushed to his chest, his mother's pendant lay, pulsing with a force that was warm yet owed nothing to any fire's heat.

Closing his eyes, his cheek hard against his wife's fiery hair, Richard dragged in a huge breath and let sensation take him. Just as his mother's necklace had always been destined to find it's way here, to reside with his sweet witch in the vale, he, too, his mother's only child, was destined to find his home, his haven, his salvation, here.

In his witch's arms.

In her.

With a long, shuddering groan, he surrendered to fate.

*

'Master!'

Richard whirled to see one of the workers from the farm at the mouth of the vale come hurrying across the stable yard. 'What is it, Kimpton?'

The man halted before him and touched his cap. 'You asked that we should report anything not right, sir.'

'I did. What's amiss?'

'The gate on the south paddock.' The man looked Richard in the eye. ''Twas fast last night when I did my rounds, but 'twas wide this morning, when my youngest went down that way.'

Richard's gaze sharpened. 'Did he close it?'

'Aye, sir.' The man nodded. 'And I checked it, too. Nothing wrong with the latch.'

Richard smiled. 'Very good. Let's see what happens.'


Sir Olwyn Glean arrived just after lunch.

He brusquely thrust his hat at Henderson and charged straight for Catriona's office.

He started blustering the instant he flung open the door. 'Miss Hennessey! I really must protest—'

'To whom are you referring, sir?'

Catriona's chill tones brought Sir Olwyn up short; he struggled for an instant to breathe, then drew in a huge breath. And nodded in a belated attempt at polite form.

'Mrs. Cynster.'

After her exertions of that morning, let alone all the mornings before, Catriona was of the firm opinion she fully deserved the title. Regally, she inclined her head and folded her hands on her ledger. 'To what do I owe this visit, sir?'

'As always,' Sir Olwyn declared with relish, 'to your cattle! Having them scattered about foraging two and three to a field through winter means you can never keep a sufficiently good eye on them. Fence latches break, or get loose – and then what happens?'

'I have no idea' – Catriona looked at him serenely – 'but whatever it is, if the matter concerns the vale's livestock, you should speak with my husband.' She waved toward the door. 'He's in charge of the herds.'

'Much good that is,' Sir Olwyn retorted, 'with him away in London.'

'Oh, no, Sir Olwyn – I'm much nearer than that.'

Sir Olwyn jumped and whirled. From just behind him, Richard smiled urbanely, every inch a wolf about to take a large chunk out of a marauding dog.

Catriona fought valiantly to keep a straight face; she nearly choked swallowing her giggle. As for McArdle, he looked down at his closed ledger and didn't look up again. The tips of his ears, however, grew redder and redder.

Smoothly continuing into the room, Richard drawled: 'What's this about the vale's cattle?'

Red-faced, Sir Olwyn belligerently spluttered: 'The vale's cattle have strayed into my cabbages and ruined the crop.'

'Indeed?' Richard's brows rose high. 'And when did this happen?'

'Early this morning.'

'Ah.' Richard turned to Henderson, who stood in the doorway. 'Please fetch McAlvie, Henderson.'

'Aye, sir.'

McAlvie must have been waiting, for he was back with Henderson before the silence in the office stretched too thin.

'Ah, McAlvie.' Richard smiled at the herdsman. 'Are we missing any cattle this morning?'

McAlvie shook his shaggy head. 'No, sir.'

'*How* would you know?' Sir Olwyn scornfully interjected. 'The vale's cattle wander all the time, especially in winter.'

'Mayhap they used to,' McAlvie stated, 'all the other times when we've paid for your cabbages. Aye, and your corn. But not any more.'

301

Sir Olwyn glowered. 'What do you mean – not any more?'

'Precisely that, Sir Olwyn.' Deliberately, Richard captured his gaze. '*Not* any more.' Then he smiled. 'We've instituted a new procedure for managing our cattle through the winter. We have a new barn – the entire herd's been confined there since before the last snowfall, so if any had won loose, the tracks would be easy to see. But they haven't.' Richard smiled again. 'No tracks. If you'd like to go with McAlvie, I'm sure he'd be happy to count the herd with you and show you about our new facilities.'

Sir Olwyn simply stared.

'However,' Richard drawled, 'to return to your complaint, I'm afraid if any cattle have damaged your cabbages, they really must be your own.'

Sir Olwyn's inner struggle showed on his surface – his face mottled, veins stood out on his forehead. He managed not to glare, but only just. All but visibly fuming, he swung on his heel, grabbed his hat from Henderson, went to jam it on his head, and remembered, just in time, to nod briefly to Catriona. Then he forced himself to nod, exceedingly stiffly, to Richard. 'Your pardon,' he growled. Then he stumped out.

Henderson hurried after him to open and close the front door. Returning to the office, he gruffly declared: 'Good riddance, I say!'

Doubled up with laughter, none of the others could speak.

Catriona came early to the dining hall that evening. Sliding into her seat at the main table, she watched as her household – her people – filed in and found their seats, chatting and laughing, faces bright and smiling.

The manor had always been a peaceful place, secure and stable; she was accustomed to the sense of calm serenity that had always hung a comforting blanket over this room. The serenity was still there, but, lately, another element had been

302

added. A certain vigor, a joy in life, an eager confidence to see what tomorrow held.

It was, very definitely, a male quality, owing something to assured strength, to experience, and to sheer energy. At times, it almost sparked with rude vitality. To her heightened, experienced senses, the new force melded and merged with the serenity – primarily her contribution; the result was a household more joyfully alive, more happy and content in its peace, than had existed before.

She knew from whom that new force derived; she had to wonder if he knew he was responsible. On the thought, he entered, pausing to chat with Irons and two of McAlvie's lads.

His hair black in the candlelight, his face so much harder, more angular than any others in sight, his tall figure so vital an amalgam of strength and grace that he threw every other male into the shade, he was the focus of her attention, her mind, her heart.

The focus of her love.

She raised a hand and touched the twin crystals that during the day rode between her breasts. At night, she wore only the older – she would never be without it. It was now a part of her, as it was meant to be. As he was meant to be.

Smiling serenely, she drew her eyes from him. Glancing around, she beckoned to a maid. 'Hilda – slip up to our bedchamber and make sure the fire's built high.' So the air would be warm when they retired to their bed.

The maid, one with sufficient years to read between the lines, smiled broadly. 'Aye, mum – I'll make sure it's a right blaze.' Eyes twinkling, she hurried out.

Catriona smiled. Just another little detail married ladies had to deal with. Inwardly grinning, she turned back to survey her people – and enjoy the sight of her husband among them.

303

# Chapter Sixteen

Catriona was late down to breakfast the next morning, but not quite as late as had been her wont in recent times. While Richard's morning demands hadn't abated in the slightest, she felt less drained, less exhausted from fulfilling them. Perhaps she was growing used to waking up that way.

Whatever, her energy was at a high as she descended the stairs, her feet tripping, her heart light. Smiling brightly, she swept into the dining hall, beaming at all in sight. At the main table on the dais, Richard was looking down at his plate. Her heart buoyed on a wave of sheer joy, Catriona rounded the table and went to her place beside him.

He sensed her presence and tried to turn her way – tried to straighten his back, tried to lift his head and look at her.

Catriona slowed; horrified, she took in his slack features, the pallor of his skin.

Hunched, his heavy lids hooding his blue eyes, he made a heroic effort to lift his arm toward her.

He crashed out of his chair.

With a pained cry, Catriona flung herself to her knees beside him. About them, shouts and exclamations rang; chairs scraped as everyone rose. Frantically searching for a pulse at his throat, Catriona barely heard.

Then Worboys pushed through and went heavily down on his knees on Richard's other side. *'Sir!'*

The pain in his cry was echoed in Catriona's heart. 'He's still alive.' A panic like nothing she'd ever known had locked a vise about her lungs. Dragging in what air she could, she framed Richard's face in her hands; with her thumbs, she pried open his lids.

They rose, just enough to confirm her worst fears. He was drugged – heavily, heavily drugged.

She sensed him gather his strength – he blinked and looked directly at her, his eyes focused by sheer force of will. Then, with an even greater effort, he turned his head to Worboys. 'Get Devil.' He licked his dry lips. *'Immediately!'*

'Yes, of course, sir. But ...'

Worboys' words faded as Richard, with such intense effort it was painful to watch, turned his head until, once more, he was looking at Catriona. Jaw clenching, he lifted one hand, fingers extended, to her, to her face—

A spasm twisted his features; he gave a choked gasp, and his lids fell.

His hand fell, too; his head lolled.

He was unconscious.

Only the slow beat of his heart beneath her palm stopped Catriona from wailing. Others did, believing the worst – she hushed them with a word.

'He still lives. Quickly – some wine! Then I'll need to get him to our bed.'


That first night was not going to be the worst – Catriona knew it. Richard's life hung by a thread – a steadily fraying one. Only the fact that she'd been there, on the spot when the poison first took hold, had saved him – if she'd been even five minutes later, it would have been too late.

Even now, she might have been too late.

Dragging in a breath, she wrapped her arms about her, and continued her slow pace beside the bed. Before the fire would

305

be warmer, but she didn't dare go so far away. She needed to be close, to do whatever she could quickly, when the time came. It hadn't come yet, but soon, soon . . .

Outside the wind howled and sobbed; she fought not to do the same. She'd done all she could thus far.

Before letting them move him, she'd tipped two glasses of the light morning wine down his throat before his instinct to swallow had faded. All through the day and into the night, she'd painstakingly coaxed liquids into him. Garlic water, honey water, and goat's milk mulled with mustard seed – all the standard remedies. Her efforts had been enough to hold him to life thus far, but it was only the beginning of his battle.

This time, his fate rested squarely in the lap of The Lady.

So she prayed, and paced, and waited – for the crisis she knew must come.

And tried not to think about the other crises looming – the ones to be faced when he regained consciousness, or even before.

The thought that he believed she'd drugged him again, this time with deadly intent, hurt beyond description, but she couldn't interpret his movements, his words, in those instants before he'd lost consciousness in any other way. He'd looked at her so strangely, so intently, so deliberately, then he'd told Worboys to fetch his brother immediately. Then he'd tried to point to her.

Whether the pain that had crossed his face had been due to the drug, or to hurt at her supposed betrayal, she couldn't decide.

But . . . dragging in a huge breath, she pressed her lips tight; kicking her skirts out of her way, she paced on. She was not going to let his temporary insanity get her down. She was not going to waste her time, diffuse her energies, in feeling hurt or insulted, nor in wringing her hands or indulging in tears.

306

The stupid man couldn't afford it – he might die if she wasn't at her best. At her strongest.

He might die anyway.

Thrusting that thought aside, she reiterated to herself her decision on how best to deal with her husband's mental breakdown. Once his wits returned, she would simply hold him to his vow – and force him to talk to her, and she would talk to him. And keep talking until she had straightened out his wayward thinking. It was, of course, nonsensical to imagine she had poisoned him – no one else in the household, not even Worboys, believed that.

But only Richard knew that she'd drugged him before – she could appreciate that in that dizzy moment when the drug had fought to rip his wits from him, he might have remembered that fact and extrapolated without thinking things through.

She could forgive him – but she wasn't about to let her past misdemeanor combine with his drug-induced daze to set a wall between them.

She would talk until the wall fell down.

There was, however, a hurdle looming in her path – very likely a large hurdle; at least, she imagined his brother would be large. Large and forceful. Powerful. Used to being obeyed, to having his edicts complied with.

Grimacing, Catriona swung about and marched around the bed, just for a change of scenery. Of perspective.

She wasn't now sure she'd done the right thing in encouraging Worboys to carry out Richard's order and summon his brother the duke. At the time, she'd been of the mind that as she'd nothing to hide, there was no reason she couldn't face the inquisition. Unfortunately, *she* hadn't thought things through in that instance – thought about what might happen if Richard's brother – a man known to everyone as Devil and presumably a potent source of authority – insisted on removing Richard from her care. Decreed that Richard, still

307

unconscious, would be better tended in London.

Could she – would she be able to – refuse?

If he was taken away before she made sure he understood she hadn't poisoned him, would she get the chance to right his mind later – would he return if he believed, for whatever twisted reasons, that she was behind his poisoning?

The thought went around and around as she paced up and down. And got nowhere. She couldn't, in fact, concentrate on that point, too overwhelmed by the far more scarifying prospect raised by the possibility of Richard being taken from her care.

If he was, he might not live.

And she doubted she could explain that to his brother, or anyone not acquainted with the ways of The Lady.

Sighing, she halted and reached a hand to Richard's wrist. His pulse was still steady, if far too weak. Once again, she mentally reviewed her treatment, searched for any options she had not yet tried. But she'd done all she could – without knowing the specific poison for certain, she couldn't risk doing any more.

She knew, of course, *who* had poisoned him, but the culprit was no longer in the manor, in the vale, for her to question. It seemed Algaria had slipped the poison – a poison only she and Catriona had access to – into Richard's mug, then left immediately, ostensibly to travel to her own cottage, which she sometimes did, but never without informing Catriona first.

The fact that Algaria hadn't waited to gauge her potion's effect suggested she'd been in no doubt it would work. Quelling a shudder, Catriona resumed her pacing and considered the three possible poisons – hemlock, henbane, and wolfsbane. All were deadly, but the last was the hardest to treat. She couldn't, however, overlook the possiblity that a mixture had been used, so she'd had to combine remedies for all three.

308

She knew that wouldn't be enough.

Which was why she was there by the bed, would always be there, every minute until he awakened. Until she knew he was safe. She had to be there to anchor him to this world if need be, if his connection with it grew too weak. She'd never done such a thing before, but she knew about the region she mentally dubbed 'neither nor.' The region in which life ceased to have meaning, the threshold between the real world and that other.

She'd stood on that threshold once before, on the night after her parents had died. Her mother had come to her in her sleep – from the dream state to 'neither nor' was no great step. Having died in the arms of a man who had loved her deeply, and who she had loved in return, her mother had had no real cause to linger – she'd held back only to bid her adieu.

So she knew the way to that region, knew it was cold, swirling with chill grey mists, treacherous in that it had no reality to which human senses could cling. Any who stepped into it had to rely on their other senses, and their link to any other in that void would only hold true if there was a strong connection between the two souls – like a mother and child, or a husband and wife bound by love.

If the connection wasn't there, then in trying to reach Richard and hold him to life, she would risk losing herself.

She didn't care – if he died, life wouldn't be worth living, but she'd have to live it anyway, without him. The thought was guaranteed to stiffen her spine, to fire her determination. She would not lose him. Or herself. She had faith enough for both of them – faith in his need of her, as much as in her love for him.

The first trial came in the early watches of the morning, when his breathing slowed and he slipped into the greyness. On her knees beside the bed, Catriona drew in a deep breath and resolutely closed her eyes. With one fist clenched about the twin pendants between her breasts, with the other she held his hand and followed him, into the void beyond the world.

He was there, but blind and weak, helpless as a day-old kitten; gently, she turned him around and brought him home.

Over the next days, and the next nights, she fought by his side, time and again stepping into that grey nothingness to lead him back, to give him her strength, her life, so he could continue to live.

The effort drained her. She could have done with Algaria beside her, but that, of course, was not to be. About them, the manor lay quiet, hushed, yet she was conscious of a soothing, steady stream of support, of prayers and wishes for his health and hers. Without him, life still went on, but it was as if, with his retreat from their world, the heightened sense of life he'd brought to them had sunk into hibernation.

Mrs. Broom and McArdle brought her food and drink; Worboys was in constant, surprisingly helpful, attendance. He knew his master's state was serious, yet, after that first moment of weakness, he had remained the staunchest in his certainty that Richard would shortly wake hale and whole.

'Invincible, the lot of them,' he'd assured her when she'd commented on his unswerving confidence. He'd gone on to relate the Cynsters' successes at Waterloo.

It had given her comfort, and some hope, for which she was grateful.

But she alone knew what harmful forces had been unleashed against him – what powerful poison had been fed to him – and only she could heal him and hold him fast to this world.

With a sickening jolt, Catriona awoke on the third morning after their ordeal had begun.

She'd fallen asleep on her knees by the side of the bed, her arms stretched across Richard. With a start, she jerked upright.

310

Her heart in her mouth, she stared at his face.

His color was that of one alive, pale, but still with her; she only breathed again after seeing his chest rise shallowly, then fall.

With an immense sigh of relief, she eased back on her knees. He hadn't slipped away from her while she slept.

Thanking The Lady, she struggled to her feet, wincing as cramped muscles protested. She hobbled to a nearby chair and fell into it, her gaze locked on Richard.

He was still held fast by the poison; he still needed her as his anchor.

Catriona sighed, then painfully rose and hobbled to the bellpull. She was going to have to share the watches with others, others she could trust, and put her faith in them to call her the next time he started slipping away.

She couldn't risk falling asleep and leaving him unwatched again.

Courtesy of Mrs. Broom and Cook, she slept the next night through – which was just as well as the morning brought with it a challenge she hadn't expected to face for at least a few more days.

'How on earth did they get here this soon?' Standing beside McArdle on the front steps, she watched the huge black travelling carriage drawn by six powerful black horses come rolling up through the park. There was no need for her to see the crest worked in gold on the carriage's doors to guess who was calling.

'They must ha' traveled through the night – no way elsewise they'd be here now.' McArdle's gruff tones held a hint of approval. 'Must be right powerfully attached to his brother.'

That was Catriona's unwelcome conclusion – dealing with Richard's brother was shaping to be a battle, one she didn't

311

know if she had the strength to win. Suppressing the urge to clutch her pendants, she drew herself up; summoning every last weary ounce of her power, she lifted her chin and prepared to make the acquaintance of her brother-in-law.

As it happened, she was to meet her sister-in-law first. A tall, powerful figure uncurled long legs and stepped down from the carriage the instant it halted, but beyond throwing a hard, raking glance about the courtyard, he didn't advance, but turned back to hand a lady from the carriage – he had to lift her as she was quite clearly not about to wait for the steps to be let down.

The instant her feet touched the cobbles, she glided forward, her gaze fixed on Catriona. The lady was severely but elegantly attired in a warm woolen cloak over a carriage dress of rich brown, chestnut hair escaping from a simple chignon. She was taller than Catriona; her features were fine and presently set in a noncommittal expression. Her gaze was direct, her whole bearing declared she was a lady used to command. Catriona braced as the woman looked down, lifting her hems as she negotiated the steps.

Reaching the top, she dropped her skirts and looked Catriona directly in the eye. 'My poor dear.'

The next instant, Catriona was enveloped in a scented embrace.

'How dreadful for you! You must let us help in whatever way we can.'

Released, Catriona tried to steady her reeling head.

'Is this your steward?' The lady – presumably Honoria, Duchess of St. Ives – smiled kindly at McArdle.

'Yes,' Catriona managed. 'McArdle.'

'A pleasure, Your Grace.'

McArdle tried to bend his arthritic spine into a bow of the required degree – Honoria put a hand on his arm. 'Oh, no – don't bother. We're family, after all.'

312

McArdle shot her a grateful look.

'If you wouldn't mind, my dear ...?'

The deep, rumbling resigned tones had the duchess whirling. 'Yes, of course. My dear' – she looked at Catriona and gestured to the presence that had followed her up the steps – 'Sylvester – Devil to us all.'

Holding her calm before her like a shield, Catriona turned, a welcoming smile on her lips – and had to quell an impulse to take a large step back. She was used to Richard and his towering propensities – Devil was worse – about two inches worse.

She blinked into a hard face that was so much like Richard's it made her heart stop, then she looked into his eyes – a lucent green quite unlike Richard's burning blue. In color. The cast of his harsh features, until then severe, eased. As he smiled, she saw the likeness rise again – in the set of the lips, that untrustworthy glint in the eyes. They were, quite clearly, alike in many ways. She blinked again. 'Ah ...'

Despite his sobriety, his smile held a hint of the devil he must be. 'It's a pleasure to meet you, my dear. I thought Richard must have lied but he hasn't.' With effortless grace, he captured her hand, planted a kiss on her fingertips, then, his other arm having stolen about her shoulders, bent his head and brushed a perfectly chaste, oddly reassuring kiss on her cheek. 'Welcome to the family.'

Catriona stared into his eyes. 'Th ... thank you.' She blinked, and looked at Honoria – who was waiting to catch her eye.

'Don't let it bother you – they're all like that.'

Imperiously waving her husband back, she linked arms with Catriona and turned to the door. 'Quite clearly my feckless brother-in-law is still alive, or you wouldn't be greeting us so calmly.'

'Indeed.' Finding herself back in her own hall, Catriona

313

quickly introduced Henderson and Mrs. Broom. She grasped the moment while her overpowering relatives were divesting themselves of their coats to relocate and strengthen her habitual serenity. 'Mrs. Broom has prepared a room for you – I'm afraid you'll find the household not quite what you're accustomed to. It's a good deal smaller, of course, and we're also much less formal.'

'Oh, good.' Handing her gloves to Mrs. Broom, Honoria looked up and smiled. 'I'm afraid Cynsters aren't much for formality within the family. And as for this' – with a graceful wave she indicated the house about them – 'not being what we're accustomed to, you must remember I was only a lowly governess until just over a year ago.'

Catriona blinked. 'You were?'

Honoria studied her surprise. 'Didn't Richard tell you?' Shaking her head, she linked arms with Catriona; together they turned for the stairs. 'Isn't that just like a man – never tells one the important things. I'll have to fill you in.'

From behind them, where Devil prowled in their wake, Catriona heard: 'Lowly governess? *Lowly?* You've never been lowly in your life.'

Despite her woes, Catriona's lips twitched; she couldn't resist glancing at Honoria.

Who waved dismissively. 'Don't mind him – he's the worst of them all.'

They halted at the foot of the stairs; sobering, Catriona drew her arm from Honoria's and turned to face them both. 'As Worboys informed you, Richard was poisoned – precisely with what I don't know, but I've been treating him generally, and ...' Her voice quavered; she broke off and drew in a breath. Lifting her chin, she fixed her gaze on Devil's green eyes. 'I want you to know that I had nothing to do with it – I did *not* poison Richard.'

They both looked at her, studied her, their expressions

blank, their eyes filled with sharp intelligence. Then, just as Catriona was about to speak again – to say something to break the silence – Devil reached out, took her hand, and patted it. 'Don't worry – we're here to help. You're obviously over-tired.'

'Have you been nursing him all by yourself?'

The tone of Honoria's question demanded an answer.

'Well, I . . . until yesterday.'

'Humph! Just as well we almost crippled the horses to get here. One member of the family in a sickbed is quite enough.' Taking Catriona's arm again, Honoria took to the stairs. 'Now show us where he is, then you can tell us what needs to be done.'

Swept up the stairs by an irresistible force, it was all Catriona could do to steady her whirling head. She'd expected censure, certainly a reserved stiffness, at least some degree of suspicion; instead, all she could sense from her new relatives was a warm tide of sympathy and support. She led them to the turret room, to where Richard lay, straight and still in the bed.

Standing at the foot of the bed, her eyes fixed on Richard's face, she waited while Honoria and Devil greeted Worboys, who had been watching over his master. Then they joined her, one on either side, and looked down at Richard.

'He's still breathing freely and his pulse is steady, but he hasn't regained consciousness since he collapsed.'

Catriona heard the tiredness in her voice, and felt, again, Devil's hand slide around hers. He squeezed her fingers gently, comfortingly. She felt Honoria's sympathetic gaze on her face, then sensed an exchanged glance pass over her head.

'I'll sit with him for the next few hours.' Devil released her hand.

'Perhaps,' Honoria said, 'you could show me to our room?'

She didn't really want to leave Richard, but ... Catriona gripped her fingers tightly and lifted her gaze to Devil's face. 'If his breathing starts to slow, or grow weaker, you must promise to call me immediately. It's important.' Her eyes locked on his, she reinforced that thought. 'I might need to ...' She gestured vaguely.

Devil nodded and looked at the bed. 'I'll send Worboys or one of the others for you at the slightest sign.' Then he looked back, a slight smile curving his long lips. 'But if he hasn't already died, the chances are he won't.' His gaze drifted to Honoria; the look in his eyes deepened. 'There are any number of people who can tell you that Cynsters lead charmed lives.'

His comforting gaze came back to her face as Honoria humphed.

'Indeed! Believe me,' she said, gently turning Catriona from the bed, 'there's little point worrying about them, although, of course, we do.' She steered Catriona to the door. 'Now come and show me where I can wash – I've been in that carriage for more hours than I care to count.'

Ten minutes later, sunk in an armchair in the room Mrs. Broom had readied for the ducal couple, Catriona knew that, far from taking care of her guests, her guests were taking care of her. She was too tired to resist, and they did it so well, so effortlessly. They made it so easy for her to just stop for a moment, to stop thinking and simply be. She needed the rest – so she took it, let the steady flow of Honoria's description of their trip north flow past her, and waited for her guest to finish her ablutions.

That done, as she'd expected, Honoria sank gracefully into the chair beside hers, leaned forward and took one of her hands. 'Now tell me – why did you imagine we'd imagine you'd had any hand in poisoning Richard?'

Meeting Honoria's misty-blue gaze, Catriona hesitated,

316

then sighed and closed her eyes. 'I got a trifle in advance of myself.' Opening her eyes, she looked at Honoria. 'You see, I think Richard believes I poisoned him – that might be what he believes when he awakes. I was trying to prepare you for that, trying to assure you he was wrong.'

'Well, quite obviously he's wrong – but why would he think such a thing?'

Catriona grimaced. 'Possibly because I drugged him once before.'

'You did?' Honoria regarded her with more interest than puzzlement. 'Why? And how?'

Catriona colored. She tried to hedge, prevaricate, avoid the questions, but, she discovered, Her Grace of St. Ives could be ruthless. Honoria dragged the answers from her – then slumped back in her chair and regarded her with awe. 'You're very brave,' she eventually stated. 'I don't know of many women who would be game to feed an aphrodisiac to a Cynster – and then climb into bed with him.'

Catriona raised her brows in resignation. 'Blame it on total innocence.'

Honoria's lips had yet to return to straight; she shot her a measuring, not-at-all-discouraging, look. 'You know, that's really a very good story, but one I fear we'll have to keep within the family – the female part of it, that is.'

Having by now realized that Her Grace of St. Ives, having been married to His Grace for more than a year, was unshockable, Catriona accepted the comment with an equanimity that, half an hour before, would have astounded her.

'However, to return to your fears over what Richard might think once he wakes, I really do think that you're underestimating him.' Head on one side, Honoria stared past her, clearly considering. 'He's not usually thickheaded. And he's certainly not blind – none of them are, although you'll find they sometimes try to pretend they are.' She looked directly at Catriona.

'Do you have any reason to think he believes you were involved, or is it – forgive me – merely a worry on your part?'

Catriona sighed. 'I don't think so.' Briefly, she described Richard's actions before he lost consciousness.

'Hmm.' Honoria wrinkled her nose. 'You could be wrong – it's perfectly possible he had some other, male-Cynster-type reason for sending so emphatically for Devil. And for staring at you in that way. However,' she stated, setting her hands on her knees, 'that's neither here nor there. If he wakes with such a stupid idea in his head, you may be sure I'll set him right without delay.'

Honoria stood and shook out her skirts; rather more wearily, Catriona rose, too. 'He might not listen.'

'He'll listen to me.' Honoria met her eye and grinned. 'They all do, you know. It's one of the benefits of being married to Devil. As he's the head of the family, there's always the possibility that I might have the last word.'

Despite herself, for the second time that day, Catriona felt her lips twitch. Honoria saw, and smiled. 'And now, if you'll do me the honor of listening to me as well, I really think you should rest. Devil and Worboys and I will watch over Richard – you need to gather your strength in case he needs your healer's skills.'

Catriona looked into Honoria's eyes and knew she was right. She drew in a deep breath and felt like she was breathing freely for the first time since Richard had collapsed. Putting out a hand to Honoria's, she squeezed gently, blinked quickly, then nodded. 'All right.'

Smiling, Honoria kissed her cheek. 'We'll call you if he needs you.'

Catriona slept deeply into the afternoon; she awoke, still worried, but even more determimed to haul her weakened spouse back to this world – and his rightful place at her side.

318

'He's been unconscious for too long,' she declared, pacing once more by his bedside, her gaze on his sleeping face. 'We need to do something to rouse him.'

'What?' was Devil's only question.

She was about to admit that she didn't know, when a flicker of an eyelid stopped her. She stared at Richard's face, then rushed to the bed. 'Richard?'

Another definite flicker – he was trying to respond, but couldn't lift his lids.

Devil, close beside her, placed a hand on her arm when she would have spoken again. 'Richard,' he said, his tone a warning, '*Maman*'s coming!'

Richard's reaction was clearly visible. He tried desperately to open his eyes, but couldn't. A frown creased his brow, then slowly eased as he drifted back into unconsciousness.

'We can walk him!' Fired anew, Catriona dragged back the covers. 'If he can respond, then forcing him to use his muscles will help work the poison from his system.'

Devil helped her haul Richard to his feet, but Richard was still too incapable to support his own weight; while Devil could hold him upright, he couldn't make him walk. When Catriona tried to slide under Richard's other arm and help, Devil pulled a lock of her hair. 'No!' He frowned at her. 'Get Henderson.'

There was enough implacability in his face to make her heave an exasperated sigh and run from the room.

Henderson came quickly. With him under one of Richard's arms and Devil under the other, they started walking Richard up and down the room. At first, it was no more than a dragging stagger, as one foot dragged, then fell in front of the other. They walked him for ten minutes, then rested, then tried again. And won a fraction more response from Richard. Heartened, they kept up the treatment, walking, resting, then walking again.

319

Noticing a flicker of Richard's lashes when she spoke to Henderson, Catriona spoke directly to Richard, exhorting him to greater efforts. But, after a time, he only shook his head irritatedly and became even less cooperative.

'Enough.' Devil steered their burden to the bed. 'Let's have dinner, then we'll try again.'

They did, with greater response but even less cooperation. Richard wanted to be left in peace. He didn't say so, but his meaning was quite clear; he became increasingly difficult to manage, swearing in inventive mumbles at his tormentors.

But he walked – back and forth with increasing control over his limbs. When, all but exhausted himself, Devil called a halt and let Richard fall back across the bed, he had regained enough muscle control to grope blindly back onto the pillows and snuggle down.

Smiling for the first time in five days, Catriona drew up the covers and tucked him in.

As she straightened, Devil draped a brotherly arm about her shoulders and gave her a hug. 'If he can remember all those French curses, he'll be back with us soon.'

Catriona's smile wavered; she grasped Devil's hand and squeezed. 'Thank you.'

He grinned and flicked her cheek. 'No need. He's mine, too, you know.' With that enigmatic comment, he led her to the door. 'Honoria's already asleep – she said she'd watch through the small hours. I'll stay here now and wake her about midnight. You can get some sleep, then you can relieve her in the morning.'

Catriona hesitated. 'Are you sure—'

'Positive.' Devil held the door and elegantly waved her through. 'I'll see you in the morning.'

He did – early in the morning. When Catriona returned to the turret room to relieve Honoria a good hour before dawn, she

320

found, not Honoria, but Devil yawning over a game of Patience set out on the covers beside Richard, still comatose.

Catriona stared at Devil. 'What happened to Honoria?'

Devil looked up at her, then squinted at the clock on the mantelpiece. 'Good heavens! Is that the time?' He grinned engagingly, but undeniably wearily, up at her. 'It seems I forgot to summon my dear wife. Never mind.' He stood and stretched. 'I'll go and wake her now.'

He looked down at Richard. 'Time flies when one's having fun, but he never was much of a conversationalist.'

With a last, weary smile, he left her.

Shaking her head resignedly, Catriona tugged the armchair into place so, sunk in its comfort, she could see Richard's face. His beard had grown, concealing the gauntness of his cheeks; he looked more than faintly disreputable, slumped almost face down in the bed with his hair falling over his fore-head and his arms flung out.

Catriona smiled and pulled her workbasket to her side. They would walk him again after breakfast; she'd ring for Worboys to relieve her, then go and summon Henderson and Irons. With their help, perhaps she could get Richard to throw off the lingering effects of the wolfsbane today.

Looking up at him, she listened to his breathing, steady and even, as familiar as her own. Reassured, she picked up her needle and settled to darn.

Head bent, Catriona was plying her needle in the chair beside the bed when Richard finally managed to lever up his lids. Quite why they'd been so unconscionably heavy he couldn't understand, but, at long last, they'd done what he wanted of them and opened.

The sight of his witchy wife in a pose of sweet domestic-ity was undeniably pleasant; he drank it in, let it soothe away the last of the panic that had gripped him when he'd drifted in the grey cold and wondered if he would die. He hadn't wanted to die, but he'd been so cold, so weak, he hadn't felt able to cling to life.

But then she'd come, slipping her warm hand in his and leading him back, out of the grey cold and into the warm darkness of their bed. She hadn't wanted him to die either – she hadn't let him go, she'd helped him cling, helped him stay. Helped him live.

He was still here, with her; looking further, he confirmed that he was in their bed, and that morning light was seeping through the curtains. He drew in a deep breath, and brought his gaze back to her well-beloved face – and noticed the dark smudges beneath her eyes. In that instant, she yawned, lifting a hand to smother it, then she blinked her eyes wide and refocused on her darning.

Richard frowned; his witchy wife was undeniably pale, undeniably drawn. She didn't, now he looked more closely, look all that well.

His frown deepened.

Catriona felt it and looked up; startled, the first thing she saw was the blue of his eyes. Her heart soared, only to plummet a second later. He was frowning direfully. At her. He opened his lips – she stayed him with a raised hand. 'No! Let me speak first. No matter what you think, I did *not* poison you.'

He blinked, but his frown returned immediately. He opened his lips again—

'I realize you might have jumped to that conclusion, and I can see why you might, but you're wrong. It's absolutely ridiculous to imagine that after all you've done for me and the vale, all that's passed between us, that I would suddenly turn around and poison you. If you really think that—'

'I *don't!*'

Catriona blinked and discovered Richard was no longer

frowning at her – he was glowering at her.

'Of course, I don't think you poisoned me!' His gaze raked her, then returned to her face; his glower turned black. 'What nonsensical notion have you been worrying yourself with?'

When she didn't answer, he swore. 'I'd heard women got silly ideas when pregnant, but that takes the prize.' He looked at her more closely – then swore again. 'Is that what you've been worrying yourself sick over? That I'd be fool enough to think it was you?'

Dazedly, somewhat warily, Catriona nodded. Which brought forth another round of curses.

'What a stupid, foolish notion—'

'Why did you send for your brother, then?'

'So he'd be here to protect *you* if I wasn't about to do it, of course! *Lord—!*'

Running out of curses, he leaned forward, grabbed her hand and hauled her onto the bed. Pins, needle and mending went flying. Catriona gasped as she landed amid the covers.

Before she could react, he'd framed her face and was studying it closely.

'You haven't been taking care of yourself—'

'*You* were the one poisoned—' She struggled to get free, to sit up; even in his weakened state, he held her easily.

'We'll sort that out later. You obviously haven't been getting enough sleep. Pregnant women are supposed to sleep more – I would have thought you'd know that. You've staff and helpers about you . . .' He broke off, then looked into her eyes. 'How long have I been unconscious?'

'*Five days,*' Catriona informed him.

'Five *days?*' Richard stared at her, then his gaze softened and dropped to her lips . . . 'No wonder I'm so hungry.'

This time, Catriona knew precisely which appetite he was referring to. She opened her lips – but didn't manage to say a word.

He kissed her, gently, tenderly, then with gathering rapaciousness. Catriona felt the covers about her slide, felt the pillows shift, felt his hand slide up her leg to her garter, then stroke the soft skin above. He leaned into her, pressing her deeper into the soft mattress; she clung to the moment, savored it briefly, then thumped him on the shoulder. Hard.

He shifted slightly – she managed to drag her lips free and gasp: '*Richard!* You're not strong enough!'

He raised his head and looked down at her – as if what she'd just said was utterly impossible – then he hesitated, considered, then groaned, grimaced, closed his eyes, and rolled off her.

'Unfortunately, much as it pains me to admit it, I think you might be right.'

'Of course, I'm right!' Struggling up on one elbow, Catriona tugged the covers back over him. 'You've been at death's door – literally! – for five days. You're not simply going to open your eyes and' – she gestured wildly – 'get right back into things.'

He caught her eye and waggled his brows at her; ignoring her blush, she humphed. 'You just stay there and rest.' She went to slide away, to back off the bed, but his arm, around her, didn't give. She looked at his face.

'I'll stay here,' he said, gently, reasonably, 'provided you stay with me.' Catriona frowned; inexorably, he drew her closer. 'You need to rest, too.' Drawing her down, back into his arms, he settled her head on his shoulder, then pressed a kiss to her forehead. 'Just let me hold you while you sleep.'

He did. Swamped by relief so deep it shook her, touched that his last conscious thoughts, and now his first, had been for her, wrapped in his arms, with him safe beside her, Catriona slept.

# Chapter Seventeen

'I am *not* an invalid!' Richard eyed the mushy food on the tray balanced across his thighs with disgust.

'You are,' Catriona declared. 'And Cook made that especially for you – she's an expert at building people up.'

'I don't need building up.' His expression mutinous, Richard poked at the greyish mass with his fork. 'I need letting up.'

'I think you'll find you're mistaken.'

Richard looked up. 'Honoria!' His sister-in-law swept in, clearly intending to lend Catriona her support; Richard glanced back at the doorway, and to his relief saw the shadow he wanted darkening the door. 'Thank God – come in commonsense.'

Brows rising, Devil strolled in. 'I don't know that I've ever been called "common" before.' He grinned. 'You need a shave.'

'Never mind that – have you seen what they're feeding me?'

Devil looked. 'Better you than me, brother mine.'

'You have to save me.' Richard pointed to the mushy mass. 'You can't leave me to this fate.'

Straightening, Devil looked across the bed – at Catriona, staring mulishly, arms folded; at his wife, her expression implacable, her fine eyes on him. 'Hmm – actually, in this case, I think I must defer to higher authority.'

Richard stared at him. 'You've never done that before.'

'Ah – but you weren't married before.' Strolling around the bed, Devil collected Honoria in one arm and turned toward the door. Looking back, he added, 'And neither was I. I'll come back after lunch.'

Richard glared at the empty doorway, flicked a glance at Catriona, then looked down at the mush on his plate. He scooped up a forkful and ate. Swallowing, he frowned at his wife. 'I'm only doing this for you, you know.'

'Good.' Some moments later, she added: 'All of it.'

Richard complied. Aside from anything else, the food tasted a lot better than it looked – and he was hungry enough to eat a horse.


Both Devil and Honoria returned after lunch, after he'd cleared the tray and Catriona had taken it away.

'I have to say that seeing your eyes open is a great improvement.' Devil perched on the end of the bed. 'I've had quite enough of watching over you while you sleep.'

Richard grinned. Devil was three years older; they'd shared a nursery – his comment harked back to the untold nights when, scared of the dark, he'd only fallen asleep because he'd known Devil was there to protect him from imagined monsters.

'You gave us a shock.' Honoria leaned down and kissed his stubbled cheek. 'At least you had the good sense to marry a lady who could save you.'

Richard smiled and accepted the compliment graciously. Over the next half hour, they exchanged family news, heavily biased toward the emerging talents of one Sebastian Sylvester Cynster, Marquess of Earith, Devil's heir.

'We would have brought him,' Honoria declared, 'but we didn't know what the state of things here might be.'

That, of course, was the cue for Richard to fill them in, which he did in glowing terms, quite unable to contain his satisfaction on that score – his happiness in his new life. 'Now you're here, I'll be able to show you around.'

'Once you're released from *durance vile*.' Devil nodded at the bed.

'Tomorrow,' Richard said.

Devil grimaced. 'Don't get your hopes up. You didn't seem too strong while we were walking you yesterday.'

'Walking me . . .?' Richard frowned, then shook his head. 'I didn't even know you were here . . .' Still frowning, he glanced at Devil. 'Actually, I do remember – was it you who warned me *Maman* was coming?'

Devil grinned. 'We were testing to see if you'd respond.'

Richard shuddered. 'Just as long as it's not true.' He caught Devil's eye. 'You didn't tell her, did you?'

Devil raised his brows exaggeratedly. 'What do you think?'

Rising, Honoria shook out her skirts. 'Naturally, we left a note.'

Devil's head snapped around. 'We did?'

Honoria stared at him. 'Well, of course. We couldn't simply leave and not tell Helena, not even leave a message – she is his mother, after all.'

Richard groaned and fell back against his pillows.

Honoria turned her gaze on him. 'She was away with the Ashfordleighs – she'd think it very strange to return to Somersham and find Sebastian alone with the staff. So I simply explained and told her not to worry.'

Devil raised his eyes to the ceiling. 'Honoria—'

Sudden shouts from outside cut across his words; a second later, the rattle of carriagewheels and the sharp clack of hooves rose from the courtyard.

Richard groaned again; Devil grimaced.

Honoria stared at them. 'It can't be.'

'It can,' Devil assured her.

'It is,' Richard gloomily prophesied.

It was. In the courtyard, a cavalcade of two carriages with outriders drew up.

Hearing the commotion as she crossed the front hall on her way back to Richard's side, Catriona went out onto the front porch to investigate.

The scene in the courtyard was bewildering – as if a house-party from London had lost its way and turned up at the manor. Coachboys, outriders, grooms and maids rushed hither and yon, opening carriage doors and setting steps in place, tugging at the straps that secured bags and trunks to the backs and tops of the carriages. A tall, exceedingly elegant gentleman stepped down from the second carriage; he cast a swift glance about the teeming courtyard – his gaze halted, and lingered, on her, before returning to the scene of chaos about the first carriage. Despite his fairer coloring – brown hair, not black – Catriona felt certain the gentleman was another Cynster.

Just as she felt certain the small, dark-and-silver-haired lady he helped down from the first carriage was the Dowager Duchess of St. Ives – Helena, Richard's stepmother. With the brisk energy of a whirlwind, the Dowager waved the elegant gentleman back to his own carriage, where a second lady was waiting to descend. Behind the Dowager, two young ladies, their lowered hoods revealing a wealth of golden curls, were gaily piling out of the first carriage. Claiming the arm of one of her grooms, the Dowager made straight for the front porch, her cloak billowing about her.

She came up the front steps with the force of a military charge. 'My dear!'

Catriona only just had time to brace herself; flinging her arms wide, the Dowager enveloped her in a warm embrace.

328

'Now you may tell me he is better – he is better, is he not? But of course, he is! You would not otherwise be standing here so calmly, welcoming a garrulous old woman!' Green eyes twinkling, the Dowager hugged her again, then released her; holding both her hands wide, she stepped back and, with every evidence of shrewd consideration, quickly looked her over.

'Oh, yes!' Looking up, the Dowager caught Catriona's eye. 'You will do very well for him, I think.' She smiled, brilliantly. 'And you will not let him down – you will always be there for him, yes?' For one instant, green and hazel eyes held, and touched, then the Dowager beamed. With Gallic exuberance, she kissed Catriona on both cheeks. 'Welcome to the family, my dear.'

Touched to the heart by the profound love that shone from the Dowager's eyes, Catriona blinked rapidly. 'Thank you, ma'am.'

'Helena,' the Dowager firmly declared. 'I am Helena to both my sons' wives. But tell me – Devil and Honoria have arrived, have they not? And how is Richard – is he eating? Has he risen? Has—'

'Aunt Helena, you're liable to give poor Catriona a very strange notion of the family.'

Turning, Catriona beheld the elegant gentleman with a graceful lady on his arm. They both smiled warmly; he bowed. 'Vane Cynster, my dear – and I assure you we don't all rattle on so.'

'I am *not* "rattling on,"' Helena declared. 'I am merely exercising the right of any mother to learn of her son's health.'

'But he isn't about to die, is he?' The question came from one of the blonde beauties, now lined up behind the Dowager.

'Surely not Richard?' The second young lady fixed Catriona with huge blue eyes. 'But you're a healer aren't you? You'd save him.'

There was an element of absolute confidence in that last, uttered with a nod, that touched Catriona anew.

The graceful lady sighed and touched the Dowager's arm. 'Perhaps, Helena, if we move inside – I rather think there's another snow shower coming.'

Catriona stepped back and gestured the Dowager in; as the Dowager swept majestically across the threshold, the graceful lady touched Catriona's arm and met her glance with a smile.

'I'm Patience, my dear. Recently married to Vane, another of the family's reprobates. And these are Amanda and Amelia – and' – she paused to draw breath and met Catriona's eye – 'I'll explain how it all happened later.'

They followed the Dowager in; the scene in the hall quickly achieved the same degree of chaos that had held sway in the courtyard. Boxes and trunks were ferried in and piled in corners under Henderson's dour direction. Mrs. Broom looked as stunned as Catriona felt; wide-eyed, the house-keeper struggled to take in her instructions, then rushed off, calling to maids and footmen to open up and air rooms for the latest guests.

A cacophony unlike anything the serene manor had known rose in the hall as the two young ladies checked which bandbox was whose and where the Dowager's shawl had gone; Vane and both coachmen were in earnest discussion with Irons over where to stable the extra horses. The Dowager had discovered McArdle and was inquiring after his stiff limbs as if she'd known him all his life – and he was respond-ing as if she had. Rushing maids and footmen stopped now here, now there, to put a question, then dashed off about their duties.

Catriona stood just inside the front doors and took it all in, let it wash over her. The noise, the boisterousness, the enor-mous well of energy that swelled within her hall; it was an immensely powerful force. It was there in the swift, neat

330

movements of the Dowager, in the set of her head as she tilted it the better to consider McArdle's replies. There in the crisp directions Vane Cynster issued, in the innate grace, redolent of harnessed power, with which he moved. There in the glow that lit the young ladies' faces and invested their bodies with a taut grace reminiscent of fawns about to spring into flight.

Coming to stand beside her, Patience looked over the hall. 'The Cynsters are here – what more need be said?' But she was smiling. She turned to Catriona. 'I do apologize for descending on you like this, but as you were going to have to cope with Helena come what may, it's probably just as well the rest of us are here to help you.'

The clear affection in Patience's tone, in her eyes, as they returned to the Dowager, stripped her comments of any implied criticism.

'Perhaps,' Catriona murmured, 'I'd better take her up to see Richard.'

Patience nodded. 'Do. It'll set her mind at rest. Don't worry about the rest of us.' She smiled at Catriona. 'If you don't mind, I'll speak directly to your housekeeper if there's any problem – I rather think you must have enough on your plate.'

Catriona returned her smile. 'Please do.' Looking back at the Dowager, she drew in a deep breath. 'It's possible I may be rather busy for a while.'

With that, she stepped boldly into the fray and fetched up by the Dowager's side. 'Helena, if you wish, I'll take you to see Richard – I'm sure he'll be anxious to see you.'

The Dowager shot her a shrewd glance. 'No, no, *ma petite* – it is I who am anxious to see him. He' – with a Gallic gesture, she dismissed all males – 'is but a man. He does not understand these things.'

As she took the arm Helena offered, Catriona saw two blonde heads lift; two pairs of blue eyes fastened on them.

'Amelia! Amanda!'

Both heads turned; Patience beckoned. With a sigh and a last look, they went.

'Vane, you can see Richard later – I want to get our rooms sorted out first.'

Her gaze on the stairs, Catriona smiled and bore the Dowager upstairs to see her second son.

Richard felt trapped – deserted by Devil and Honoria – left to face his stepmother alone. When the door opened and swung wide, he contemplated groaning and acting much iller than he was, but then he glimpsed his wife's fiery halo and thought better of any deception.

Only God and Her Lady knew where it might land him.

'Richard!' Helena – she who he'd always known as *Maman* – came sweeping down upon him.

Smiling reassuringly, he returned her hug, and squirmed when he glimpsed tears in her eyes. To his relief, she blinked quickly and they were gone, and she beamed her brilliant smile at him.

'*Bon!* You are already much recovered, I can see.'

To his surprise, instead of taking possession of him, his sickbed and his room in short order, she contented herself with taking possession of his hand, and cast a questioning glance at Catriona, standing at the end of the bed.

Catriona inclined her head. 'He is much better – he was unconscious for five days, but with Devil's help, we managed to walk him so the poison wore off sooner.'

'This poison.' Helena tilted her head, still regarding Catriona. 'How was it given him?'

Catriona looked at Richard. 'In his morning coffee.'

'And the person who put it there? Will they try again?'

'No.' Steadily, Catriona held Richard's gaze. 'The poisoner is no longer in the manor, or the vale.'

332

'Ah!' Helena nodded sagely. 'They have run to safety, yes?' She looked at Richard, then squeezed his hand. 'You will go after them, I know – but not until you are well again, *hein?*'

'I'll be perfectly well by tomorrow.' Richard tried to catch Catriona's eye but failed – she was looking at Helena.

'You will know best, of course,' his impossible stepmother was saying, 'but how quickly he recovers will depend on the poison, yes?'

'Indeed.' Looking back at Richard, far too calmly for his liking, Catriona informed him: 'You were given wolfsbane, and probably henbane as well. But it's the wolfsbane that's the most lingering. It weakens muscles, and it takes far longer than one thinks to release its effect. For the amount you must have taken in, it would generally take weeks for full recovery.'

'Weeks?' Horrified, Richard stared at her.

She smiled reassuringly. 'In your case, you have a very robust and ... er, vigorous constitution. If you remain in bed and eat what Cook sends you until you can stand and walk alone, you may be well enough to leave this room inside of a week.'

'*Eh, bien* – your wife has spoken. She is the healer here and you must pay attention.' Placing his hand under the sheets, Helena covered it and patted his arm. 'You will be good and recover quickly, so that I will not worry, no?'

Richard stared at her, then he looked at Catriona and saw the militant light in her eye.

With a long-suffering groan, he sank back into his pillows. He was rolled up – horse, foot and guns.


'Damn it – why couldn't you stop her!' Grumpily, Richard mock-glared at Vane.

Who merely grinned. 'Me and which army?' Settling on one corner of the bed, his back against the post, Vane raised

333

a resigned brow. 'You've known what she's like all your life.'

Richard humphed.

'And if you'd seen what faced us when we arrived at Somersham, you'd be thanking me for managing to leave Mrs. Hull and Webster behind. As it is' – Vane glanced at Devil, similarly ensconced on the other side of the bed – 'I'm sure the only reason they consented to remain at Somersham was because Sebastian was there.'

Richard looked at Vane in only partly feigned horror, then shook his head. 'What I can't understand is what you're all doing here.'

'*We,*' Vane said, clearly referring to himself and Patience, 'were returning from visiting the Beuclaires in Norwich and thought we'd stop by to tell Devil and Honoria our news.'

Devil raised his brows. 'What news?'

'The impending extension of our family.'

'Really?' Devil grinned and thumped Vane on the shoulder. 'Excellent. Another playmate for Sebastian.'

Both Richard, beaming and shaking hands with Vane, and Vane himself, stopped and turned to stare at Devil.

'Another?' Vane asked.

Devil grinned even more as he resettled his shoulders against the bedpost. 'Well, you didn't think I'd stop at just one, did you?'

They hadn't, but ... 'When?' Richard asked.

Devil shrugged nonchalantly. 'Sometime in summer.'

Richard hesitated, then raised a brow and sank back. 'Sounds like our respective mothers and aunts will be in alt. Nothing they like better than a baby or two.' Or three. But he kept his lips shut on that point and looked at Vane. 'So what happened when you got to Somersham?'

'We arrived mid-morning, one hour after Helena and the twins, who she's been chaperoning about, got in from the Ashfordleighs – we didn't even get a chance to get out of our coats. Your mother had read Honoria's note and got the bit well and truly between her teeth even before we arrived. Nothing would do but she must rush north to your side – to your deathbed, as she put it. As usual, it was impossible to gainsay her – and, of course, I couldn't let her go rushing through the snow with just the twins for escort. Well,' Vane gestured, 'you can imagine what it was like. Mrs. Hull on the stairs with Sebastian in her arms declaring you were at death's door. Webster all but wringing his hands and making unhelpful suggestions as to how best to reach the Lowlands. The twins oohing and aahing and trying not to remember Tolly's death. And your mother, center stage, vowing she would fight through drifts on her hands and knees to get to your side in time. In time for what, I didn't ask.'

'To make a long story short, I didn't stop them because I couldn't. The push north had gathered so much momentum before we arrived that it was beyond my poor ability to deflect.'

Richard grimaced in exasperated understanding. 'Couldn't you at least have left the twins behind?'

Vane eyed him straitly. 'Have you tried recently to turn the twins – independently or in concert?'

Richard blinked at him. 'But they're only girls.'

'That's what I keep trying to tell them – they seem to have different ideas.'

'Humph!' Richard settled deeper into his prison. 'Well, they won't be able to test their wings here – it's as quiet as a nunnery.'

An hour later, Catriona presided over the noisiest dinner she could ever recall. It wasn't that anyone raised their voices, or spoke above the tone of polite conversation. But the sudden injection of Cynster elegance, wit and curiosity had spawned innumerable conversations, both at the main table, where all

335

the guests sat, and at all the tables in the hall, filled by her household.

Everyone was chattering animatedly.

The wash of sound did not give her a headache – not at all. It was comforting, in some ill-defined way. There was warmth in the laughter, in the interest and attention, in the real affection so openly displayed. There was a human element the Cynsters had brought to the vale that, somehow, had been missing before. She wasn't quite sure what it was, but . . .

In her habitual role as head of the household, she kept an eye on the courses, making sure her guests needs were met. Everything ran smoothly – indeed, despite the totally unexpected influx, no serious problem had occurred.

Her gaze, at that instant, resting on the Dowager, Catriona inwardly grinned. Everything had gone right, because nothing dared go wrong, not before the Dowager and Honoria. Patience was less forceful a personality, at least on the surface, but even she could command when she wished. She'd called both the twins and her husband to order very effectively that morning.

Catriona inwardly frowned. Vibrant, effective matriarchs did not fit her earlier vision of what Cynster wives must be like. Recalling what had given rise to that transparently inaccurate view, she waited until Honoria, beside her, was free, then caught her eye. 'I know,' she murmured, leaning closer and lowering her voice, 'what the bare circumstances of Richard's birth were. What I can't quite understand' – her gaze flicked to the Dowager – 'is how his acceptance into the family came about.'

Honoria grinned. 'It is difficult to see – unless one has previously met Helena. Then . . . anything becomes possible.' She lowered her voice. 'Devil told me that when Richard was dumped, a squalling babe of a few months, on the ducal doorstep, Helena heard the ruckus, and before Devil's father had a chance to hide matters, Helena simply – literally – took Richard out of his hands.' She paused and sent an affectionate glance up the table to the Dowager. 'You see, Helena loves children, but after Devil, she couldn't have any more of her own. The one thing she most yearned for was another – especially another son. So, when Richard arrived, in her inimitable way she decided it was all Providence's doing and claimed him as her own. The trick was, by then, she was well established as Devil's father's duchess – a veritable power within the ton. Quite simply, none had the gall to gainsay her – where was the point? Helena could have socially destroyed most people with nothing more than a raised brow.'

'I'm surprised Devil's father was so . . . acquiescent.'

'Acquiescent? From all I've heard of him, I doubt the term would apply. But he sincerely loved Helena – the accident that resulted in Richard's birth was more in the way of him comforting Richard's mother than in any intended infidelity. And so he indulged Helena – he loved her enough to allow her the one thing she asked of him in recompense: he allowed her to claim Richard and bring him up as her own, something which unquestionably gave her great and abiding pleasure.'

Again, Honoria glanced affectionately at the Dowager. Catriona did the same.

'So,' Honoria concluded, 'Richard's birth has been an open secret for thirty years, and, really, no one cares any more. He's simply Richard Cynster, Devil's brother – and as the family approve of that, who's to argue?'

Catriona shared a glance with Honoria, then smiled and touched her arm. 'Thank you for telling me.'

Honoria returned the smile, then looked around, alerted by the deep rumble of her spouse's voice. She promptly called him to order, taking up verbal cudgels in the twins' defense. The head of their house was dissatisfied with their appearance – in what way he refused to clarify.

337

Catriona stifled a grin. Cynster wives were definitely not mere cyphers, pretty trophies to be displayed on their husbands' arms. With three others in the room, she couldn't escape the conclusion that, for whatever inscrutable male reasons, Cynster men had a soul-deep affinity for strong women.

And, furthermore, despite their occasional comments to the contrary, they wouldn't have it any other way. They took real delight in indulging their wives; one only needed to catch the look in Devil's eyes as they rested on Honoria, or in Vane's as he watched Patience.

Or in Richard's as he watched her.

The realization stopped her thoughts – something inside her quivered. The reason Cynster men so indulged their wives was there in their eyes. Much indulged their wives might be; much loved they certainly were.

And, as Devil loved Honoria, and Vane loved Patience, so Richard loved her.

It was that simple.

Dragging in a tight breath into lungs suddenly parched, Catriona barely heard the flow of noise and chatter about her. Her sight was turned inward.

Richard had fulfilled his vow to play second fiddle to her – to honor and indulge her position as lady of the vale – which was a large concession from a man like him – a warrior like him. She'd realized that from the start – that without such a concession, their marriage could never work, could never be the success they both needed it to be.

He'd made that concession because he loved her.

The sudden clarity, the absolute certainty that filled her mind was dazzling, breathtaking.

She'd known that he needed her, that he now knew he belonged here, in his appointed place at her side. But she hadn't, until that quivering instant, realized that he loved her as well.

338

Glancing at Devil, she saw him grin and flick a finger to Honoria's cheek, then he turned to address Vane, but his hand closed over Honoria's where it rested on the table. Vane was lounging in his chair, one hand on Patience's back, his fingers idly toying with her curls.

Only by that light in his eyes, and, perhaps, if she had any experience by which to judge, his intensity in their bed, did Richard show his love for her. He was reserved – she'd known that before she'd met him; he always wore a mask in public. He didn't display his love openly, as the others did so easily, apparently without thought. She needed instead to pay attention to his actions, and the motives behind them, to see what force was driving him.

She should, perhaps, have seen it before, but he yielded his secrets grudgingly. That he knew was beyond question; as Honoria had mentioned, Cynster males weren't blind, although they sometimes pretended they were. He had, she recalled, been very definite that he wanted her as his cause.

Turning to speak to the twins, she hugged her newfound discovery to her heart and, throughout dinner, took it out now and then to ponder. To consider. Again and again, she observed that special something that flowed openly between Devil and Honoria, and Vane and Patience – and wanted it for her own.

Quite how she might bring it about – give Richard the confidence he needed to show his love openly, presumably by convincing him she returned it fullfold – was something she'd yet to determine.

But it was something she vowed she would do.

Smiling sunnily, she chatted with the twins – thanks to The Lady, she now had ample time to work on Richard.

The next morning, Richard lay in bed and tried to disguise his fretfulness. Lying in bed doing nothing was his least favorite pastime, but at the moment, that was all he could do. Nothing.

At least he'd managed to coax his wife into sleeping beside him once more; she'd apparently been sleeping in the room next door ever since his poisoning, so as not to disturb him. He had made it very plain that now he'd regained his senses, not having her beside him would disturb him even more. He'd won that round, but no other.

There was no point in arguing – he couldn't stand on his own, much less walk. He'd tried, surreptitiously, in one of the few moments he'd been left alone. Luckily, he'd crashed back on the bed and not the floor. His muscles were not just weak but, as his witchy wife had warned him, still feeling the effects of the poison. Even holding his eyelids up was an effort.

Inwardly cursing she who had drugged him, he kept his face relaxed and listened to Vane's news of shared friends. With his usual instinctive grasp, Devil had refrained from pressing the question of who had poisoned him, waiting until he'd recovered enough to inquire. While Richard and Catriona had not discussed the matter beyond their exchange before Helena, Richard had, with complete confidence, assured Devil that the poisoner was not a threat now, and that he and Catriona would deal with the matter once he'd fully recovered.

Devil had accepted that; Richard knew he could rely on his brother to quash any further interest in the matter. It was definitely a situation he and his witchy wife needed to deal with on their own.

Not, however, yet.

Stifling a sigh, Richard smiled at Vane's description of a race held at Beuclaire Hall. Then he let his gaze drift past his cousin, to where Catriona sat on the windowseat, industriously darning, her hair turned to a blaze of glory by the sunlight streaming in through the window.

At least there was nothing wrong with his eyes.

340

Five minutes later, heralded by the most peremptory of knocks, the door opened. A tall, broad-shouldered, ineffably elegant figure sauntered in.

His gaze fell first on Catriona – and went no further.

The ends of his long lips lifting in a smile both Richard and Vane knew well, the gentleman advanced, then swept Catriona a bow.

'Gabriel Cynster, my dear.'

Catriona instinctively held out her hand; he took it and drew her effortlessly to her feet, into his arms, and kissed her. Raising his head, he smiled wolfishly down at her. 'Richard's cousin.'

'Another one,' Vane commented drily.

Smoothly releasing Catriona and gracefully reseating her with an irresistible smile, Gabriel turned to the bed and raised a languid brow. 'You here, too? If I'd known, I wouldn't have half-killed my horse getting here.'

Blinking, Catriona picked up her needle, but kept her gaze on the tableau about the bed.

'How the devil did you hear?' Richard asked. 'Don't tell me it's common knowledge among the ton.'

Halting by the bed, Gabriel looked down at Richard. 'Well, you're obviously still alive – Mama must have got her skeins tangled. She was quite adamant I'd find you at death's door.' Gracefully, he sat on the end of the bed. 'As for the news being bruited about, I can't say, but it wouldn't surprise me. Mama wrote me a series of orders, couched in a manner to discourage disobedience, and bade me hie north at speed. I was at a very select gathering in a hunting lodge in Leicestershire. How the devil she knew where to find me I really don't like to think.'

Vane humphed.

Richard grinned sleepily.

Gabriel shook his head. 'It's a sad day when one can't even

escape to a select, supposedly secret orgy without having one's mother summon one – without a verbal blink.'

Both Richard and Vane chuckled. Gabriel raised his brows resignedly.

Catriona shook out her mending and started to fold it. 'I'll certainly write to Lady Celia and thank her for her kind thoughts.'

A sudden hiatus gripped the three about the bed.

'And now,' Catriona declared, 'Richard needs to rest.'

The three exchanged a meaningful look; Catriona stood and smiled at Vane and Gabriel. 'If you would, gentlemen?'

She waved to the door; they left with smooth smiles and no argument. Bustling to the bed, she tucked Richard in. He wished he could frown, but he really was tired.

'Come and lie down with me.' He tried to catch her, but he was far too slow.

She whisked away, raised one finger to waggle at him, then changed her mind and smiled. A smile that softened her face and set his pulse racing, a smile that should have sealed her fate – if he'd been in any way up to it.

'Later,' she said. 'When you're well again.'

There was a softness in her eyes, an echo of something in her tone, that eased and soothed his irritation. She drew the curtains and left him; Richard drifted off, into dreams of a highly selected orgy, restricted to just two.


By the next morning, he had really had enough. He felt strong enough while lying relaxed on his back, but even lifting his arms was an effort. He couldn't make love to his wife. He couldn't get out of bed.

As far as he was concerned, he needed practice on both counts.

To that end, he persuaded Devil, so often his partner in crime in days past, now left to bear him company while their ladies took the air in the park, to help him up.

'If I can just get my legs functioning properly . . .'

Ducking one shoulder beneath Richard's arm, Devil helped him balance his weight as he rose from the side of the bed. 'Let's try it to the fireplace and back. We need to avoid the window – they might glance back and see us.'

Richard grabbed Devil's shoulder and lifted his foot to take the first step –

The door opened. 'It's drizzling—' The Dowager, in advance of her daughters-in-law, halted and viewed her sons – caught in an act of disobedience – through narrowing eyes. 'What is this?'

They both blushed. The degree of accent in Helena's speech gave them warning she was not amused.

'I would 'ave thought you were both now old enough to 'ave more sense,' she declared.

'Sense?' Her expression mirroring her skeptical tone, Honoria stepped around the Dowager. Devil quickly slid Richard back down on the bed and straightened. Honoria marched up to him, met his gaze directly, then took his hand. 'Come – I believe you've been relieved of duty here. Permanently.' With that, she towed him to the door.

Devil cast a glance back at Richard and shrugged helplessly.

Richard fell back on his pillows with a groan – as the two most important women in his life descended on him.

They lectured and fussed and lectured again, in between tucking him in tenderly. He bore it stoically – with a final sharp but concerned glance, Catriona had to leave him.

Helena pulled up the chair, picked up Catriona's discarded mending, and settled down to watch over him.

Richard sighed. 'I promise I won't try to get up again – not until my wife gives her permission.'

'Be quiet. Go to sleep.'

Helena's stern tone told him she had not forgiven him his indiscretion yet.

Richard swallowed a grunt. After a moment, he said: 'You never fuss over Devil.'

'That's because he never needed to be fussed over. You do – now be silent and sleep. And leave me to fuss.'

Thus adjured, he shut up and found himself, to his surprise, drifting into a doze. Before he succumbed, he asked: 'What do you think of Catriona?'

'She's the perfect wife for you. She will fuss very well in my stead.'

Richard felt his lips twitch resignedly; he took her advice, shut up and slept.

He awoke some hours later to discover the twins, one perched in a straight-backed chair to the left, the other in a matching chair to the right, bright blue eyes wide, watching over him.

Astonished, he stared at them. 'What the devil are you doing here?'

They smiled. 'Guarding you.'

Richard glowered; he looked them over, noting the full curves that filled out their bodices, the trim figures revealed by their muslin skirts – and glowered even more. 'Your necklines are too low – you'll catch your deaths.'

They bent identical disgusted looks on him.

'You're as bad as Devil.

'And Vane.'

'*Almost* as bad as Demon – he's been underfoot everywhere we go!'

'What *is* the matter with all of you?'

He humphed and shut his eyes – and refrained from telling them. 'This is the Lowlands,' he stated incontrovertibly. 'It's colder up here.' He wondered if Catriona had some spare shawls they could pin over their shoulders, closed to the neck.

Still, at least they were up here, with him, Devil, Vane and Gabriel about, not gallivanting in the south, flaunting themselves like plump lambs before God knew how many hungry wolves, with only Helena for protection.

Keeping his eyes shut, he sank deeper into his bed. Perhaps there was some sense to this madness after all.

# Chapter Eighteen

The week passed slowly for Richard, confined to his bed, and in a whirl of unaccustomed gaiety for the other inhabitants of the vale.

They'd never encountered people like the Cynsters before.

Entering the stable yard four mornings later, Catriona was conscious of the smile on her face – it rarely dimmed these days, despite Richard's posioning and what she would, once their guests left, have to face. For now, all was running smoothly, with a bubbling, effervescent sense of life. Thanks to their guests.

They were everywhere, helping with everything, yet they had, with a characteristic tact that was in itself overwhelming, managed to do so without stepping on anyone's sensitivities.

A feat that commanded her respect.

On her way back to the house after checking the still slumbering gardens, she paused to take in the activity in the yard. Devil was there with McAlvie and his lads; beside them, Vane and Corby were mounted, about to ride out to check the orchards. Vane was looking down, Devil was looking up – all the other men seemed not just smaller, but somehow less alive. Then Devil nodded and stepped back. Vane wheeled his mount; with Corby at his heels, he clattered out of the yard. Turning away, Devil collected McAlvie; with the herdsman's lads following close behind, they strode down the slope to the cattle barn.

Smiling to herself, Catriona resumed her progress to the house. Devil watched over the livestock, Vane the orchards. Without the slightest comment, they'd left the crops to her. They'd divided Richard's responsibilities between them and were acting in his stead. As for Gabriel, he'd appointed himself Richard's amanuensis; he was presently sitting with Richard and dealing with the accumulated correspondence concerning his business affairs. She hadn't realized how extensive Richard's investments were until Gabriel had found the pile of letters in the library and come storming upstairs, waving them and insisting Richard deal with them.

She was learning new things every day.

Like the fact that, while in no way susceptible in the common sense, the other women in the vale were very definitely appreciative of men like the Cynsters. A group of them had gathered in the doorway of the dairy to enjoy the sight of Devil and Vane. All the Cynster men drew the same response – they were always so elegantly dressed and shod, yet thought nothing of picking up an axe and splitting logs, or helping with a fence, or herding cows. The local women had grown used to Richard, but ... their wide smiles and their comments, drifting on the breeze – 'And there are more of them yet, Cook says.' 'Oh, my!' as, with smiling nods to her, they turned back into the dairy – suggested they were far from bored with the sight.

Her smile converting to a grin, Catriona climbed the steps and pushed through the heavy back door. Cynsters, she'd decided, were simply larger than life.

Two of them were baking bread. Up to their elbows in flour, Amelia and Amanda stood at the kitchen table, giggling with Cook's girls as they all kneaded dough. All the girls were flushed, Amelia's and Amanda's ringlets were dancing, their huge cornflower blue eyes brilliant with laughter. Even with flour smudges over their pert noses, they were beauties.

Beautiful young English ladies from one of the very best of the old families.

They could still giggle with the best of them. While certainly not unconscious of their charms, neither twin seemed to have a 'conscious' bone in her body – while neither would ever forget who they were, they were openly friendly and ready to be pleased.

Cook's girls were in awe, but equally ready to join in the fun.

'Perhaps we could do the loaves in braids – like this.' Amelia created a distinctly skewed braid with her dough.

'Aunt Helena likes bread made like that,' Amanda explained, 'but perhaps we should try some different shapes – braids might not be to the gentlemen's taste.'

Smiling broadly, Catriona passed on, leaving them devising all manner of fancy loaves. Those sitting down to lunch would have a new interest.

Heading into the house, she passed the archway to the second kitchen, which housed the main ovens of the manor. And halted – arrested by the sight of two derrieres, side by side, one cloaked in serviceable drab, the other in fashionable twill.

'Hmm – I think it needs a touch more rosemary.' Bent over, peering into the dark cavern of the roasting oven, Honoria passed the basting ladle to Cook.

Who nodded her grey head. 'P'raps, p'raps. And maybe a pinch more tarragon and a clove or two. Just to pick it up a bit, like.'

Neither heard her, neither turned around; both continued to study the roast with absolute concentration. Smiling still, Catriona glided on.

'I have always found that a *soupçon* of lavender in the polish is the perfect touch. It freshens a room without overpowering.'

'I do so agree, madam. And it makes the beeswax just that bit softer, to go just that bit farther. Can I help you to a little bit more sherry, Your Grace?'

From the shadows of the corridor, Catriona watched Mrs. Broom refill the sherry glass clasped between the Dowager's fine fingers. A ring of emeralds and diamonds flashed as the Dowager gestured her thanks.

'I have noticed,' she said, as Mrs. Broom returned to her chair, 'that your silver has a very nice luster. What polish do you use?'

'Ah, well, now – that's a bit of a vale secret, that is. Howsoever, seeing as you're family now . . .'

Shaking her head, Catriona glided silently on, storing the moment in her memory to describe to Richard later. The Dowager could very well have sat in the drawing room and commanded Mrs. Broom's presence; instead, she'd elected to take sherry with the housekeeper in her snug little parlor. The better to learn her secrets.

The Dowager was incorrigible.

Her smile wreathing her face, Catriona stepped into the hall – and remembered those she had not seen in her journey through the nether regions. The manor's tribe of children. They'd been noticeably absent – not one small body had she seen, not one shrill shriek had she heard.

Which was not necessarily a good thing.

Where were they? And what were they up to?

She detoured via the games room – and found her answers. Patience was sitting on the rug before the hearth, her elegant skirts spread wide to accommodate the kittens, playing, rolling, batting at fingers and hands. The children were all gathered about, quietly enthralled.

'Ooh, look!' one said in wonder. 'This one likes my hair.'

'Their claws are sharp.'

'Indeed,' Patience warned, 'and so are their teeth.'

She looked up at that moment and saw Catriona – Patience raised her brows in question. Catriona smiled and shook her head.

'Ow!'

Patience turned back. 'Now be careful – they're only very young and don't mean to hurt.'

With her manor filled to bursting, and yet, at peace, Catriona headed on to the stillroom.

She was there an hour later when Patience put her head around the door. 'Can I interrupt?'

Catriona grinned. 'Please do – I'm only refreshing the linen sachets.'

'Perhaps I could help.' Pulling a stool up to the other side of the table at which Catriona sat, Patience settled and picked up one of the small linen bags. 'I'll sew them up, if you like.'

'You can interrupt me any time,' Catriona informed her, pushing the needle and thread over the table. 'That's the part I hate.'

Once they'd settled to their tasks, Patience said: 'Actually, I was wondering if you could recommend anything to help settle my stomach.' She caught Catriona's eye and grimaced. 'Just in the mornings.'

'Ah.' Catriona smiled and dusted off her hands. 'I have a tea that should help.' She had the canister to hand. 'It's mainly chamomile.'

The family had celebrated Patience and Vane's good news with a boisterous round of toasts around Richard's bed some nights before. Honoria had tried to take a backseat, claiming a second pregnancy was less news than a first – they hadn't let her succeed. However, other than exchanging warm glances, she and Richard had said nothing; both, independently, had felt the need to keep their news to themselves for a time – to savor it fully before sharing it with others. Setting the canister down, she found a cloth bag and filled it with the leaves. 'Have the maid brew this for you every morning and drink it before getting out of bed – it should soothe you.'

It worked for her.

Patience took the bag gladly. 'Thank you. Honoria doesn't seem to be affected – she says she only feels woozy for about a week.'

'All women are different,' Catriona assured her as she returned to her task of stuffing dried herbs into the linen sachets.

A companionable silence descended, then the door opened; Honoria looked in. She smiled. 'There you are. Perfect. I wanted to ask if you had any remedies made up for teething infants.' Pulling up another stool to the table, she picked up an empty sachet and started to stuff it. 'Sebastian's cut his first two teeth, but the rest seem to be causing him more bother. He gets so fractious – and, if anything, he can out-bellow his father.'

Patience chuckled.

Catriona grinned and slipped from her stool. 'Cloves should help. I have an ointment made up here somewhere.'

While she poked about and found the jar, then filled a smaller jar for Honoria, the other two industriously stuffed and sewed.

'Actually,' Honoria said, handing a stuffed sachet to Patience, 'when you come to visit I must get you to go through our stillroom. I know the basics, of course, but I'm sure you could give me a few lessons to good effect.'

'Hmm.' Patience looked around at the neat rows of bottles and jars, all filled, all labelled. 'And when you've finished in Cambridgeshire, you can come and visit in Kent.'

Ordinarily, she would instantly have said that she never left the vale; instead, visited by an impulse she couldn't de?ne, Catriona smiled warmly. 'We'll see.'

*

351

They all gathered for lunch that day – when the gong sounded, the three ladies left the stillroom where they'd spent a companionable hour finishing the linen sachets and comparing household notes. As she strolled with her sister-in-law and cousin-in-law to the dining hall, Catriona could not recall any similar experience. She'd never been party to such a discussion before, never been exposed to the warmth of shared confidences and freely offered advice.

She'd never felt as close to any other lady as she now did to Honoria and Patience. Yet another revelation of what she had not known could be.

The dining hall was its now customary hub of noise and energy. As she took her seat, she looked over her guests with an affection she'd never before experienced. A growing affection.

They, of course, simply took it as their due; they smiled, grinned and even winked at her, then settled to entertain themselves and everyone else. They were all so powerfully alive, so sure of themselves, so innately confident, yet not high in the instep at all; the manor folk, the vale folk – all her people – had taken them to their hearts.

The Dowager sat beside McArdle and lectured him on taking more exercise, something Catriona had tried to hint to him for years. The Dowager didn't hint – she told him. With extravagant gestures cloaked in Gallic charm.

And, of course, McArdle listened, and nodded his head in agreement.

Cook and Honoria compared notes on the success of their efforts with the roasted meats, while the twins called everyone's attention to the highly varied loaves scattered about the tables, prettily sharing all compliments thus gained with Cook's three girls, who turned beet-red with confusion.

Henderson, Devil and McAlvie sat at another table, deep in discussion of who knew what; farther along, Vane and

Gabriel were chatting with Corby, Huggins and the stablelads – about horses if their gestures were any guide.

Outside the weather was still raw and cold, but inside, the manor was aglow with warmth and laughter. Smiling benignly, Catriona looked out over her extended household and silently blessed them, every one.

Later that afternoon, she left Richard, grumbling, to rest, and went out to watch the riding lessons.

Vane had discovered Richard's attempts in that direction – he'd told Devil and Gabriel.

The children were now in alt. They were getting riding lessons every day, sometimes twice a day, from their very own instructors, all ex-cavalry officers. Catriona had learned that last from a breathless Tom, later confirmed by Devil.

'I'm probably the strongest rider,' he'd said, 'but Demon's the best.' He'd glanced down at her and smiled. 'You haven't met him yet – he's Vane's brother.'

Catriona was quietly grateful Demon hadn't turned up at the manor, too – multiple Cynsters were a lot to get used to all at once.

But they were very good riders – and very good with children.

Slipping unobtrusively into the yard, she perched on the corner of the water trough in its center and watched the three groups into which they'd divided the children. The youngest were with Devil – totally unafraid of him – giggling and laughing as he patiently held them on and taught them how to sit, how to hold the reins. The next group in age, including young Tom, were with Vane, being coached in the rudiments of active riding. The last group, composed of the stablelads and young farmhands who could ride after a fashion but were definitely not up to the Cynster mark, were drilling under Gabriel's eagle eye.

Catriona watched for some time, trying to comprehend the rapport that seemed so effortless, between Cynster men and horses, and also small humans. In the end, she inwardly shrugged, smiled and accepted it – they were, transparently, naturals in both spheres – that was all there was to it.

And she, and all the vale, were going to miss them when they left.

Later that evening, Richard lay on a daybed in their bedchamber, ten feet away from the bed. That was the present limit of his strength, a fact he found disgusting. At least his witchy wife had let him get out of bed; he could now stand, but beyond a few paces, his strength seemed to fail.

Apparently delighted with his mild progress, and finally convinced the poison had departed his system for good, Catriona had brought him up a special herbal brew, guaranteed, so she'd said, to help him regain his strength. Nothing else, she declared, now stood between him and a full recovery.

And freedom. The wild expanse beyond their windows.

The potion tasted vile, but Richard doggedly sipped – and planned how to celebrate his vigor once it returned.

His musings were interrupted by Devil, who opened the door and strolled in, followed by Vane and Gabriel.

'While our wives and esteemed parent are busy hatching plans, we thought we'd come up and commiserate.' Devil grinned. 'How are you feeling?'

'Better.' Draining the last of the potion and swallowing it with a grimace, Richard realized that was true. He set the beaker aside. 'I suspect I'll have to endure a few more days, but . . .'

'Just make sure you recover fully,' Gabriel cautioned. 'Be damned if I'm riding this far north again if you suffer a relapse.'

Vane chuckled. 'Your wife seems convinced you'll be your old self any day, and I rather suspect she knows best.'

'Hmm.' Richard eyed them speculatively. 'Actually, I was just planning a little adventure, so to speak, to celebrate my return to the living.'

'Adventure?'

'How little?'

'What sort?'

Richard grinned. 'Nothing too outrageous, but we haven't had any serious excursions, not since Waterloo. I don't know about you, but two weeks in a bed has sharpened my appetite.'

'*That's* hardly suprising,' Devil returned, 'in the circumstances. But what about this adventure?'

Richard threw a cushion at him, which landed on target and made him feel much better. 'If you don't keep a civil tongue in your head, I won't tell you. I'll just ride off one morning and you'll have to wait until I get back.'

'Ride?'

'Where to?'

'I promise to be excessively civil.'

'Well . . .' – Richard pulled at his earlobe – 'it so happens I'll need help for this venture – at least a couple more riders. If, of course, you think you can spare the time for a little lark before heading south to more civilized climes?'

Devil raised his brows in mock exasperation. 'Forget the jokes – what's the plan?'


'Catriona?'

Caught in the act of pushing away from the desk in her office, Catriona looked up. Devil stood in the doorway, with Vane just behind him. 'Is anything wrong?' she asked.

'No, no!' Devil entered; Vane followed. Devil smiled ingenuously. 'We just wondered if you could spare a few minutes to explain a few things to us.'

He wanted something; Catriona could tell by that smile. Calmly settling back in her chair, she waved them to the two chairs facing her. Melchett had just departed, having looked in to tell her all was on track for the spring plantings to be done as she'd directed. Upstairs, Richard was with Worboys, getting dressed for his first attempt at the stairs. Her world was serene, on course. And the two before her were now part of it. 'How can I help you?' she asked. 'Whatever it is, if it's in my power, naturally, you have only to ask.'

Devil's smile broadened. 'It's about the crop yields. Richard told me what you achieve here—'

'And Corby happened to mention the tonnage you clear from your orchards – and how old your trees are.' Vane raised his brows. 'Frankly, if I didn't know he wasn't lying, I'd have said he'd dreamed the figures up.'

Catriona smiled. 'We do very well, that's true.'

'Not very well,' Devil corrected her. 'Astonishingly well.' He met her gaze. 'We'd like to know how you manage it.'

Catriona held his gaze and swiftly considered her options. She had said she would give them anything in her power; there was no reason she couldn't answer their question. Her only worry was that they wouldn't believe her – or wouldn't have a sufficiently open mind to understand. Then again, they had come to her and asked. And, as one of The Lady's disciples, it behooved her to spread Her message as widely as she could.

Drawing a slow breath, she nodded. 'Very well. But you'll need to bear in mind that what I tell you is a ... a philosophy rather than a prescription.' She glanced at Vane. 'So the answer is the same for both crops and orchards, indeed, for anything that grows. And the philosophy holds true for all arable lands, whether in the shadow of Merrick, or in Cambridgeshire, or in Kent.'

They both nodded. 'So ...' Devil prompted.

'So,' she said, 'it's a question of balance.'

'Balance?'

'What you take out must be put back, if you wish to take out again.' Catriona leaned forward, resting her arms on the desk. 'Each patch of soil has certain characteristics, certain nutrients which allow it to bear crops of such and such a nature. Once the crop is grown, however, the nutrients used in the bearing are depleted in the soil. If the soil is continually planted, it will continue to deplete and bear poorer and poorer crops until it fails. Crop rotation helps, but even that does not return the nutrients to the soil. So if you want to continuously crop, and crop well, then you need to renew the soil, replace the nutrients used, after each cropping. That's the fundamental point – the need for balance – in and out.'

Vane was frowning. 'Just go back a minute. Do you mean that for each particular crop, in each particular field, you need to work out a ... a ...'

'An understanding of the balance of the nutrients involved?' Catriona nodded. 'Precisely.'

'This balance,' Devil leaned forward. 'How's it measured?'

They questioned her, and she answered and explained; Devil asked for paper and sketched some of his fields – Vane listed the fruits and nuts he grew. They discussed, and even argued, but not once did they doubt, or give any hint that they dismissed her guidance. Quite the opposite.

'I'll try it,' Devil declared, 'and you'll have to come and talk to my foremen when you visit.' He folded the sheet of paper on which he'd jotted notes. 'If we can achieve even half of what you do here, I'll die happy.'

Considering his own sheet of notes, Vane grinned. 'My men are going to think I've taken leave of my senses, but ... it's my fields – and my gain.' Looking up, he smiled at

357

Catriona. 'Thank you, my dear, for sharing your secret with us.'

'Indeed.' Rising as she did, Devil waggled his brows at Catriona. 'Doubtless the most useful lady's secret I've ever learned.'

Laughing, she waved them out; they went with sweeping bows. Sitting back down, she couldn't stop smiling. After a minute, she tidied her desk, then went upstairs to gauge Richard's strength.


'Ah – *there* you are.'

Catriona looked up from the garden bed she'd been contemplating, one she hoped would soon show a few green shoots. Gabriel was making his way between the beds toward her, patently trying to see what she'd been studying in the winter brown earth.

'Is there anything there?'

'No.' Catriona grinned. 'I was merely checking. Is there something you need?'

He straightened and smiled. 'Not exactly – I heard of the advice you gave to Devil and Vane.'

'Ah, I see.' Catriona waved him to join her as she ambled on down the path. 'And what do you grow?'

'I don't – at least, not in the same sense.' He grinned down at her. 'I grow money – from money.'

'Oh.' Catriona blinked. 'I don't think I can give you any advice there.'

'Probably not,' he affably agreed. 'Not but what that balance idea of yours is quite close to the mark – but in investing it's risk and return that create the balance.'

Catriona held his gaze. 'I'm afraid,' she said, 'that I don't really know much about investing.'

His grin widened. 'Few people do – which brings me to my point. In light of your sterling advice to the others – which in turn benefits me, as Devil's wealth underpins the family ducal purse and both he and Vane invest through me, so the more funds they have to put in, the wealthier we all, myself included, become – I'd like to offer you my help in making investments in the same way I help all the rest.' He stopped and smiled at her. 'You're family now, so it's only fair.'

Catriona stared into his eyes, a light hazelly brown, and let his words and his smile warm her. 'I . . .' She hesitated, then nodded. 'I think I'd like that. Richard invests with you, doesn't he?'

'All the family do. I oversee the investments, and Heathcote Montague, our joint man of business, acts as our executor.' Gabriel grinned. 'That means I do all the talking and investigating and he takes care of the boring formalities.'

Catriona nodded. 'Tell me more about what you do. How do these investments of yours work?'

They ambled through the gardens for close to an hour, by which time she'd learned more than enough to know that he, at least, knew precisely what he was talking about. 'Very well.' With a nod, she halted at the entrance to the gardens. Here was an opportunity to establish the vale's future income for all time. Gabriel would invest their excess funds for her – the income would be there to tide the vale over any lean years, should such ever come to pass. She nodded again and refocused on Gabriel's face. 'I'll talk to McArdle and get the funds transferred – Richard will know the direction.'

Gabriel's easy smile lit his face; hand over his heart, he bowed. 'You won't regret it, I swear.' He straightened, eyes twinkling. 'Welcome to yet another aspect of our family.'


Richard entered the dining hall that evening to a rousing chorus of cheers. The whole household stood and clapped. His slow stroll disguising his lack of strength, he grinned and nodded gracefully, his expression one of amused affability.

359

But when he met Catriona's gaze as he reclaimed his seat beside her, she could see the warmth, the joy, the affectionate acceptance, burning in the blue of his eyes.

She smiled mistily and quickly sat so that he could sit, too. The cheering subsided, and the first course was brought out.

Beneath the table's edge, Richard clasped her hand briefly, then frowned at the serving dish placed before him. 'Good heavens! Is that turbot?'

'Hmm-mm.' Drawing the dish closer, Catriona heaped some on his plate. 'Cook said it was one of your favorite dishes.'

'It is.' Bemused, Richard stared at it, then looked at her. 'But wherever did she get turbot up here?'

Catriona raised her brows haughtily. 'We have our ways.'

He hesitated, then grinned, and gave his attention to the turbot.

The entire meal was a succession of Richard's favorite dishes – a fact that did not escape him. He caught Cook's eye and saluted her, which made her blush vividly even while she nodded graciously.

He leaned closer to Catriona. 'I'd go down and thank her, but . . .' He grimaced.

Catriona smiled, and fleetingly leaned her shoulder against his. 'You can speak to her tomorrow, or the day after, when next you go through the kitchens.'

He trapped her gaze and slowly arched a black brow. 'That soon?'

The words hung between them, layered with meaning. The air about them grew dense, shutting everyone else out. Catriona felt her lungs lock. 'Oh, I think so,' she managed, conscious of that sudden skittering excitement that she hadn't felt for too long. The rest of the room had vanished; all she could see was the blue of his eyes. 'You should be able to . . . get up . . . er, completely, any day now.'

His lips quirked; a wicked glint lit his eyes. 'You've no idea,' he drawled, 'how thankful I am to hear that.'

Breaking eye contact, Catriona reached for her wineglass and took a much-needed sip. 'Yes, well – there you are.'

'Hmmm – and where will you be?'

Flat on her back beneath him. 'Busy,' Catriona stated repressively.

'Oh, I think I can guarantee that,' the reprobate she'd married agreed.

Catriona awoke the next morning, and saw – knew – what it was that the Cynsters had brought to the vale. The knowledge came as a revelation – a flash of insight, a crystal clear certainty. And in the same revealing moment, she saw their marriage – hers and Richard's – in its entirety, its full meaning, its full glory. Saw why The Lady had directed her to his arms.

She was there still; she knew, in that moment, that she would remain there for all time. He slept behind her, wrapped around her, his breath, softly huffing, caressing her nape, one arm possessively protective, over her waist.

He'd needed her – to provide an anchor for his restless soul, to give him the home and position he'd needed, to be his warrior's cause.

But she'd needed him, too – in more ways than one. He'd recognized from the beginning, and forced her to see, too, that she needed him to protect her and to ease the burdens that were hers through her responsiblities to the vale. What she hadn't seen – couldn't have seen – and what he may not have guessed, was that she needed more than that.

She needed to learn about family – large ruling families – something she and the vale knew nothing about. With Cynsters all around, she'd observed firsthand the enormous positive energy that, as a group, they commanded. They were not really moral, or religious in any way, yet they all, day by day, act by act, served one goal – the family, both their own smaller groups, as well as the larger whole. While their decisions were usually direct and straightforward, down-to-earth and obvious, they were also far-sighted, always made in the best interests of the family.

From the first, she'd been impressed by the incredible strength of the group, far greater than the sum of its parts. That strength derived from the simple fact that they were all moving in the same direction, all focused on the same ultimate goal.

The Lady's ways were profound.

There'd been no large family at the manor for generations – the lady of the vale had, by custom, only one child, a girl child to take on her mantle. But times were changing – there would be fresh challenges to face, greater challenges. Challenges requiring more than the isolation of the vale to counter them.

Lifting a hand to her breast, Catriona fingered the pendant that hung there – Richard's mother's legacy. Through their marriage, a line older than hers had come into the vale; their child – their first daughter – would be the first of a new line, a greater line, sprung from the merging of the two.

She would be the first of a new family.

Catriona lay still and pondered that fact, while beyond the windows the sun rose. As dawn washed the land, she slipped from Richard's arms and left him softly snoring.

Her revelations were still much in her mind when, later that morning, she repaired to the stillroom.

She'd been there an hour when the door opened and two bright faces looked in.

'May we ask you something?'

Smiling, Catriona waved the twins to stools before the table

362

at which she was working. 'How can I help you?'

'We have this burning question,' Amanda informed her, wriggling onto the stool.

'We want to know what we should look for in a husband,' Amelia stated.

Catriona opened her eyes wide. 'That is a big question.'

'As you're a healer, we thought you might be able to advise us.'

'We're being paraded around at present – you know, so that all the eligible gentlemen can look us over and see if we might suit them.'

'But we've decided that that really isn't sensible.'

'No. We need to decide if *they* will suit *us*.'

Catriona couldn't stop her smile.

'Which,' Amanda declared, unabashed, 'means we have to decide what it is we should be looking for.'

Catriona nodded. 'I can see that – I have to say you're approaching this in a very clear-headed way.'

'We decided that was the only way to approach it – that's why we've come to see you.'

'We can't ask Aunt Helena – she's too old.'

'And Honoria was married over a year ago. These days, she's so caught up with being a duchess and taking care of Sebastian, she probably can't remember what she thought was important then.'

'And Patience isn't feeling well. And she's rather ... absorbed – as if she's thinking of her new baby.'

'But we thought you'd know – you're a healer and they always know everything, and you've only just married Richard, so you should be able to remember why you did.'

Unarguable logic. Catriona had to laugh. But her laugh was kindly and gentle; inside, she felt deeply touched, humble, and a little awed. She'd been thinking about how she should learn about 'family,' as if it was something she could study at a distance – and now here were the twins, reminding her that 'family' wasn't at a distance, it was here. She was, their blue eyes declared, already one hub in the giant Cynster web, accepted as such, available to answer questions on matters vitally important to the younger generation. That was how families operated.

Drawing in a breath, she eyed the twins, read the earnestness in their eyes. 'As I understand your question,' she said, looking down at the paste she was mixing, 'you want to know, not why I married Richard, so much as what's important to look for in a prospective husband.'

'Precisely.'

'That's our dilemma in a nutshell.'

'So,' Catriona said, 'your question is really philosophical, and as such that's something I can answer.' Frowning, she swirled the paste with the pestle; the twins remained encouragingly silent.

'A good husband,' she declared, 'must be protective. That's often the easiest point to ascertain. If he frowns at you when you do something barely reckless, then he's noticing you in that way.'

The twins nodded in unison.

Catriona didn't notice, intent on her paste, intent on her answer. 'For some reason, the best men also tend to be possessive – and that's also easy to see. He'll scowl at any other eligible men about you and get irritated if you don't pay sufficient attention to him. The *next* point, however, is a difficult one – one you need to be careful to get right. It's often not obvious.' She rolled the pestle about. 'He should be pleased with you – even proud of you – as you are. He shouldn't seek to change you, or . . .' She gestured.

'Think you need to take lessons from his sister in how to go on?'

Catriona looked at Amanda. 'Precisely.' Amanda's tone,

and the militant light in her eye, suggested she'd already stubbed her toe on that step.

'The last point, one which, in your cases especially, I would strongly urge you to consider, is his attitude to family.' It was on the tip of her tongue to explain that she hadn't considered that herself – because she hadn't known to do so. But The Lady had ordained her marriage – and The Lady had looked out for her. Pausing in her labors, she studied the twins. 'You were born into and raised within a large and close family – not everyone has that advantage. But you would miss it dreadfully, and find life very difficult, if the man you chose did not value your family, and the concept of family, as you do.'

Two pairs of huge blue eyes blinked at her; in that instant she knew their thoughts. Family? They weren't aware they valued the concept – it had simply been there, a constant all their lives; they had, perhaps until now, taken it for granted.

'Hmmm.' Amanda frowned.

'And, of course,' Catriona pointed out, 'any gentleman wishing to marry either of you will have to run the gauntlet of your family.'

Both girls rolled their eyes.

'As if we could *ever* forget!'

'That's always a worry,' Amelia said. 'What if the gentleman *we* want doesn't pass the family's inspection?'

Catriona smiled and looked down at her paste. 'If the one you want meets those four criteria, I think you'll find the Cynsters will welcome him with open arms.'

# Chapter Nineteen

Catriona was not called upon to make any declaration on the question of her husband's complete recovery; the next morning, Richard demonstrated his return to full vigor by ensuring he reached the breakfast table a full hour before she did.

When, distinctly breathless, having lifted heavy lids and found him – and the dawn – long gone, Catriona rushed into the dining hall, she was greeted with wide smiles by the other Cynster ladies and knowing grins by the Cynster men. Straightening her spine, she swept up to the main table; her incorrigible spouse uncurled his long length and rose to pull out her chair.

'I wondered when you'd wake.'

The words, murmured in a tone of absolute innocence, brushed her ear as she sat; Catriona stifled a too-vivid recollection of what he'd done to ensure she hadn't.

Lifting her gaze, she met the Dowager's bright eyes.

'*Bon!* He is recovered, is he not? So all is well, and we really must return south – the Season will start soon, and Louise will be wanting to take the twins to the modistes.'

'Indeed,' Honoria agreed. As Patience turned to speak to the twins, Honoria turned to Catriona. 'I know you'll understand – I want to get back to Sebastian. We've never before left him for so long.'

Catriona smiled serenely, sincerely. 'I'm so grateful that you came and have stayed for so long. Naturally, you need to get back. And' – with her eyes she indicated Richard, on her other side, talking to Devil and Vane – 'there's really no reason you need stay.'

Honoria smiled widely, squeezed her hand in empathy, then looked across the table at Devil. 'So we can all leave tomorrow.'

'We may as well,' Patience agreed, turning from the twins.

His gaze briefly touching Vane's, then Richard's, Devil sat back in his chair. And regarded his wife. 'Actually, it's not that simple. I'll need a day or so to talk things over with Richard – there's some matters I've set in train that I need to work through with him.'

'And I want to go over the trees in the orchard,' Vane said. 'There's some grafting work you should consider.'

'Don't forget those funds that we must discuss before I leave,' Gabriel put in.

Honoria, Patience and the Dowager stared up the table.

'Does this mean,' Honoria eventually asked, 'that you're not yet ready to leave?'

Devil grinned. 'It'll just take a day or two.' He transferred his limpid gaze to Catriona. 'We wouldn't want Richard to overdo things and suffer a relapse.'

All the ladies turned to look at Richard, who returned their scrutiny with a look of helpless innocence. Honoria barely stifled a snort; she stood. 'I suppose,' she conceded, 'a day or two more won't hurt.'

Honoria looked up as Patience slid into her chair at the break-fast table the next morning. 'Have you seen Devil?'

Patience shook her head. 'I was about to ask if you'd seen Vane.'

Honoria frowned, then both she and Patience looked up.

Gliding more slowly than usual, Catriona joined them. She sank into her carved chair. And looked at the teapot. Then she reached out, lifted the pot, and, with careful concentration, filled her cup. Setting the teapot down, she studied the full cup, then reached for the sugarbowl, and dropped in two lumps.

Honoria grinned and exchanged a swift glance with Patience before turning to Catriona. 'Where's Richard?'

Eyes closed as she savored her tea, Catriona shook her head. 'I don't know – and I don't want to know. Not until I've recovered.'

Honoria grinned; Patience chuckled.

Catriona frowned. 'Actually, I vaguely – very vaguely, you understand – recall him saying something about having to be busy about 'Cynster business' today.' She cracked open her lids. 'I assumed he meant with Gabriel.'

They all looked down the table, to the four empty places usually filled by the cousins at breakfast time. From the detritus, it was clear they'd already broken their fast.

Honoria frowned. 'They're not in the library. I looked.'

Patience frowned, too. 'What I can't understand is why Vane left so early – he came down before dawn.'

'Devil, too.'

Catriona frowned, then shook her head. 'I can't recall.'

Just then, McArdle appeared, stumping slowly along. With his stiff joints, he was always a late riser. Heading for the end of the table, he stopped by Catriona's chair. 'The master asked me to give you this, mistress.'

Eyes opening fully, Catriona took the single folded sheet and nodded her thanks; McArdle stumped on. For one instant, she studied the missive; Richard had never written to her before. Unfolding it, she scanned the five lines within – she blinked; her eyes kindled. Lips firming, she set her teacup down with a definite click.

'What is it?' Honoria asked.

'*Just* listen.' Drawing a deep breath, Catriona read: 'Dear C – Please tell H and P. We have gone to conclude a business deal. We'll be away for four days. You are not to worry. R.' She looked at Patience and Honoria. 'The 'not' is underlined three times.'

They fumed and swore vengeance, then, all three together, they bustled out to the stable.

Catriona led the way. 'Huggins – when did the master leave?'

Huggins straightened, letting down the hoof he was checking. 'Rode out just at dawn, the boy said.'

'And the others?' Honoria asked.

Huggins touched his cap in a half bow. 'With him, Your Grace. 'Twas the master, His Grace, and both the other Mister Cynsters, ma'am. They rode out all together.'

'Which way?' Catriona demanded.

Huggins nodded to the east. Catriona turned and looked, even though the house blocked her view. She glanced back at Huggins. 'They rode *out* of the vale?'

Huggins raised his brows. 'Don't know as to that, but they took the road that ways.'

'Did they take any provisions?' Patience asked. 'Saddlebags, blankets?'

Huggins grimaced. 'They saddled their own horses, I believe, ma'am. There's usually only one sleepy lad in the stables that early. I doubt he'd 'ave noticed.'

'Never mind. Thank you, Huggins.' Catriona motioned the other two away. Together, they crossed the yard and went into the gardens, to where, once past the side of the house, they could look down the vale, into the now wellrisen sun. Catriona gestured to the vale's mouth. 'If they left near dawn, they'll be well beyond the vale by now.'

369

'Well beyond our reach,' Honoria observed darkly.

Patience frowned. 'What on earth are they about?'

'And where on earth,' Catriona waspishly added, 'have they gone to be about it?'


'*Mistress!* Come quickly!'

Three days later, working at the table in the stillroom, Catriona looked up to see Tom jigging in the doorway.

'Come see! Come see!' A smile splitting his face, he beckoned her wildly, then dashed toward the front hall.

Catriona dusted her hands and set off in pursuit.

'What is it?' Patience came out of the library as Tom's running footsteps echoed through the hall.

Catriona lifted her arms in a shrug.

'There's something going on outside.' With Patience, Catriona turned to see Honoria hurrying down the stairs. 'All the children have rushed down into the park. There's some sort of commotion going on down there.'

They all looked at each other, then turned and glided, as fast as dignity allowed, to the front door. Between them, they hauled the door wide, then went out onto the porch.

The sight that met their eyes did not, at first, convey much – they were just in time to glimpse the last of Tom as he flew down the drive into the park. His cohorts, nowhere in sight, were presumably ahead of him. Around both sides of the house, other members of the household and manor farm streamed, deserting the kitchens, the workrooms, the stables and barns, all rushing for the drive.

McArdle stumped up to the steps, nodding toward the park. 'We've some new arrivals, seemingly.'

His face was relaxed, his lips curving; Catriona was about to quiz him, when she sensed a presence at her back. She turned and beheld the Dowager.

Patience and Honoria moved aside to give her space; in her

most regal voice, Helena demanded: '*What* is going on here?'

'*Mooo-rhooo!*'

The bellow had them all turning, staring at where the drive came up from the park. A huge hulking bull came lolloping up out of the trees, a long rope trailing from a ring in his nose. In his wake, a noisy gaggle of children, grooms and farmhands came tumbling, tripping and laughing, calling and screeching. The bull ignored them; sighting the party on the steps, he rolled happily forward, tossing his head, heavy rolls of muscle rippling. Cloven feet clacking loudly on the cobbles, he cantered to the steps, then, planting his front feet wide, came to a skidding halt. He looked the ladies over, then stared directly at Catriona, raised his huge head, uttered a mammoth bellow, shook his head vigorously, then looked down and exhaled in a huge, shuddering snort.

The party on the steps simply stared.

'Got 'im!' The eldest farmhand pounced on the rope, then reeled it in, shortening it to lead the bull away. Looking the animal over, the lad glanced up at Catriona, his eyes shining. 'He's a prime 'un, ain't he, mistress?'

'Indeed.' Catriona knew enough to know a prize bull when she saw one. 'But where . . .?' Looking up, her eyes widened as more cattle came into view. Two yearling bulls led the way, trotting happily along under Gabriel's watchful eye. They were followed by a long line of cows and heifers, ambling contentedly, mooing and lowing; Catriona had lost count by the time three other riders came into view toward the end of the long procession.

Devil and Vane rode on either side of the stream of cattle, keeping them moving, watching for stragglers but even more watching out for the children now running alongside the beasts, hands out to fleetingly touch the soft hides as, heads swinging, the cows plodded on.

Right at the end rode Richard, McAlvie at his stirrup,

371

McAlvie's lads flanking them, striding along, eyes on the cattle, proud grins on their faces. McAlvie looked fit to burst with enthusiasm. He was talking animatedly to Richard, who, smiling, replied with an indulgent air.

From the instant he appeared, Catriona could look at nothing else; driven by the worry of the past three days, she scanned his tall figure critically, but could see no signs of exhaustion. He rode easily, long limbs relaxed, holding himself in the saddle with his usual indolent grace.

He was well. She knew that even before, reaching the courtyard, he looked up and saw her. The smile that lifted his lips, the light that lit his eyes as he viewed her – despite the distance between them she could feel it like a touch – assured her as little else could that his three days away had done nothing to harm him.

'McAlvie!' Gabriel hailed the herdsman. 'Where do you want these two?' He indicated the yearling bulls, now coralled by the crowd to one side of the steps; with a word, McAlvie left Richard and hurried to take charge.

The courtyard was a sea of excitement, of ordered pandemonium, with cows mooing, shifting and stamping, surrounded by the household and farmhands, smiling and pointing, chattering and commenting, all waiting to assist in moving the new herd down to the new cattle barn.

Which, Catriona recalled, had been built large enough to hold them.

But first, by vale tradition, they had to be named. McArdle, by right of being the oldest man in the vale, named the bull Henry. Irons declared one of the yearlings was Rupert; Henderson named the other Oswald. The women deferred to their offspring, and thus were born Rose and Misty, Wobbles and Goldy. Tom frowned and bit his lip, then named his cow Checkers.

And so it went on; called on to approve each and every

name, Catriona nodded and smiled and laughed. But her senses were elsewhere, trying, through the noise and bustle, to keep track of Richard. He'd dismounted, but she could no longer see his dark head.

To her right, she was distantly aware of Devil strolling up the steps and being pounced on by Honoria. In accents only a duchess could command, her sister-in-law inquired where they'd been. Devil merely grinned. His gaze intent, he turned her and, deftly blocking her attempts to do otherwise, herded her into the house – all further discussion to be undertaken in private. If he gave her an answer, Catriona didn't hear it.

Behind her, to one side, the Dowager was in earnest discussion with McArdle, gesturing at the herd and asking questions. With a frustrated humph, Patience picked up her skirts and darted down the steps. Vane, handing his reins to one of the grooms, turned as she hurried up. Reaching out, he helped her forward when she would have stopped, one arm sliding around her as he turned her and smoothly guided her toward the gardens.

From her manner, Patience was scolding; from his, Vane wasn't listening.

Brows lifting resignedly, Catriona straightened and scanned the courtyard again. With the cows all named, McAlvie was preparing to move them around the house and down to the barn. People were milling everywhere, but she could usually see Richard easily – he was taller than any of her people. But no dark head stood out. Hands rising to her hips, a frown forming in her eyes, an emptiness in her heart, Catriona reached out with her senses – a talent she rarely used as it disturbed those, like Cook, who had latent talent of their own.

Richard was not in the courtyard in front of her.

'Do you approve of your wedding present?'

The deep purr in her ear, the touch of his breath on the sensitive skin of her temple, came simultaneously with the possessive slide of his hand splaying across her waist and belly. She started, then stilled. He held her, and their child, against him for an instant; she felt his strength envelop her. For one blissful moment, she closed her eyes and let herself slide into it, then his hand slid to her hip and he turned her.

Her eyes snapped open. 'Wedding present?'

He was grinning. 'I didn't give you one, remember?' The light in his eyes was victorious, triumphant. 'I couldn't think what to get you.' His gaze softened. 'A witch who considers an escort to her prayers as precious as diamonds.' Smiling, he tapped her nose with one finger. 'It was a challenge – to find something you'd truly appreciate.'

A shadow fell across his face; Catriona realized that, with his arm about her waist, he'd steered her back into the front hall.

'You bought me a bull as a wedding present?' She wasn't at all sure she believed that – the herd he'd driven in was worth a small fortune, was probably worth even more than she estimated. The vale could not have afforded that sort of addition to its ailing herd. A fact her husband knew.

'Not just the bull – I bought the whole herd.' He looked at her innocently. 'Don't you like Henry?'

Catriona smothered a snort. 'I daresay he's a very good bull.'

'Oh, an excellent bull – I have guarantees and glowing references as to his performance.'

His lips were very definitely not straight. The front hall was empty – from outside, a cheer went up as the new herd started their last amble to their new home. Richard's lips curved more definitely, more devilishly; his arm about her tightened. 'Why don't we adjourn to our room? I can explain the finer points of Henry's reputation, and you can give me your opinion.'

'My opinion?' Arching one brow, Catriona met his glowing

374

gaze. Her feet, of their own accord, were carrying her toward the stairs.

'Your opinion – and, perhaps, a token or two of your affection – your appreciation.' His smile had turned devilish with salacious anticipation. 'Just to reassure me that you really do like Henry.'

Catriona looked into his eyes – the sounds of the crowd walking the new herd to the barn were fading in the distance. She could imagine how victorious their progress up the vale had been – she'd seen any number of workers from the farms among the crowd. And the manor folk had given them a rousing welcome – a hero's welcome. The look in Richard's eyes – the same look she'd glimpsed briefly in Devil's and Vane's – suggested they were expecting a similar welcome from their wives.

Her gaze locked on his, as they reached the top of the stairs, she smiled. Finding his hand, she twined her fingers with his, then, her own eyes alight, she slid her gaze from his and turned toward their chamber. 'Come, then – and I'll consider your reward.'

He deserved it.


Later, after having overseen his bath and shared a dinner fit for a conqueror which, to her amazement, had arrived without explanation on a tray, Catriona rewarded her husband thoroughly, an exercise that left her totally naked, totally drained, slumped, facedown and boneless, amid the rumpled sheets of their bed.

*Much* later, she mumbled: 'Where did you go?'

Sprawled, similarly naked, beside her, Richard glanced at her face. She hadn't yet opened her eyes, not since he'd shut them for her. He settled back on the pillows and enjoyed the sight – of her luscious ivory back and bottom delectably displayed alongside him. 'Hexham.'

375

'Hexham?' A frown tangled Catriona's brows. 'That's in England.'

'I know.'

'You mean those are *English* cattle?'

'The very *best* of English cattle. There's a breeder who lives outside Hexham – we went to visit him.'

'Visit?'

Richard chuckled. 'I have to admit it felt rather like olden times – raiders from the Lowlands sweeping south to steal cattle. Except, of course, that I paid for them.' He considered, then his brows quirked. 'Mind you, I'm not sure Mr. Scroggs won't decide we've stolen them anyway – we got them at a very good price.'

Catriona lifted her heavy head, and her heavy lids, and stared at him. 'Why was that?'

Richard grinned. 'Devil's inimitable ways. His presence here was too good an opportunity to pass up – he's a master at negotiating. He doesn't precisely *lean* on people – not physically – but they do tend to give ground. Rather unexpectedly, to them.'

Catriona humphed and lowered her head back onto the tangled covers. 'We weren't expecting you for another day – you said four in your note.'

'Ah, yes.' Noting the increasing strength in her voice, Richard's interest in their adventure waned. 'We expected to get back today – one day to ride to Hexham, two days to drive the cattle back, but' – he slid down the bed, then swung up and straddled her knees – 'we thought if we said four days rather than three, you'd worry less.' Sliding his palms along her thighs, he gripped her hips and gently flipped her onto her back. 'Or,' he said, sitting back on his ankles, his hot gaze roving her delectable nakedness, 'at least, not yet have whipped yourselves into a righteous frenzy when we got back on the third day.'

376

So sated she could not tense a single muscle, Catriona lay on her back and stared up at him. 'You purposely told us four days, so we wouldn't be prepared to ... to deal with you as you deserved—'

A swift grin cut off her words; he swooped down and kissed her. 'We wanted to surprise you.'

For more reasons than one, Catriona knew, but as he kissed her lingeringly again, and eased his long body down over hers, she couldn't summon enough temper to care. He lay on her as they kissed, then eased to one side, lying half over her, half beside her, one dark, hair-dusted thigh wedged between hers.

Propped on one elbow, he turned his head and splayed his hand over her belly. Gently, he stroked, gauged. 'Have you told them yet?'

Her gaze on his face, Catriona shook her head. 'I ... wanted to wait a little – we haven't had time—'

'I haven't said anything, either.' His hand resting heavy over where their child grew, secure within her womb, he turned his head and met her gaze. 'I want to think about it – see how things settle – how it feels, if it ... fits.'

He looked back at his hand; Catriona studied his face, dark planes gilded by the firelight. Then she raised a hand and gently smoothed back the lock of hair that always fell over his forehead. He looked back at her; she smiled into his eyes. 'It fits.' Her heart swelling, she held his gaze. 'You, me, our child, the manor, the vale – we all fit.'

For one long instant, she was lost in the blue – the blue of summer skies over Merrick's high head. Then she smiled, mistily, and traced his cheek. 'This is how it's meant to be.'

Her gaze had dropped to his lips; half-lifting her head, she rose – he bent his head and their lips met, in a kiss so achingly tender, so honest, so vulnerable, there were tears in her eyes when it ended.

377

He looked down at her for a moment, then his lips kicked up at the ends. 'Come show me.' Drawing back, he sat on his haunches and pulled her up to her knees.

'Show you what?' Turning her head, she looked over her shoulder as he swung her about so her back was to him.

His eyes burned, his grin grew wicked as he drew her back, sliding her knees outside of his, drawing her bottom against his ridged abdomen. 'Show me how things fit.'

He needed little instruction on that point; hot and hard, he pressed into her. Her body flowered and opened for him; she gave a soft sigh as he slid fully home.

He settled her, her thighs over his, her bottom wedged against his hips. Impaled upon him, with his chest against her back and his steely arms around her, she was open and vulnerable; her breasts, her belly, the springy curls at its base, the soft inner surfaces of her thighs, already taut, were his to stroke and fondle, to caress as he willed.

And he willed.

Held almost upright, she couldn't rise much upon him; instead, buried deep within her, he rocked. Slowly, languorously.

Catriona bit her lip against a groan as his fingers tightened about her budded nipples and she felt him surge slowly within her.

Then he chuckled; fingers gripping her hips, he lifted her a little, then slowly thrust upward and filled her. Catriona shivered.

'I was just thinking . . .' he murmured.

Flicking a glance over her shoulder, she saw him looking down as he lifted her slightly again.

'We can't risk telling anyone our news yet.'

He filled her; Catriona dragged in a desperate breath. 'Why not?'

'Because if *Maman* finds out, she might not leave.' He

drew her fully down and rolled his hips beneath her. He reached for her breasts. 'And much as I love her, having Helena about for any appreciable time would try the patience of a saint.'

He filled his palms and kneaded.

'Devil seems to manage.'

'She doesn't fuss about him.'

He started to rock her again, a tantalizingly slow ride. His hands drifted over her skin and she heated, and grew hotter. Grew wilder.

She hadn't yet got used to his manner of loving, of the slow, relentless giving, the gradual, inexorable rise toward bliss. If she tried to run ahead, he would hold her back, prolong the delicious torture until she was all but beyond herself – until, when he let her fly free, she screamed.

She'd had trouble with those screams from the first. She'd tried to muffle them, tried to suppress them, tried to at least keep them within bounds – keep them from disturbing the household. *He* didn't seem to care – but then, as Helena would say, he was a man.

The thought focused her mind on the evidence of that, on the thick, heavy, rigid reality filling her, stretching her, completing her – she felt excitement fuse, felt the thrill shimmer and grow.

Desperately, she opened her eyes and focused – on her dressing table across the room. In the mirror, lit only by the weak light of the fire, she saw him, a dark presence in the shadows behind her, saw her body lift rhythmically in his embrace, saw his body coil and flex, driving hers.

Upward. Onward. Into that realm of pleasure where the physical and emotional and spiritual merged.

But he kept their journey to a rigidly slow pace.

Dragging in a breath, her senses at full stretch, her wits all but scattered, she sought for some distraction – something to help her survive the slow disintegration of her senses. 'Your nickname.'

'Hmm?'

He wasn't listening.

'Scandal,' she gasped. She'd heard Devil, Vane and Gabriel all use it to his face, although naturally, all the ladies called him Richard. Clutching the arm wrapped across her hips, she let her head fall back and licked her dry lips. 'How did you come by it?'

She'd wanted to know since first she'd heard it.

'Why do you want to know?' There was a touch of amusement in his voice – a teasing lilt.

*Why?* 'Because we might go to London. In the circumstances, I think I have a right to know.'

'You never leave the vale.'

'But you might have to go south for some reason.'

After a moment, he chuckled. His steady rocking penetration had not faltered. 'It's not what you think.'

'Oh?' She was clinging to sanity by her fingernails.

'Devil coined the tag – it wasn't because I cause scandal, but because I was: "A Scandal That Never Was."'

Her wits were reeling, her senses fracturing – beneath her heated skin, her nerves had stretched taut. As if he understood, he nuzzled her ear. 'Because of Helena's actions in claiming me as hers, I was a scandal that never eventuated.'

'Oh.' She breathed the syllable – it shattered in the warm stillness as she gasped. And tightened, every muscle coiling.

He bent her forward, drove deeply into her – and sent her flying, tumbling over the edge of the world.

Richard held her before him, heard her scream – listened to it die to a sob. He held still – briefly – buried within her, savoring the strong ripples of her release, then let go his own reins, let his body have its way, and followed her into ecstasy.

*

380

By the time she joined the breakfast table the next morning, Catriona was a walking testament to the fact that three days spent primarily out of doors had completely restored Richard's strength.

There was nothing wrong with his stamina; she could swear to that on The Lady's name.

A fact apparently so obvious, no one needed to ask; all the Cynsters were busy with their preparations to leave.

If anything, their leaving created even more commotion than their arrival.

Two hours later, standing on the steps, ready to wave them off, Catriona turned as the Dowager came bustling out, lecturing McArdle to the last.

'Once down to the cattle barn and back at least once a day – I will check in my letters to see that you are doing it.'

McArdle's assurance that he wouldn't forget was lost in the clatter as Vane's elegant carriage, drawn by matched greys, came rattling around the house to join the Dowager's carriage and the ducal equipage, both already waiting on the cobbles.

Devil and Honoria had already taken their leave; Richard stood beside Devil as he handed Honoria into their carriage, then, with a last word to Richard, and a last rakish smile and a wave to Catriona, Devil climbed up and Richard shut the door. He paused for a moment, watching Gabriel hand the twins into the Dowager's carriage. His horse tied to the carriage's back, Gabriel would travel with them to Somersham, then escort the twins back to London.

Vane and Patience were heading for London, too, but they would stop at Somersham first to allow Patience to rest before joining Vane's family in the capital. Richard returned Patience's wave as Vane handed her into the carriage; with a salute, Vane followed her in.

A groom shut the door – others scurried around checking straps and harness. Smiling, Richard strolled back to the front steps. He arrived to see Helena release Catriona from one of her extravagant embraces.

'You must promise me you will visit in summer.' Clinging to Catriona's hands, Helena looked into her eyes. 'The Season, I can understand, might be difficult and not to your liking, but in summer, you must come.' She shook Catriona's hands. 'You have not been part of a big family before – there is much you yet need to learn.'

Catriona saw the worry in Helena's fine eyes; smiling serenely, she leaned forward and touched cheeks. 'Of course, we'll come. Exactly when' – she drew one hand free and gestured – 'is in the lap of The Lady, but we will come, you may be sure.'

Helena searched her eyes briefly, then beamed. '*Bon!* It is good.' With that, she pressed Catriona's hand and turned to her second son. 'Come – you may lead me to my carriage.'

Surprised by his wife's promise, Richard masked his concern and suavely offered his arm.

Helena took it; he led her down the steps and over the cobbles to where Gabriel and the twins were waiting. With a last hug, and a last cling, Helena let him go; accepting Gabriel's hand, she climbed into the carriage. Gabriel followed and Richard shut the door. Helena leaned out of the window as Catriona, who had strolled in their wake, linked her arm with Richard's.

'You will not forget!' Helena wagged a finger at Catriona.

Who laughed. 'I won't. June – July – who knows? But sometime in summer.'

'Good.' Helena beamed her brilliant smile and sat back. The coachman cracked his whip.

'Farewell!'

'Safe journey!'

The carriages rolled smoothly out, the ducal carriage in the lead, followed by the Dowager's with Vane and Patience's carriage bringing up the rear. The grooms and outriders rode alongside, all in the ducal livery. It was a scene from a pageant, a sight the vale had never seen before; the manor household lined the courtyard and the drive, waving their unexpected but very welcome visitors on their way.

Catriona watched them go, waving until the drive dipped and they were lost to view, conscious of a sadness of a type she'd never felt before. She didn't try to push it from her – this was one of the things she needed to learn. Pensive, smiling rather mistily, she let Richard turn her; arm in arm, they strolled back to the house.

She felt his gaze on her face as they climbed the steps. At the top, he halted; looking up, she met his gaze and found it serious and concerned.

He hesitated, then asked: 'Did you mean what you said about going to London?'

'Yes.' She smiled reassuringly. 'I don't intend to let Helena down.'

'But . . .' He frowned. 'I thought you never left the vale – or at least, only under legal edict.'

'Ah, well.' Her smile deepening, she tried to find words in which to explain something he'd never stopped to think about, something he'd known all his life. Even more, to explain that through the evil of his poisoning, good had come – that having his family here had opened many doors into the future. Not just for the vale, but for the two of them, too. Instead, after searching his eyes, she smiled, deliberately enigmatic; raising a hand, she traced his cheek, then stretched on her toes to plant a kiss by the side of his mouth. 'Times change.' Turning, she glanced toward the mouth of the vale, to where a collection of dark specks travelled down the road. And smiled. 'It's time for the lady of the vale to learn about the wider world.'

\*

383

When the road curved, finally hiding the manor from view, Devil grinned and sat back. An instant later, he reached out an arm, drew his wife to him and kissed her soundly.

'What was that for?' Honoria asked, prepared to be suspicious. She didn't think she'd yet forgiven him for his three-day disappearance, but she couldn't entirely remember what she'd said the night before.

He grinned in unlikely innocence. 'Just because.'

The carriage jolted; he glanced out of the window. 'Well, that's Scandal well settled.'

'Hmmm.' Honoria closed her eyes and settled against his shoulder. 'She's just what he needs.'

Devil gazed at the fields and woods beyond the window, then murmured: 'This place is what he needs, too. She's given him a home, in the right place, at the right time.'

A moment of silence ensued, then, in precisely the same tone, Honoria, her eyes still closed, murmured: 'There are times when I could almost imagine you believed in fate.'

Devil shot her a sideways glance, one she didn't see. Noting her closed eyes, he let his lips curve, then he looked out of the window – and let the question in her words pass unanswered.

# Chapter Twenty

Together, Catriona and Richard reentered the front hall.

'Excuse me, sir.' Henderson came up. 'Corby was wondering if he could have a word before he goes back to Lower Farm.'

'Of course.' Releasing Catriona, Richard beckoned to Corby, who'd hung back by the wall.

By Richard's side, Catriona hesitated, then quietly glided away. Leaving Richard conferring about the orchard fence, she silently made her way upstairs.

She had unfinished buisness to attend to.

It had been easy to set aside the question of Richard's poisoner while his family – their family – had been here. In truth, it would have been difficult to deal with the matter appropriately while they'd been about.

But they were gone now.

There wasn't a single person in the vale who did not know who had poisoned Richard. But all her people would, with their usual unwavering confidence, leave the matter in her hands – to be settled as The Lady willed.

Which was as it should be, but she wasn't looking forward to it – to what might have to be.

Reaching the top of the stairs, Catriona looked back, down into the hall to where Richard's dark head was bent as he spoke to Corby. She looked for one long moment, then drew in a deep breath, straightened her spine, straightened her shoulders, and turning, headed for their chamber.

Richard knew the instant she left his side. From the corner of his eye, he saw her climb the stairs, her steps slow and measured, saw her reach the top, hesitate as she looked back at him, then quietly walk away.

The instant he finished with Corby, he followed her.

He opened the door to their room and immediately saw her, standing at the end of the bed, pushing a thick shawl into a saddle bag.

She looked up and saw him, then continued with her packing.

He shut the door and advanced on the bed, on her. 'Where is she?'

Catriona looked up as he halted beside her; she met his gaze, then raised a questioning brow.

Richard's lips thinned. 'Algaria. It's obvious it was she who poisoned me.'

Catriona hesitated, then grimaced. 'We can't say that for certain.'

'It hasn't escaped my notice that, other than you, only she knows enough of those elixirs and potions you store in the stillroom to mix whatever it was in that coffee.'

'Wolfsbane. Plus a little henbane. But that doesn't convict her.'

'No, but it makes her the obvious suspect.' He hesitated, then asked, rather more quietly, 'Besides, if it wasn't she, where are you going?'

Her gaze on her saddle bag, Catriona grimaced again.

She heard Richard sigh, then felt him shift. He reached past her, bracing one arm on the bedpost; sliding the other around her, he turned her, trapped her – lifting her hands to his chest, she looked up.

He trapped her gaze. 'Don't you trust me yet?'

She looked into his eyes and saw nothing but devotion – selfless, committed, and unshakable; with a sigh, she closed her eyes and leaned her forehead on his chest. 'You know I do.'

'Then I'll come with you. No—' He held up a hand when she looked up, her mouth opened to argue. 'Consider me your protector, your champion – your consort. I'll hold myself at your command.' He studied her eyes. 'In this matter, I won't act without it.'

Determination and commitment were etched in his face, enshrined in his blue, blue eyes. Catriona studied them, then drew a deep breath and nodded. 'We'll be gone for two days.'

Mounted – she on her mare, he on Thunderer – they reached the mouth of the vale just after midday. Richard followed as Catriona turned the mare's head north; he waited until they were trotting steadily before asking: 'Where exactly are we going?'

'Algaria has a small cottage.' Catriona gestured with her chin. 'It's almost directly north. It's not all that far as the crow flies, but the tracks are not easy.'

That was an understatement. They followed the road from the vale, a relatively well-surfaced lane, until it joined the road to Ayr. Crossing this, Catriona led the way up a narrow sheep track, the little mare picking her way daintily. Thunderer hurrumphed – and clomped in the mare's wake.

From there on, it was nothing but sheep tracks, barely a trail worn into the rocky ground. Studying the poor land through which they passed, Richard noticed a field, some way away, planted with a low-lying crop. Crossing the field was a straggling line of gaunt cattle.

After considering the sight for a moment, he transferred his gaze to his witchy wife's hips. 'Aren't these Sir Olwyn's fields?'

387

'Yes.' She nodded without looking around. 'Both to the north and south.'

Richard looked to the south, to where the cattle now stood morosely hanging their heads. 'Looks like he's just lost some more cabbages.'

Catriona looked around, then followed his gaze to the distant field. She studied the evidence, then humphed. 'He never would listen when I tried to help him.'

Surveying the bleak scene about them, an amazing contrast to the vale, no more than a few miles behind them, Richard raised his brows. 'I can see why he wanted to marry you.'

Catriona merely humphed again.

They plodded slowly on through the afternoon; Richard called a halt, an enforced rest, on the crest of a small hill. The track wound about the top then descended into shadow. Sitting in the sunshine, he looked across the rocky, largely barren landscape through which they'd travelled. In the distance, a purple haze hid the vale. Catriona came up, dusting her hands on her skirts after feeding dried apples to Thunderer and her mare. With a soft sigh, she slid down beside him, settling against him when he lifted an arm about her shoulders.

They looked out in silence. Eventually, he said: 'It's beautiful here. Not pretty, but majestic. It's all so hard, harsh and rocky, it makes a place like the vale all the more wondrous, all the more precious.'

Catriona smiled and leaned more heavily against him. 'Yes.'

They looked some more, then Richard asked: 'Are we still on Sir Olwyn's lands?'

'Theoretically yes, but he's never farmed this area. Algaria's cottage lies just inside his northern boundary.'

Resting his chin in her hair, Richard frowned. 'So Sir Olwyn is Algaria's landlord?'

Catriona looked up at him. 'Well – yes, I suppose that's

388

true.' Turning back to the scenery, she clasped her hands over his at her waist. After a moment, she sighed. 'If there's one thing I know about Algaria, it's that she must have had a very strong reason to poison you. She would not have done it lightly – not just because she didn't like you – not even because she felt so strongly that you weren't the right husband for me.'

'She never made any secret of that.'

'No – that's not her way. She never hides what she thinks. But to act as she did, she must have had some compelling reason.'

Hearing the fervor in her voice, Richard hugged her tighter. 'Why are you so sure?'

It was a simple question, accepting rather than dismissive.

'Because the only excuse for any disciple of The Lady to take a life is in the service of others. That is, she must be acting in defense, usually of others.'

'Others – such as you?'

Catriona nodded. 'Me. Or the people of the vale.' After a moment, she sighed. 'But that doesn't make sense – because no matter what Algaria *thought* you might do, you haven't *done* anything to harm me or the vale. Quite the opposite.'

Turning in his arms, she looked into Richard's face, into his blue eyes. 'Can you think of anything – any act at all – that you've committed since coming to the vale that she could misconstrue as a real threat?'

Richard saw the worry in her eyes and knew it wasn't for him. He would have eased even that burden for her if he could. But . . . framing her face, he looked deep into her eyes. 'Since the day we wed, I've only had one aim in life – your well-being – and that isn't compatible with harming you or the vale.'

She sighed; turning her head, she pressed a kiss into his palm, then wriggled around and settled back into his arms. 'I know. That's what bothers me so.'

They pressed on as the afternoon slowly waned into evening; as the chill in the air deepened, Catriona turned into the mouth of a narrow cleft and pulled up before a rude hut. To Richard's questioning glance, she replied: 'We would have made it in a day if we'd started early enough, but we can't go on in the dark.'

Richard didn't argue – the track they were now following was little more than a ribbon worn into the rocky hillside, and aside from the cold, there were gullies and clefts aplenty, traps for the unwary. He dismounted, then lifted Catriona down. 'What is this place?'

'It's an old shepherd's hut. I doubt it's been used since last I was here.'

Unstrapping their bags, Richard glanced at her. 'Since last ...? I thought you never left the vale.'

Taking the bags from him, Catriona pulled a face. 'I don't count my herb trips.'

'Herb trips?'

'At least once every spring and again in late summer, I travel to collect herbs and roots which don't grow in the vale.'

Unsaddling Thunderer, Richard narrowed his eyes at her. 'I foresee a developing interest in botany.'

Catriona grinned. Hefting the bags, she threw him a provocative glance. 'There's quite a lot I could teach you.'

Richard raised his brows. 'Indeed?' Hauling the saddle from Thunderer's back, he met her gaze squarely. 'Why don't you go and sweep the spiders out, then I'll get a fire going – and you can teach me all you will.'

Catriona's grin widened; her eyes danced as she turned away. 'Why not?'

Richard watched her hips sway as she climbed to the cottage, then he grinned and turned back to the horses.

The first lessons his witchy wife taught him had nothing to

do with botany. The first thing he learned was that despite her delicate appearance and her usually cossetted state, she ranked with the most experienced camp-follower in the not-at-all-easy task of making a rude shepherd's hut seem comfortable and warm. In conjuring a warm and sustaining meal out of what they'd carried in their saddlebags and the roots and leaves she'd gathered before the light died.

In making him feel relaxed and rather cossetted himself.

It was a distinctly pleasant feeling.

Smiling serenely, Catriona watched the heavy muscles in his shoulders ease, watched the glow of comfort suffuse his expression. And inwardly smiled all the more.

She hadn't been sure whether to bring him with her on this journey, not until he'd asked and sworn his allegiance. Then she'd known it was right – that he should be by her side when she faced Algaria at her cottage, and whatever truths awaited them there.

But she could do nothing about Algaria tonight, and, regardless of what transpired with Algaria, her own life would go on – and she had a goal, a personal aim, one vitally important to her.

She needed to show Richard she loved him. Needed to convince him of that fact – drum it through his Cynster skull so that, someday, he would be confident enough to openly show his love for her. She wasn't holding her breath, of course – she knew it would take time. Men as reserved as he did not change their habits overnight. But she was prepared to be patient; she would persevere.

The first thing to do was to start.

And now was as good a time as any.

Sliding the wooden eating bowls back into her saddlebag, she set it aside, then approached Richard where he sat on a round stool before the fire, staring at the flames. Resting her hands lightly on his shoulders, she brushed her lips along his cheek. 'Come to bed.'

The soft whisper had him standing immediately; he'd already banked the fire. Taking his hand, a soft smile playing on her lips, Catriona led him to the pallet lying on a crude frame in the corner. She'd had him fetch fresh spruce to slide into the dry straw, then she'd covered the whole with a blanket, keeping two others to wrap about them. The warmth in the cottage released a faint tang from the spruce; their warm bodies crushing it would release even more.

Stopping by the bed, he drew his fingers from hers and immediately reached for her laces. Laying aside the warm shawl she'd draped over her shoulders, she let him do what he did so well. He divested her of her gown and petticoats, then considered her fine lawn chemise.

'You might want to keep that on.'

Catriona considered her own plans for the night and shook her head. 'Not tonight.' Quickly, fingers flying, she slid the tiny buttons undone, noting his blink, his sudden stiffening as she opened the bodice. Then she grasped the hem and whisked the chemise off over her head. She dropped it on a stool with the rest of her clothes, then grabbed one waiting blanket, shook it out, and slid onto the bed beneath it.

Richard watched her, blinked at her, then undressed and joined her in record time. He pinched out the candle just before he did, plunging the room into a mysterious dark lit by flickering firelight. The pallet dipped beside her as he stretched beneath the second blanket; he was all dark, mysterious male when he loomed on his elbow beside her. And reached for her.

'No.' Catriona braced one hand against his chest when he would have rolled her beneath him. She wriggled the other way, pressing him back to the pallet. 'This time, I want to love you – not the other way about.'

Richard blinked again and swallowed the reassurance that had risen to his tongue. She always loved him – took him into

392

her body with a joyous delight, a witchy neediness, that was all the loving he needed. But ... if she wanted to love him even more, he'd grit his teeth and bear it. 'Just what form,' he murmured, as he rolled obediently onto his back, 'is this loving of yours going to take?'

'This, for a start.' Scrambling over him, Catriona found his lips with hers, and kissed him – gently at first, then with greater confidence as he parted his lips and welcomed her in, playing the role that was usually hers. She took his, wriggling so she was higher over him to deepen the kiss, to coax, to incite, to sexually stir him.

Not that he needed any stirring. Against her thigh, cocooned in the warmth of the blankets, she could feel the steady, pulsing throb of his erection – hard and heavy and all hers. Inwardly grinning, she shifted, trapping it between her thighs, artfully caressing.

It grew hotter, harder. His hands, splayed across her back, tensed.

She pulled back from their kiss. 'I want,' she whispered, already slightly breathless, 'you to tell me what you like.'

'What I like?' His voice was a gravelly murmur in her ear. 'What I like, sweet witch, is to feel your body close tightly about me, all hot and wet and urgent.'

'Hmmm, yes. But before that,' she insisted. 'Do you like this?' Discovering a flat nipple hidden beneath the crisp mat of his hair, she burrowed her head down and licked it – lovingly.

And felt him tense, just a little, beneath her. 'Very nice.' The words sounded a touch strained. In wriggling lower, she'd slithered over his erection; it was now cradled in her curls, pulsing against the rounded softness of her belly.

'Good.' Artfully sliding this way, then that, using her whole body as well as her hands to caress him, she pressed hot, open-mouthed kisses across his chest, down the ridged muscles of his abdomen, interspersing her kisses with wellplaced licks and the occasional suck.

Beneath her, his body was hardening; muscles here and there flickered restlessly. Recalling in fine detail all the caresses he'd pressed on her – and which ones drove her the most demented – Catriona decided that what was good for the goose probably worked equally well with the gander.

The sudden hiss of his indrawn breath as, sliding swiftly further down, she curled her fingers about his rigid length, then caressed it with the warm swells of her breasts, suggested her reasoning was sound. Smiling to herself, she slid further yet, deliberately guiding his long length up from the valley between her breasts, along the smooth skin of her upper chest, then up, sinuously lifting her head to caress him with her throat.

Before turning her head and caressing him with her lips.

He jerked; every muscle in his body locked tight. His hands shifted from her shoulders; his fingers sank into her curls. 'Catriona?'

He sounded shocked. Inwardly grinning, Catriona was too busy to answer him. She didn't, however, have any real clue what she was doing, how much pleasure he was feeling, so, after kissing, licking and sucking to her own content, she decided to inquire about his.

'Do you like this?' She planted a soft, wet kiss on his pulsing tip.

Richard bit back a groan. 'No,' he lied. But he couldn't force his fingers to grip her tresses and haul her away.

'Oh. Well, perhaps you like this better?'

He did; Richard gave up and groaned as she closed her mouth, all soft, hot heat, around him. He withstood her torture for two more, exquisitely wracked minutes, before realizing that, no matter that he could tease her to *extremis,* his own constitution wasn't up to it.

394

'Catriona—' In an explosive movement, he half-sat – for one fractured instant driving his shaft deeper into her mouth – then he caught her, lifted her, scattering the blankets they no longer needed. They were both burning with an inner heat.

An inner heat that poured over his teased and sensitive flesh as he set her on her knees, straddling his hips.

She blinked down at him. 'I was only trying to please you.'

He scowled at her; despite the poor light, he could see the witchy smile on her lips. 'You please me every time you take me in, you damn witch.'

His knowing fingers found her softness, deftly probed, stroked and readied her. It took only one flick to replace his fingers with his throbbing shaft. Gripping her hips, he eased her down, closing his eyes in ecstasy as she slowly slid down and enveloped him.

'That,' he stated his voice deep but weak, 'is what pleases me the most.'

He heard her witchy chuckle, then she rose on him and slid down, clasping him tight again. Sliding his hands about the globes of her derriere, he gripped and helped her rise – and felt the dew spring up beneath his hands as he stroked and caressed.

They settled into their usual slow rhythm; only then did he lift his heavy lids. Small hands braced on his chest, she rode him happily, a serene, definitely witchy, lustfully knowing smile on her lips. Her gaze was fixed on his face, watching, gauging, assessing his response to that ultimate, most intimate caress.

He only just managed to suppress his wolfish grin. He was blessed, and he knew it. 'If you really want to please me, one thing you could do is always come to me stark naked, with your hair down.' As it currently was, a rich, vibrant corona about her head, rippling fire over her white shoulders and down her slim arms. When he took her from behind, it was like a living veil, sliding sensuously over her back. He loved her hair.

Her eyes glinted; she inclined her head. 'Any other requests?'

'Just one. Stop trying to muffle your moans and screams.'

She frowned slightly; he smiled winningly and she humphed. 'That's all very well for you to say, but if anyone else heard me – well' – she caught his eye and frowned – 'it's rather revealing, you know.'

He grinned. 'I do, indeed, which is why I like to hear them – those little sounds of your appreciation.' He gripped her bottom and lifted her high, then thrust deeply into her as he lowered her again. Eyes closing, she bit her lip to hold back a groan. 'Like that. They're little sounds of pleasure – and they're precious to me. They're like trophies that I win for pleasuring you.' After a moment, he added: 'How else do I know if I'm hitting the mark?'

'You *always* hit the mark,' Catriona retorted, her lids still too heavy to lift. 'You always pleasure me to oblivion.'

'Perhaps – but I like to hear you admit it.'

Opening her eyes, Catriona studied his as she continued to move upon him. Then he shifted her, pulling her thighs wider so he could sink more deeply into her; a moan welled in her throat – this time, she let it go. And sensed the real pleasure the sound gave him.

'Very well.' Leaning forward, she kissed him, letting their hungry lips feast. As she drew back, eyes closed in concentration as he started moving more powerfully beneath her, she mumured, 'I'll try.'

It wasn't hard, especially given their location, with no one within miles to hear her screams. But he reveled in her commitment and took advantage to the full.

He garnered a whole swag of trophies that night.

*

396

Courtesy of Richard's developing fondness for the amenities of the shepherd's hut, it was mid-afteroon before they reached Algaria's cottage.

She'd seen them coming. She stood in the doorway as they rode up, Catriona just a little in the lead. Algaria met Catriona's gaze, then, deliberately, her hands clasped before her, bowed her head. Turning, she went into the cottage, leaving the door open.

Richard dismounted, then lifted Catriona down. She paused, held between his hands, and met his gaze. 'Remember your promise.'

He grimaced. 'I won't forget. I'm your right arm – your protector. I'll follow your lead.' He gestured her toward the house.

Drawing a deep breath, drawing herself up, Catriona led the way inside.

It was a two-room cottage, one up, one down, with the kitchen facilities in a lean-to at the rear, and a small stable against the side. Pausing on the threshold to let her eyes adjust, Catriona scanned the room and saw Algaria standing, hands clasped before her, her head still bowed in the attitude of a penitent, on the other side of the deal table with her back to the cold hearth.

Catriona moved into the room, until she stood at the opposite side of the table, facing Algaria. Richard's shadow blocked the light from the door momentarily, then she sensed his presence at her back.

Lifting one hand, she extended it across the table. 'Algaria—'

'As you love me, let me speak.' Slowly, Algaria lifted her head. She looked first at Richard, standing silent at Catriona's shoulder, then shifted her black gaze to Catriona's face. 'I now know what I did was wrong, but at the time, it seemed right – what The Lady required of me. But rather than you, it was I who made the mistakes in interpreting Her signs. I acted wrongly, and I deeply regret the pain and suffering I caused.' She drew breath, her gaze locked on Catriona's, and pressed her hands tightly together. 'I ask for your understanding and will abide by your judgment.'

Lowering her proud head, she looked down.

Catriona waited a moment, then asked: 'What made you realize you were wrong?'

Algaria lifted her head; the glance she bent on Richard was hardly affectionate but contained a respect that had not previously been there. 'He lived.' She looked at Catriona. 'If you knew how much wolfsbane I put in that cup ...' She pressed her lips together, flicked Richard another glance, then stated: 'Not even your intervention should have been able to save him. Yet he lived. The Lady's intention is clear – she could not have spoken any louder.'

Catriona nodded. 'As you say. It took him a long time to recover, yet every day longer made his living more remarkable.'

Algaria inclined her head and looked down once more. 'It is clear The Lady wishes him as your consort – the error of my actions could not be more plain.' She lifted her head and met Catriona's gaze levelly. 'I am sincerely contrite' – she drew a tight breath – 'and ready to accept whatever judgment you make.'

'Why?' Catriona asked. 'Why did you think it necessary to remove Richard, especially knowing you were acting against my wishes?'

Algaria grimaced. The look she flicked Richard held an element of apology. 'Because I believed he was responsible for the fire.'

'*What?*' Catriona felt Richard shift behind her, but true to his word, he held silent. 'He was in Carlisle – or riding back – at the time the fire started.'

398

Algaria held up a hand. 'Bear with me – I knew that was what we'd been told. However,' she paused and drew a deep breath, 'if you recall, three days after the fire, we were running low on tansy, and I offered to go and check the patch south of the woods.' Catriona nodded; Algaria glanced at Richard. 'The patch in the woods always sprouts ahead of the main bed at the manor itself.'

Richard inclined his head; Algaria went on: 'On that side of the park lives an old man known to us all as Royce. You and he, now I've thought back on it, haven't yet met – he's something of a hermit in winter.'

'He's a marvel with animals, particularly with birthing lambs,' Catriona put in. 'He lives in a small hut on the south side of the park.'

'I saw Royce that day when I went looking for the tansy – it was sunny and he was stretching his stiff limbs. He sat on a rock and talked – despite living so alone, he loves to talk to people, so I waited and listened.'

'He talked about the fire only in passing – he'd missed all the excitement. He couldn't see the smoke because of the park – he'd only heard about it later. What he *did* say, however, was that on the day when he came to the manor to fetch bones for broth, while returning home, he saw a stranger – a tall, dark-haired gentleman riding a dark horse. This man rode through the park, but not up to the manor. It was late afternoon, heading into evening – the stranger tethered his horse in the park, took something from his saddle pocket, then skirted the manor itself, and went around behind the forge. He didn't see Royce watching. Royce thought it strange, but . . .' Algaria grimaced. 'He assumed the gentleman was you. Later the gentleman came back, mounted his horse, and rode down the vale – that time, Royce was close enough to see the man had blue eyes.' She paused and met Richard's undeniably blue eyes. 'I knew Royce got his bones on the day of the fire – I

399

gave them to him myself. He didn't know about the timing of the fire, so he didn't know you didn't apparently arrive until black night.'

'You thought it was me?'

Lifting her chin, Algaria nodded. 'I reasoned that in order to tighten your hold on Catriona, you'd been seen to leave, then you rode back, earlier than anyone thought, set the fire, waited until it was blazing, then rode in and rescued the situation.' She eyed Richard; her lips tightened. 'If that had been your plan, from all I saw afterward, it worked.'

Richard considered, then nodded. 'I can prove it wasn't me. Two of Melchett's lads saw me riding into the vale, and we spoke briefly – we could already see the smoke rising.' He could remember that moment of dread panic very well.

Algaria waved dismissively. 'I accept without question that my interpretation was wrong – else you would have died. It wasn't you old Royce saw.'

'So who was it?' Catriona asked. Algaria lifted her shoulders; in the same instant, Catriona's face lit. 'Dougal Douglas!' Swinging about, she looked at Richard. 'It must be him.'

Richard grimaced. 'He fits the general description, but tall, dark-haired, blue-eyed gentlemen aren't really all that rare, even in the Lowlands.' He paused, his gaze on Catriona's. 'Algaria jumped to an erroneous conclusion – we shouldn't repeat the mistake.' He studied her face – he could almost see her intransigence, her witch's wiles working. Inwardly, he sighed. '*But* . . . Ido know that Dougal Douglas knew I'd left the vale. He thought I was heading south, that I'd be well on the road to London by lunchtime that day.'

Her eyes narrowed, Catriona humphed. 'I know it was Dougal Douglas.' Transferring her gaze to Algaria, she raised her brows. 'So you poisoned Richard because you believed he was responsible for the fire?'

400

Algaria drew herself up. 'Yes.'

Catriona considered – considered Algaria and her rigid discipline, her rigid pride. Considered Richard, a vital force beside her, his heartbeat as familiar to her as her own. They were both dear to her, both with so much to give. She and the vale needed both of them. Straightening, she turned to Richard. 'You have heard all I've heard – you know as much as I know. It was your life Algaria sought to take – as my consort and protector, I give you the right to pass judgment and sentence upon her.'

She looked into Richard's eyes, then, without another glance at Algaria, turned and left the cottage.

Leaving Richard staring over the deal table at Algaria.

Who stiffened and lifted her chin proudly, her black gaze smoldering. She was still a potent force – he could sense it – but expecting the worst. Yet the old witch would never beg his pardon, or ask for mercy.

He wasn't inclined to be all that merciful but ... he had survived – and he and his witchy wife were much closer, more one, than they had been. She'd trusted him enough to leave her mentor's fate in his hands.

And, despite the fact that he wasn't at all comfortable with Algaria, she'd behaved much as he, in the same situation, might have himself – although not with poison. A well-aimed fist would have been more his style.

But what to do with her – what possible sentence could he devise? The answer popped into his mind with such vigor, such force, he grinned.

Which made Algaria nervous; he grinned even more. 'After much consideration,' he stated, 'I've decided that the most appropriate penance, the most suitable punishment, will be for you to return to the vale, to act as overall nursemaid to our children.' Being responsible for a household of Cynster brats – oh, yes – that was perfect. And he'd so enjoy contributing to her punishment – and she'd so disapprove of the enjoyment he derived from the process. 'And,' he added, 'should you have any spare hours, you must devote them to easing *our* lady's burden by relieving her of some of her healer's chores.'

He smiled, rather pleased with himself.

Algaria raised her brows. 'That's it?'

Richard nodded – she didn't know anything about Cynsters – she didn't know what she was destined for. When Algaria's face lit with relief, he quickly added: 'Just as long as you're quite sure you won't again decide to make away with me.'

'What? Fly in the face of The Lady's expressed wishes?' Algaria waved derisively. 'That's not a mistake I'm likely to make twice.'

'Good.' Richard waved himself, gesturing her to the door. 'Then I'll leave you to make your peace with our lady.'

He was sitting, relaxing, on a stone at the back of the cottage, out of the wind, when Catriona came searching for him. She came up behind him and slid her arms about his shoulders and hugged him.

'Your sentence was inspired – she's so relieved. In fact, she's almost happy. I even saw her smile.'

Richard squeezed her arm. 'If that pleases you, then I'm glad.' He looked out at the rugged hills before them. 'Actually, I was thinking of inviting Helena to come for a visit, maybe in November. She can tell Algaria all the stories of what Devil and I and all the rest used to get up to – to prepare her for what's to come.'

Catriona chuckled, then sobered. 'Incidentally, I remembered, and Algaria does, too, that Dougal Douglas used to visit the vale as a youth. Algaira says his family was keen on a match between him and me.'

'Is that so?' Despite his lazy drawl, Richard was already

making plans to call on Dougal Douglas. Once he determined who had set the blacksmith's cottage ablaze, he fully intended to exact retribution.

'Well.' With a sigh, Catriona straightened. 'We'll spend the night here, then start back early tomorrow. We should reach the vale before dusk.'

'Good.' Richard stood, suddenly eager to be home again, to get his witchy wife back where she belonged. Turning, he gathered Catriona in one arm and they started to stroll back to the cottage. 'No one in London would ever believe this – me sitting down to dinner with not one, but two witches.'

'*Not* witches.' Mock-chidingly, Catriona poked him in the ribs. 'Two disciples of The Lady, one of whom is bearing your child.'

Richard grinned. 'I stand corrected.' Tipping up her face, he kissed her – a kiss she returned very sweetly. Then Algaria called from the cottage, and Catriona broke away.

His brows lightly rising, Richard took care to hide his sudden thoughts; when Catriona took his arm and towed him to the cottage, he didn't resist.

The next morning, they left Algaria's cottage at the crack of dawn, Catriona still sleepy, Algaria grouchy, Richard with a wide smile on his face. The attitudes of all three were connected; Algaria had given up her bed for Catriona's use, casting dark looks Richard's way when he'd bid her good night and joined Catriona upstairs. Algaria had slept on the old settle downstairs – that, however, was not the reason she'd slept poorly.

Richard had provided that – provided reason enough for his witchy wife, despite her disapproval, to moan and sob her pleasure for quite half the night.

He was, this morning, in a very good mood.

Keeping Thunderer to a lazy amble, he followed Catriona's

403

mare and Algaria's old grey. The two women rode side by side, talking of herbs and potions.

Richard grinned – and wondered if witches ever talked of anything else.

Idly speculating, he ambled along in pleasant content, his gaze locked on his wife's swinging hips—

*Ph-whizz! Thwack!*

Thunderer balked and whinnied; Richard abruptly drew rein. Ahead, Catriona and Algaria milled, their faces blanking in shock as they looked back and saw what he was staring at.

A crossbow bolt.

It had whizzed across, a mere inch before his chest, then struck a rock and glanced off. It now lay in the heather, glinting evilly, in the soft morning light.

Fists clenching about the reins, Richard jerked his head up and looked about. Algaria and Catriona followed his lead, visually scouring the slopes below them to their left.

'There!' Algaria pointed to a fleeing rider.

Catriona stood in her stirrups to look. 'It's that *fiend* Dougal Douglas!'

'That pestilential man!'

Calmly, Richard scanned the long valley below them. 'Wait here!' With that curt order, he swung Thunderer about and tapped his heels to the horse's sides. The huge grey surged, perfectly happy to thunder hell for leather over the heather, leaping small streams, jumping rocks. They descended to the valley on a direct course to intercept the fleeing Douglas like retribution falling from on high.

They met as Richard had planned, with him on Thunderer higher up the slope from Douglas on his black horse. Leaping from Thunderer's saddle, he collected Douglas and rolled, making no attempt to hang on to his prey, more intent on landing safely himself. He managed to avoid hitting his head on any rocks; with only a bruise or two pending, he swung around. And saw Douglas, still prone some yards away, groggily shaking his head. Richard's lips curled. Snarling, he surged to his feet.

Whether Douglas knew what hit him – either what had brought him from his saddle or who it was that hauled him to his feet by his collar, shook him like a rag, then buried a solid fist in his gut – Richard neither knew nor cared. Having a crossbow bolt fired at him gave him, he considered, a certain license.

They were much of a height, much of a size – it was no wonder the old hermit had thought Douglas was him. Richard had no compunction in treating Douglas to a little home-brewed – the way they brewed it south of the border. That first rush took the edge from his fury; grasping the downed Douglas by his collar yet again, he hauled him once more to his feet.

'Was it you,' Richard inquired, recalling several incidents that hadn't, to his mind, been sufficiently explained, 'who left the paddock gates opened and broke branches in the orchard?'

Gasping and wheezing, Douglas spat out a tooth. 'Damn it, mon – she had to be brought to see she needed a mon about the place.'

'Ah, well,' Richard said, drawing back his fist. 'Now she has me.' He steadied Douglas, then knocked him down again.

He gave him a moment, then hauled him to his feet again. And shook him until his teeth – those he still had left – rattled. Closing his fist about Douglas's collar, he lifted him, just a little, and, very gently, inquired, 'And the fire?'

Dangling and choking, Dougal Douglas rolled his eyes, flailed his arms weakly, then, forced to it, desperately gasped: 'No one was supposed to get hurt.'

For one instant, Richard saw red – the red glow of the fire

405

as he'd ridden into the courtyard – the red maw that had roared and gaped as he'd seen his wife, her hair bright as the flames, fling a blanket over her head and dash into the fury. 'Catriona nearly got caught in the blaze.'

His tone sounded distant, even to him; refocusing on Dougals's face, he saw real fear in the man's eyes.

Douglas paled – he struggled frantically.

Catriona rode up to see Richard bury his fist in Dougal Douglas's stomach. The fiend doubled over; Catriona winced as Richard's fist swung up and, with his full weight behind it, crunched into Douglas's jaw. Dougal Douglas fell backward into the heather. And didn't move.

Richard watched, but saw no sign of returning life. Shaking out his fingers, he turned. To see Catriona. He sighed. 'Damn it, woman – didn't I tell you—'

Her eyes flew wide. '*Richard!*'

Richard whirled – just as Dougal Douglas came to his feet in a lunge, a knife in his fist. Swift as a thought, Richard side-stepped and caught Douglas's wrist.

*Snap!*

'*Aargh!*' Dougal Douglas fell to his knees, cradling his broken wrist.

'You *fiend!*'

Abruptly, Richard found himself thrust aside; hands on her hips, green eyes blazing, Catriona interposed herself between Dougal Douglas and him.

'*How dare you?*' Green fire and fury poured over Dougal Douglas. 'You were once welcomed as a friend of the vale and *this* is how you repay The Lady's graciousness? You conspire against me and the vale – *worse!* you attempt to harm my chosen consort – the one The Lady finally sent for me. You're an evil worm – a loathsome toad! I've half a mind to turn you into an eel and leave you here to gasp to death, or better yet, to be picked to death by the birds. *That* would be

a suitable end for you – a just repayment for your unconscionable acts.'

She paused for breath; Douglas, on his knees before her,
simply stared. 'Damn it, ye daft woman – the man's a damned
Sassenach!'

'*Sassenach?* What does *that* have to do with it? He's a *man*
– far more of one than you'll ever be.' She stepped forward;
eyes locked on hers, Dougal Douglas cowered back.

Catriona pointed a finger directly at his nose. 'Hear me
well.' Her voice had changed to one of mezmerizing power.
'If you ever again act against me, the vale or any of my
people – and especially my consort – those jewels you hide
beneath your sporran will shrivel, and shrink, until they're the
size of apricot kernels. Then they'll fall off. And as for the
rest of your apparatus, should you entertain so much as a
black thought against any of The Lady's people, it will grow
black, too. And wither away. And if you speak ill of anyone
from the vale, or even connected with the vale, then for every
ill word a boil will grow – on that part of you that has more
will than your brain.'

She paused for breath; Richard reached out, closed his
hands about her shoulders and lifted her aside. Setting her
down just behind him, a little to the side, he leaned down so
his face was level with hers and whispered: 'I think he's got
your message. Any more, and he might faint.' He glanced at
Dougal Douglas, who, aghast and pasty-faced, was watching
them both like a trapped rabbit. Richard grinned and turned
back to his wife. 'Much as I enjoyed your performance, leave
the rest to me.' He trapped her wide gaze. 'It's my job to
protect *you*, remember?'

She humphed, and crossed her arms over her chest, and
glowered at Dougal Douglas, but she consented to remain
silent and still.

Richard turned back to survey their malefactor. 'Might I

suggest,' he said, 'that before my wife further develops her theme, you might care to be on your way?' The relief on Douglas's face was plain; he started to get to his feet. Richard stayed him with one raised finger. 'However, do make sure that, henceforth, you stay out of our way, and out of the vale. On pain of The Lady's wrath. Furthermore, just in case you're inclined, once you're well away from here, to forget how potentially violent The Lady can be, you would do well to dwell on this, more mortal threat.'

All hint of expression leaching from his face, Richard held Dougals's gaze calmly. 'All the details of your recent interference in the vale, all the facts plus witnesses' accounts, will be forwarded to my brother, Devil Cynster, His Grace of St. Ives. Should any inexplicable harm subsequently befall anyone in the Vale of Casphairn, it will be laid at your door. And the Cynsters will come after you.' He paused, then added, his voice still even and low: 'You should also bear in mind that we've centuries of experience in asking for no permissions, but exacting vengeance swiftly – and looking innocent later.'

Exactly which one of them Dougal Douglas found more intimidating would have been hard to say. With a dismissive gesture, Richard waved him away. Cradling his wrist, he stumbled to his feet, then lurched off to catch his horse, which was ambling off down the valley.

Richard heard an odd sound from beside him – something between a snort and a cough, crossed with a disgusted humph. He wondered whether his witchy wife was fixing her curse on Dougal Douglas, but decided he didn't need to know – didn't want to know.

He whistled, and Thunderer came ambling up, heartened by his brisk ride. Turning, Richard saw Algaria trotting up, leading Catriona's mare. Draping an arm about Catriona's shoulders, he steered her to the mare.

'It's a great pity we can't lay charges with the magistrate – but we can't.' Catriona stopped and looked up, waiting for Richard to lift her to her saddle.

'Indeed not,' Algaria agreed. 'The last thing we need is to draw official attention to the vale. But your combined threats should hold him.' She regarded Richard with real approval. 'That last threat of yours was a masterstroke. No matter what curses Catriona levels, men always understand legal threats best.'

Richard smiled and lifted Catriona to the saddle – and forebore to point out that his threat was not precisely legal – rather the opposite, in fact – a distinction he felt sure Dougal Douglas had understood. But even more to the point, he could attest that Catriona's curses would make any man think twice. Equipment shrinking, then dropping off, turning black, boils – what else she might have dreamed up he hadn't wanted to hear.

The thought made him shudder as he swung up to his saddle; his wife noticed and looked her question – he smiled and shook his head.

Then he clicked the reins, and they headed home – back to the Vale of Casphairn.

Later that night, snug and safe in their bed, soothed and sated and quietly happy, Richard looked down at his wife's red head, comfortably settled on his chest. Raising one hand, he lifted one fiery lock from her cheek. 'Tell me,' he murmured, careful to keep his voice low so he wouldn't break the spell, 'when you were ranting at Dougal Douglas, were you angry on The Lady's behalf, or your own?'

Catriona humphed and wriggled deeper into his arms, pressing herself to him, holding him tightly. 'That was the *third* time I nearly lost you! If you must know, I didn't even *think* of The Lady. Or her edicts. Although in this case, it's

409

really all the same thing. But just because *she* issues the directives, that doesn't mean *I* don't have my own opinions. She sent me to you – you were destined for me. But I agreed to have you. And now you're here and you're mine.' She tightened her arms about him. 'I'm not letting you go. I want you beside me – and I have no intention of letting anyone interfere, not Sir Olwyn, Dougal Douglas, Algaria, or anyone else!'

Lying back on the pillows, Richard grinned into the dark. After a moment, he murmured: 'Incidentally, I'm only half-Sassenach. The other half derives from the Lowlands.'

His witchy wife shifted, lifting away from him. 'Hmmm ... interesting.' A moment later, she asked: 'Which half?'

A week later, Richard was shaken to life – literally – by his witchy wife.

'*Wake up,* do!'

Obligingly, he reached for her.

'No, *no!* Not that! We have to get up! Out of bed, I mean.'

She illustrated by leaping out from under the warm covers, letting in a blast of icy air.

Richard groaned feelingly and cracked open his lids. He blinked into deep gloom. '*By The Lady!* It's pitch dark – what the devil's got into you, you daft witch?'

'I'm not daft. Just get up! *Please?* It's important.'

He groaned again, with even more feeling – and got up.

Catriona pushed and prodded him into his clothes and down the stairs. Clutching one sleeve, she dragged him into the dining hall, and up onto the dais, and around to the wall behind the main table. She stopped and pointed to a huge old broadsword hanging on the wall. 'Can you lift it down?'

Richard looked at it, then at her, then reached for the sword.

It was heavy. As he lowered it and settled his hand about

410

the pommel, he knew it was not just old but ancient. There was no scabbard. But he got no time to dwell on the weapon, because his wife was urging him on.

They went out to the stables and he saddled their sleepy mounts while she held the sword balanced before her. Then they mounted, and he hefted the sword; in the crisp chill of pre-dawn they set out for the circle.

'Tether the horses,' Catriona said as he lifted her to the ground. 'Then bring the sword.'

Richard threw her a glance, but did as she asked. She was gripping and releasing her fingers, her gaze flicking again and again to the line of light slowly advancing up the vale. As far as he could see, she still had plenty of time, and yet . . . his witchy wife was nervous.

The instant he'd finished with the horses and hefted the sword, she gripped his other hand and towed him urgently toward the circle. She didn't drop his hand as they came to the place where he usually sat and waited for her. She didn't stop until they stood at the very entrance to the circle.

Only then did she release his hand and swing to face him.

Catriona looked down the vale, at the slowly advancing line of light; at her back, she could sense the power within the circle start to awaken, to unfurl in anticipation of the first touch of the sun. It was cold and frosty, but the day would be fine. Drawing a deep breath, feeling the age-old power in her veins, she looked up at Richard.

And smiled, unaware that the light of her love filled her face with a glow he found wondrous. Dazzling. A glow he, the warrior, would have moved heaven and earth just to see.

'There's a great deal I have to give thanks for.' Her voice was clear, calm, yet vibrant. 'As my chosen and accepted consort, as my husband and my lover, it's your right to enter the sacred circle and watch over me while I pray. My father used to stand guard over my mother.' She paused, her eyes

411

locked on the blue of his. 'Will you perform that office for me?'

It was an offer she needed to make – it was her final acknowledgment that he belonged beside her – always beside her, even here, at the epicenter of her life. They belonged to each other, and nowhere more so than here, before The Lady.

They were one and always would be, both with each other and with the vale.

This, she knew beyond certainty, was how it was meant to be.

Richard stilled. Unable to think, all he could do was feel – sense – the power that held him. And her. He had no wish to break it – to reject it – to fight against its bonds; instead, he welcomed it with all his heart. He drew in a slow breath and wondered at the headiness in the air. 'Aye, my lady.' Bending his head, he touched his lips to hers, then drew back. 'My witchy wife.'

He held her sparkling gaze for an instant, then gestured with the sword. 'Lead on.'

They entered the circle just as the sun reached them, bathing them in her golden glow. He followed her in, hers to the death, the far-sighted warrior who had found his cause.

# Epilogue

*March 1, 1820*
*Albemarle Street, London*

'And so there you have it.' Leaning back in a chair drawn up to the table, Vane raised his ale mug in a toast. 'Richard and Catriona – and all the London belles can bid Scandal good-bye.'

'Humph!' Languidly asprawl at the other end of the table, resplendent in a navy silk dressing gown embroidered with peacocks, Demon Harry eyed his elder brother with apparent equanimity – and underlying unease. 'How's Patience?'

Vane grinned. 'Blooming.'

The sight of his brother's transparent happiness made Demon shift in his seat.

'Mama, of course, is *aux anges* over the impending addition.'

'Hmm – she would be.' Demon wondered whether that would divert her attention from him – he doubted he could rely on it.

'And there's already plans afoot for a huge celebration sometime this summer – Richard and Catriona have committed to coming down, and, of course, all the aunts and connections will want to see them, and the new arrivals.

Demon frowned. He'd missed something. 'Arrivals?'

Vane's grin surfaced. 'Devil, again – what else? Honoria's due about the same time as Patience, so it'll be quite a summer celebration.'

Babies and wives all over. Demon could just imagine.

Having brought him up to date, Vane heard creaks upstairs and, with a raised brow and an understanding smile, made his excuses and left. But instead of repairing upstairs, to further indulge himself with the feminine charms of the luscious body he'd left sprawled in his bed, Demon remained at the table, considering all Vane had told him – chilled, more and more, by the shadow of impending fate.

Which just went to show.

Demon drummed well-manicured fingernails on the table; he was going to have to do something about his situation. The situation he now found himself in.

First Devil, then Vane, now Richard. Who would be next?

There were only three of them left – him, Gabriel and Lucifer – and he was the eldest. There was no doubt in his mind who the aunts and connections would next expect to front the altar.

The odds were narrowing – to a degree he didn't like.

But he'd already made his vows – to himself. He'd vowed he'd never marry – never put his trust, his faith, his heart in any woman's hands. And the notion of limiting himself to one woman sexually was beyond his ability to comprehend. How the others managed to do so – Devil, Vane and now Richard – he couldn't imagine. They certainly hadn't before.

It was one of life's mysteries he had long ago decided he didn't need to unravel.

The question now before him, on this brisk sunny morning, was how to avoid fate – a fate that was steadily closing in on him.

His position wasn't good. Here he was, in London, with the Season about to start, with his mother and all his aunts in residence, with the scent of blood firing them . . .

Drastic action was called for.

Strategic retreat to safer surrounds.

Abruptly ceasing his tattoo on the table, Demon raised his head. 'Gillies?'

A moment later, an unprepossessing face popped around the door. 'Yessir?'

'Fig out the bays. We're going to Newmarket.'

Gillies blinked. 'But . . .?' Deliberately, he raised his eyes to the ceiling. 'What about the countess?'

'Hmm.' Demon looked up, then he grinned and stood, cinching his robe tight. 'Give me an hour to satisfy the countess – then be ready to roll.'

Newmarket, and assured safety, were only a few hours away, but once there, he'd be starved for the usual rake's fare – he may as well indulge his appetite before leaving.

As he climbed the stairs two at a time, Demon grinned. The countess was no threat – and Newmarket was safe.

He was well on the road to being the one Cynster in all the generations to finally escape fate – and the trap she laid for all Cynsters.

*More titles
in the exciting
Cynster series
from
Stephanie Laurens,
available now from
Piatkus Books!*

# WHAT PRICE LOVE?

Despite his dangerous air, Dillon Caxton is now a man of sterling reputation, but it wasn't always so. Years ago, an illicit scheme turned into a nefarious swindle, and only the help of his cousin, Felicity, and her husband, Demon, saved Dillon from ruin. Now impeccably honest, his hard-won reputation zealously guarded, he's the Keeper of the Register of all racing horses in England, the very register Lady Priscilla Dalloway is desperate to see. She has come to Newmarket, determined to come to the rescue of her horse-mad brother who has fallen into bad company.

Together, Dillon and Pris uncover a massive betting swindle. Assisted by Demon, Felicity, and Barnaby Adair, they embark on a journey riddled with danger and undeniable passion as they seek to expose the deadly perpetrators. And along the way they discover the answer to that age old question: What price love?

978-0-7499-3712-6

# A SECRET LOVE

When a mysterious lady, her face hidden by a black veil, begs Gabriel Cynster for his help, he cannot refuse her plea. For despite her disguise, Gabriel finds the woman alluring and he is powerless to deny her. But he exacts payment as only a Cynster would demand: with each piece of information he uncovers, she must pay him – in the form of a kiss.

Lady Alathea Morwellan knows Gabriel is intrigued, but despite the sparks that fly between them, they have never passed a civil moment together. Yet as the stakes get higher, so does Gabriel's desire for payment. And with each overpowering kiss, each passionate embrace, Alathea knows that she will not be able to resist his ultimate seduction . . . but what will happen when she reveals the truth?

'Her lush sensuality takes my breath away!' Lisa Kleypas

978-0-7499-3720-1

# ALL ABOUT LOVE

Six notorious cousins, known to the ton as the Bar Cynster, have cut a swath through the ballrooms of London. Yet one by one, each has fallen in love and married the woman of his heart, until only one of them is left unclaimed . . . Alasdair Cynster.

Known to his intimates as Lucifer, Alasdair had decided to rusticate in the country before the matchmaking skills of London's mamas become firmly focused on him, the last unwed Cynster. But an escape to Devon leads him straight to his destiny in the irresistible form of Phyllida Tallent, a willful, independent beauty of means who brings all his masterful Cynster instincts rioting to the fore. Lucifer tries to deny the desire Phyllida evokes – acting on it will land him in a parson's mousetrap, one place he's sworn never to go. But destiny intervenes, leaving him to face the greatest Cynster challenge – wooing a reluctant bride.

'Laurens is one of my favourites!' Linda Howard

978-0-7499-3721-8

# DEVIL'S BRIDE

When Devil – the most infamous member of the
Cynster family – is caught in a compromising position
with plucky governess Honoria Wetherby, he astonishes
the entire ton by offering his hand in marriage. No one
had dreamed this scandalous rake would so tamely take
a bride. As society's mamas swoon at the loss of
England's most eligible bachelor, Devil's infamous
Cynster cousins begin to place wagers on the
wedding date.

But Honoria isn't about to bend to society's demands
and marry a man just because they've been found
together unchaperoned. No. She craves adventure.
Solving the murder of a young Cynster cousin fit the bill
for a while, but once the crime is solved, Honoria is set
on seeing the world. But the scalding heat of her
unsated desire for Devil soon has Honoria craving a
very different sort of excitement. Could her passion for
Devil cause her to embrace the enchanting peril of a
lifelong adventure of the heart?

978-0-7499-3716-4

# A RAKE'S VOW

***He vowed he'd never marry*:**
The other Cynster men might not mind stepping up to
the altar, but Vane Cynster never wants to be shackled
to any woman, no matter how comely. Bellamy Hall
seems like the perfect place to temporarily hide from
London's husband hunters. But when he encounters
irresistible Patience Debbington, Vane realises he's
met his match and soon he has more than seduction
on his mind.

***She vowed no man would catch her*:**
Patience isn't about to succumb to Vane's sensuous
propositions. Yes, his kisses leave her dizzy but he's
arrogant, presumptuous . . . and, despite his protests,
bound to be unfaithful, just like every other man.
Patience has promised herself that she'll never become
vulnerable to a broken heart. But is this one vow that
was meant to be broken?

978-0-7499-3717-1

# A ROGUE'S PROPOSAL

Demon Cynster has seen love bring his brethren to their knees, and he's vowed that he will not share their fate – until he spies Felicity Parteger sneaking around his country estate. Demon remembers Felicity as a mere chit of a girl, but now she stands before him – begging for his help – all lush curves, sparkling eyes – and so temptingly worthy of the love he's vowed never to surrender to any woman.

Felicity knew Demon was one of the ton's most eligible bachelors and a rogue of the worst sort, but he was the only one capable of getting her friend out of trouble. Her fascination with him had nothing to do with the power lurking just beneath his devil-may-care facade – or with the desire that flares when he takes her in his arms. She knows he'll never yield to her the love she desperately seeks, but could a marriage with passion alone – even with a man like Demon – be enough?

978-0-7499-3719-5

# ALL ABOUT PASSION

*'If one is not marrying for love, one may as well marry*
*for something else. My future countess has to be*
*sufficiently docile and endowed with at least passable*
*grace of form, deportment and address.'*

Gyles Rawlings, fifth Earl of Chillingworth and honrary
member of the Cynster clan, is determined not to
succumb to the dangers of falling in love. To that end,
he makes an offer of marriage – sight unseen – to the
niece of an old friend. He believes he's chosen a
biddable lady who will bear him an heir and leave his
emotions unattached. He arrives for his own wedding
without ever actually meeting his fiancée and at the
altar is astonished to discover that he's offered for the
wrong woman. His new wife is a passionate hoyden
who makes his head spin. Francesca isn't docile,
certainly not biddable, and she has no intention of
settling for anything less than her husband's heart.

978-0-7499-3722-5

# ON A WILD NIGHT

*'Where are all the exciting men in London?'*

After spending years in the glittering ballrooms of the ton, Amanda Cynster is utterly bored by the current crop of bland suitors. Determined to take matters into her own hands, one night she shockingly goes where no respectable lady ever should, but where many an intriguing gentleman might be found.

But titillating excitement quickly turns to panic when Amanda discovers she's quite out of her depth. She looks around for help – and is unexpectedly rescued by the Earl of Dexter. Lean, sensuous and mysterious, he has delayed re-entering society, preferring instead a more interesting existence on its fringes.

He's the epitome of the boldly passionate gentleman Amanda has been searching for, but although his very touch makes it clear he's willing to educate her in the art of love, Amanda has to wonder if such a masterful rake can be sufficiently tamed into the ways of marriage.

978-0-7499-3723-2